Shauna is a first-time author who took time out of her career to pursue motherhood and to chase her dreams of telling her own stories and seeing them in print. Her first book came to her as she was battling her own demons of depression and anxiety. Writing became an outlet that helped her through the dark times and to overcome the struggles she had dealt with.

Dedication

To my husband, Raymond, your constant support and encouragement is the reason my dreams have become reality. None of this would have been possible without you, you truly are a blessing in every possible way.

Shauna Richmond

The Wrath of Raghnall

Austin Macauley Publishers™
London • Cambridge • New York • Sharjah

A CIP catalogue record for this title is available from the British Library.

ISBN 9781788784351 (Paperback)
ISBN 9781788784368 (Hardback)
ISBN 9781788784375 (E-Book)

www.austinmacauley.com

First Published (2019)
Austin Macauley Publishers Ltd
25 Canada Square
Canary Wharf
London
E14 5LQ

House Olden

In the years of old, House Olden is well known for its courage and strength on the battlefield. Castle Mourne is located on the base of a mountain with great stone walls that rise up into the sky and stretch as far as the eye can see. The weather is often cold and damp, despite the blue sky that hangs above the land. The sun lights up the land for miles, emerald green fields shine in the daylight, acres of land sit quietly where the farmers grow the crops. Sheep, pigs and cows fill the farmland that sits beneath graceful rolling hills of the mountain. The scent of freshly cut grass and fertiliser from the nearby farms fill the air. A narrow road that could only fit two horses side by side leads through the middle of the land, separating the animals from the crops that lead to a herd of trees which lead to the village. The closer to the village you get, the less greenery can be seen. The beautiful land was converted to stone buildings and dirt roads, a mixture of smoke and fresh baked goods now filled the air, the small folk filled the streets with laughter and tales of their ancestors and past battles, this land was sanctuary for many and they all thanked the Lord of the land Theodore Olden.

Theodore is a tall man standing at six foot four, he is fair skinned with dark hazel brown hair and chestnut brown eyes, and he always has himself well presented and maintains a tightly trimmed beard and tidy hair that stops just before his shoulders. He is an amicable man, who is known to joke with his men and also reward their hard work. He is extremely strict when it comes to the upkeep of his land, training his men for battle and raising his four children. He is loved by his people as he is fair and kind to the small folk, who have not been as lucky as he, with titles and wealth, but he knows without the small folk he would not be able to rule his land as they provide the food and fuel needed for the survival of the house. As a youth, Theodore famously saved Richard Byrnell's life at the battle of Rosefort, and help secure

Geoffrey Draconian's place as the rightful Lord to the Land. As a reward for his courage, Richard promoted Theodore from his squire to one of his soldiers. Theodore excelled with his marksmanship and fought ferociously in hand to hand combat, a born leader that was not to be trifled with.

When Jamie Olden, Theodore's father passed away, he ascended to Lordship and married Mary Byrnell a sallow skin, thin woman with a long neck and light brown hair with eyes to match. She was bred well to be the wife of a Lord, but was far more serious than that of her husband, she also happened to be Richard's younger sister forming a strong Allianz between both houses. Quickly after the marriage, Mary became pregnant and later gave birth to their first born son Nicholas. Mary was known for jealously guarding her children. Their safety was her top priority alongside their education.

Growing up, Nicholas was groomed to be the Future Lord of house Olden, he was trained from the age of seven to take the burden of leadership. As he grew older, he was known to be extremely intimidating both on and off the battlefield. A very confident young man who took on a lot of his father's traits both in appearance and personality. Nicholas stood at six foot five, he towered over most of his father's men, his thin frame made him appear taller to some. His angelic face, dark brown hair and blue eyes were indeed enough to make the ladies of the land swoon, he made friends easily as like his father and he joked around with the men quite often. Strict on his routine with himself and his men, he is known to be one of the best soldiers in the land as he served as his father's banner man, knowing one day he would have to lead his father's men and their sons when he became Lord of House Olden.

When the Banners of war were called by his Uncle Richard, Nicholas was the first to go riding out with his father's army into battle with such force that he is now feared by rival houses and he has earned the name Nicholas the courageous; a reputation he knew made his parents proud. Unlike his younger siblings, Nicholas did not have as much freedom as them, everything in his life had been carefully picked out for him; his education, clothes, right down to his future wife. He knew his mother had been carefully looking at surrounding houses, trying to choose who she thought the perfect woman was for her son.

Finn Olden is the second born son to house Olden. He is quick to temper and quite rebellious with a reputation for having a vulgar mouth which generally ended with him brawling in taverns, sleeping with whores and any woman that strayed from their husband, sneaking out at night and generally finding ways to anger his father. After he was caught stumbling out of the millers wife's chambers, Theodore had no choice but to have his son receive twenty lashes across his back, the scars now serve as a caution to avoid sleeping with another man's wife, or his punishment next time will prove to be far worse.

When his younger sister Cara-Lea was being tormented by the pig farmer's son, he grabbed him by the neck and beat the boy until he was unrecognisable to his own mother, while his father was vexed at his actions he was also proud at how Finn stood up for his younger sister.

An expert swordsman, some say a born killer, what he lacks in patience he makes up for with his skills in combat. Finn stands at a shorter six foot two than that of his brother and father; however, his broad muscular build along with his speed were enough to deter much unwanted attention as not many men dared to anger him. His dishevelled dirty blonde hair and celestial blue eyes mixed with his charm and quick wit proved him hard to resist, although with the reputation of a Brute, he has a heart of gold with a loyalty to his family which never wavers. Finn loves his family dearly, although he resents his older brother Nicholas for being the apple of his father's eye. Theodore always seemed to favour Nicholas above Finn even when they were little, the only way Finn learned to get his father's attention successfully was to act out, he never minded the punishments it was the only time his father truly seemed to take interest in him. His mother worried that she may never find a suitor for him as most of the surrounding houses feared him and did not want their daughters to wed somebody as unpredictable and uncontrollable as Finn Olden.

Edward and Cara-Lea are the third born children to Theodore and Mary Olden. Edward, unlike his brothers, is more of an intellectual than a fighter, he is tall for his age with light brown hair and brown eyes and he aspires to be like his father yet has no intention to fight on the battlefield. He takes comfort in the safety of his books, Edward would much rather be lost in the tales of battles than actually participate in one. His sister Cara-Lea is known for her musical talents and her priority to put the family above everything else, she is known for her stubborn personality and intellect. Like her twin, she is often found with her head in a book, both Edward and Cara-Lea resemble their mother more than Nicholas and Finn.

Edward looked up to Nicholas and his father, he would often follow them around to hear the fascinating tales of battle they had to tell, he loved the strategy of it, all being able to out-smart the enemy and lure them to traps, which meant less death on your houses end. He would listen and take notes from his father and brother, and learn all he could about all the other houses. If he had to serve as his brothers banner man one day, he would surely be well equipped with knowledge of how they fight and how to defeat them.

Cara-Lea is a soft spoken girl, a young beauty with the voice of an angel, she would often make up songs and preform them for her mother, or at events in her house. Unlike her twin, she looked up to Finn, she loved his brutal honesty; his sarcasm always made her laugh even when she was not supposed to. While her other brothers where busy discussing war tactics and all things boring to her, Finn took her to the stables and taught her how to ride a horse "properly" as he called it.

'Being lady like is all well and good, until you need to get somewhere in a hurry.' he used to tell her. She always felt safe with Finn, she knew nobody would dare go near her with her older brother at her side.

The Olden household had always had a strong name with a Proud Heritage with the new generation of Olden's making sure that name is upheld to the highest standards. All Theodore's children were set a strict routine they had to follow. The day began at dawn, this was time to rise from their slumber and get dressed for the day ahead. They would attend Mass before they attended breakfast. Nicholas and his father would then attend to business matters in relation to the land while Finn would attend weapons practise, while his two younger siblings would spend their time studying poetry and music. Mid-morning prayers would follow and a meal. The afternoon would see Finn and Nicholas off hunting and hawking while Lord and Lady Olden went inspecting the estate. Evening Prayer which was often missed by Finn would be had, following supper in the Great Hall. After supper usually followed some form of entertainment like music, dancing, jugglers or jesters. When it was time to retire to bed, bedtime prayers were to be said before starting it all again the next day. Although, following a strict routine living under the leadership of Theodore Olden proved to be very pleasant for the people in the land.

Freya

Rose Fort is such a beautiful land, the luxurious castle that she now called home is brought to life in the morning sun with the ivy that covered the walls of the castle and the flowers in bloom, but the thought of her pending marriage had her mind troubled. Her husband-to-be, Roderick Draconian, was a cruel man. He beat the servants, hung his own men if he felt they weren't battle ready, how could her father promised her hand to a beast like this? She feared for her own safety, she knew once she sired him an heir he would most likely have her head, but it was done, he had already paid the fee and the marriage would take place as soon as the paper work came through.

It was a damp, cold day as she made her way over the slippery wooden bridge through the now dense fog, she sensed something is not right, suddenly, it felt like someone was watching her. Torn between the decision to stop and look around, or run in terror, she chose to keep going and ignore her nauseating feeling of being watched. As she made her way toward the entrance of the Castle, she heard some rustling in the bushes and that uneasy feeling that she was being watched returned, trying to keep her breathing as light as possible to hear if anyone was indeed following her. She heard a branch break and some more rustling in the bushes. Beginning to panic, she turned to see if she could see anyone behind her, but couldn't make out anything other than trees and fog. Suddenly, she heard it, something moving heavily and like lightning behind her, with that Freya began to run faster and harder than she ever had before she could hear heavy breathing through the fog, but she was uncertain if it belonged to whatever she heard or herself feeling her heartbeat in her chest, trying to convince herself it was just one of Roderick's hounds she heard, but too terrified to stop running and look back to confirm that she was over reacting, reaching the entrance of her home she runs through the doors to safety. Making her way up the marble staircase, thinking it had to be one of the hounds that got out, angry at herself for getting so frightened but reminding herself she was just a girl of twelve, her heart sinks when she realises that she is not a girl anymore but a woman, she will be a wife and have to sire and heir for her husband.

As she turns the corner at the top of the staircase, Freya feels a sharp dagger like pain across her back, screaming while blood starts to pour from her wounds. Afraid for her life, she attempts to fight it off. She pushes and shoves with every ounce of strength she has, managing to break free enough to turn and see the animal that attacked her. That's when she sees it, one of her betrotheds hounds. Stunned and terrified it stands before her snarling, giant yellow fangs, the length of a small dagger mesmerised and horrified Freya. She has seen what these animals are capable of. Hell fire eyes met her gaze, with her blood dripping from this beast's mouth. The full repulsiveness of the merciless creature, getting ready to attack again, she knows she cannot out run this thing. She could only fight it off, Freya frantically looks for something to hit it with, even just to stun it while she can try to escape. She starts to feel the tears well up in her eyes with fear and the pain of her injuries, fear of not wanting to die like a mouse to a cat. In one moment, before she could lift her arms in defence, the strength and weight of the monster's body knocked her down, its enormous paws pinning her down to the ground, the revolting, slobbering mouth and scorching rancid breath hit her face. As she looked into its eyes, she knew this was a creature from hell and that it was going to take her life, helpless beneath the weight of the monster she starts sobbing.

'Somebody help me!' she begged.

Before she could call out again, the creature sinks its dagger like teeth into her shoulder, it was then she began to black out the last image she could see was a pair of legs running towards her before everything went dark.

Freya awoke, to find herself in her bed chambers, her body burned with the pain of a thousand daggers, she had hoped at first it was a bad dream but the pain was too real to have been dreamt.

'You've been a very naughty girl, Freya.' That slow sadistic voice made the hair on the back of her neck stand up, quickly turning in the direction the voice had come from, there he stood.

'My lord?' she asked anxiously.

'Vikings! Always acting the fool,' his mouth pressing into a hard line. 'You killed one of my hounds!' The anger in his voice terrified her.

'No! My lord, I was attacked by…'

'Are you calling me a liar?'

'No my lord, of course not.'

'Good! One of my guards killed Brutus to save your life, I do not see how your life was worth more than that of my hound, do you?' he asked sadistically.

'He tried to kill me,' tears filled her eyes as she feared what he might do to her, she had seen him flay a servant girl for pouring him the wrong wine, what had this monster planned for her.

'You know as well as I, my hounds only attack when I give command,' his voice so formal, but his expression had changed, a hint of a smirk showed on his face.

'You sent that beast after me?' Her mind now racing, why would the man offer to marry her just to try to kill her before it was official?

'Did I say that? I really don't think I said that,' the amusement in his voice turned her stomach. Why would anyone do such a thing? 'You looked puzzled, my love, I should help you see things more clearly,' his voice softened. 'You see I was initially going to kill you on the wedding night, but then your father wouldn't be around, it's so much harder to torture someone to death when they are not available.' He slowly started walking towards Freya, his dark brown hair swept across his face, his clothes stained in blood, as the mountain of a man sat down at her side, Freya felt her body go numb. 'With you and your father out of the way North shore is mine for the taking. I should really thank those Viking raiders that killed your mother and brothers, it makes my job so much easier.' That sadistic grin appeared on his face, the one she knew too well. Before she could move, Roderick's hands wrapped around Freya's neck and began to squeeze tightly. She fought hard to try wriggle from his grasp but he was far too strong. She tried desperately to suck in some air but to no avail, she had to try break free to warn her father, to save her own life. A mist descended over her eyes, her heart beating ever faster in her chest, she could not die like this.

A figure in red made its way quickly behind Roderick and threw him from the bed, Freya was left choking in the air that had failed to find its way past her lips but a moment ago. A loud crash echoed around the room, when she was able to turn to see who her saviour was, Bjorn the Brave, Freya's father stood over her betrothed, his boot pressing down on Roderick's neck.

'You piece of shit!' Bjorn hissed looking down at the man struggling under the weight of his massive boot.

'You think you can attack my daughter, make an attempt on my life and walk away, you're a disgrace.' Bjorn's long sand coloured hair draped over his face and his angry words filled the room. Freya watched as her father's red glove moved his bright red cape to the side as he reached for his long sword. As he gracefully wrapped his hand around the gold hilt, a magnificent sword indeed one he had named Sting, he pulled the sword from the sheath slowly.

'Father!' she begged.

Bjorn turned to his daughter. 'You do not expect me to spear this coward's life?' The sound of confusion and anger filled his voice.

'No, I expect you to let me end it.' Bjorn glanced momentarily at his daughter before handing her his dagger. Bjorn removed his boot from Roderick's neck and instead pressed it into his chest.

'I will not die at the hands of a fucking woman!' he spat.

'No, you will die at the hands of a fucking Viking!' With her words barely passing her lips, she took her father's dagger and knelt down beside the beast that tried to take her life and drove the dagger straight through his heart.

With a gasp, Freya opened her eyes; she had been sleeping. Every night for the past two years she kept reliving that horrific night. Sitting up in her bed, she noticed the pool of sweat that lay beneath her from her night terror. Swinging herself around in her bed she leaped to the floor, all the while clutching her head trying to ease the sense of dizziness that came with the throbbing in her head behind both eyes. Her father had never stopped begging her forgiveness for choosing such a suitor and had agreed to let Freya decide whom she would wed, if she decided to get married after that ordeal. She knew her father was thinking in grief when he chose Roderick as her betrothed, he wanted the Allianz to build a great army, he had not giving much thought to his character.

Looking around her at a room covered in beasts lying on the floor staring at her. Four pups she took and raised, she loved them dearly—three boys and just one bitch. Toby was the pick of the litter, he was built like an ox and as fast as he was strong. She loved him because he was different, he stood out from the rest of the litter, he was a soft reddish brown with a white chest, white paws and a black and white face he was beautiful. Christian and Captain were his two brothers, they were black and tan with longer snouts they looked more vicious than their brother, their hair was longer than Toby's and their ears stood upright to attention while Toby's had flopped. Mandy was the bitch of the litter, she was jet black all over, almost impossible to see in the dark of night. Her ears had flopped like Toby's, she had large brown eyes that seemed to always be watching you, she was short haired with fangs that reminded her off the beast that had once attacked her, no matter how similar the dogs were to remind Freya of Brutus she knew they were nothing like him. They had loved her and protected her since she had taken them in. They were beasts indeed, but they were her beasts.

Walking out of her chambers and through the halls of her home, she admired the beauty of the castle. Shining suits of armour filled the corridor with the banners of her house, hanging proud on the walls the three heads of a wolf, bear and wild boar sat in the centre of the green banner with gold embellishments. Rosefort was now her home, the last of the Draconian's had died attempting to end her bloodline. Freya stayed in the castle after her attack, her father had seen to it that anyone loyal to Roderick Draconian was put to death, as to not cause a revolt. His hounds had been killed all except for their young that had yet to be trained, Freya was not one to punish others for their family's mistakes that included animals. Her uncle and his wife came to Rosefort to help clean up the mess her betrothed had left behind. Her Uncle Henry was her mother's brother and had a gift for ensuring loyalty from the men who fought for him, while his wife Clara was a healer she tended to Freya, and the injured small folk belonging to Rosefort. It took months for Freya to heal after her attack. While she was recovering, she learned from her aunt how to heal others. Henry was a beast of a man, as tall and vicious as a bear some would say, but Freya found him quite loveable. She had known Henry as her uncle, one of her protectors, one of the few people she could trust with her life.

Freya had to talk to the small folk when she was feeling better, she called everyone to the Throne room to announce her family had taken the land, Rosefort, now belonged to House Raghnall. As people gathered in the room, she felt her nerves and did not know what to say, without thinking she start to sing

'It's time to move on now, it's time to find a new cause. Get on to your feet now and give a round of applause. He had a good run, now he's dead and wasting away. Don't dwell on the pains of the past, Draconian has passed away.'

The small folk gathered around the hall applauding and chanting Freya's name. The cruel Lord they had all feared, had been killed. Now a new household had taking over Rosefort to give them a better life.

One cold and wet day, Freya was walking through the forest, gathering up some plants and other items her aunt had requested, when she came across a boy around her age. His skin was white as snow, his eyes sky blue, and his hair jet black and shoulder length, it looked like he had not had a meal in weeks. Approaching him slowly, she noted his body quivering, no doubt from the cold and torn clothes.

'Do not fear me, I mean you no harm,' she said softly.

'What is your name boy?' Cautiously approaching him, she studied his expression.

'Andrew, my name is Andrew,' his teeth chattered as he fought to speak. She handed him her cloak and brought him back to Rosefort for food and shelter. It was there she had learned that his family had been attacked by Roderick's men a few weeks prior to his death. Andrew had been hiding away in the forest since then, afraid of being found, he had not learned of the Lords death or that of his men.

Pulling herself from her thoughts, Freya approached the marvellous marble fire in the library of her home, she loved it for the way it stood tall yet peaceful like in the middle of the room and for the comforting warmth it let out when ablaze. Freya listened as the wood crackled in the flames, somebody had been tending this, she thought to herself.

'You're up early,' a loud friendly voice came from behind her. Freya needn't turn around to know who it belonged to.

'Asger, from what maiden's bed did you crawl from this night?'

'I don't believe I got her name,' he said mockingly.

'You have been tending this fire?' the look of pain unmoving from on her face.

'Well there is some stew left in the cauldron, I was planning to heat up to break the fast of the night, care to join me?'

Freya did not answer, she just nodded and turned back to the fire. Asger was her only surviving sibling, he had not been at home when the raid had taken place, and instead Bjorn had sent him to train with his uncle when he was ten. After what happened in Rosefort, her brother came home to find his sister scared, bruised and withdrawn. After a few months had past and her wounds healed, Freya start training with her brother, she already knew how to shoot a bow as her father had shown all his children from a young age for the purpose of hunting. It was swordsmanship she needed to learn and there was no better person to show her than Asger. He was the best fighter out of Henrys men mainly because of his brute strength, he had easily taken on ten men at a time and still come out the victor.

Eventually breaking her thought, she turned to her brother. 'Father got an invite from house Olden to attend a great feast.'

Regarding his sister's gloomy tone, 'Oh? You do not wish to go?'

'It's not that, it's just, everyone thinks you're dead, nobody has seen you since you were sent away, they all think you died with Mother and the others.' Tears start to fill her eyes. Asger puts a hand on his sister's face and wipes away the tears that have escaped her eyes.

'Little cub, do not be saddened by this, can you imagine the look on everyone's face when I walk in there. It would be far too much of a shame to let that opportunity go to waste.'

Little cub, she thought, her mother always called her that. A smile started to appear on Freya's face, a welcomed expression by both herself and her beloved brother.

'You must go, buy some fine silks for the feast, cannot have you arriving in your battle wear, the village would think it was under attack.' A soft laugh escaped her as she imagined Asger arriving with all the noble's dressed in his bear skin fur with his leather straps, there would be an outcry of rage and fear.

'Not a bad idea sweet sister, but I don't know about silks. I mean I am a Norseman, I shall like to arrive looking like one so there is no confusion about who I am. I suppose we should find you a nice head dress?' he said in jest.

The look of disgust on his sister's face said it all. 'Head dress? Oh no! Not for Oden, or any one of the Gods. I am a Viking, we do not wear head dresses, I like my hair free flowing and wild thank you very much, besides I am sure Loki is behind those atrocities. Only a fool would put one on their head and call it respectable.' Laughing away together as they served up their stew, Freya could not help but think this feast may be the distraction she needs, to escape from her past.

Nicholas

Rising from his slumber, well rested and ready for the day ahead, Nicholas leaps from the bed and quickly dresses as to not feel the icy bite of the morning air against his warm skin. He fixes his tousled hair before leaving his chambers and makes his way down to morning mass. With his stomach grumbling, he was hoping the priest would be quick in his sermon today, as he was looking forward to breaking the nights fast. Upon arrival to the church, he was greeted by the twins, Edward looked like he had not quite woken up while Cara-Lea looked impeccable as always.

Up all night reading again?' Nicholas raised a curious eyebrow at his younger brother, who regarded him with a nervous smirk.

'Father will not be pleased if you do not follow his curfew,' Edward searches himself before answering.

'Finn never follows Father's rules. And look where that got him, you just need to look at his back and see that there are consequences for not obeying your Lord, even if you are his own flesh and blood.' Looking around, Nicholas could not seem to locate his brother. *Late again*, he thought to himself.

'Let's go inside, before Father has our hides and Mother has our heads.'

Standing in the front row of the church, the smell of burning sage filled the air, everyone in the church dressed in their best clothes, the small folk filled the back rows of the building.

'Nicholas, where is your brother?' Looking over at his mother's concerned expression, he did not have the heart to say what he was really thinking, that Finn was probably still passed out in a tavern or brothel somewhere in town.

'I'm sure he will be here any minute Mother,' Judging by his father's angered expression for Finn's sake he'd hoped he was right.

'Finn!' Cara-Lea exclaimed with excitement when she saw her older brother march quickly down the aisle towards her. It was no secret that although she loved all her brothers dearly, Cara-Lea always put Finn on a pedestal, but for the life of him Nicholas could never figure out why that was.

'Mother, Apologies for my lateness I seemed to have lost track of time.' Nicholas watched, as his brother leaned in to kiss his mother on the cheek and take his place beside his brother. Examining his rebellious brother, taking note of his bloodshot eyes and stench of stale ale.

'This is you at your best brother?' he asked with a disappointed tone in his voice.

'Well it's not me at my worst, although as cow heavy as I felt this morning, coming from my chambers I feel like I'm not far off.' Both brothers exchanged an amused glance.

'Nothing a good meal can't' fix,' said Nicholas.

'Or a good woman,' said Finn, lowering his voice as not to let anyone overhear.

'A good woman? You won't find one of those in a brothel,' Nicholas replied.

'Hush! Now both of you before anyone hears you, Father would be vexed to hear you both right now.' Although the two brothers were left sniggering at her, Nicholas acknowledged his little sister's concern.

'Apologies my dear sister, it won't happen again.'

After morning mass, it was time to eat, the smell of freshly baked bread was so alluring to Nicholas and his growling stomach that he could not wait to get his hands on it. Taking a seat at the table, he reached over for his cup of wine while waiting on his bread and fish serving. Finn quickly sat down next to him, armed with his cup of ale.

'Glad to know we can count on you to be on time for something,' Nicholas jested.

'Where is the food, already my stomach thinks my throat is cut,' Finn said, aggravated ignoring his brother's previous comments.

'It's on the way, patience is a virtue brother.'

'So is a full stomach,' Finn snapped.

'Nicholas, what was it like, the battle with Father and Uncle Richard?' came a little voice beside him.

‘Edward? Why do you ask such things?’ Nicholas asked.

‘They say you are the bravest of all the men that you have no fear. I wish I were like you and Father.’ Edward beamed at his brother with pride.

‘Everyone on a battlefield is afraid Edward, whoever says otherwise is lying, and real bravery is not the absence of fear dear brother, its standing your ground and facing it head on, in spite of fear. Battles are not for the faint hearted, I have seen grown men reduced to tears and vomiting before a battle, and yet be the first man willing to put his life on the line when it is time to fight. I pray you will only ever know battle from your books, it is a cruel thing to witness first hand.’ And with a reassuring grin, he put his hand on his brother’s head and messed up his hair. Nicholas had always had a certain fondness for Edward, he can tell he has a different nature from himself and certainly from Finn, an innocence he would like him to keep for as long as possible, so he does not have to grow up as quickly as he did. As the siblings at the table bantered with one another, they almost missed the food being served, he must have been hungrier than he had thought because Nicholas had cleared his plate almost immediately. He was glad to notice that he was not the only one at the table who had practically inhaled his meal, Finn basically had his head in the dish that was served to him.

After breakfast it was time to attend to matters of the estate, making sure taxes were collected on time, receiving reports of crops, harvests and supplies for the land, and settling complaints and disputes regarding tenants before moving on to more political discussions and decisions. The least favourite part of his day, sometimes Nicholas envied his younger siblings, although they had their own responsibilities, they did not have the burden of someday being Lord to the Land.

‘Nicholas! My boy,’ his father’s voice came from behind him as he left the great hall.

‘Father? Have I forgotten something?’ Nicholas asked.

‘No, No, nothing like that, I have been meaning to discuss something with you, your mother and I think it is time to find you a wife, after all you are a man grown now and it’s about time you started a family, I was already married to your mother at your age… Lord Preston wants you to marry his daughter

Amelia, I did not know what way to say it, so there I just said it.' Theodore explained.

'Lord Preston, he is a friend of Mother's, is he not? I take it, Mother already accepted for me?' Nicholas asked rolling his eyes.

'The women is relentless, she wants grandchildren. Nothing is set in stone but it would do great things for this house. Henry is a good man, he has honour and is loyal, and such an Allianz is not something to take turn away.' Theodore reasoned.

'Amelia is an exquisite girl, I remember her from Uncle Richards' last tournament. I accept the offer of marriage but I would like to see my betrothed before the wedding, perhaps a feast can be arranged?' Nicholas asked hopefully.

'Your mother is already arranging it as we speak, like I said, relentless.' Theodore joked.

'There is just one more thing father, if there is to be a feast then what is to happen to Finn?' Nicholas asked concerned.

'Finn! That boy will be the death of me, your mother won't allow me to lock him in the dungeon either. I'll just have to keep a close eye on him while the guests are staying here.' said Theodore.

'If I may, he is well behaved when Mother and Cara-Lea are around maybe have them stick close by, make sure he stays out of trouble,' Nicholas explained.

'Ah yes, figures the only thing he will listen to is a woman, lucky for me he fears your mother,' Theodore joked.

'As do we all,' Nicholas agreed.

'Indeed, but you will have a wife to fear now instead and in some ways that's much worse, believe me.'

Lady Mary Byrnell

Going through her check list with her hand maiden Margaret, she could not help but feel excited. After all it is not every day a house as distinguished as the Preston's asks to join their house to another.

Nicholas would be her first child to wed and sire children. It has been ten years too long, since she last heard the pitter-patter of tiny feet running through the halls, although her twins were not quite grown, they were not babies anymore. Edward was highly intelligent and had a gift at reading people, a smile etched on her face as Mary recalled Edward telling Finn his biggest weakness was ale and women, the child could not have been any more than six at the time, and Cara-Lea her only daughter was so radiant, a girl that was blessed with grace and beauty as well as having a magnificent voice for song.

Finn was her Dark Horse, she had called him that since he was four years old. He was always getting into trouble, she would send him out in his best clothes and he would come back covered in dirt and mud, and his clothes shredded. Not always approving of his behaviour, she knew that if anyone in the family needed him, Finn would be there, she hoped one day he would settle down and marry but she wasn't so sure any noble woman would take him due to his reputation.

'Margaret! Please tell the cooks to ensure that the potage is piping hot and full of flavour and also pears marinated in red wine are Lord Preston's favourite. Do ensure his serving is quite large and best, have a little extra put aside in case he craves extra, everything needs to be perfect.' Lady Olden ordered.

'As you wish my Lady,' nodding Margaret quickly took her leave. The feast had been organised along with the entertainment for the night, now there was only one thing left to do, talk to Finn.

Finn was at weapons training when his mother found him, with his little sister watching from the side lines she had always been found at her brother's side when she had finished her studies.

'Cara-Lea!' Her mother called with a tone she knew all too well. 'I need to speak to your brother alone, I'm sure you can find some needlework that needs to be done, or book that has yet to be read.' With that, her daughter glanced at Finn, wondering what sort of trouble he was in this time, turning back to her mother she gave her a quick nod before turning around and retreating back towards her chambers.

'Mother to what do I owe the honour of having you in my presence?' Mary turned towards her second born who was sliding his sword back into its sheath all the while keeping his gaze fixated on her.

'Nicholas is to marry Amelia Preston, there shall be a great feast to celebrate the betrothal, and all of the arrangements have been made, the guests invited…' she began.

'And you're here to ask that I don't fuck it up?' Finn asked.

'Finn Olden, hold your tongue.' she said sharply. 'I have raised you better than to speak in front of a Lady like that, never mind your own mother!'

'Apologies Mother, I should be more considerate when I speak to you, but that is why you are here, is it not?' Finn asked charmingly.

'As I was saying there is to be great festivities to celebrate the joining of our houses, the guests include the Preston's obviously, The Byrnell's, The Whitmarsh's and The Raghnall's,' she explained.

'The Vikings? Mother I…' But before he could finish his sentence, Finn was interrupted.

'I know how unpredictable you can be with women and with alcohol to add to it, I can only imagine the trouble you can get in, please do not do anything to bring shame on this house even if provoked,' she begged. Finn could see the concern in his mother's eyes, she needed this to go well.

'I promise… I promise to do my best not to fuck up, my Lady,' Finn glanced down at his mother with a mischievous grin on his face.

'Good, and at least you were more polite about it that time, go back to your training I shall see you at dinner,' turning away from her son, Mary sauntered back towards the great hall in hopes of finding her husband there.

Finn was always rebellious but when he made a promise to his mother, he kept it no matter how hard it was for him to do. Mary knew her son would not let her down and the fact that he gave her his word made her feel at ease. Nicholas agreed to the marriage, Finn agreed to be on his best behaviour. Lord Preston's favourite food would be served and the entertainment for the night was arranged in a few nights from now. This grand event would take place with her House being celebrated by the Lords in the surrounding lands, nothing could ruin this moment for her.

'My Lady you look more ravishing every day, I do believe I will have to conceal you from sight when our guests arrive, for mine can't be the only breath you steal,' her husband's voice followed behind her in a sultry tone. Feeling Theodore pull her into a warm embrace still sent shivers up her spine.

'My love, should you not be attending to matters of your estate?' curious as to how her husband had free time for once.

'No my Lady, Nicholas took the last few matters under his wing, he is coming into his role excellently which gives me some time to woo the enchantress before me.'

'Woo me at a time like this? My Lord there is much to be done for this feast, everything for Henry and Amelia is set but for Bjorn and Freya… I do not know what to do after all they have been through, I am sure a roasted Boar and some stuffed peacock will not be enough to heighten their spirits,' Theodore pulled himself out of his wife's embrace and regarded her for a moment.

'My love, Bjorn is a good man, what happened to him and his family is a tragedy, one we cannot mend, he has accepted the invitation, he will be here in a few nights, maybe the stay away from home is what him and Freya need to distract themselves from the pain,' Theodore reasoned.

'As always you are right, we must ensure to have a plentiful supply of ale, you know how those Vikings love to drink. Catherine was always there for me, I just want to be able to do the same for her family, as she did for mine.'

As Mary was pulled back into her husband's warm embrace, her thoughts drifted back to her late friend Catherine Raghnall, she was an old friend, a Norse girl who was sent to be one of

Catherine's hand maiden's while Catherine was growing up and preparing for marriage, although not from a distinguished background, she was very head strong and free spirited, which were some of the traits Mary loved about her. To find out a few years prior, that her friend and all but one child had been murdered while her husband was away, broke her heart. Vikings never saw another tribe as equal and often raided one another, but because Bjorn came from a noble home, it was more shocking than hearing of a raid in a small farming village which was generally the case. She had always thought more of the death of the family than that of a raid. After all Catherine was a renowned shield maiden and her husband's family were royalty before a mutiny forced them out of their land and into hiding. Although saddened by the thought of her late friend, Mary could not wait to see her daughter Freya and her father Bjorn the last time she recalled seeing them her eldest sons where still boys of just five and seven, now she is getting ready to say goodbye to one of her sons as he embarks on his new life as a married man.

Asger

Asger approached the training field where he had asked a close friend to help his sister with hand to hand combat, knowing his sister was lethal with a bow, he wanted to brush her up on skills that would help if she ever found herself without it again. He is a tall man, with broad shoulders and huge arms, shoulder length auburn hair and a short beard to match, some of the men joked that he resembled a bear, comments that were made mainly when he was in battle as his brute strength was noted by all of his men and all soldiers that had seen him in battle. As he was believed to be dead and nobody bar his uncle and his men had seen him since he was ten, he fought under the name 'Ufi' meaning wolf, a name his father called him growing up as he had not quite filled out, he was thin and tall back then, but as quick as a wolf and his infamous temper had never left, he just learned how to channel it better.

While watching Freya train with Nari, he could not help but feel proud, the gods have been good to him, spared his life by getting him sent away just a day before the raids of his home occurred, and sparing that of the life of his young sister not once but twice. He had asked Nari to train Freya as Nari was better at handling a sword than Asger. They were very similar in many ways as friends, but yet very different. Asger stood tall and broad while Nari was an average height with a slender figure and dark hair, he often tried to lighten as most Vikings did, while Nari had a more placid temperament. Asger was indeed a force to be reckoned with, he always had a fierce temper that was the reason his father sent him away, to channel that aggression and learn to fight with his uncle and his soldiers.

'Asger, a word if I may.' Gilli, an old childhood friend was approaching, he was broad with an average height with slightly more meat in his face than Asger.

'Gilli, to what do I owe the pleasure?'

'Your father sends word that you are to attend an event at house Olden?'

'That is correct, yes we leave at dawn, why do you ask?'

'It is just, my Lord, everyone thinks you are dead, do you think it wise to make yourself known again after all this time?' he could tell his friend showed great concern for him.

'Ah my dear friend if you remember correctly my father wanted my presence hidden in case of backlash from what happened to my sister, there were a great deal of people upset about the death of that snake.' Just the thought of what had happened left a bitterness in his mouth that he could not shake off.

'But you are the only heir your father has, if anything was to happen to you…'

'Speak no more, dear friend if you have misplaced your mind, my sister lives therefore I am not the only heir.'

'Forgive me, but your sister is in fact a woman, yes she is Bjorn's child but if she marries her husband will get everything if you are not there to claim your place as heir to the throne. When people discover you live there will be a great price on your head, look what they did to your family my Lord, I could not bear for the same to be said of you or your sister.'

'Freya is grown now, in the two years since the incident she has become one of the best fighters I have come to see, she is by far the best archer out of every one of the men, she just needs more practise with that sword. As for what happened to my family, my Grandfathers mutiny by those who called themselves loyal was a great tragedy one we will correct in time but we need numbers, and as for my mother and brothers when I catch the cowards responsible for their deaths, they will surely live to rue the day they ever walked onto our land.'

Asger always had great guilt over not been there when his family were slaughtered, he blamed himself for not being there to protect them, all the while knowing that if he had been there when the attack occurred he would not be alive today.

'The Gods kept me alive for a reason, to claim back my family's kingdom, to avenge my family, and to cause one hell of an uproar when word gets out that the Prince of Thule is alive.'

'And the princess? What of her?'

'If any man is stupid enough to so much as look at her sideways it will be the last thing he does, however I cannot be with her all of the time which is why you Gilli and Nari will be accompanying us on our trip.'

'Me my Lord?' the shock in his voice was evident.

'Yes Gilli you, you have eyes like a hawk and are one of the best marksman I have ever seen, I would feel better with you around, especially if we happen to walk into an ambush after word gets out I am alive, I am trusting you with my sister's life, if anything is to happen to me you get her as far away from danger as you can, that is an order.' Asger had rarely ordered anybody he was not training, but Gilli knew when it came to Freya, she would always be her brother's top priority.

'You have my word, but if I am to accompany you what do I wear, I have never been to a feast before.'

'As long as you are equipped with your bow and arrow I could care less what you wear, you could show up naked and rub your cock against Olden's leg if it made you happy.'

'I thought that was your plan, my Lord.'

'It was until my sister informed me of the many maidens that will be attending this feast. I think I'll save the cock rubbing until I secure one back in my chambers.'

Too busy mocking one another, both men did not realise that Freya was finished her training and standing right behind them.

'Well, I really could have went the day without hearing that,' Freya interrupted making both her brother and Gilli jump.

'Sister, how much did you hear?'

'Enough to be completely disgusted, by the way, you may want to keep it in your trousers while we are attending this feast, or Father will cut it off.' Asger blushed, he hated to think of his sister hearing any conversations he had about his own appendages.

'Apologies, I only say such things as a jest, I will head back to my hut and start gathering my things there is much to prepare for our trip, it will take us it will be nearly a day's ride to the ship then another three days before we arrive at house Olden,' kissing his sisters forehead as he prepared to leave, he couldn't help but think of the events to take place in the days ahead.

On his way back to his hut, on the training grounds Asger noticed a familiar face, he was tall and broad with long, dark hair and a tightly trimmed beard.

'Drew!' he called, the man turned to face him, he was much bigger than the scared little skeleton that his sister had brought home one afternoon.

'Asger!' he regarded him kindly with a smile.

'Freya and I will have to go to house Olden which means the land will be short a ruler for the next few weeks, I need you to fill in, in our absence.'

'Me?' Andrew asked puzzled.

'I know my sister would want the same, we trust you and so do the people here, you will be left with all the men to make sure they continue training and fulfil their other duties while we are away, Nari and Gilli will be accompanying myself and my sister. My father will meet us at the ships.'

'I am honoured deeply, I will not let you down.'

'I know you won't, you have come a long way in the past two years.'

'I owe your family my life, I will put that life into protecting your home while you are away, and no outsiders will pass the walls unless you are here to witness them.'

'Gratitude brother, after all, Freya has adopted you as her own as have we all, you are a part of this family now, I best go gather my things before our sister has my head. Oh and one more thing, I doubt the Oldens would appreciate all of my sister's animals coming with us, I will need you to take good care of them while we are away.'

'All of them my Lord?' Drew asked surprised.

'All, but the first four they will be accompanying us on our travels.'

Cara-Lea

Today was the day her mother had prepared for, for days maybe even weeks for all she knew. Her new dress, her mother had purchased just for this occasion, was magnificent a bright rich green with gold embellishments around the lower part of the dress, the neck and borders of the sleeves which came down tight to her wrists. Her chestnut coloured hair was styled upwards with a braid of hair acting as a band to hold the style in place, and off of her face. Finally, a gold circlet headpiece with emerald jewels was placed on her head, she felt like royalty, Mother had never spent so much money on her alone, she had always looked her best but never had her own headpiece, or such an exquisite dress.

Leaving her chambers and walking towards the great hall, she was met by her twin brother, who her mother had dressed so they would match. His emerald tunic and cape set off his dark brown eyes and complimented his sallow skin, a gold horseshoe shaped brooch similar to her headpiece held Edwards cape closed.

'Can you believe these clothes Edward?' excitement filled her voice.

'Mother has higher hopes than I had thought for tonight. After all it is Nicholas to be wed, I would have expected this kind of lavishness with Finn, Mother would need to buy a kingdom to have him wed off.' The twins giggled as they descended down the stone stairs.

'Finn is not that bad, he is quite caring, he would do anything for us in spite of the consequences, and he just needs to learn to stop acting out to get a rise out of Father.' She could tell Edward was thinking for a moment.

'I suppose you are right, as always… Nicholas!' Edward shouted suddenly, as he spotted his older brother ahead of them. Turning in the direction of her brother's excited scream, she noticed her eldest brother looked rather dashing, mother may have spent a lot on their clothes but she spared no expense on her first born. He was dressed in deep blue silks with sky blue and lilac trimmings with pointed shoes. A gold chain with Sapphires which held up his silk and velvet cape draped from his shoulders down to his chest.

'I had to look twice at you, I could not believe that was my brother before me.' Turning to his little sister smiling.

'I know, I know, I am as handsome as ever, she will have a hard time refusing me. Look at you both, Edward you look like a proper little Lord and Cara-Lea you look as beautiful as ever.' Blushing she walked with her brothers noting that one was missing.

'Finn late as usual, he better make it to the great hall before the guests, or mother will have more than his head.'

Turning the corner of the long corridor that led to the great hall, Cara-Lea was surprised when she saw him.

'Finn!' she exclaimed.

He turned in the direction of her voice grinning, he had never been on time for anything, even her brothers where left baffled. She could not believe her eyes, Finn never really made much of an effort with his appearance, he was so blessed he didn't really have to, she had never seen him look so much like a gentleman. His hair had been cut although remaining tousled, he was dressed in a fine black velvet cape which was lined with a gold silk underneath and had gold detailed trimmings along its side that complimented his blonde hair and blue eyes. A tunic that fastened all the way to the neck with four large gold buttons on either side. Pale gold embroidery in the shape of an upside down leaf ran from his collar to his belt and from his wrists to just below his elbows with the rest of his tunic was a shiny black fabric almost like leather. His leather belt with large gold buckle fastened around his waist, whilst the lower part of his tunic was trimmed in that same bright gold embellishment as his cape. Finished with black trousers and leather boots to match. Running up to throw her arms around her brother, she looked at him in amazement.

'You look incredible. Mother will be so happy,' her voice cracked as her brother's arms pulled her into his chest for a short embrace.

'Little sister, is that a tear in your eye?' Finn asked.

'I am just so proud of you,' are the only words she could think to say.

'Hush now, there will be no tears today,' he said reassuringly, 'Let me look at you,' pausing for a moment, he examined his sister's appearance, 'You look like a princess, I should have to stay close to you tonight or some little Lord might try to take you away from me,' giving his sister a warm smile, he turned as his brothers approached.

'Should I fetch the priest to read you your last rights now, or wait until after dinner?'

'Playing the fool again brother?' Nicholas and Finn had forever mocked one another, in fact she could not remember them ever been sincere when they were together.

'Shall we go in,' she interrupted.

'But of course my lady will lead the way,' Finn bowed before his sister, before following her into the Great Hall.

Looking around at all the guests as they were announced, Cara-Lea was left beaming she had never seen so many notable families in one place. Her mother and father where standing in front of the top table, greeting the guests as they entered. Her father was in a white tunic with fawn trousers and cape to match his chain was made of pure gold, her mother was in a white and gold embroidered gown with a long veil finely worked and fastened on her head that covered her shoulders and hung down to her feet. Lord Preston, his wife Ann and their daughter Amelia approached the top table as their two sons Mark and Eugene, and daughter Annabelle took a seat with the other guests. Cara-Lea regarded her brother, who seemed exceedingly happy with his mother's choice for a wife and what was not to like. Amelia was the definition of elegance, her dress was orange with gold trimmings her veil and sleeves were snow white and wrapped in such a way as Lady Olden's, she also wore a gold headpiece that sat on the top of her forehead just where her veil started. She had a very traditional beauty, like so many of the other maidens her eyebrows where overly plucked which was the fashion for women to have a high forehead, pale pink thin lips and large hazel eyes. Nicholas joined his parents to welcome the Preston's and with a chivalrous kiss on the hand, led Amelia to her seat next to him.

'Bjorn the Brave and his daughter Freya,' she heard the announcement over the banter that was going on at her table. Suddenly the room went quiet as every eye stared at the people walking in, Bjorn was a large man as tall as a horse and very muscular with a blonde beard and hair past his shoulders. There were others with him, three men that were not announced, one was a tall man solid young man dressed in the finest black velvet with gold embroidery and the symbol of house Raghnall placed on the right breast of his tunic, the three headed beast shone in the light. The men that accompanied him, were dressed in an emerald green tunics with gold embroidery. Glancing at her brother Edward, she noticed his expression lit up, he had always loved his mother's stories about the fearless Vikings and how Bjorn saved his father's life in battle by throwing a man from a cliff and crushing another's head with a rock when he was outnumbered. Nicholas had a serious expression on his face like he was expecting something bad to happen, but Finn his jaw swung open and the look of astonishment on his face was something she had never witnessed before.

'Brother I do believe you have dropped something?' Nicholas whispered.

Finn looked down at the ground then turned to his brother, 'What are you talking about?'

'You dropped your jaw,' Nicholas sniggered as he turned back to face the approaching guests.

Freya caught every eye in the room as she approached with two dogs either side of her, she was breath taking. Her dress was the first thing Cara-Lea noticed, it was hard to miss her gown was cherry red covered in onyx stones and embroidery, it sat off the shoulder with puffed up arms that slid in tightly from her bicep to her forearm, the red material draped down from there to her knee while the continuing sleeve puffed out again until it reached her wrist. The corset attached had she tightly pulled in, exaggerating her curvaceous figure, the skirt of the dress was quite large fell to the floor with some gathered red material running up either side meeting the corset at her hips. A black choker with a large round ruby sitting in the centre was placed on her neck. Her hair was a tricolour of red brown and blonde blended into one to the point it seemed that her hair changed colour under different lighting. She had a heart shaped face, small but intense sapphire blue eyes and a fuller bottom lip while the top lip was thinner. Her skin was pale but glowing, she truly is a rear beauty.

'Theodore, Mary it has been far too long.' Bjorn gave a hearty call to his old friends, outstretching his arms to lady Olden and shaking Lord Olden's hand.

'Thank you for having us.'

'The pleasure is ours old friend,' Theodore said sincerely.

'I hope you don't mind the extra guests, but I do believe my son Asger was left off the invite.'

'Asger!' Lady Olden gasped. 'We thought you were dead,' she paused for a moment, 'Oh my dear boy.' Lady Olden ran down the steps taking the Norseman into her arms before examining him.

'Who is he?' Cara-Lea asked looking at Nicholas to provide her with some answer.

'Bjorn's first born son, we had heard he was killed with the others, he has been believed to be dead for years,' her brother explained, looking more puzzled the more he thought about it.

'And Freya look at you, you look so much like your mother, she would be proud, come sit tonight is truly a celebration to be had by all.' She had never heard such excitement in her mother's voice. Whatever their story, these Vikings had definitely caught her attention. Examining the room again with Finn's jaw continuing to scrape the floor and the whispers that had started at the surrounding tables, it looked like she was not the only person to be intrigued by these guests, and this should prove to be a very interesting night indeed.

Finn

Asger had been seated next to him, noting the look the young Lord's face he smiled, 'What's the matter? Never seen a dead man before?' Finns expression brightened as a row of laughter came from his end of the table. The first course of food had been served, it smelled delicious and although hungry as he was eating, was the last thing on his mind. Asger had been placed beside him while his sister had been seated next to Cara-Lea, the two that had accompanied them, had been seated next to the other guests.

'So how does it feel to be back from the dead?'

'Not as good as one would hope, I will have to think of a new party trick for next time,' raising an eyebrow and giving Finn a slightly crooked grin.

'Forgive me, but how is it you survived?'

'That was my father's doing, like you I have a certain quality for lack of a better word for vexing my father, I was sent away to train with my uncle and his men the day before the raids took place, everyone who knew about my departure was killed with my father and sister being the exception to that of course, he figured since I was still but a boy and giving my family's history for people wanting to kill us, keeping the fact that I lived a secret was the best thing we could do be sure I would not be hunted.'

'I am truly sorry for your loss, but how is it you know about me?'

'I am to be king, not your king of course but a king none the less, it is my job to find out as much about the other houses. I can to be sure I keep good company when I regain my throne.'

'That is a very bold statement to make.'

'Indeed, but men are not remembered for doing things quietly.'

'Well said,' raising a cup of ale, both men washed their first course down.

As the second course of stuffed peacock arrived, Finn repeatedly glanced over to where his sister was seated, the girls were giggling but for the life of him he could not figure out what they were talking about, his eyes ran over the table his mother in deep conversation with Ann Preston, and his father with Henry Preston and Bjorn. Nicholas, Edward and Amelia seemed to be getting on well. Knowing his love for his own sister and remembering his promise to his mother, he refused to query the Vikings past too much in case he caused offence, unless of course Asger mentioned it first. Pouring more ale for his guest and himself, he had hoped that would loosen Asger's tongue a bit, they spent the past while discussing different weapons and fighting styles along with what their opinions were on different the other houses that had joined the festivities, he caught his mother's eye from across the table, who gave him a proud smile which made him feel content in himself.

'So when will it be your turn to be married off,' Asger asked mockingly.

'Me?' he was shocked, but also found the question rather amusing.

'The only thing Finn loves more than himself is his ale and swords,' Nicholas interrupted.

'Nice of you to join us brother, to be honest I've never thought about it.'

'No maidens that catch your attention eh?'

'Not exactly, I mean look at the women here, why would I want a woman who's missing her eyebrows, I would never be able to tell if she was smiling, or frowning.' A loud laugh came from the men seated around him.

'I see your point Finn, thank the Gods that Freya has not started that she can be hard enough to read with the little expressions she gives as it is, women eh? Another round of ale should help us forget about them.'

After the remaining three courses of roasted wild boar, pears in red wine and a selection of nuts had been served, Finn felt fit to burst the music had just begun and surely enough there were already a few up dancing, Asger being one of the first swinging Annabelle Preston around the room, it was evident he had not much experience in dancing with women. The realisation had kicked in that he had consumed more ale than food as he felt it start to go to his head, thinking it best to step outside for a moment so as not to do anything to upset his mother, he excused himself from his table and casually walked out of the great hall to the back of his family home to the gardens where there would be a seat he was hoping to pass out on. As he got outside, he noticed a crisp chill in the air that was oddly refreshing everyone had been inside so if he would do anything foolish out here there would be nobody to see him. Finding a bench he lay down and hoped his double vision would leave him soon. After a while he heard footsteps, sitting up he looked around until he saw her, down by the fountain the maiden in the red dress with her four dogs he could only make out three but he knew one was as black as night and would be harder to make out especially to inebriated eyes. Slowly he approached her.

'A fine gown that is my lady,' Freya turned and looked startled at first, she said nothing just kept her eyes fixed on Finn.

'I think it would look better on the floor of my chambers?' before he realised what came out of his mouth, he felt a sharp pain across his face as her hand shot hard across it, Freya turned and stormed off. Laughter came from the other side of him.

'She didn't take too kindly to that, did she?' it was Gilli.

'What a woman!' Finn exclaimed as both men laughed.

'What were you thinking?' Finn still holding his face.

'That's just it, I wasn't, it just came out.'

'I think she likes me,' he said jesting.

After a while of speaking with Gilli outside, Finn re-entered the great hall, he quickly glanced around him and saw Nicholas and Amelia speaking with Cara-Lea and Freya, taking a deep breath he marched over towards them.

'Apologies for the interruption, my lady may I have a word,' taking Freya by the hand Finn led her away from his siblings and over to a secluded corner where he would not be overheard.

'Forgive me, I have realised large quantities of ale can make my mouth say things my mind did not wish them to.'

'I have heard many things about you Finn Olden and being a gentleman is not one of them, so stop trying to act like one now, that was the real you in the garden but a few moments ago not this persona now.'

'No, I mean yes that is the way I would normally behave but my words are genuine I am sorry if I have caused offence, is there anything I can do to make it up to you?' But before she could answer Cara-Lea had grabbed Freya by the hand and brought her up to dance with Edward and the others.

'You don't want to go there brother,' Edward's voice said quietly.

'What are you talking about Edward?'

'I have seen the way you have stared all night at her, you like the Viking.'

'Don't be so daft,' he replied, shaking off his brothers comments.

'She killed her betrothed do you know that? The scars that sit on her shoulders are from his hounds, now with the Prince being alive and the only surviving Draconian dead, this could be the start of a war brother, stay away from Freya,' and with that warning Edward had disappeared into the crowd.

After his brothers warning, Finn found himself consuming more ale until he was left stumbling out of the great hall walking up the corridor to the stone steps which led to his chambers he heard a commotion.

'She is only a chamber maid after all.'

'Does her heart not beat like every others?' Looking around he found that Freya and a guard arguing with a girl crying on the floor.

'What is the meaning of this?' he said sternly.

'Your man just tried to rape this poor girl!' Her voice cracked. Finn could tell she was flustered. Finn called for the other guards, when they arrived he ordered his arrest and had him taken away.

'Are you alright?' he asked the sobbing girl on the cold stone steps.

'I am sorry my lord.'

'Sorry? You have nothing to be sorry for.' As she stumbled to her feet, Finn noticed her dress was ripped and her face bruised, removing his cape he draped it around the chamber maids shoulders.

'I will see to her wounds,' Freya's words were low, as Finn passed the girl over to Freya.

'Do you know where your room is?' he asked Freya.

'Just up that staircase to the left your sister showed me earlier.' He watched as Freya walked away with the still sobbing girl before ascending up the stone staircase to his chambers.

A loud knock on his door woke him from his slumber the next morning, rising from his bed still half asleep he opened the door to find Nicholas standing outside.

'Good morning beautiful,' he said loudly as he entered his room.

'Sleeping naked again I see?'

'What do you want Nicholas, didn't mother tell you morning mass is not a must while the guests are here.'

'So I have been told, not the reason I am here. Freya told us how you saved that girl from been attacked last night.'

'I'd hardly call it saved, I showed up when she was on the floor it was Freya who discovered her.'

'Nonetheless, Father is actually applauding you since he found out, you are wanted to come down to break the fast with us immediately, which means as much as you adore looking at your own body you will need to put some clothes on, I suggest something warm, we are to go hunting later with our new guests.'

Edward

He had never been hunting before, never wanting to go but Father insisted this time. ‘But Mother, I do not know how to hunt,’ he complained.

‘Just stay near your father and brothers and you will be fine.’ Reassuring words from his mother, she was right Finn and Nicholas are great hunters and Father thought them both.

The woods were cold and damp even while wearing his furs the icy bite of the air sunk its teeth into the slightest bit of exposed skin. He saw his breath in front of him as he tried to keep his balance on the slippery ground beneath him, this was not Edwards idea of fun, he would much rather be at home in the library with his head in a book. He had already seen Bjorn drop a rock on a fox and crush its skull, Nicholas kill a family of rabbits, Asger bring down a few hawks and they had barely left home. They still had a bit to travel before they would spot anything of note. Hearing a rustle in the trees as he walked by, he looked up and spotted a squirrel sitting on the branch of an old pine tree. Taking his bow, he tried to line up his shot closing one eye and breathing rapidly he was about to make his first kill.

‘You will shoot much well with both eyes open,’ Freya was standing beside him smiling.

‘I’ll show you,’ she knelt down beside Edward and helped him line up his bow.

‘Keep both eyes open…breathe out…and release.’ The bow string cut into his soft fingers he had very little experience with weapons, not realising that shooting a bow would prove to be painful on his cold hands.

‘Father I did it, I did it. Father Look!’ Running up to him with the dead squirrel in hand.

‘Well done Edward’, he looked up at his father beaming with pride, while the others looked on smiling.

'Well done, little man.' Nicholas tossed his hair as he rubbed Edwards head.

After half a day of hunting the men returned to house Olden. Among the animals brought back, Theodore brought back a wolf, Bjorn brought back three fox's, Nicholas and Finn brought back a family of rabbits and a wild boar, Freya and Asger came back with two deer and four hawks and Edward came back with his squirrel.

Sitting at the table enjoying the warmth of his evening meal, Edward overheard a conversation Finn and his father were having.

'And the Guard from last night what of him?'

'He will be castrated for his crimes, the girl is ok just a bit shaken up lucky Freya and you showed up when you did, I am proud of you son.'

'There is nothing to be proud of Father with all due respect I showed up after Freya had disrupted the attack.'

'Finn you know as well as I that if you hadn't been there that poor girl could have been attacked too, it has happened in the past, some men when they get the slightest bit of power, go mad with it and want to use that as a weapon against people they see as beneath them.' Edward could not make out what they were saying after that as they were walking further away from him.

The next day after his morning studies, Edward and his sister went down to the training grounds to see the men in competition. 'I found the Norsemen very intriguing, so I did a little reading, and their history is fascinating, did you know they have warriors that have been said to transform into bears, wolves and wild boars.'

'Edward please for someone so intelligent you cannot believe that a person can transform into an animal.'

'It is what is in the book! Anyway the name Freya is from a Goddess they believe to be the most beautiful and she is the goddess of love, but naming your child after someone your supposed to worship would that not be blasphemy for them?'

'I know not brother you are just going to have to ask them yourself.'

When they arrived, it was Finn and Asger armed with blunt swords and shields. As they were coming at one another, it was clear that Finn was the better swordsman but Asger was more powerful, blow after blow was being delivered by Finn almost knocking Asger to the ground but one good hit from Asger knocked Finn half way across the training ground. Edward had never seen Finn be overpowered like that before, but he kept coming back no matter how hard he got hit, Finn would just come back faster and stronger.

Eventually, it looked like both men were too exhausted to lift their shields to block or their swords to swing. Turning to Nicholas, he asked. 'How long have they been fighting?'

'Well over an hour now, at least they had already started before we came out.' Nicholas looked at Freya to see if she knew.' At least, I have never seen anyone able to handle Asger like that.' Amelia was standing beside Freya.

'Your brother does not back down easily my love.' Regarding her betrothed.

'Finn never backs down, if you want to stop him you'd have to kill him.' Cara-Lea's voice rang with pride at her older brother's performance.

'As Father always said, it's not how good the dog can fight, it's how much fight is in the dog and Finns bite is worse than his bark.' Edward always admired Finn but he also feared him because of his unpredictability, but he knew as well as everyone in the family that if anything ever happened, Finn is the one to run too and that is all the security his little heart needed as long as his brothers were around nobody could possibly hurt his family, and he was delighted that the onlookers from the other households got to see first-hand there is a reason that his family name has been around for generations.

Edward knew his brothers were getting ready to go hunting again and that Freya would be going with them. He would have to act fast in order to find out the answers, he so desperately wanted. 'Umm, Freya… I was reading a book earlier about Vikings and umm.' his stomach was churning, he felt his face flush, how was he going to ask his questions without causing offence?

'Oh for goodness' sake Edward!' His twin interrupted.

'What he is trying to ask is, how exactly is it you got your name?' Shooting her brother a look of contempt. He slowly raised his head to look at Freya who seemed amused by his curiosity.

‘My mother, she chose my name some would say she had a very strange way off thinking, others thought she would anger the Gods by calling me by such name, but my mother never gave it a second thought,’ she said smiling as she remembered Catherine.

‘If I dare be so bold? Why did she not care if she angered the Gods?’

‘Because my mother did not believe in them, she like you believed in a God that died upon a cross, she chose my name because she liked it, it is that simple.’

‘But if your parents had different faiths how did that not cause strife?’ Edward noted Cara-Lea’s face fill with anger, and his brothers entertained expressions, no doubt at his cherry red face.

‘They did, they would argue all the time but they loved each other nonetheless. Many think my parents’ marriage was arranged but it was not, they chose to be together, went against their families. My father was cast out and became a humble farmer like every other Viking while my mother raised myself and four brothers, it was only after my grandfather found out their where traitors in the people he believed loyal to him that he accepted my family back. The mutiny was not long after so Asger has told me anyway I was too young to remember it, Soon after my grandfather was killed the raids started, two of my uncles and their families were killed, and mine was next. Father had been away at that time, he left the day before with Asger to see him get safely to my uncle. I remember the sky was filled with fire and a thick smoke, my brothers screaming, my mother could fight better than most men but there were too many of them, she was slain trying to protect her children.’

‘How did you survive my lady?’

‘My brother Nate, he grabbed me and ran for what felt like hour, he was older than I, knew how to hunt and to set traps he protected me, we were safe. One morning, I woke to find Nate had not, I tried everything but he would not wake, I do not recall much after that just waking to find my father carrying me. I later found out he had not been gone but a forth night, it felt like years. Nate had died, he had been injured in the raid and his wounds became infected. Father said Nate would have felt greatly sick, but he never showed it.' Edward watched as her eyes filled with tears.

'Forgive me,' he said, reaching for her hand. 'I did not mean to pry, or to cause pain.' Freya gathered herself as she realised it that she had an audience, excusing herself, she turned heel quickly while Edward was left feeling guilt about his previous presumptions, he had heard she had been responsible for the death of betrothed and like so many assumed it was because she was a violent Viking, but having listening to her speak, he felt there was more to the story then what he had heard.

Bjorn

As he walked down the corridor, he could not help but appreciate that it was full of paintings of all the previous Olden lords, just before the great hall was the painting of Theodore and his family, Nicholas and Finn were much younger in it and the twins barely out of the womb. While admiring the Olden family portrait, he could not help but feel sorrow as he missed his own family dearly. 'The Gods had spared the lives of his only daughter and his eldest son, but his beautiful wife Catherine and sons Nate, Gram, Abi and Asfrith had been taken from him.

'It should have been me,' he said quietly to himself.

'You were not wanted,' a voice familiar voice came from behind him. Theodore stood behind him, gazing at his family portrait.

'I will never know the hurt you have felt my friend, and I cannot imagine the scars your soul has been left with.'

'If only I was there Theo, I could have done something, saved my boys… My wife.' His voice was full of anger yet his eyes were full of hurt.

'You would have been killed if you were there.'

'I would have welcomed it! A glorious death.'

'And who might I ask would have been there to save Freya? You live for a reason, you are not being called home yet… She looks just like her mother.'

'So she does, she has her temperament too.'

'Catherine was a force to be reckoned with.'

'You can say that again, try been married to the woman! I remember I was gravely ill, my sleeping must have offended her at the time because she cracked open my skull with a spade and told me to get out of bed.' Both men burst out laughing.

'It was the best cure for an illness I ever had, never been ill again since that day.'

'I cannot imagine Freya mimicking that.'

'You don't know her Theo, she is too much like her mother, she may seem placid to you but deep down there is the same bloodlust that runs through her as it did Catherine, I handed her the dagger you know when that bastard tried to kill her.' Theodore just looked at his friend not knowing what to say. 'Since then I have sent her to Asger, he has trained her well it struck me that day that I will not always be there to protect her no matter how much I want to, the evil in this world is too powerful to overcome. Freya is afraid not of hurting another but of enjoying it, she fears the darkness in her soul that has been growing since she witnessed her mother slaughtered.'

'You must not blame yourself, anyone who has been through what your daughter has would have their heart darkened, Freya is not evil nor a threat to anyone bar my sons face.' A wide eyed Bjorn paused and glanced at his friend nervously.

'Oh you heard about that? Do not worry, it's about time someone smacked some sense into him…' Before he could finish his sentence, Theodore was interrupted loud muffled shouting in coming from the entrance of his home, both men quickly ran in the direction off of the commotion. It was Gilli and Nicholas, they were covered in blood.

'My boy what happened?' Theodore panted.

'Bandits! We were out hunting we must have disturbed them.' Gilli shouted confused and afraid.

'Father Finn, and Asger have not returned.' Nicholas seemed calm, Theodore knew his son was concerned about his brother.

'My son?' Bjorn gasped.

'Gilli fetch me my sword.' Bjorn barked as he ran out to get a horse. He was not going to lose another child.

He could feel his heartbeat hard in his chest, his mind raced, 'Not my Asger, You have taken so much from me Oden, Don't you dare take my son too.' The horse galloped fast up towards the gates of house Olden, he knew once he was outside of the walls, the forest entrance would greet him but moments after. The sound of Theodore's stallion dashing along behind him was the only other noise he could hear.

Upon entering the forest, it was clear to see how an ambush could have taken place. There was a heavy mist surrounding him and with the trees already blocking out the suns light, he found it hard to study his surroundings.

'Asger!' the echo followed his voice, he listened a moment but no answer came.

'We last seen them down near the river.' Gilli's voice cracked behind him.

'We should proceed with caution my friend, those bandits could still be lurking around…our boys are safe I know it.' Admiring Theodore and his ability to stay calm in any situation, he slowly trotted through the trees towards the river. Bjorn noticed a trail of bodies leading up in the direction they were going, none of which were Asger or Finn thankfully, pools of blood covered the once green grass, tainting the soil beneath, none of the men spoke, no words where needed this was a battle, he counted twenty bodies so far to the five that went hunting. A branch broke meters away from him, he turned in the direction.

'My Lord!' The voice panted.

'Thank the Gods,' as the voice got closer Bjorn was able to make out who it belonged to. Bjorn dismounted from his horse.

'Nari, where is my son?'

'The last I saw he was near the bridge at the lake, there was too many bandits, we got separated.' Tears filled the young man's eyes he was injured barely standing blood was dripping from his leg and the side of his face had been slashed. 'Gilli get Nari back to house Olden and get Freya to see to his wounds, she will know what to do.' Bjorn lifted Nari onto Gilli's horse and sent them back the way they came.

Approaching the Bridge Nari spoke of, the men all listened out to see if they could hear any signs of Finn or Asger. Bjorn had hoped Nari would be ok he had known him since he was but a boy, not his own son but he always treated him like one, he had grown close to the family since the raids, Asger always joked that Nari and Gilli were the unofficial members of the Bjorn's family. Just as he was beginning to give up on the thoughts of finding his son here, he heard loud rustling and fast paced footsteps heading in his direction. 'Bandits.' he thought the boys would be quieter than that surely. Reaching for his sword as the footsteps grew ever closer, he was not going to be taken out by some outlaws.

'Finn!' Theodore cried.

Bjorn looked up and saw Finn approaching, he had something on his shoulders but through the mist Bjorn could not figure out what is was. Finn looked exhausted blood and sweat ran down his face, there was a gash just above his left eye and another on his forearm. Looking up again at the object on Finn's shoulders, a sick feeling overcame him as he realised it was his son Finn had been carrying back, he felt his heart sink as he watched his only remaining son motionlessly being brought back to him.

Nicholas

His mind ran wild, 'What were the bandits after? Why attack them with no intent to steal? Where was his brother?'
The last he had seen Finn they were approaching the wooden bridge in the middle of the forest tracking a deer when an arrow shot by his head missing his eye by mere inches. He was blessed that their archer was not a skilled shot, as he turned in the direction the arrow came from a swarm of men were quickly descending down the hill at the unsuspecting hunters. They had no armour and the only weapons they were equipped with were the crossbows arrows they used for hunting.

'There are too many of them,' Gilli shouted.

'We have to retreat to house Olden,' Nari followed.

'The only way back is up that hill,' Nicholas protested.

'Today is a great day to die! But I'll be taking as many of those scum with me,' Asger growled as he shot a few arrows into the mob quickly approaching them. His thoughts left him as he heard a loud shriek, looking up he saw Amelia running towards him.

'My love!' she panted. 'I had just heard the news, thanks be to God that you are okay. You are hurt?' she asked frightfully as she drank in his blood soaked appearance.

'I am not,' he said bluntly. 'It is not my blood.' Nicholas examined his betrotheds stunned appearance for a moment.

'Is there news of my brother?' Amelia hung her head.

'There is no news my love, your father has yet to return.' There was a knock on the door, as one of the chamber maids had entered the room with a basin water and some cloth.

'How dare you enter my, betroths room without being invited in…'

'Amelia I had sent the girl to fetch me something I could clean myself up with.' Nicholas snapped.

'Apologies my love.'

'It is not I, you owe an apology too,' Amelia's expression changed from one of regret to one of offence. 'You expect me to apologies to the help?' she spat.

'I expect you to be obedient and do as I ask, you are not my wife yet and nor shall you be if think you are above the small folk, they may not have been born with titles or prosperity but they are the people who provide your food, make your clothes and provide healing for the sick all of which you would not survive without, now leave us.' Amelia dare not argue, her husband to be was infuriated, she thought it best to do as he asked and exit his chambers.

After a few moments, Nicholas heard shouting in the village square, he looked out the window to see it was Gilli, shouting for help. He had Nari alongside him. Quickly putting on a fresh tunic, Nicholas raced out of his chambers, down the long stone staircase and out of his home to the village square. Trying to push his way past the gathering crowds.

'Freya? Where is Freya?' Gilli desperately called, as Nicholas grew closer to them, he noticed Nari had been seriously wounded he had half an arrow snapped in the side of his leg and was holding a blood soaked rag to one half of his face no doubt cloth Gilli had torn from his own clothes to offer his friend to try stop the bleeding.

'Gilli? Where are the others? Where is my brother?' Nicholas begged.

'Bjorn and your father continue their search, I was told to bring Nari back here, please I beg of you, where is Freya?'

At that moment just as Nicholas had done, Cara-Lea and Freya pushed their way through the gathering crowds towards her friends.

'Gilli? What happened here? Where is Asger? Where is my brother?'

'I know not my Lady, your father and Lord Olden are out looking for him and Finn as we speak, but please Nari is hurt. He needs your help.'

Freya slowly approached her wounded friend, who Gilli had been supporting up, removing his hand from his face so she could get a better look.

'You have lost a lot of blood.' she whispered before turning to Gilli.

‘He won’t make it up to his chambers, can you carry him?’

‘I think so, my lady,’ he replied hesitantly.

‘I will help,’ Nicholas announced, stepping forward towards the injured Norseman.

As Freya turned to Cara-Lea, ‘I will need a lot off ale or whatever alcohol you can find me.’

‘Do you really think now is the best time to be drinking?’ Nicholas asked shocked.

‘It’s for his wounds!’ Freya snapped.

‘I will also need something to dress them and a spoon and needle, can you get them for me.’ He watched as his sister nodded at her new friend and disappeared into the crowd.

Once they had reached the room that Nari had been staying in, Nicholas placed the injured guest on the bed, as Cara-Lea quickly followed with the items she had been asked for, looking on in awe at how quickly Freya worked to help mend her friends injuries. Picking up a large jug of alcohol, Freya instructed her friend to close his eyes and she poured it onto his face and again to his leg.

‘Gilli! Nicholas! I need you to hold Nari down while I get this thing out of his leg.’ Cara-Lea, I need milk of the poppy.’

‘No Freya,’ Nari whimpered.

‘Hush now my friend it will help ease your pain.’ Not knowing what action to take next, Nicholas glanced down at Gilli, who was holding down Nari’s legs. ‘This is going to sting, I will try make this as brief as I can,’ with that Freya placed one hand on the broken arrow in her friends leg and the other on his hip, as she pressed down on his hip she pulled the remainder of the arrow out of Nari. Grunts of pain filled the room, Nicholas turned to look at Freya who was holding the shaft of the arrow in her hand.

‘Where is the head?’ he begged. Gilli looked horrified as the realisation hit him.

‘It’s still inside him! What do we do?’ Freya noting the panic in Gilli’s voice remained calm. ‘I thought that might happen, now where that spoon I asked for?’ Searching her surroundings for a moment before placing her hand on it, she raised the spoon to examine it before washing it down with alcohol.

‘I am sorry dear friend, this is going to hurt, hold him down!’ Nari’s screamed echoed through the halls.

Cara-Lea ran into the room as the screaming subsided. 'I have the milk of the poppy,' she announced.

'Turns out he doesn't need it now,' Gilli joked.

Nicholas loosened his grip as he realised the man he had been holding down had passed out.

'Thank you for all your help, I can see to mending his wounds from here,' Freya said as she placed the arrow head on the chest at the bottom of the bed.

Closing the door behind them, Nicholas turned to Gilli, 'How did she learn to do that? What make men pass out, bit of a gift our women have to offer,' he laughed.

'After Rosefort, her injuries took a long while to heal up, when her father would have to leave home to travel her uncle and his wife Clara took care of Freya. Turns out Clara is a Volva.'

'A Volva?' Nicholas asked.

'A witch,' Cara-Lea interrupted.

'Some might say that yes,' Gilli continued, 'A healer to us none the less, anyway she helped mend Freya's injuries and that of the men in the village that would pick them up in battle, as Freya could do nothing else until she was fully healed she followed Clara around and learned how to treat various illnesses and injuries which of course has it's uses to us.'

'Do you think Nari will be okay?' Cara-Lea asked innocently.

'I have every faith in Freya, is she dismissed us and was happy to proceed alone, I do believe he will recover nicely.' It was the first time since before they were attacked that Nicholas felt relatively at ease.

'Lord Olden approaches,' the guard's announced, as they walked back to the village square. The crowd that had dispersed earlier, had flocked back together again. *Please don't be dead,* he thought to himself as he watched his father in the distance grow ever closer, knowing full well that his father would not return without Finn dead or alive. Feeling his sisters hands wrap tightly around his arm, he knew he should say something to reassure her. 'Finn will be fine, I have seen him face far worse odds than what we were up against.' Only half a lie he told himself, it's true his brother had angered many people before with his behaviour and foul mouth but in every fight he was properly armed unlike today, a crossbow was a great weapon but not for fighting heavy numbers up close, it took too long to ready.

The streets were filled with small folk looking on at their Lord approaching with his men. Nicholas could see his father's horse Steal trot up toward him, Finn was motionless his face buried in the horse's main as his arms hung on either side of its neck, being held on by his father who was seating behind his sons body.

'He lives,' Theodore announced as he spotted his children's worried expressions as they gazed upon their brothers unconscious body, a great feeling of relief hit Nicholas, knowing his brother was alive, a feeling that did not last as he noticed Bjorn pull his son from his horse.

'Asger,' Gilli screamed as he pushed past the crowd towards his friend. 'Is he?' looking upon his friend he could not bear to finish his sentence.

'He lives, but only just, where is my daughter?' Bjorn fought back the sadness in his voice, but could not hide the look of sorrow on his face. 'She is with Nari, my Lord.'

'Bring her to me at once, I will bring my son to the room which he is staying.'

'Yes my Lord,' Gilli's voice quivered as he answered Bjorn.

'Nicholas,' his father beckoned. 'Take your brother to his chambers, and see to it that he gets seen too immediately, I could care less what monk or priestess sees to him as long as they do it quickly.'

'Yes Father as you wish.' Reaching up for his brother's body, he noticed the guards behind his father also had someone riding with them. He watched for a moment as they dragged the man off the horse and up towards his home.

'See to it that brute gets a warm welcome before showing him to his cell, I will be there momentarily.'

Nicholas noticed he was wearing the same clothes as those that had attacked them earlier, it was a strange thing for his father to keep a bandit alive especially for making an attempt on the lives of two of his own children. As he pulled Finn down off the horse his legs almost buckled under the weight of his brothers body, with him being unconscious Finn was dead weight, he signalled to one of the guards to come and help him get his brother to his chambers.

'Sister go and get somebody to help Finn, I will see to it that we don't drop him getting him up the stairs.' Cara-Lea let out a small laugh as she watched her brother and one of her father's guards hoist Finn up and carry him away.

Theodore

As he sat under a large oak tree just outside of the gardens of his home with his head in his hands, he contemplated what to do with the prisoner, normally he would have killed him the moment he found him but Theodore longed for answers, what were bandits doing so close to his home? They had not been seen near house Olden since Nicholas was but a boy. Why attack men who clearly had nothing to steal aside from a handful of hunting weapons? There was something more to the attack that took place that day, he could feel it in his bones.

'I knew I would find you here.' His wife said softly as she sat down beside her husband.

'I find great peace here,' he said, looking around to admire the view of the emerald green grass that sprung up from the rich soil that covered the land.

There was a view of the entrance to the gardens which illuminated in the sunlight, with the shrubbery that enfolded around the garden like the wall of a hedge maze, multi-coloured flowers shone all through the garden with a with marble fountain carved with angels along its base acted as the centrepiece. Anytime Theodore would find his mind troubled he would always stroll up to that oak tree and find tranquillity where he sat.

'What is to happen to that man, which occupies the dungeon?' she asked calmly.

'I have yet to decide,' he answered honestly. 'I require answers in which he alone can give, but he will not talk easily.'

'There are ways around a stubborn tongue my love.'

'Do you think me a coward my lady? Torture is an option, when a man has no honour. I have seen the men that take pride in inflicting pain on others and take pride in it, they are lower than the worms that consume the flesh of the dead,' he spat.

‘Forgive me my Lord, I am but a stupid woman, I did not mean to anger you.’ Taking a deep breath in.

‘It is I that should be asking for your forgiveness my lady, I need not take my frustrations out on you, but to the people who tried to kill our sons.’

‘I feared the worst for Finn when he had not returned with Nicholas,’ Mary muttered as she welled up.

If he was not so damned stubborn, he could have easily been killed out there. For once his rebellious nature turned out to be positive. He chuckled at the thought.

Finn was always more than a handful, he refused to do anything that did not suit him and the men that had set out to take his life, would have surely found it frustrating when he refused to die for them.

‘Thanks be to God that it was Finn and not Nicholas who got cornered with Asger,’ he said softly as he watched as his wife shot him a look of disgust. ‘I have no doubt both of our boys can fight and fight well, but giving the circumstances I don’t think Nicholas would have made it out of there alive,’ he explained. He watched as his wife thought for a moment.

‘I would not count Nicholas out so easily, my love, he was with Finn when they got attacked.’

After deciding not to make any rash decisions, Theodore figured it best to go check in on his sons and Asger first. The guest rooms where the first to meet him as he got to the top of the staircase, Bjorn and Gilli were pacing outside the floor of the room Asger had been occupying.

‘How is he?’ Bjorn whose back was facing him looked around at his friend, Echoed Screams filled the halls and threw Theodore momentarily.

‘If she can stop the bleeding, Freya thinks he will be able to make a recovery.’ Gilli answered uncomfortably trying to ignore the cries of his friend.

‘She has had to use fire,’ Bjorn’s voice was mournful.

‘Dear God,’ Theodore gasped. He had witnessed men having their wounds closed by burning the area in which they were injured. The smell of burning flesh seeped out of the room, they stood outside and all went quiet. Moments later, Cara-Lea opened the door and entered the hall she nearly fell down when she noticed her father was standing in front of her gazing in astonishment.

'Father, I wanted to help.' she explained. 'I need Turmeric paste.'

'Cara-Lea we do not have anything like that here.'

'I have some it's in my room,' Gilli announced as he led Cara-Lea back down the hallway.

'Turmeric?' was the only thing Theodore could think to say, Bjorn just regarded him with a half-smile.

After leaving Bjorn down the hallway and growing ever closer to his son's room, he was left dumbfounded, since when had his daughter such an interest in the healing of others? Where would you find Turmeric on this side of the earth? Surely Gilli did not travel for months just for one spice?

'Father are you okay?' Nicholas asked.

'Turmeric?' he whispered under his breath all the while staring at the floor. 'Nothing, it's fine. How is your brother?' shrugging off his confusion.

'Unconscious last I saw, one of the monks are in there now Cara-Lea found him at the church, he says Finn will be fine it will take a few weeks for him to recover and the gash on his head should not cause any scaring, he will be happy to know when he wakes.'

'I will go grace our prisoner with my presence, if anything changes send word.'

'As you wish Father.'

The dungeon was damp and cold, when Theodore arrived. It had been years since he was down here, the foul smell of decomposed rodents struck him the further he walked in. His guards waited outside the cell off the man who went to take his sons lives, immediately he felt like beheading him but he could not, not if he wanted his answers.

'You stand accused of attempted murder of five men, two of which happen to be my sons and heirs to house Olden.' Theodore's voice ran deep, his posture straightened and chest pressed out, to any man sitting, he would look like a giant. No answer came, the bandit just sat on the floor staring at the ground. 'Why did you come here?' he asked again, no answer from the bandit. 'I suggest you find your tongue boy, before I have it removed.' That got his attention, he slowly looked up at Lord

Olden, a sadistic grin shot across his face. 'Behold Lord Olden in all his glory, and the King of Kings Bjorn the Brave,' he taunted.

'So you know who you attacked.' Theodore replied bluntly.

'I know who was attacked, but the question is do you know? Do you know what they are? Killers the lot of them!'

'You and your men attacked them!' He barked.

'And look what happened, all my men are dead, yet your five survive, if it was any other five they would have perished.' The prisoner hissed as he fixated on Theodore, his face was grey, like it had not seen sunlight before, his dark hair and eyebrows set off his light blue eyes which looked glazed over, the sadistic look on his face sent chills down Theodore's spine, the hair on the back of his neck stood up and his blood ran cold. If evil had a face surely it was the one that he was looking upon at this moment.

'Those men you attacked are well versed in the art of combat.'

'As were mine, but yet five of your highly skilled soldiers managed to escape with their lives against thirty of my men, what are the odds.' His twisted face brightened up as his voice went ever higher.

'However impressed I am, your sons where just bad timing, it was the Vikings we came for and if it wasn't for the stupidity of that animal you call a son, coming back to aid the Viking prince we would have succeeded.'

'Why do you want them dead?'

'They want the throne, have plans to reclaim it, our people cannot allow that.'

'Bjorn is the rightful King!' Theodore barked.

'Indeed!' the prisoner shouted excitedly. 'Which is why we must finish what we started, their bloodline will end, those things you have in your guestrooms will fall one by one until their bloodline is extinct.'

'I've heard enough,' Theodore raised his right hand. 'For your crimes I, Theodore Olden, son of Jaime Olden and Lord of the land, sentence you to death by the hangman's noose, my word on this soil is law and will be done, may God have mercy on your soul.' As he marched out of the cell, the prisoner's voice followed him.

‘You cannot stop this Lord Olden! Eventually they will all be dead and your family with them if you try to shield them!’ As he got to the top of the dungeons he slammed the door behind him, the bandit knew too much for just a passer-by, he had not been through the walls, or Theodore would have noticed. Were their bandit spies in his land, or worse a traitor living among his family? He would have to find answers soon and prepare the men for another attack.

Drew

It had only been days, since Asger left him in charge of Rosefort but it felt like weeks, the people were coming to him with their problems and wanting resolutions. He worried about the decisions he made but more than that he worried about his Princess and his Kings safety surely there would be a target on them once it was discovered Asger had lived? Walking through the kingdom, he counted his blessings that he had not perished out there in the woods alone, that Roderick Draconian had been killed and Freya had lived, that Rosefort was now hers to control and that the people in the Kingdom now felt safe and happy, and he got to be a part of that.

Rosefort was the most secure out of all Kingdoms, there were three sets of walls and gates to pass through before you ever got the city each within ten miles of each other, each gate heavier and thicker than the last. The final wall was light grey in colour with bright green ivy climbing ever higher. Once inside Rosefort, a maze of hedges and rose bushes greeting you to your left and a babbling brook shimmered to the right. The flowers were in bloom Tulips of every colour stood to attention, leading towards the castle which was situated on the top of the steep mountain side overlooking the Realm.

There were acres of land set aside and separated for the different animals to run free from cages, a horse ranch positioned to the left of the city, Mines at the back of the land as to not interrupt the beauty of the empire. Apple trees were planted just outside of town so the small folk could always go and gather some if they were in need of food. The soil was known to be the richest and fertile of all the lands, it was said you could grow almost anything in Rosefort.

As he walked back through the city towards the castle, Drew noticed a commotion outside one of the taverns, as he approached he noticed a child being tossed in the air between two soldiers.

'Put him down at once,' he commanded the men stopped and turned towards Drew. The little one was put down, it was then he realised it was not a child but a small man.

'What is the meaning of this?'

'Nothing going on here Andrew just a harmless bit of Dwarf tossing,' one of the men giggled.

'Harmless? This man could have been seriously hurt, and you find it funny?' Baffled by the actions of Asger's men, he turned to the Dwarf.

'My deepest apologies, this should not have happened.'

'No, it shouldn't,' the little man snapped. 'But it always does, men like that find it amusing to pick on those different from themselves it has happened before and it will happen again.'

'I give you my word no one in this kingdom will ever do something like this again, take them away.' Drew barked at the other soldiers.

'You're not the Lord of this house boy, why should we listen to you?' one man hissed.

'Lord and Lady Raghnall left me in charge in their absence, my word is law until they come back when I say take them men away I mean it so do as I say, or you will be joining them understand.' He felt his blood boil and patience wearing thin. The men were restrained and taking away to the dungeons.

'What is your name?'

'Asher… I must say that was rather entertaining to watch, not many people show respect for us little people as you did, it can make you some enemies choosing a dwarf over your own kind.' They are not my kind, they may look similar and fight for the same house but those men have no honour.' Asher was standing before him for a few moments before Drew realised he had been standing with his garments ripped.

'Come, we will get you some new clothes.'

After Asher was dressed in new clothes, he looked around, 'You have a lot of dogs here, how does one keep track of them all. With great difficulty and they are not all mine they belong to the Princess, she has a great deal of animals dogs are only the start.' A small pup ran up to Asher, he was no more than a few weeks old, white with black spots all over on his side he had a large black heart shape on his fur. 'That's Loki, Freya found him in the woods about three weeks ago, she named him that because he's always up to something strange he does not take to strangers and yet he likes you.' Asher bent down to pet the pup when he looked across the room with a concerned look on his face.

'Is that a wolf cub?' A small grey cub sat under the window of the room for a moment before Loki ran at it both ran out of the room.

'One of them she has more. Asger went hunting when he came across a bunch of them starving the Mother had been nowhere in sight most likely killed, he took them back here for Freya.'

'This Princess seems to have a fondness for taking in strays, doesn't she?'

'She believes in second chances, in fact these are not even half of her animals, I could use a hand in feeding them all if you don't mind, I will see to it you get paid for your efforts.' Asher gave Drew a quick smile in agreement before they left the room to go find the other animals.

Drew led Asher to the stables first, then to the kennels before taking him out toward the acres of land that sat beside the castle the first thing they came across was a half dozen rabbits followed by a heard of boar piglets that were half the size of little Asher, one in particular caught his attention, the largest of the piglets kept following Asher everywhere he went.

'I think she likes you,' Drew mocked, it was clear Asher had a fondness for that piglet.

'Does she have a name?' the little man asked.

'Not yet, none of the piglets do.'

'She looks like a Rose-Mary,' Asher stated, Drew turned and looked at him stumped for words.

'Reminds me of a girl I was supposed to marry only this one's much more attractive.'

Finally after half a day of looking after all the animals they were down to their last stop before dinner, Asher trotted alongside Drew doing his best to keep up he was entering the castle at the opposite end in which he had entered it that day.

'I thought you said there was one more set of animals to feed?' he asked.

'There is, they live in the castle.'

'Surely it would have been a good idea to start with them instead?'

'Not exactly I was afraid once you seen them you would not help me with the others.' Rosemary oinked happily alongside Asher, she refused to stay with the other piglets when it was time for them to leave.

'Just this door down the hall,' Drew gestured. When the door was opened, Rose Mary squealed and Asher felt the blood drain from his face, reaching down he grabbed the little piglet. 'Have you lost your senses.' He stood holding the piglet tightly as he looked upon the beasts in the room even the cubs were bigger than he. 'They are not vicious,' Drew explained. 'Really because I was brought to believe that bears can rip men apart with ease and I'm only half of one,' Drew laughed as he closed the door behind them sealing all three of them in the room.

After the bear cubs had been fed and Asher was over joyed that they did not mistake him for a meal, himself and Drew headed down the long gleaming corridor for their own dinner.

'If I can be so bold, why does the princess have so many animals?' Asher asked as he strutted down the corridor next to the mountain of the man who had befriended him.

'I guess it's that she has a certain understanding for them, she can relate in a way that and she has a kind heart she would not turn anything away that needed help human or animal. But when you do happen to meet Freya try to refrain from calling her Princess she is not exactly one for titles.' Asher stopped and turned to Drew the baffled expression on his face said it all.

'Freya is royalty yes but she didn't know that until a few years ago after her family were slaughtered, Bjorn had a hard time explaining to a child why people would do something so horrid. She always believed she was just a farm girl as she grew up on her mother's land, she prefers to be as independent as she can she will allow servants to help her bathe and dress, and that sort of thing but the majority of the time she prefers her own company, she does not want to be treated like she is better than others because she now has a title she is still the same person she was when she was a girl just not as naïve,' Drew elaborated.

After Dinner Drew took his leave up to the library, he wanted to write to house Olden to ensure Freya and the others had a safe journey across and if they needed him to arrange passage back home.

Dearest Freya,

I hope this letter reaches you before you leave house Olden.

I have not heard word from you or the others, I worry that your journey did not go well.

I hope the decisions I have made in your absence will make you proud, there is a certain matter at hand regarding two of your soldiers, I have left for you personally as I know you would prefer to deal with it in person. I hope that you made it to house Olden swiftly and secure. I wonder if you have discovered Finn Olden and if he lives up to his reputation?

All of your animals are well cared for here and I have found someone I think you will like to take in, he is a good man who undoubtedly has had a hard life. The animals took to him one in particular a piglet he has named Rose-Mary, I am sure you will find extremely amusing seeing them together.

Should I arrange passage back home for you? I pray for your safe return.

Regards

Andrew

He took the seal of house Raghnall and sealed the letter with the mark of the three headed beast.

Cara-Lea

Sitting on the windowsill of her brothers chambers, she studied his unconscious body. He was bruised and had small gashes from his hands spreading up his arms. How he managed to carry Asger in that condition she could not imagine, he had to have been in tremendous pain but thanks to him the Viking's son lived. He risked his life to save another. She always knew her brother was a good person, had always defended him when others spoke ill of him but she is now smugly proud that she had been telling people of her brothers courage and heart since as long as she can remember, but know everyone finally seen it. Glancing down at her lap, Cara-Lea realised she had been covered in blood from helping Freya with the others. After walking into the room with Nari, she was frozen in fear, she had seen men after battle and heard the stories but to actually see the gore of it all up close made her stomach turn as sour as four day old milk that had been left to spoil in the summer sun. Freya had helped her snap out of her shocked state and allowed her to help, something she was sure her mother would not approve of, a high born lady getting her hands dirty and helping others was not something that was done, at least not in these parts. She had been intrigued at how this young Viking girl had such knowledge and healers hands in a way she had envied her.

Turning her head out the window, she looked upon the view that captivated her from Finn's chambers you could see as far as the docks. She had always found water very calming. The sun shimmered on the ocean while the waves rocked gently back and forth, the ships bobbed from side to side in the water as the traders and fishermen that pulled into port had unloaded their cargo. She hummed gracefully, a tune she found was fitting to the ever changeable ocean.

'Lovely song, I hope you're not planning on singing it at my funeral.' She turned to see her brother had woken and was looking upon her with a sweet smile on his face.

'Finn!' She gasped before jumping to her feet and running to his side. Flinging her arms round his neck, she was overwhelmed with emotions. 'Don't you ever frighten me like that again,' she barked. Cara-Lea felt her brother wince when she embraced him. 'Oh, sorry, I'm just so thankful to have you back.'

'Did I go somewhere?' He mocked as he brushed off the pain from his injuries. That was her brother she thought, he would always protect her even when it meant brushing off his own pain so that she would not have to feel any.

'Do you need anything? I can send for food, or a drink, or milk of the poppy?' she asked excitedly.

'Milk of the poppy?' Her brother looked on at her confused.

'I helped with the others,' her voice rang with satisfaction.

'The others?' Finn asked his expression turned to that of grief at the thought.

'Don't worry they live, Nari passed out when Freya was healing him, Nicholas and Gilli had to hold him down, I went to fetch him something for the pain but when I got back he looked lifeless but they said he would be alright and I had done a great job helping.' Cara-Lea started searching her face for her brother's approval. His demeanour changed, he was now more at ease after hearing from his sister, and he started to look more like himself again.

'Well done little sister, I always knew you were special.' A burst of joy filled her, as her brother approved of her actions, her mother will not be happy but at least Finn would always be proud of her.

A short while later, Cara-Lea left her brothers chambers allowing him to rest after his ordeal, it dawned on her that there was one more person who she had yet to check in on, Asger. A surge of guilt hit, the Vikings were so good in helping finding her brother and in helping to mend the wounded and yet she was so wrapped up in ensuring Finn was okay that the thought of checking on Asger never crossed her mind until now.

After entering the guest chambers and examining the room she had entered, she noticed Freya sitting on the floor of her brother's bed leaning into it, her expression motionless as she sang a song in a whisper while holding her brothers hand. Pausing for but a moment to decide if she should come in past the threshold of the door, or to turn back, she decided to approach the bed. Kneeling down beside her new friend she had no words, knowing too well the anguish Freya had to be feeling right now, reaching out and placing her hand upon Freya's she gave a gentle squeeze.

'He will live.' Freya said softly. 'He is a fighter.' 'And how are you?' she asked expressing her concern.

'Honestly, I'm exhausted. It's been a hard day maybe you should rest?' Freya giggled at the thought.

'It's not just today Cara, its life, my life, I must have been some bad bastard in a past life because it seems I'm been punished in this one.'

'You're no bastard,' Cara-Lea snapped.

'I grew up believing I was farm girl, and I was happy with that. Mother would take me down to care for the animals and help her grow crops. I had no servants, no expectations just to be me. Then the raids happened and my family were killed, my brother and I escaped but he died shortly after from an injury he received from trying to save me.' Tears filled her eyes as the memories from her past flooded her mind. 'After my father found me, he told me we were royalty, he took my mother and brothers and fled after his family were killed he did not want us to be killed for any crown, after healing I was promised to a Lord who unbeknownst to my father was a cruel, evil man, he tried to have me and my father killed to claim his right to our families rightful kingdom. It's happening again every time I feel safe something bad happens if anything were to happen to Asger or my father.' Tears slowly fell from her eyes at the thought, Cara-Lea even felt herself well up at the thoughts of what had happened to this family.

'No one will hurt you or yours, I promise you, and my father and brothers would not allow it.' Looking up she noticed the hand, Freya had been holding, was starting to twitch.

'I think he's waking up, I will leave you two alone but I will be right down the hall if you need me.' Assuring her friend as she got up off the floor to leave the room.

Back in her own chambers she undressed and washed the blood off her body. Dark Oak covered the walls of her Chambers, her bed had the finest cream silk sheets with green embroidery with matching velvet curtains than gracefully gathered at the window. A knock came from the door, the door slowly opened as her mother entered.

'I have heard you have not attended your music lessons today.' Cara-Lea watched as her mother's lips pressed into a hard line, she could tell she was upset.

'No I lost track of time,' she explained.

'Playing a healer,' Lady Olden's eyes widened she had never been this upset with her before.

'Those people needed help,' she begged.

'Not from a young Lady,' her mother barked. 'There are plenty of people out there who could have helped them look at your clothes covered in blood and who knows what else.'

'I wanted to help Mother,' Cara-Lea barked back.

'This is not to happen again, understood? You are high born start acting like it, no man will want a wife who cannot be obedient.'

'What if it had been one of us Mother, you would have wanted anyone to come to our aid.'

'This discussion is over, you are an Olden not a hand maiden. I expect you at dinner looking and acting like a lady.' Lady Olden stormed out of the room, Cara-Lea felt her blood boil and her hands tremble, she had never been so angry at her mother, how dare she make her feel like such a disappointment for wanting to help and where was she until now?

A short while later a knock came on the door of her chambers, she approached the door expecting her mother to have returned to yell at her again. Taking a deep breathe she opened the door, but the person on the other side was not her mother but Amelia.

'May I come in?' she asked after gazing upon Cara-Lea's vacant expression.

'Yes of course,' she stepped aside to let Amelia enter the room.

'I am afraid I need your advice, I seem to have upset your brother, I need a way to make it right, and you know him better than anyone.'

'Okay? What did you do to upset him exactly?' Amelia hung her head.

‘I snapped at a servant girl, I was so worried about him after I heard about the attack and she just came into the room without being invited, it was only a servant girl but he got so upset with me.’ Cara-Lea rolled her eyes and fought back a laugh, she thought she was naïve and spoilt until she had heard this. ‘Do you find my distress amusing?’

‘Yes actually I do,’ she snapped, already today I could have lost two of my brothers I had to help with a surgery and tend to wounds, I was covered in blood, there are good men that nearly died and on top of that my mother came in and chewed my ear about not being lady like because I helped those that needed it and you come to me upset about something so silly. My brother was under a lot of stress today I am sure you will be forgiving, now I have to ask you to please leave, I must get ready for dinner. Cara-Lea swung the door of her chambers open while Amelia passed her by speechless and then quickly swung it shut. Had the world gone mad? Or has it always been this way and she was only seeing clearly now? She ran her hands over her face, took a deep breathe in and stared at the clothes laid out for her to wear to dinner. If today was anything to go by dinner would be a battle in its own, how was she going to make it through a table full of entitled people who couldn’t see past the end of their noses?

Finn

As he sat on the edge of his bed with a fur blanket wrapped around his waist, he felt his head throb and had a burning sensation above his left eye, on his forearm, his chest and his right thigh. No stranger to pain he knew the sensation all too well, it should have been much worse than this Asger had saved his life, he was cornered by three men in the forest trapped like a mouse to a cat they were playing with their prey before going for the kill. The larger of the men swung his sword high in the air, standing unarmed and out of options there was nothing more to do than accept his fate. As the blade of the sword start to descend, he took a deep breath in feeling the icy chill of the air fill his lungs one last time, it was then that the air was knocked out of him. Asger had launched himself with such force at Finns executioner that he had sent himself and the bandit flying into Finn which had knocked him back into the rocks behind him where he had struck the back off his head. His vision became a blur as he heard the men screaming around him and as he heard a carnal roar like that of a wild animal. He must have passed out as when he opened his eyes, his vision had restored and he found Asger with his clothes ripped apart and blood dripping from the numerous lacerations from his body, but the real carnage was what lay around them. The bandits had not only been killed but ripped apart, he watched as crows feasted on the flesh of the dead. Two questions remained, how long was he unconscious? And what happened to the men who tried to kill them?

His mother insisted Finn stay in bed to rest after his ordeal but it was not like him to follow orders. He dressed and made his way toward the great hall where dinner would be being served. On his short walk to the staircase, he noticed a door to one of the guest chambers was open, curiosity got the better of him, and he approached cautiously surely everyone should be at dinner? Slowly pushing the door open he noticed a girl on the floor sobbing, it was dark and her back was towards him, he could not make out who it was at first. Taking a few steps into the room, he noticed three hounds watching him as he approached. 'Freya?' he asked softly. The girl gasped and turned quickly to face him, almost immediately the hounds ran towards him growling and baring their teeth.

'It's okay, Finn is a friend,' she told them softly one by one they turned back to their original spots and continued to stare at Finn. 'I was told you saved my brother,' wiping the tears from her face she stood up slowly, it was then the fourth hound revealed itself, it had been at her side the entire time.

'More like he saved my life, to be honest I have no recollection of what happened, or how we are still alive, all I know is I should be dead, I hit my head and lost consciousness when I awoke Asger was on the ground bleeding I couldn't leave him like that, I had to get him back.'

'Thank you for returning him to me,' she leaned in and kissed his cheek. Finn could smell fresh Rosemary from her hair.

'You're welcome,' he said softly feeling her warm breath on his neck.

'Sorry for my appearance, I must look awful.' Running her hands over her hair and clothes quickly trying to compose herself.

'You do look like you have been dragged over a hedge,' Finn agreed. Freya giggled.

'I better go change for Dinner.'

'I can help you with that.' Freya shook her head and smiled.

'I will have a bath made up for you after dinner, that way you can relax and banish demons from mind.' Reaching down, Finn caressed her hand before leaning down and gently placing a kiss upon it.

Arriving at dinner he was surprised he was early for once his mother and father were seated at the top table, along with Nicholas and Amelia who seemed to be lost in conversation and Edward and Cara-Lea who were laughing at a book Edward had.

'Finn, I thought I told you to stay in bed,' his mother barked.

'Nice to see you too Mother.' Finn pulled out a seat and placed himself beside his sister, who was beaming at him proudly. He turned to Cara-Lea and winked.

'How are you feeling?' Amelia asked from across the table.

'Like I have yet to have my fill of wine,' looking into his empty chalice.

'Finn my boy,' a deep voice yelled from across the room. He looked up and seen Bjorn standing at the end of the table with his arms spread open wearing a smile from ear to ear. Immediately standing up to greet the Viking Bjorn locked Finn in a bear hug, all the while chuckling while Finn's eyes widened and his jaw clenched feeling the pressure of the colossal man's embrace on top of his injuries. Bjorn eventually released his grip.

'I can never repay you for what you did today. I am truly flattered my lord, but I should be thanking you, your son saved my life out there, all I did was just brought him back when he hadn't got the strength. I never took you for being so humble, either way my family owe you a great debt, you are always welcome at our table wherever it may be.' Bjorn slapped Finn on the back before retreating to him seat beside Lord Olden while Finn walked back to his own seat where his younger siblings looked on at him beaming.

Finn noticed Nicholas had escaped from the attack virtually unharmed, he was a little scuffed up but nothing that would indicate he had been anything more but a brawl.

'That looked like it hurt.' Nicholas motioned towards Bjorn.

'Nothing I can't handle,' picking up his chalice to have his first drink. The wine was dry and potent, he felt its sensuous burn gracefully pass from his lips to his throat, his first taste of normality today.

'I heard Finn fought twenty men unarmed, he ripped one man's arm off and beat him with it, and then he ripped another's leg off and made him kick himself in the arse with his own leg.' Edward was always one for having an active imagination, this is the first time Finn could recall his little brother bragging about him.

'Edward!' Lady Olden snapped. 'That is no way for a young Lord to speak, especially not at dinner!' she scowled. Little Edward's face turned crimson in colour, he had forgotten he had been seated so close to his mother.

'I am sorry Mother.' He hung his head in embarrassment, while his elder brothers looked on laughing.

'And you two, don't be encouraging him!' Lady Olden was in quite a vexed mood.

‘Apologies Mother.’ Nicholas tried to compose himself.

‘Kicked him up the arse with his own leg, I love this child,’ Finn sniggered. His mother disapprovingly stared at him, normally he would try to behave in front of her but after the day he had, he could use a bit of humour.

‘Boys will be Boys,’ Theodore interrupted his wife before she could speak. ‘After today we could all use a bit of merriment.’

‘Your Edward reminds me of one of my boys, he was just as imaginative as himself,’ Bjorn smiled at Lady Olden who quickly changed her attitude, Finn knew she was feeling guilty as the Viking had lost most of his family and here was his mother snapping at her own children.

‘How is your son?’ she asked.

‘He’s seen better days but thanks to Finn and Freya he will live.’ He picked up his chalice in his enormous hands and took a big gulp of wine.

‘I have sent some broth and bread up to his room and to his friend.’

‘You are too kind m’lady.’ Freya and Gilli had entered the room and took their places next to Bjorn.

A short time later, a dish of poached fish had been served, it had not been salted which means it was newly caught and made it more succulent, feeling his stomach growl with the hunger, Finn wanted to just pick up his food and tear into in, but knowing his mother would most likely snap at him for doing it he decided to use the utensils provided. Shovelling a mouthful of bread on top of the forkful of fish, he chomped his way quickly through his meal with every few bites a large mouthful of wine followed, as he ate he had time to reflect on the events from today, what had happened out in the forest, did one of Freya’s hounds sense the danger her brother he was in and come to his aid? Or did some other animal attack those men? Was there even an animal at all? Feeling his head throb the more he thought about it, he figured the only way he would find out was to find out what Asger knew, after all he was the one fighting while Finn had been knocked out.

When he finished his meal, Finn decided to go investigate the forest again with fresher eyes. Saddling up his horse Onyx, who was as black as night with a silky black mane to match, he was ready to go. Climbing onto his horse, he slowly made his way out of the stables this time he had brought his sword in case there were more bandits out there. Trotting his way past the gates of house Olden, the horse quickened into a gallop and they approached the entrance to the forest almost immediately, the moonlight faded into the branches of the trees, pulling on the reins Onyx came to a complete halt. Finn dismounted from the horse, before moving he listened to the sounds of the forest, listening for footsteps or any signs that he was not alone. Slowly he began to make his way towards the bridge where he and Asger had battled the bandits. The deeper he walked through the woodland, the darker it became, but Finn was not worried. He knew his families land like the back of his hand, he had walked them every day since he was but a child. He came to the bridge where he had fought for his life earlier that same day, looking around there was blood spatter everywhere, it looked black in the moonlight. The bodies and the parts of them that had been ripped off had now gone, most likely Theodore had them taken away and burned. He thought been back here would jolt his memory but he was more confused than ever, he had been in battles before, seen death and carnage but nothing explained the gore that had laid before his eyes, he could only imagine what this would look like in the light of the sun.

He heard the snap of a branch, looking around he could not see anyone in the distance he pulled his sword from his scabbard and prepared for another ambush. Moving closer to the direction of the noise, Onyx start to tug back pulling on Finns injured arm, He released the reins, the horse galloped away. Something had obviously spooked him, a wolf maybe? The trees started to part as the light of the moon split through illuminating the land before him. Finn knew where he was, he was at the edge of the forest near the cliffs. He heard children laughing, this was strange they should be at home eating dinner with their families before bed not out in a dark forest where bandits could be lurking. Approaching the sound of the children's laughter, he noticed the trees had parted. He saw two children playing near the edge of the cliff.

'What are you doing out here?' a voice called Finn swung around to notice Freya was standing behind him armed with her bow and arrows strapped to her back.

'I could ask you the same thing.'

'Came to find answers I take it?'

'Maybe I did…what do you make of this.' Finn pointed towards the children playing by the cliffs. Freya looked shocked

'What are they doing out here?' Finn shook his head.

'No idea.' They watched in silence for a few moments. 'I wish I could be that age again,' Freya muttered.

'The age of innocence,' Finn announced. Freya turned to Finn.

'Ever think of having your own?' he said nothing for a moment searching his mind for an answer.

'Me with a family?' he asked.

'Why not?'

'I doubt many Lords would have me as a son in law,' smirking he turned to Freya.

'Is that a horse?' she asked looking ahead where the children were playing. Finn glanced up and saw a silver horse standing in the moonlight on the edge of the cliff.

'Looks like it?' he said. One of the children walked towards it and patted its head, it seemed gentle.

'Maybe that's why they came up here, they must have seen it closer to home and followed it here… It seems too gentle to be wild.' Freya sounded confused. Finn started to feel uneasy a nauseating feeling ran through his body, he brushed it off. After today it's no mystery as to why he doesn't feel himself. 'Why is the horse wet?' Freya asked.

Finn turned quickly and noticed water dripping from the animal's mane.

'No!' He gasped as he ran towards the children. Freya started to run with him although it was clear she did not know why they were running. The child that had been petting the horse reached up to lift itself onto its back. 'Don't touch it,' he yelled the children turned in Finns direction. The horse looked up and swung around facing Finn and Freya who were running at it. Finn dove at the children knocking himself and a little girl out of the way. Freya had grabbed the little boy who had tried to mount the creature. It let out an unforgiving shriek, turned to face the edge of the cliff then leapt off.

Freya cautiously approached the edge of the cliff and looked down upon the ocean below.

'What the hell was wrong with that horse?' she panted. Finn looked at the children who were shaking with fright.

'It was no horse.' Staggering to his feet fearing he done more harm to himself by diving into the ground he explained. 'It was a Kelpie.'

'What in God's name is a Kelpie?' Freya barked.

'A kelpie is a shape shifter, a sea demon who takes on a certain form to lure it's victims in, once they have their prey they drown them, then they eat them. They are normally black and their mane sticky as to attach victims to it when they pet it but this was not? It must have been young.' Finn looked back at the children. 'Let's get you home,' Finn removed his cloak and wrapped it around the young girl, 'So where are your hounds tonight?' he asked Freya.

Captain and Christian are guarding Asger's room,' she explained.

'You think someone in my family would harm your brother?'

'It's not that, if he needed anything, or something happened they would come find me.'

'You have them well trained…that accounts for two, where are the other two?'

'Do my dogs frighten you?' She looked upon, Finn grinning from ear to ear.

'Me, no! They just have a tendency to sneak up on a person is all especially the black one,' Finn exclaimed.

'Mandy is harmless,' she chuckled.

'Until she's not,' He interrupted.

'Well Toby is looking after your horse, he seemed a little frantic, practically ran us over at the entrance to this demon possessed graveyard.'

'He had to of sensed the Kelpie, I have not seen one since I was a boy.'

'It tried to take you?' she asked.

'No, Edward, since then he has read every book he could on creatures from different lands, he isolated himself and became a bit of a book worm, he doesn't like to fight, would prefer to devise a plan and have you bring on your own ruin then to fight with a weapon. He is a smart child, I'll give him that.' Finn stopped to look around, the little girl was struggling to keep up with them under the weight of his massive cloak, and he picked her up. 'What is your name?' he asked her gently.

'Annabelle,' she answered unsure if she should be frightened, or not.

'And how old are you Annabelle?'

'I will be six years on my name day, Gryff is eight years m'Lord.' She pointed down towards her brother. They proceeded to walk towards the entrance to the woodland.

'What is that?' she asked pointing to Finns left, there was something moving in the shadows of the trees. Finn heard branches crack and leaves rustle, heavy panting followed as the noise got closer. 'Mandy.' Freya called. The hound as black as ash appeared before them, it was extremely difficult to make her out in the dark of night.

'And there is number four,' Finn stated. Annabelle giggled as Finn turned and gave her a bemused look.

Galloping up to house Olden with the two hounds dashing along behind them, the four noticed some commotion in the village square.

'We've looked everywhere, they can't have gone far.' The voices of the small folk were filled with concern, Finn noticed a woman sobbing hysterically into her husband's arms. He looked down at the little girl who was sitting in front of him on his horse.

'You see what you do by running off?' he asked. She frowned.

'We didn't mean to worry Mother, we just wanted to play with the horse.' Finn dismounted and helped Annabelle off Onyx.

'Lose something?' he called. The small folk turned towards him, the grief stricken mother looked up and immediately ran towards them.

'My babies!' she cried.

'We found them down by the cliffs on the other side of the forest.' Freya explained.

'Thank you.' The woman had tears running down her cheeks but looked relieved knowing her children were safe.

'What were you thinking worrying your mother like that,' the Father barked as he grabbed his son by the collar and dragged him from Freya.

'They were lured by a Kelpie. Finn interrupted. A flurry of gasps filled the air where the small folk stood. 'You should keep a better eye on your children and warn them of the demons tricks. These children were lucky, we happened to stumble across them but the next will surely perish, the creature will be back it has yet to feed.'

As he put Onyx back into his stable Freya sat and watched. 'If I didn't know any better.' Finn began 'I would swear you were taking me up on my offer helping you out of your clothes.'

'There it is,' Freya laughed. 'I was wondering when the cad in you would come out, you have been too much of a gentleman today.'

'Me a cad? Never! I've been told I can be quite charming.'

'Whores will tell you anything as long as you pay them right.'

'I don't need whores, I have been told I'm quite handsome.' Raising his head high, he looked at Freya and winked.

'You may not need whores but it doesn't stop you from laying with them,' she replied amused.

'Why does it matter to you who I lay with, princess?' he watched as her expression darkened.

'Please do not refer to me as princess, it is just a title some people desire to make them feel important, and it matters not who you lay with, not to me anyway, I just find it fascinating.'

'What's so fascinating me, or the whores?'

'The tales of you, before we came here I had been warned numerous times of you in particular.'

'Been warned of me? I should be flattered.'

'Flattered?' Freya cried. 'Of the tales of your cock and its abilities to get you into trouble.' Finn was amused at hearing the way Freya spoke of him, he composed himself and approached her slowly.

'Well you know I have always found my cock very intriguing.' A sly grin appeared on his face. 'I'd be happy to show you, I'm sure you would find its abilities quite fascinating.' He said in a sultry tone. Freya's cheeks flushed as she looked down at her feet with her eyes wide open.

'I should go check on my brother.' She backed up and knocked over a stool behind her, sending her tumbling back into a haystack.

‘I may be wrong but I’m sure your brothers not in there, although I must say the stables would prove to be a first for us both, how about I pretend to be the young stable boy and you can be the mistress of the household who has her way with me.’ Finn lay down beside Freya who looked completely flustered staring at him. ‘What do you say?’ with that Freya jumped up and bolted from the stables. Finn lay in the haystack laughing hysterically.

‘Well done little brother, I think you scarred the poor girl for life.’ Finn sat up to find his brother standing a short distance away at the end of the stable.

‘Oh! I was only having some fun,’ Finn chuckled.

‘I must say it is a first to see a woman run away from you.’

‘I think she likes me,’ Finn announced with a devilish smile.

‘What makes you say that?’ his brother asked.

‘She didn’t slap me this time.’

Back in his chambers getting ready for bed sober for the first time in a long time, Finn reflected on the day that had occurred. First, his training with Asger wore him out, then the ambush which nearly killed them both, then seeing a Kelpie for the first time in years and re-injuring himself trying to save the children. At least his day ended on a high note. But still questions remained, what had happened when he got knocked out, why are the sea demons returning? Have they been cursed for this to be happening? Why were the bandits attacking them? What did they want? Who are these Vikings? They certainly were a peculiar bunch. Too many questions rattled through his head and none of which he had the answer to. But one thing is for certain, he was going to find out one way or another he would have answers.

Edward

Standing up half asleep in church, he tried not to yawn. After hearing Finn speak of the kelpie last night, Edward got frightened, he remembered when a kelpie nearly took him when he was young only for his father intervening he would have been killed. Edward stayed up all night taking solace in his books. The priest finally finished his ramblings that had nothing to do with the bible and they were permitted to leave. Making his way home for his morning meal, he sat next to his twin. No sooner had he sat down his stomach growled loudly, he turned to his sister. 'I'm famished.' he said rubbing his stomach. She looked upset. No doubt over the fight she had with her mother the day before. She had told Edward of how she helped with the injured and how her mother yelled at and belittled her for it. Edward had noticed his mother was very grouchy the past few days but he put it down to stress of having to host these lavish banquets for their guests. The Preston's were due to leave tomorrow and the Vikings would be leaving as soon as they were well enough to travel.

Bjorn and his father had entered the hall for their meal. They seemed quite content in themselves. Edward knew the bandit they had captured yesterday was to die shortly after their meal. It would be the first time he would see a man hanged, he was worried that he would get upset and shame his father and brothers.

Nicholas and Amelia had entered shortly after, they seemed to have made up after yesterday, maybe Cara-Lea shouting at Amelia managed to knock some sense into her. Finn strolled in on time again these last few days, seems to have given his brother an attitude adjustment. Edward watched and listened as Amelia pulled his twin aside.

'I am so sorry about my behaviour yesterday, I am so embarrassed. You were right in what you said my problems were nothing compared to yours, I hope you can forgive me.' Amelia begged.

'Of course I can, yesterday seemed to get the better of us all and we are to be sisters after all.' His twin smiled at his brothers betrothed and gave her a quick embrace.

The last to enter the room was surprisingly Lady Olden herself. She excused herself claiming she had been feeling rather ill then took her seat. Finn as usual was looking for the wine and stuffing a rather large piece of white bread into his mouth. Edward liked to listen to people at meal times as he found it provided useful information, on different houses and people.

'Finn my boy.' Bjorn had seemed to have taken a shine to his brother. 'I was wondering if you could do me the honour of taking my daughter under your wing today.' Edward watched as Nicholas start to choke on his wine.

'Apologies, must have went down the wrong way.' Finn looked at Nicholas then at the Viking. 'What would you have me do with your daughter?' Finn asked wearily.

'Well Nari and Asger have been training Freya how to use a sword, the girl could shoot every eye out of a spiders head but swordsmanship is not exactly her strong point, since both are injured I was hoping you could show her a few things, I hear you're the top man around here when it comes to weapons and my son spoke highly of you after your training yesterday.' The Viking was beaming with pride as if Finn was his own son. The same mischievous grin Edward had grown to know appeared on his brother's face.

'Is that so, well in that case I would be more than happy to show your daughter how to handle a sword,' he raised his chalice up and winked at Nicholas, who proceeded to spit out his wine.

'Gods man, who thought you how to drink.' Bjorn barked.

The Village square was overflowing with small folk this had been the first execution in these lands in twelve years. The Bandit stood smiling on top of a stool with his head in a rope.

'Why is he smiling' Edward asked Nicholas.

'Because he wants to die well,' His brother replied. 'You must watch Edward, you are nearly a man grown you must be able to face death.' Nicholas warned.

Feeling his heart beat in his chest, he was terrified the words that were been spoke by his father had not registered, he could scarcely hear any words at all over the crowd, then everything all of a sudden went silent. He took a deep breath in and looked on any minute now. The only sound he could hear were that of the crows circling above them, his father always told him animals could smell death. Nicholas put a hand on Edwards shoulder this was it, the chair was kicked from under the man and he was left flopping around on the end of the rope like fish out of water.

'His neck didn't break,' Edward gasped.

'No, but he will be dead soon in a few moments.' His brother replied. After what seemed like hours the body stopped moving and just dangled from the rope.

'You did well little brother,' Nicholas reassured him.

The image of the dead man at the end of the rope was haunting his mind he could not forget about it like everyone else seemed to do immediately.

'Do you want to come watch Finn train Freya?' his twin interrupted.

'I've never seen a woman train with a weapon before,' he lit up at the thoughts of a distraction.

'Did she not teach you how to hunt?' Cara-Lea asked.

'Well yes but this is different this is a sword,' he said excited. They rushed down to the training grounds, it seemed like they were not the only ones intrigued by having a woman fight, Nicholas and Amelia were there and Gilli, but he was there to support Freya. They watched as Freya swung at Finn again and again but Finn was too quick even injured he could dodge her attacks with ease.

'A woman with a sword! Now I've seen everything.' Amelia's brother Eugene mocked.

'Come on lovey, can't you hit him just once.' Amelia's other brother Mark jeered.

Finn stopped and threw his shield and sword down. 'How about one of you come in here and face me,' he spat.

'We wouldn't want to interrupt your little lover's dispute.' Mark hissed and both men laughed.

Amelia looked ashamed of her brother's behaviour. The men were too busy laughing they didn't notice Mandy or Toby approach them. The dogs start to snarl and bare their teeth.

'Hey that's not funny, call these beasts off,' Eugene begged.

'They're only having a lovers quarrel,' Gilli said mockingly.

Everyone turned and watched the two men run from the hounds, Gilli let them get a few yards up before he called the two dogs back.

'I will never get the hang of this,' Freya cried.

'Hold out your sword,' Finn demanded. Intrigued Edward watched closely. Freya slowly lifted up her sword and held it steady. Finn paced around her a few times like a wolf toying with its prey. Finally Edward watched as Finn came behind Freya and pressed himself up against her, she looked nervous.

'See that,' Finn said as he ran his hand down her arm and grasped her wrist. 'That dip right there, the blade is not balanced in your hands it is far too heavy for you, the problem is not your technique or your abilities, the problem is the sword you are using it was not made for you, it was made for someone much stronger… A man maybe, this sword will get you killed,' He warned, 'I will have a new one made, one you can manage better one made for you.'

'I hate to admit it but he is the best man around here when it comes to weapons, and he has a point why carry someone else's sword when it just slows you down?' Nicholas interrupted.

Freya agreed to let Finn forge her a new sword.

'I think she's amazing,' Cara-Lea announced. 'She hunts, fights, heals is there anything she cannot do.'

'I don't understand why she feels the need to do such things it is for the men to provide and the women to raise the children.' Amelia interjected.

'Vikings are different than us and as far as I know her mother was not a Viking either but from some other background, she would have learned three different ways of living,' Nicholas explained. 'Besides, after what happened to her family and with that Draconian, she is better off knowing how to defend herself.'

'I think more women should learn, I mean what happens when all the men are at war and you get invaded.' Edward was always one for thinking ahead.

'That would never happen,' Amelia brushing his comment off.

'It did to her,' Edward snapped. Cara-Lea and Edward glanced and each other before excusing themselves.

'Can you believe that woman is going to marry into our family?' Edward spat.

'I don't think she is all bad, just naïve,' his twin explained.

'Think about it, the Preston's are this prestigious household that has not had to battle since Father was a boy. They have had everything handed to them and brought up to believe they are the best in the world. High born with no sense.' Edward thought for a moment when he realised she was right. 'Well that will change when she marries Nicholas,' Edward announced.

'Not if Mother has anything to do about it.' Cara-Lea hung her head, she was still upset over the argument she had with her mother.

'Mother is not marrying her Nicholas is, and he will not stand for some spoilt brat barking orders and acting like she is above everyone, it is true we are high born but Father raised us to help others not look down on them,' Edward demanded. A knock came on the door, Lord Olden had sent for his daughter, which meant Edward was alone once again.

The thought of the dead man was lurking in his mind, this would surely drive him mad, if he could not find a distraction. Walking down the corridor he came to Finns room, Edward reached out and knocked on the hard mahogany door, he heard footsteps approaching. Finn slowly opened the door to find his little brother standing outside gazing up at him.

'Edward? Is something wrong?' he sounded concerned.

'No, nothing wrong, can I come in?' Finn stepped aside to allow his brother access to his chambers.

'What's bothering you?' Finn asked as he picked up a chalice of ale.

'That man today, I can't get the image out of my head,' Edward explained. 'Death is a horrid thing little brother, the image can stay with you for a long time.'

'But have you not killed?' Edward asked.

'I have, I have taken many lives but it was them, or me and I chose me, having said that the people I have killed haunt me every night their soul is tied to mine, for it is my blade than struck them from this world.'

'So even you get haunted by the image of death?'

'Everyone does Edward, those who tell you otherwise are lying,' Finn explained. Edward felt more at ease now he thought he was being punished for being scared of death.

'Why are you here Edward, I would have thought you would have gone to Nicholas with this kind of thing?'

'I was going to but…' he looked down and started fidgeting with his fingers.

'But?' Finn continued.

'He's having sex,' Edward explained. Finn froze with his chalice in mid-air.

'He what now? How do you even know what sex is?' Finn enquired.

'Well you are my brother, you have been doing it for years, and that and I kind of walked in on him and Amelia.' Edward blushed. Finn cackled.

'Golden boy breaking the rules with the fair maiden of house Preston, if Mother only knew.'

'You won't tell her will you?' Edward begged.

'No, I won't Edward, besides even if I did she wouldn't believe me, I would end up getting the blame for it in the end.'

'But you desire Freya not Amelia.' Edward watched his brother look upon him some what impressed.

'What makes you think that?' he questioned.

'I have seen the way you look at her, and you have not been with another woman since she got here.'

'I am not an animal Edward I don't need a new woman in my bed every night.' Finn explained.

'Even still this is the longest you have gone without getting in trouble for fighting, or being with a woman. You desire the Viking girl, I can see it, and Cara-Lea and Nicholas can see it you have never lusted after any woman before at least not like this. Is it because she has eyebrows?' Edward asked straight faced. Finn burst out laughing. 'Still eavesdropping on conversations are we? Good I need you to do something for me.' Edward looked upon his brother confused Finn had never asked him for a favour before.

'Those bandits attacked us for no good reason we were unarmed and had nothing of value on us, it's out of character for them. Somebody knows something around here, I want to know everything you can find out about those bandits and about the attack.' Edward agreed to help his brother he had always loved pretending to be a spy and he was good at it. This was just the distraction he needed to forget about what he had seen today.

Lady Olden

She paced up and down her chambers, barking orders at one her hand maidens 'The Preston's leave tomorrow, they will desire a good breakfast with our best wine that should satisfy Henry after them animals attacked his sons. Eliza, I want you to find me a trader who sells the best jewels and bring him to me a gift from our home to the Preston's for honouring our home with their presence and joining ours to them, this needs to go well the Preston's control Red Oak and Silverside.' Eliza nodded and took her leave.

'Costing me more money?' Theodore jested.

'This marriage needs to happen, Henry could call it off at any time he wished,' she pleaded.

'If he thinks our son is not good enough for his daughter, let him call it off he won't find better, but you should not have to pay him off to keep him satisfied.' Theodore was a reasonable man, Mary could see he was reaching his limit with her spending.

'My love, we need the supplies from Red Oak and from silverside, they can provide us with so much resources we may never want again.' 'I did not realise we were wanting now,' he snapped.

'Do you know of your daughter's actions yesterday?' she asked hoping it would take his mind off her spending.

'She helped Freya with mend the men's wounds, what of it.' Mary felt sick to her stomach, he had known of their daughter skipping lessons and running wild and he showed no signs that it bothered him.

'It's not right, a young lady should be prim and proper, obedient not running around destroying her clothes and acting like someone else's slave fetching things for them!' Theodore rubbed his hand along his forehead as if containing himself.

'She was only trying to help, we could use a bit more of that around here.'

'If she wants to help she can visit an orphanage, or the small folk, or any lady like ways to give back, we have monks and others who are trained to heal, I do not need my daughter acting so common.'

'Is she not my daughter also? I see nothing wrong in her behaviour, in fact I am proud that she took it upon herself as a highborn to look past her title and give a damn about someone other than herself unlike her mother.' Theodore slammed his fists at the table he had been sat at. 'I will hear no more of this,' he warned. Mary watched as her husband stormed off out of the room leaving her speechless, he had never spoken to her like that before.

Eliza returned shortly with the tradesman. Walking over behind her mistress this tall, skinny, pale girl stood in awe as the trader start to show her Lady Olden his treasures. Emeralds and Sapphires shone in the light of the sun that beamed through the high arched windows of the room, everything was so extravagant but Mary had decided on a necklace made of silver that curled like the locks of Eliza's hair into each other in the centre lay a large single pearl.

'That one.' Mary chose, she seemed very satisfied in her decision.

'Eliza go fetch Amelia for me.' Eliza quickly walked out of the room in search of Mary's future daughter in law.

'I beg your pardon, my lady but this letter has just arrive for you.' Evangeline another one of Mary's hand maidens stood in the doorway, she was a short girl with long ginger hair, she was very placid in nature, and she just stood in the threshold of the room clutching the letter awaiting direction. 'Thank you Evangeline that will be all.' Mary dismissed the girl, she turned the letter open and saw the seal. An Ox, the mark of the Byrnell family gazed back at her. She felt her heart sink. Opening the letter she carefully read word by word again and again.

Dearest Daughter, It has come to my attention that the Viking and his children live and have been treated as guests in your home. Is this true?

Her father was a powerful man who loathed the Vikings. She had always suspected him of having a hand in the slaughter of Bjorn's family. He had wanted Catherine to marry Richard, but she refused and took Bjorn as her husband instead. This was unacceptable to him the girl who had served in his home and his daughter for so long that she go and marry a pagan in place of a highborn. Caleb Byrnell was known for his temper, although Mary loved her father she also feared him. Yes she suspected he had been the one responsible for the death of her old friend but she could not prove it. Nor would she say it, Bjorn could turn on her out of rage if it were true, because it was her blood that took his away. One thing she did know, who ever wanted his family dead will surely be back to finish what they started all those years ago. Now her sons were nearly killed for befriending them, her daughter had also befriended Freya she would not have her children killed for the company they kept. As much as she still had love for Catherine and Bjorn, she would need to put a wedge in between the families to keep hers safe.

Amelia had entered the room. 'You wished to speak to me Lady Olden.' she asked meekly.

'Yes my dear, come in.' Mary greeted her with a smile and asked her to take a seat. She took the necklace from the table opposite and presented it to Amelia.

'For you my dear.' Amelia beamed and quickly tossed the cloth back that had been covering her gift.

'Lady Olden you are far too generous.' Amelia looked at the necklace in surprise and gratitude, she ran her fingers over its silver bends of the jewellery, drinking the moment in.

'Nonsense you will be an Olden too soon, I look forward to your marriage to my son, I thought it would be something for you to wear on your wedding day.' Mary smiled gently down at Amelia, she would no doubt produce many grandchildren for her, strong highborn sons for the family's lineage.

'I would be honoured, it is beautiful. Suiting the girl who should wear it.' Mary said as she lifted it up and fastened it around Amelia's neck.

'May I go show my father?' she asked.

'Of course dearest, it is yours to do as you wish.' Mary watched as Amelia skipped joyfully from the room, she had done it she knew it then and there that her son would be wed to the Preston girl. Now her only problem was what to do with the letter from her father she could not ignore it but if she said the Vikings remained guests at her home someone would surely come to spill their blood.

Freya

Sitting at her sat at her brother's bedside, she couldn't think of anything but Rosefort. It was home to her now and she missed everything from the grounds to her animals and friends.

'Thinking of home again little cub.' Asger asked. Freya turned to look at her brother.

'Is it that obvious?' He gave her a sweet smile and placed a hand on her shoulder.

'We will be home soon.' He said reassuringly. Asger was now stitched up and conscious which was all she had wished when her father returned yesterday with him. 'Finn has been asking a lot of questions, about what happened yesterday.' Asger tilted his head.

'Is he now, and have you answered those questions?'

'No, I haven't but I think you should. People fear what they do not understand little cub, if anyone finds out what we can do we might as well paint a target on our backs.'

'Too late, there is already one there,' she joked.

'He is right Freya, they would never understand,' Gilli added. 'You did, so did Nari. She has us there,' Gilli raised his hands in the air. 'Speaking of I better go check on him, make sure he's not pulling at your patchwork, oh and Freya this letter came for you today looks like it's from back home.' Gilli handed Freya the letter and left the room.

'It's from Andrew,' she told Asger as she read. 'He wanted to check in to make sure we got here safe.'

'Safe and sound,' Asger joked.

'He's asking about Finn,' she laughed.

'Finn eh? Now why would he ask about him?' a mischievous smile appeared on her brother's face.

'Behave yourself brother,' she warned. 'I will go to the library and write him back can you look after yourself for a while?'

'I think you should send some nice girls in to look after me instead.'

'No whores! You'll reopen the wounds I have sealed.'

'You're no fun,' he sulked.

'Don't pout, it doesn't become you.'

'You sound more like Mother everyday little cub.'

Dearest Andrew,

I apologise for not writing sooner, we have arrived at house Olden safe. The matter you mentioned with my soldiers should be seen to upon my arrival home in a few short days.

I am afraid my brother and Nari have been injured there was an incident with some bandits, they live and will be back to full health soon, both just need to get their strength up before our journey home.

Finn is unexpected to say the least, the first day I met him he demanded my company in his chambers to which I struck him. But then he changed, he is far from a gentleman but not as much of a brute as I have been told. There is almost something kind about him. Have you heard of a creature referred to as a Kelpie? I am afraid I have encountered one on my stay here, frightful creature. I am sure you are looking after my home and my animals just fine, do not worry. We will be home soon.

All my love

Freya.

Andrew has been her closest friend since she discovered him half dead she had, hoped he would be put more at ease knowing she had full trust in him. Looking around Freya realised she forgot to bring a seal for her letter.

'Edward do you know where I could get a seal?' she asked the young lord who had been perched upon the fireplace.

'The room next door, the scribes always have plenty in there.' He smiled happy to help. Freya thanked the boy and left in search of a seal. She knocked on the door, an old man greeted her.

'Apologies for the interruption, I was wondering if I could borrow a seal for a letter I need to send home.'

‘Of course child wait here.’ The door closed then reopened again shortly after. The old man handed her a seal. ‘Will that be all?’ he asked.

‘Yes, thank you!’ Freya said graciously.

After sending her letter off, Freya took some time to explore. She found herself back in the gardens where she had been the first night she arrived.

‘Freya, would you like to join us?’ Amelia had called her. She was sitting with her sister sipping on wine. Freya approached and took a seat she was not used to being in the company of highborn women. Mandy sat at Freya’s feet and Toby sat opposite close to the fountain. ‘Are you enjoying your stay?’ Amelia asked.

‘I am, it was nice to see a different land. I have heard Rosefort is magnificent, it is known for its beauty.’

‘It is, you should come and see it sometime.’ Amelia and Annabelle seemed pleased with their invitation.

‘It does sound so much more appealing than Castle Mourne don’t you think,’ Annabelle joked.

‘It’s no wonder they keep referring to it as house Olden sounds much more appealing.’ The girls giggled together as Freya grew increasingly more uncomfortable. ‘I will be sure to have Nicholas take me when we wed.’

‘You are so lucky he is so handsome.’ her sister approved.

‘He is, isn’t he?’ Amelia agreed.

‘And you laying together before marriage.’

‘Annabelle hush… Besides it has been arranged we will be married soon so it’s not technically breaking the rules.’

‘He looks like he knows how to please a lady.’ Annabelle Blushed.

‘That he does,’ Amelia boasted.

‘I’ve heard his brother is a stallion in bed,’ Annabelle announced.

‘Annie!’

‘Well that’s what I’ve heard, what do you think Freya?’

‘I think you should ask him yourself he seems to be coming this way.’ Freya nodded towards the fountain where Finn had been walking towards the women.

‘Good afternoon ladies, Freya I was wondering if I could have a moment of your time.’ Freya excused herself and walked with Finn through the gardens. 'I did not realise you had become such good friends with the cackling hens.'

'They are not my friends they invited me to sit with them when I came out to look around.'

'Looking for me again?' Finn smirked.

'I believe you were the one who found me Finn.'

'I was coming to see if you changed your mind.'

'What would I change my mind about?'

'Our little game from last night I'll be the stable boy you be the mistress.'

'Does that honestly work on women?'

'Okay your right Monsters and Maidens it is then now how would you like to be captured.' What was he playing at? She wasn't going to stick around to find out Freya began to speed up to get away from Finn.

'I was joking,' he called after her. Finn grabbed her by the arm. Freya turned around to face him, his piercing pale blue eyes were fixed upon her. 'Let me show you the grounds, it's too dangerous for you to be walking around alone, hounds or no hounds. I give you my word I won't try anything, unless of course you want me to?' Finn took her by the hand and led her out of the gardens she had no idea where he was planning on taking her, but curiosity convinced her to go with him.

They walked in silence for a few moments, Freya had felt eyes burning into the back of her as they left the gardens. Finn never loosened his grip on her wrist, racking her brain wondering what he had been up to, she knew she would never guess until he revealed his intentions, but she was not afraid. She had grown to trust her instincts on people true out the years, she knew he would not harm her, she found herself captivated by this man, she had heard so many stories about how much of a brute he was and that he was a renowned whore-monger, when in fact she had seen very little to back up the claims.

Mandy as usual was close by at her heels, while toby skipped ahead through the tall dewy grass. The hound would get lost amongst long grass, Freya could only notice him from the tip of his tail that occasionally made an appearance. Looking through the grassland, Freya noticed Onyx standing proudly a few meters ahead. Finn had planned this, whatever it was she was still trying to guess.

‘Where are we going?’ Freya asked.

‘I told you, I am going to show you my families land.’ Finn replied. Looking around she could not help but wonder.

‘Where is my horse?’

‘I thought we could ride together, that way you can’t run off.’ Toby had jogged up to them after the stream of tall grass had gradually shortened, he sat at Finns feet and stared at Freya as Finn helped her onto Onyx.

‘Traitor,’ she muttered, looking down at her hound who tilted his head in response. Finn had given the horse a gentle kick with his heels and Onyx took off like lightening, her hounds fought to keep up with the swift stallion, Freya had no choice but to hold on tightly to Finn as they galloped from the castle, they were not going through the gates, that she knew as they had been going in the opposite direction.

She could not help to admire the scenery of the land, it was not as bright as Rosefort but had the same enchanting atmosphere, she had not noticed before now. The noise and smells from the built up kingdom were lost behind them. They were replaced by nature. Freya could smell the Pine trees and clean air, the warmth of the kingdom had left and the chill of her now open surroundings set in but she was not phased. For the first time since she was a child she felt free from responsibility, and the heavy chains of her past.

Onyx start to slow down, looking around she realised that she had been brought up the mountain of Castle Mourne. Toby and Mandy had falling behind but she knew they would catch up eventually. Freya climbed down off Onyx and turned to find a breath taking view. She gazed upon the Kingdom that lay beneath them, even from up here the wall that guarded the people seemed like it was made by giants, it was the only thing not lost to the altitude. The evening sun sat shimmering in the sky. Red and Orange strands of sunshine gathered around the clouds filling the sky with a certain warmth.

‘You can see the entire Realm from up here,’ Finn interrupted.

‘It’s beautiful,’ Freya remained fixated on the view.

‘It is, I have to confess this is not what I brought you here for.’ Finn studied her as she turned to him.

‘What did you bring me here for? She asked hesitantly.

‘Come, I will show you,’ Finn led the way. Walking uphill through some trees the ground started to level out, to Freya’s surprise the air was getting warmer, she walked up to Finn who had now come to a halt.

‘Since the bath I had made up for you went to waste yesterday, I figured this would prove to be more enticing.’

‘Do you really think I need a bath that badly?’ she asked, gazing upon the hot spring which lay isolated with only the vision of the kingdom below for it to look upon.

‘I thought you might like to relax, especially after yesterday’s events.’ Freya adored hot springs, but the thoughts of undressing in front of Finn Olden made her feel uneasy.

‘I will not get in with you watching,’ she said. Finn bowed his head, turned and descended back down the hill.

She waited a moment to make sure she was alone, before she began to undress. Lowering herself into the hot spring she found the warmth a great comfort. The only sounds were that of her surroundings, a gentle breeze, rustling leaves and the sounds of her movement in the water as she sat back.

‘That really does look enticing.’ Finn stood behind her, she had not heard him coming.

‘I thought I asked you to leave,’ she asked trying to conceal her nakedness.

‘You did, and I left…now I’m back,’ Finn began to undress.

‘What are you doing?’ she asked.

‘Joining you what does it look like?’ Finn pulled his tunic up over his head, as he turned to place it down Freya noticed his back was covered in scars.

‘What happened to your back?’ she asked.

‘Oh that? My father, the Lord of the land done that to me, apparently I had it coming,’ he said sardonically.

‘What did you do?’

‘I lay with a married woman,’ Finn explained while he removed the rest of his garments. ‘I had just come of an age where I developed an interest in the fairer sex, I was young, had a lot of ale, she was attractive and offered herself to me.’ Finn fixed his gaze on Freya as he lowered himself into the water. ‘You probably think me a fiend for it.’

‘Not at all, these things happen, they shouldn’t but they do, you were just a boy, your punishment was harsh.’ Freya explained. 'Some people would think the wife belongs to the husband to do whatever it is to her that pleases him. Others think the wife is above her husband.'

'And what do you think?' Finn asked.

'I think both are equal in marriage, no matter the circumstance both people agreed to it, they belong equally to one another and should obey each other equally,' Finn smiled.

'Well right now we are equals,' he announced. 'I find when people are naked they are more honest with each other all their vulnerabilities are out for the other to see. They have nothing to hide.'

Finn waded his way through the water over towards her. Unnerved Freya stood and tried to walk away, but Finn caught her arm.

'I will not harm you,' he spoke softly. Freya heard truth words and stopped. Releasing his hold on her, Finn continued to move behind her, she felt his hand slide down to her hip while he placed the other on her back. 'He did this to you?' he asked. She could feel his warm breath hit the back of her neck. She gulped. No one had seen her scars since she healed.

'Yes,' she whispered. Finns arm slid down her back and around her waist, he pulled her in close to him.

'I would stand alone against a thousand armed men, if it meant you never hurt again.' She felt his Lips press against her scar his facial hair lightly rubbing her soft skin as he held her in a secure embrace. She ran her hand up the back of his neck and ran her hands through his hair, turning her head to face him. Splash! Both turned to see Freya's hounds had caught up with them. Freya laughed as Toby swam around drinking the water from the spring.

'It's starting to get dark, we should go,' Finn agreed.

Bjorn

Hardy laughter filled the halls as Theodore and Bjorn reminisced passed battles.

'He always claimed to have a hand in it.' Theodore said.

'Yes a hand around his ankle, while being dragged through the field,' Bjorn chuckled. 'Those were the days Theo.'

Lady Olden walked into the room.

'My Lord,' she bowed as she addressed her husband. 'The wedding will be going ahead as planned.' Sounding pretty pleased with herself.

'And how much, of my money have you spent securing the event,' Theodore snapped. Bjorn watched as she hung her head.

'Less than expected, My Lord,' she answered.

'Good… I presume you came here to tell me something other than that?' he asked.

'I cannot find Finn I am afraid he has gone off wondering again.' Theodore ran his fingers through his hair.

'The boy can take care of himself as he has proven before, he will return by dinner time I assure you… Why is it you wish to speak to him?'

'Arrangements for the wedding need to be made, and Loch Gorman needs to be furnished before Nicholas and Amelia can move in, the wedding is in a few weeks and we are strapped for time.'

'I have had my fill of wedding talk for one day be gone, we will discuss this another time,' Theodore dismissed.

Bjorn sat silently until Lady Olden left.

'Well that was something.'

'The woman will have my money spent and me in an early grave.' Theodore explained. 'Loch Gorman eh? The boy will be set up for life there,' Bjorn announced. 'I had land set up for my sons, before it was taken from me.' Bjorn lifted his head, 'Asger will be king, but I fear this old man will be watching him take it in Valhalla. Freya has done well for herself with Rosefort, she will be safe there and has ruled the land with grace, and the people love her,' his voice was proud.

'She is like her mother, you have a right to be proud.'

'Everyday,' Bjorn replied.

'I wonder where that girl is, I have barely laid eyes upon her today.'

'I saw her this afternoon,' Gilli's voice interrupted from the doorway.

'Gilli my boy!' Bjorn slapped his knee when he saw they young man. 'Bring her to me at once.'

'I can't,' Gilli explained.

'Oh and why is that?' Bjorn asked.

'She's gone off with Finn.' The room fell silent. Gilli stared blankly at Bjorn who turned to Theodore whose head was in his hands. Bjorn let out a hearty laugh.

'Probably gone hunting Kelpies or whatever other creatures you have lurking around this land.' He announced. Theodore looked up relieved.

'You aren't angry?' he asked.

'Of course not, I trust my daughter, maybe you should try having a bit more faith in your son he might surprise you.' He chuckled.

Having left Theodore somewhat stunned, Bjorn excused himself and went to check on 'His boys' as he called them. Nari's room was closest. Bjorn pushed the door open to find the young man staring out the window. 'The Gods have blessed you.' Bjorn called. 'I have seen men twice your size with lesser wounds been bedridden for a week.' Nari turned to Bjorn. His face was sutured up and his wounds looked clean. 'I have Freya to thank for her patchwork,' he replied. 'Her and her little friends.' Bjorn knew what Nari had meant, Freya had used maggots to clean Nari's wounds, and the first thing Rane had thought her, when she was learning how to heal. 'You look…' Bjorn Began. 'I know I know…after everything I still look better than you.' Nari Interrupted. Bjorn laughed.

'Will you be joining us for dinner tonight?' Bjorn asked.

'I look forward to it, the lady Olden was kind to send up broth but I would much prefer a proper meal.'

'Nothing like a good meal and strong ale to regain your strength,' Bjorn agreed.

Bjorn found himself arriving early for dinner time after Asger was not in his chambers when he went looking for him. Scanning the room he noticed Nicholas seated at the top table with young Edward and Asger. 'Just where have you been?' Bjorn asked. 'I got bored and found myself wandering,' Asger explained.

'Oh into what maidens bed this time?' Bjorn asked. Asger dipped his chalice towards Annabelle Preston. 'You best hope her father does not find out, or there may be a brawl tonight.' Bjorn warned.

'She was simply lifting my spirits,' Asger said. 'and her dress.'

Bjorn replied, 'I wish you would find a good Norse woman.' Bjorn begged, 'You didn't…you found mother to the west.'

'Your mother was one of a kind,' Bjorn explained.

Bjorn took his seat when he realised Christian and Captain were lying under the table between him and Asger. The room slowly filled with the remainder of the Olden's guests. Theodore and Mary were sitting in the centre of the table as always, when Finn and Freya entered the room. Bjorn stood to go greet his daughter.

'And where have you been all day?' he asked.

'Finn took me to see the sights of the kingdom,' she explained.

'Oh find anything interesting?'

'Nothing that would strike your fancy Father.'

'Why are your clothes damp? Bjorn asked.

'We found a hot spring,' Freya examined her father's face for a reaction, he looked at her blankly then looked at Finn who had taken his seat between Asger and Nicholas.

'A hot spring? he asked. 'I must try that myself before we leave.' Freya gave her father a sweet smile and kissed his cheek then took a seat next to Cara-Lea and Amelia.

By the end of dinner, the wine was free flowing and there was singing and dancing, it was evident at this point that some of the men were getting rowdy looking.

'You bitch!' Mark Preston spat at Freya. 'Do you think it's funny to release your hounds after us? Don't you know who we are?' He was spilling ale over himself and the floor as he spoke. 'Do you know who I am? she asked.

'I know who you are alright, you're a pagan cunt!' venom filled his voice as he raised his fist to Freya. Bjorn watched as his daughter caught the man's arm and swung an open hand down hitting him between the legs.

'That's my girl!' Bjorn yelled as the young man fell to the floor. Eugene tried to retaliate but he was caught by Gilli, who sent him over the table. The room divided into a group of women and children fleeing and the men brawling. Chairs were being broken, chalices smashed and blood spatter from busted up men sprayed the walls. Bjorn felt a sharp pain across his back, he turned to see one a man holding what looked like a chair he had broken across the Viking. 'You dare hit me with a chair?' Bjorn asked. 'I'll hit you so many lefts, you'll be begin for the right to knock you out.' Bjorn drew back his enormous arm as his hand folded into a fist, this would prove to be a memorable night.

Theodore

After the dust settled, Theodore and Bjorn had stumbled back to their chambers laughing like boys who just had their first taste of ale. 'Your Nicholas has some right hook,' Bjorn told him.

'What about Freya, I think I actually saw one of the Preston boys,' Theodore mocked.

'With a blow like that it would not surprise me that would knock the wind right out of any man, I should know her mother used to do it to me when I vexed her,' Bjorn laughed.

'Well this is me,' Bjorn announced.

'Sleep well old friend,' Theodore smiled.

'Who are you calling old?' Bjorn chuckled turning for the door. Passing by the guest rooms he made his way towards his own chambers. Edwards's door was open and a light shone from the room, Theodore walked in expecting to see his youngest reading as usual but upon entering the room he found Edward asleep with a book in his hand. *Close enough,* he thought to himself. Blowing out the candle light he turned to leave when he heard giggling coming from the corridor, he approached the doorway and peered out. Nicholas was entering his chambers with Amelia. *Boys will be Boys,* he thought at least they were betrothed it was not uncommon for couples who are due to get married to lay together, although it still is frowned upon. Brushing it off, Theodore closed Edward's door behind him after he had left and continued towards his own room. He heard more commotion slowing down to see where it was coming he could not locate where the sound was coming from, then it hit him, arches in the corridor looked out onto the floor below. Asger was with Annabelle, Amelia's sister. *Nothing like a brawl to bring this out in people*, he thought to himself. Entering his chambers he stumbled across the floor and fell into bed.

The next morning he woke to a pounding headache, unsure if it was the consumption of ale, or the fighting the night before.

‘They ruined everything,’ Mary shouted. He did not need his wife and her frenzies to be bothering him this soon after waking. ‘The Preston’s will never want us to join them now thanks to those damned Norsemen.’

‘They did not start that fight your precious Preston’s however did,’ Theodore snapped. His wife turned to him upset he had not sided with her.

‘Your obsession with this wedding has got you far too emotional the past few days, this must stop now!’ he warned. Jumping out of bed and quickly dressing, Theodore once again stormed out of the room. Halfway down the corridor he noticed his Cara-Lea looking unhappy. ‘What is it child?’ he asked. ‘What has happened to take your light away.’

‘I just wanted to help,’ tears filled her eyes.

‘This is about your mother, I know, I think what you did was amazing,’ he reassured her. ‘I am so proud of the woman you are becoming.’ Cara-Lea looked up at her father her expression starting to brighten once again. ‘Go now, no more tears, you are far too pretty to look so down.’ Thinking of what Finn had told him of the Kelpie’s returning, he decided to go investigate but he had not been sure where to go look, the cliffs where vast, it could have been anywhere, he thought it best to go check with Finn first. Entering Finns room he was ready to go hunt down these demons once again, Finn was asleep lying on his side. Just as Theodore went to wake his son he heard a grunt from the end of the bed, looking down he could see two of Freya’s hounds asleep. Shocked Theodore turned to the bed again to realise that his son was indeed asleep, but so was Bjorn’s daughter. His son had been cradling the girl in his arms while they slept. Not knowing what to do Theodore quickly turned and fled the room.

At breakfast Theodore could not eat, he just picked at his food. Finn and Nicholas sat beside him acting like everything was normal. This was not right, Nicholas at least was due to be married to Amelia but what was Finn thinking. Slamming his chalice down, Theodore leaped from his chair.

‘Finn!’ he cried. ‘I need to talk to you now.’ Quickly leaving the great hall Finn followed his father closely. They entered the Library which was abandoned as everyone else had been having their morning meal. ‘Just what in God’s name do you think you’re doing?’ he yelled.

Finn looked taken aback, 'Following you like you asked.'

'Do not test me I saw you this morning with Freya, have you no discipline? Must you lay with every woman who comes into our home?'

'What did you see?' Finn asked calmly.

'I said do not test me boy!' He snapped.

'What did you see Father!' Finn was furious.

'I saw that girl in your bed is what I saw.' Theodore was in no mood for Finn to make light of the situation.

'Yes you did,' Finn replied. 'You saw her in my bed asleep, I did not lay with her, I slept in the same bed, after last night I was afraid that the Preston's would harm her, I refused to leave her in a room alone,' Finn snapped. Theodore was lost for words. Finn was a lot of things but a liar wasn't one of them. 'Do you honestly think I could even be with her with those hounds always around?' Finn asked.

'Apologies, my son, I am afraid I am guilty of making a bad judgment.' Finn turned to leave.

'Wait!' Theodore called. 'I need your help,' he begged.

'What is it you want from me Father?' Finn asked.

'The kelpie, I need you to show me where you saw it.'

Marching to the stables with his two eldest boys, Theodore couldn't help but think maybe Bjorn was right, he needs to start trusting that his boys are now men, Nicholas will be married soon and his Dark horse has helped save three lives in the space of a day. They can be far from perfect, but they are his blood. Things should start making sense again soon most of their guests had left with the Preston's leaving today. Bjorn's boys seemed to be healing well, it wouldn't be long until they departed for Rosefort, and his wife can finally calm down.

As they trotted along through the Forrest, Theodore noticed his boys were unusually quiet.

'So, Amelia leaves today?' he asked Nicholas.

'She does…it won't be long now before we are wed.'

'And what are your feelings on that?' Theodore asked curiously.

'She is well bred and obedient, I believe she will make a fine wife,' Nicholas announced proudly.

'Or a dog,' Finn muttered.

'What is it you have against Amelia?' Nicholas barked.

‘Oh nothing, she seems lovely, her family are guests at our home and yet start an out and out brawl, and I have never seen more idiocy in my life than that of meeting her two brothers complete cumber world’s utterly useless.’

‘Well I am not marrying her brothers, I am to wed Amelia. If I recall correctly little brother, your new Viking friends played a part in the brawl,’ Nicholas said snidely.

‘They were defending themselves after the Preston’s attacked them,’ Finn snapped.

‘Oh that is right, they did happen to insult your new conquest, didn’t they, tell me brother is she as much of a bedswerver as you?’

‘Hold your tongue brother, or lose it!’ Finn threatened. ‘Enough!’ Theodore barked. ‘I have enough of this to listen to from your mother. I will not have my sons turning on each other! One house one family.’ Theodore felt he had always had to repeat their house motto.

‘One house, one family,’ his sons replied.

‘Besides if anyone should be upset right now it should be me, your mother has me robbed blind with the money she has already put into this wedding and the real planning has not yet started, and as for Lord Preston the richest Lord in the realm, he’s so cheap he would go up your arse for a penny.’ Nicholas and Finn laughed hysterically on their horses, Nicholas was laughing so much Theodore thought he would fall off. ‘Now show me where you saw this bloody Kelpie, I should like its head to give to the Preston’s as a farewell gift.’

Drew

Wielding his sword, Asher charged at Drew who was facing away from him. As he grew closer, Drew pulled his sword from the scabbard, turned towards Asher and blocked his attack. The sound of the blades striking one another echoed through the room. Drew brought up his right leg and caught the dwarf square in the chest, sending him falling back against the wall. The beast of a man charged at Asher who struggled to get back on his feet. As the blade of his sword swung down upon the dwarf, Asher dodged gliding in between Drew's legs. Drew felt a sharp pain in the back of his legs which sent him to his knees.

'Drop your sword,' said Asher, as he held his sword at the back of Drew's neck.

Drew complied releasing his hold on his sword. 'You know for half a man,' he panted.

'You are one hell of a swordsman, better than the men I have met here so far,' said Drew.

'That's just it we have no swordsmen now all the greats are dead, you executed them all,' Asher explained.

'We didn't take your life,' Drew said.

'I was not a Draconian man,' the dwarf explained. 'The thoughts of a dwarf fighting was amusing to him, he told me to go back to the mines where Dwarfs belong, and when I went to the mines they laughed at me yet again saying their pickaxes were larger than I, and sent me away.'

Drew got to his feet, 'Looks like you had the last laugh my friend, come there is much to do today.' Drew patted Asher on the back and led the way out of the hall.

Arriving at the Strawberry beds, Asher looked around him in awe at the acres of strawberries the sat before them.

'They look delicious,' said Asher.

'They are,' Drew agreed. 'They are Freya's favourite, I have been meaning to gather some for her return. She should be home any day now,' Drew explained. 'They are the best you can find, the rich soil they grow from makes them taste all the better.' Drew knelt down and popped a strawberry into his mouth. 'Won't you have one?' he asked.

'Forgive me, but I am just one of the common folk, I cannot afford these luxuries,' Asher hung his head.

Drew laughed, 'My friend, you think I would invite you to eat and expect you to pay me? By all means help yourself, just make sure you gather a full basket after that you're free to enjoy how many you like.' Drew handed Asher a large one he had picked then turned to go gather up some of the largest strawberries he could find. 'Here come's your shadow,' Drew said, pointing towards Rosemary who trotted up towards Asher.

'If only every woman was as loyal as that piglet,' Asher joked. After a short while Drew noticed his basket was full, he turned to find Asher and Rosemary sitting on the ground with strawberry juice dripping from their lips, as they sat in with a small stack of fruit in front of them.

They left the Strawberry beds with their baskets overflowing, the odd strawberry would fall to the ground, but Rosemary was more than happy to pick up what was dropped.

'Forgive me, but I find I am rather curious,' Asher started.

'Go on,' Drew said, intrigued by what Asher had to say.

'I have noticed our defence is rather scarce, all of the best warriors were killed when Freya took over, forgive me, but how are we to defend ourselves if we get attacked when we barely have enough men to storm a tavern.'

'You're observant, I like that,' Drew answered. 'Let's just say we are working on that, I know our population is scarce right now, it will take time to build back up the realm, all I can say is the men you thought were great warriors would be like fighting a bunch of children next to the men who will replace them.'

'And Freya will command them?' Asher asked.

'Yes she will, why do you ask?' Drew enquired.

'It is just that I have seen both Freya and Asger, Freya seems to kind to rule an army, Asger is a true warrior he can intimidate a man by just walking into a room.'

Drew smirked. 'Asger is unlike any other.' He explained, 'I have fought with him, he is a force to be reckoned with, I have seen him rip a man apart with his bare hands, there is no doubt he is more than capable of ruling any empire, however, I have seen what Freya is capable of also do not mistake her kindness for weakness, Roderick Draconian did and look what happened to him, she is a lot stronger than people think.'

'I shall like to meet her someday.' Asher said simply.

'You will, when she returns.'

Looking around, Drew noticed the Vallhund Molly trying to herd the sheep. Loki had managed to get into the meadow and had been chasing them away from where Molly had been leading them to. Drew gave two long whistles and with that the pup ran over towards them tail wagging and bright eyed.

'Loki what have you been told about bothering Molly when she's working,' Drew asked. The pup put his head down. 'Go now and keep out of trouble.'

The pup ran off towards the castle while Asher looked on in amazement, 'How did he understand you?' he asked.

'All animals can understand what you say to them, they just need to get to know you first, it's a trust issue if they don't trust you they will refuse to listen but earn their trust and they will be loyal to the end. I can tell you there are not as many people out there who are as loyal as animals.'

After checking in on Freya's animals and handling matters of her estate.

Drew rubbed his belly noticing it rumbling. 'Time for our evening meal.' He smiled looking towards Asher who was now frowning.

'Are you alright?' Drew asked concerned.

'Yes… No… I suppose,' Asher muttered.

'Well which is it?' Drew asked never being one for small talk.

'I am so grateful for your generosity the past few days, but I will not be able to join you this evening. I have lost track of time and I am supposed to dine with a friend, I have nothing prepared, I should go now and see if I can come up with something.' Asher explained.

'Bring your friend here, there is more than enough food and I would be happy with the company,' Drew said kindly. Asher lit up and ran out of the hall with Rosemary at his heels to go find his friend.

A short time later Asher returned. 'This is Koi,' he said, beaming up at Drew.

'Another Halfling?' Drew asked amused, as he looked upon the messy haired dwarf that stood beside his friend.

Drew had never seen a dwarf before he met Asher, now here he was dining with two of them.

'Please sit, any friend of Asher is a friend of mine.' Drew gestured towards the table where three chalices were being filled with wine and the meal was getting ready to serve. As they took their seats, Drew noticed an awkward silence in the room, he looked around Asher seemed excited while Koi seemed nervous. 'I have to admit I was a bit taken a back when I saw you Koi, I was expecting a female friend to be joining us tonight.' Drew explained.

'You think I would be untrue to my Rosemary, how dare you,' Asher mocked.

'So how do you know each other?' Drew asked.

'I have land just outside the third wall, where I grow crops for trade,' Koi explained.

'A few years ago I was coming back home when I noticed a drunkard chasing Asher trying to catch him in an empty sack,' Drew was shocked.

'Why was he trying to catch you in a sack?' he asked. Asher's face flushed.

'He thought I was a leprechaun,' he muttered. A roar of laughter filled the room.

'He was shouting after him wanting his pot of gold,' Koi teased.

'He didn't notice that I was standing behind him, I picked up a tree branch and struck him over the head knocking him out, we both ran back to my home where Asher stayed until he got on his feet.'

'My first day in the emerald isles and I get mistaken for a leprechaun, it was the last time I wore a green tunic,' Asher joked.

Drew knew there was something special about these two dwarfs, he sensed they would make essential Allies. Late into the evening after swapping stories and having their fill of wine, Asher and Koi where getting ready to leave when Drew called them back.

'Forgetting something?' he asked.

Both men looked at each other confused. Drew summoned in two servant girls who were carrying two full baskets of strawberries.

'Alas! Freya has not returned tonight, and I do not wish for these to spoil would you be so kind as to take them off my hands, I hate seeing good food going to waste.'

Drew gave both men a kind smile and watched as they lit up when being handed the baskets. After thanking Drew, both Asher and Koi scurried away like two joyful children with Rosemary oinking gleefully alongside Asher as they ran from the room.

Asger

After spilling his seed inside of Annabelle Preston, he rolled off the bed and proceeded to dress for his morning meal.

'I leave today,' said Annabelle.

'I know,' he answered.

'Will I see you again?' she asked hopeful.

'If the Gods will it,' Asger answered as he searched for his tunic.

'You don't seem to care that I'm leaving,' she snapped.

'I do care, who else will I lay will while I'm here,' he replied.

'Is that all I am to you some whore you can just lay with when you please,' she asked.

'Not at all, I have to pay a whore, I did not pay you,' he responded impatient.

'How can you be so cruel?' Annabelle asked as she started to weep. Throwing his eyes in the air Asger approached her.

'I told you, I am not looking for a wife, you asked if we could be together while we were here and we are together, soon you'll be home and so will I, we will not see each other again,' Asger said bluntly.

Annabelle start to cry, Asger waited for a moment then left. Walking down the hallway, saw Nari coming from his chambers.

'Brother!' He called. 'Let's go eat I'm so hungry my stomach thinks my throat is cut.'

'Was that the Preston girl's room you just emerged from?' Nari asked.

'It was she will be leaving today after our morning meal,' Asger explained.

'How did she take it?' Nari asked.

'Like they all do,' he replied. 'I don't understand women, you tell them you don't want to marry and yet they expect to be your wife, and are disappointed when you tell them no.'

'Maybe they think they can change you?' Nari replied.

'A man cannot change, I know those women are not to be my wife. When I meet her I'll know,' Asger answered frustrated.

After entering the great hall for their morning meal, Asger had taken a seat next to his father who had already started on his wine.

'Getting an early start?' he asked.

'Just enjoying the festivities my boy,' Bjorn answered.

'We will be able to leave soon, Nari is well enough to travel,' Said Asger lifting his chalice to his lips.

'I don't want to rush him, he could still succumb to his injuries, give it another night, by the sunrise we can be sure he is over the worst of it, a good strong meal and good company should build him up for the journey home.' Bjorn remained concerned about the health of his friend.

'As you wish,' Asger replied.

They had started to eat when Theodore, Nicholas and Finn entered the hall carrying something wrapped in cloth, they approached the top table where Henry Preston was sitting and Theodore dropped the item in front of him as he ate.

'Apologies for our timing my sons and I understand it is your last day and that we are late to dine with you. As you know a water demon appeared on my land for the first time in six years, I could not have it destroying the lives of my people so we went in search of it.' Theodore turned to Edward and gave him a kind smile.

'The beast is dead, this is all that is left of it,' Theodore announced.

Everyone watched as Henry peeled back the cloth revealing nothing more than a soft mass like jellyfish.

'What is this?' he asked.

'That is the Kelpies remains,' Theodore answered. 'You see I was planning on bringing you back the beasts head, but after we killed it, it turned to this.' Henry sat speechless staring at the splotch which lay in the cloth. Theodore walked gracefully around the table and took his seat beside his wife, while Nicholas took his seat beside Amelia and Finn sat a few seats away beside Gilli. Asger noticed Finn staring at his sister. 'Finn seems to have taken a shine to Freya?' he asked Nari.

'I have heard your father requested that they spend time together sparing while we were incapacitated,' Nari explained.

For the remainder of his meal, Asger sat back quietly examining the room and the people in it.

After the meal had ended, Asger got up from his seat.

'Finn!' he called.

Finn turned around to face Asger.

'I wonder if I could have a moment of your time,' Asger asked.

Finn stood up, 'Lead the way,' he answered happily.

Asger led Finn down a narrow isolated hallway. 'I've been meaning to talk to you,' Asger started. 'Freya told me you had questions about what happened the day we were attacked.'

'I did,' Finn answered.

'Do you still have questions now?' Asger asked.

'What happened after I was knocked out?' Finn asked.

'I fought the bandits. I killed the bandits.' Asger replied bluntly.

'I saw the end result, it was not like anything I have ever seen, and it was not human,' Finn pressed.

Asger thought about his answer for a moment, leaving Finn staring at him blankly. 'You know we are Vikings yes?' Asger asked.

'Of course,' Finn replied.

'Well we are a mix of Viking and Gael,' Asger explained. 'My mother came from the Emerald isles, many people thought she was Norse but they are wrong,' he went on.

'Okay, but what does that have to do with what happened?' Finn asked impatiently.

'What do you know of our warriors?' Asger asked.

'I know they are ruthless, they don't fear death.'

'Exactly, the Gaels and Vikings are a lot alike, beliefs, temperament, skill set. Have you heard of warriors that can turn into beasts? It is said they are cursed, that they are demons, some say they are Gods that have been banished for committing heinous acts of violence.' Asger examined Finns expression while he registered what he was being told.

'Berserkers?' Finn gasped. 'I thought they were just legend? he asked.

'We are a dying breed, most warriors cannot change form anymore, it is too far gone in their blood but they have the strength, they are animals in human form, just because they cannot change does not make them any less dangerous,' Asger explained. 'People fear what they cannot understand Finn. That is why my family is being hunted, once people found out what we were, there was a rebellion, my mother was slaughtered, my brothers,' he paused.

'It is said a berserker cannot be killed by Iron or fire,' Finn wondered.

'It is true we can't, we can be injured badly but not killed by it. My family wasn't run through like the stories say, it was worse than that, they cut off my mother's head and burned her body, my brothers where impaled, including Abi, the youngest, he was only two.' Asger's voice filled with rage, a snarl lurked deep in his throat, thick brown fur start to fill up his arms and neck. Finn stepped back watching in shock, as the giant of a man grew ever taller before him. Asger realised he was changing with the rage, he inhaled a few deep breathes and start to calm down, the fur start to disappear, he began to shrink back to his regular size. 'They tortured innocent children and yet we are the monsters, that is why the bandits attacked us the other day, there is a large price on my families heads and with the news that reached them that I live, will only fuel their bloodlust.'

After talking to Finn for a while, Asger felt more at ease, after his initial shock at the news, Finn seemed very understanding and compassionate for their situation.

'Tell me you have love for my sister?' Asger asked.

'Honestly, I have never met another like her, I have been captivated by her since the night you arrived.' Finn spoke softly.

'You are a lucky man Finn Olden,' Asger replied.

'Why is that?' Finn asked.

'That our culture is to place the woman above ourselves, she has more rights than she would in your world. We trust our women, I fear if we had been like some of you Christians that we would have your head for even speaking to her without our consent,' Asger's words were blunt but his smile was kind, Finn looked confused on to how to take him up. 'You have nothing to fear from me or my father, if we were going to kill you we would have done it already,' Asger laughed.

'Why did you tell me what you did?' Finn asked.

'Freya, she asked me to tell you, she trusts you Finn Olden, which is a very seldom thing for her to do, she trusts very few.'

‘Can she change also?’ Finn inquired.

‘I do not think so, I have yet to find out… In all honesty, I hope I am never around if she can change, because if she can anyone who stands before her, will surely die an agonising death.’

After speaking to Finn and reassuring him that his family is no threat to his home, Asger gathered outside with the others to see the Preston’s off. Standing behind Freya he leaned in and whispered.

‘I had words with your boyfriend,’ Freya turned slightly towards her brother.

‘He is not my boyfriend, and what of it,’ she asked.

‘He didn’t piss his pants,’ Asger replied. Gilli and Nari sniggered beside him. ‘Not sure if I scared him off though, he is a hard one break.’ Asger looked across the crowd to see Finn approach. He pushed his way in beside Freya, Asger scrutinised as he watched Finn drape his arm around Freya’s waist and pull her in close to him. Asger turned to Gilli and Nari. ‘This one’s got some ironclad balls,’ he whispered. Finn turned to Asger. ‘Why do you think they hang so low,’ he said before turning back around. Freya, Gilli and Nari fought back the laughter. ‘I like him,’ Asger approved, as he watched the Preston’s leave on horseback.

Cara-Lea

Standing at the front of the crowd she watched as Nicholas had kissed Amelia's hand and led her to her horse as her family had been ahead on horseback. Edward was standing beside her with a book clutched in his hand as usual, her father and mother stood side by side watching the horses slowly trot away into the distance, she looked around to see Finn through the crowd standing next to Freya. This would upset her mother dearly, she thought. Finn was supposed to be standing amongst his family not over with the Vikings. When the horses were finally out of sight, the crowd dispersed. Lady Olden called Finn over to her, 'Edward find out what that's all about,' She ordered her twin as she took her leave. Staying close to her father's heels she was waiting for the right moment to talk to him, it had been evident that he had been stressed for the past week.

Once he was alone she saw it as an opportunity to finally speak honestly with him without her mother having a say.

'Father!' she called.

Theodore turned towards her, 'Well are you not a sight for sore eyes,' he said kindly. 'What can I do for you my child?' he asked.

'I want to learn how to heal like Freya,' she said. 'May I go back with her to Rosefort to learn?' she asked.

'You wish to leave your family home?' Theodore asked surprised by her request.

'I wish to learn and I believe she can teach me, all my life I was brought to believe a lady had to act a certain way, and in the few days past I realised, there is another way. I can be of use to our house as something other than a deal to strike with a neighbouring house,' she explained.

'I see, forgive me Cara-Lea but you have caught an old man off guard, let me think about it and I will give you my answer soon,' her father explained. He gave her a sweet smile, she felt reassured looking at her father, she knew he was a man of his word and he would not brush her request off easily. Content in herself for having the courage to ask her father, she marched proudly down the corridor looking for Edward. She finally found him talking to Finn, but when they noticed Cara-Lea approaching, they stopped.

'Is everything alright?' she asked curiously.

'Everything is fine, I assure you,' Finn answered, he looked rattled. 'Excuse me, there are somethings I have to take care of.' Finn turned on his heel and quickly marched out of Castle Mourne.

'What happened?' Cara-Lea asked turning to Edward.

'Mother,' Edward shrugged off.

'What about Mother?' she pressed.

'I overheard her forbidding Finn to have any relationship with Freya, or any of the Vikings,' Edward explained.

'But I thought they were friends of hers?' she asked puzzled. 'It doesn't make sense, Mother was so happy to see them when they first arrived, then she scolded me for helping Freya the day of the attack and now forbidding Finn to have contact with them?'

'I know it is strange,' Edward interrupted. 'You know Finn will refuse to listen, forbidden or not.'

'He is quite headstrong our Finn,' Cara-Lea gushed.

'That and he's in love with Freya,' Edward elaborated.

'Finn in love?' she questioned.

'Think about it, have you ever known Finn go this long without visiting a whore house or to want to spend more than a few moments with a woman?' Edward answered.

'I suppose you have a valid point.' she agreed with her twin, he had a better perception of people than she did that she knew but the thoughts of Finn in love was more confusing to her than her mother, suddenly turning on her friends.

The next morning, after having her fill of food from her morning meal Cara-Lea raced outside, she had wanted to get a good view of the docks as the Vikings were set to sail home today. As she past the stables, she noticed Finn and Freya were inside, Finn was sat on a haystack with his arms wrapped around Freya who was standing in front of him. She stopped to try see what was going on. Edward was right she had never seen her brother to act like this around a woman. Cara-Lea watched as Finn reached behind him and handed Freya a sword. 'It must be the one he had made for her,' she thought to herself. Judging by Freya's expression she seemed overjoyed with her gift. Cara-Lea smiled to herself as she walked away to give them privacy.

'Cara-Lea!' a voice called.

She turned to see where it was coming from when she noticed Bjorn waving her over toward him. On approach she noticed he was as jolly as ever.

'I hear you will be joining us at Rosefort, you are welcome to stay for as long as you wish,' the Viking beamed down at Cara-Lea, who was having trouble registering what he had just said.

Her father approached.

'Bjorn! You were always one to spoil the surprise,' he called. 'I had wanted to tell my daughter myself.' Cara-Lea launched herself at her father embracing him tightly.

'Thank you Father,' she whispered as tears poured from her eyes.

'You leave after the wedding,' her father continued patting her on the head. Eventually letting go she walked with Bjorn and her father down to the ship that would take Bjorn and his family back to Rosefort.

Farewells were being said as one by one, the men climbed aboard the ship. The last to say her goodbyes was Freya she shook everyone's hand and thanked them for her stay, then when she got to Cara-Lea she leant into her pulling her into a warm embrace.

'You will always have a place in our home,' she whispered before releasing her grip.

She shot Cara-Lea one last smile before turning towards the ship. Just before Freya made it to the ship, Finn ran out from the crowd and grabbed her hand. Cara-Lea watched as her brother had took off a necklace he had been wearing and placed it onto Freya's neck, he then said his goodbyes and pulled her into passionate kiss before letting her enter the ship. She watched stunned as her brother remained at the edge of the dock until the ship had departed.

‘What do you think you are doing?’ Lady Olden spat at Finn after she realised she was out of earshot of the Vikings. ‘I forbade you to go near that girl,’ she sounded vexed.

Finn turned around towards his mother with a look of disdain etched on his face.

‘I love her mother,’ He snapped.

‘I don’t care who you think you love, you are never to see her again do you understand?’ she snapped.

‘What are you going to do Mother, banish me? Do it! If you must but I will find my way back to her arms, with or without your blessing.’ Finn stormed off past his mother.

Cara-Lea watched in horror she had never known Finn to be so annoyed at their mother, nor answer her back in that manner.

‘Finn!’ Lady Olden called. ‘Don’t you walk away from me,’ she warned.

‘Enough!’ Theodore snapped, and his wife fell silent. ‘Bjorn is a good man, his daughter is a good woman and if Finn chooses to be with her and she is willing to have him they have my blessing. As for you my wife you have been very fond of barking orders and talking down to our children the past week, if I find you at it again you will have me to answer to,’ he snapped and marched off after his son. Lady Olden was left at the docks speechless.

Cara-Lea was worried. ‘What happened to one house, one family?’ she asked turning to Edward.

‘It looks that our one family is starting to divide,’ he answered. The twins looked at one another sharing concerned expressions. What is to become of their house if they do not find a way to reunite? All they could do was hope, all would resolve itself soon before things got worse.

Home at Last

After three days at sea and another days ride, they were finally home. Walking through the final gate into Rosefort, Freya felt relieved that their journey had been successful and yet felt somewhat melancholy that she had to leave her new friends behind. Fidgeting with the necklace Finn had gifted her, she looked around for a familiar face.

'Freya!' a familiar voice called from a distance.

Freya jumped from her horse and ran towards Drew leaping into his arms. 'It's so good to see you,' she said as he squeezed her tightly. 'Freya I would like for you to meet some people, this is Asher and Koi.' Freya turned to see two Halflings standing behind Drew, they looked rather nervous.

'Is that a piglet?' Asger questioned when he saw Rosemary at Asher's side.

Freya giggled, 'I think she likes you.'

'Are you hungry?' Drew asked. 'There is a meal of wild Boar that will be served soon.'

'Why didn't you say that in the first place, I'm famished.' Bjorn yelled. Freya looked around at the two dwarfs.

'Won't you join us? I am certain we should have plenty of food to go around.' Both Asher and Koi beamed at Freya and ran ahead towards the castle.

'They seem very excited,' she grinned, turning to Drew.

'They are, what I wanted to talk to you about,' said Drew. 'They were here under Draconian rule, obviously treated like rodents because they are different to others.'

'But that is what makes them unique,' Freya interrupted regarding her friend with an innocent smile.

'Exactly my point, Asher is incredible with a sword, I sparred him while you were away, he was able to use his height to an advantage and take me down,' Drew explained.

'Impressive,' Freya said turning to look up at the little men running through the town square with great speed. 'I think they could make good Allies, Lord knows we need as many as we can get to rebuild your realm.' Freya nodded while listening intently. 'You had said there was a matter regarding the soldiers here?' said Freya turning to her friend.

'I did. On the day I met Asher I found two soldiers tossing him in the air like a sack of potatoes, I ordered them to release him and they questioned me before doing so.' Freya turned away clearly displeased.

'Where are they now?' she asked.

'In the dungeons,' Drew explained.

'I shall deal with them at first light, I will make an example of them.'

As the dawn approached quickly the next morning, everyone in Rosefort was called to the Great Hall.

'You are here today because I have called you to witness what happens when there is injustice under my rule,' Freya announced. 'It has come to my attention that in my absence some people thought it ok to not follow Andrews orders in my place.' The two soldiers were kneeling before Freya smugly.

'These two men thought it was allowed to act in such a disgusting manor that they picked on another for being different to them. Let me make myself clear, Dwarf tossing will not be condoned under any circumstance. What do you have to say for yourselves?' she asked them.

'We were only having a bit of fun,' one man replied.

'You think it is fun to possibly harm one of the small folk you are here to protect? She asked, the other man sniggered. 'Send them to the stocks,' she cried. 'They are no longer soldiers in my army, they are to be stripped of all wealth, lands and weapons. Only real men will fight with this house and they clearly are not.' One of the men turned begging to Freya for forgiveness the other turned nasty.

'Bitch!' he spat. 'Who are you to lead anyone, you're only a woman! Give me that blade I'll fuck her with it!' he bellowed. 'Draconian should have had your head a long time ago, you cunt!' Venom fuelled his words.

'Stop!' Freya ordered as Gilli and Nari dragged the screaming man from the hall. 'The other one to the stocks, I have other plans for him.'

The man who repented for his actions was locked in the stocks, while the other was dragged out towards the mines and tied with wet leather straps to a wooden rack. As the leather dried it tightened onto the man's wrists and ankles, he was stripped of his clothes.

'I want his tongue.' Freya called to Nari who began ripping at the man's head. After his tongue was removed, Nari fed it to Captain. 'I will take his sword hand also.' Freya ordered. 'Let this be a lesson to any who stand among you, I will not condone Treason, Rape or Injustice of any kind. This man will live, but he will not harm another by his hand or his tongue, He should be thankful I have not taken his life.' Freya dismissed the small folk. 'Do you know why I did this?' She asked Asher. 'You cannot risk an uprising, you are a fair and just ruler m'lady, you done this to protect your people from those that mean to harm them.' She turned to Asher smiling. 'Come lets share some good wine and good food, I am sure we have much to discuss.'

As they finished their meal, everyone including Rosemary was making their voices heard with song.

'So Asher, Andrew tells me you have a weakness for strawberries,' Freya joked.

'I adore them,' Asher slurred after having a bit too much wine.

'Good to know,' she said, as she signalled for desert. Large bowls of strawberries dripping in honey was served, to everyone in the room. Everyone chuckled at how fast Koi and Asher start to eat their servings. 'I could use more good men around here, how would you two like to come and live here with me?' Freya asked them.

'But m'lady we are only common folk,' Asher gasped.

'We are far from nobility your grace,' Koi agreed.

'Do your hearts not beat the same as any other?' Freya asked. The men looked at each in amazement.

'It would be an honour to serve you m'lady,' Asher replied, the room roared with laughter once again.

'I do not invite you hear to serve me,' Freya explained. 'I invite you here as my allies, together we should do great things with Rosefort.'

After showing Asher and Koi their new chambers, Freya and Drew walked through the corridors reminiscing about good times they had when Drew first moved to the castle.

Drew turned to Freya. 'What is this?' he asked reaching for her necklace.

'A gift,' she answered.

Drew examined it for a moment it was a white quartz crystal amulet wrapped in the centre with a bronze wiry design, hanging on the end of a bronze chain, simple but eye catching.

'A gift from who?' Drew asked.

'Finn,' Freya answered simply.

'Freya you have not succumbed to his charms?' he asked worried.

'He's not like that Andrew, at least not with me, at first he was unkind and rude, but then he showed this other side he's got a sweet side, you will see when you meet him.'

'Meet him?' Andrew asked stunned.

'Yes his sister is coming here to learn our ways after his brother's wedding and Finn is accompanying her to ensure she has safe passage,' Freya explained.

'Trust me, the Olden's are not like the other houses, they are loyal and misunderstood from what I have seen,' Drew grunted. 'I trust you, it's them I don't trust, but I will give them a chance, if you see well in them they cannot be all bad.' Drew rolled his eyes sarcastically, Freya noticed and shoved him and they giggled together before Drew pulled her in to cuddle her. 'I missed you,' he whispered while placing a gentle kiss on her forehead.

'I missed you too brother bear,' she replied squeezing him in tightly.

'But what of Bartholomew?' Drew asked interrupting her embrace.

'What of him?' she asked.

'He is in love with you, how do you think he will take the news of your new found relationship with Finn Olden?' Freya searched herself for a minute.

‘I never promised myself to Bartholomew, he wanted my hand, I said no, He is a good man but any issue he has that comes of this will be brought to light soon and then I can address it. Drew pulled Freya in tightly again giving her a gentle peck on the forehead.

Family Bonds

After her argument with her son, Mary thought it best to try and talk to him. Ashamed of her outburst a few days before, it had caused a great distance between herself and her children. She was only trying to protect them but realising she had gone about it the wrong way, she had a lot of things to set straight. She had mended things with her husband, she loved him dearly and after explaining her actions to him, she could tell her understood why she had been acting out of character lately. He reassured her that her children would be making their own path in life, that they as parents where only there to guide them, and that Finn has angered enough people in his short life time to have one hundred men want his head, but was capable enough to ensure his own safety.

Rapping her knuckles on the door of Finn's chambers, Mary patiently waited for him to answer the door. The door creaked open.

'Mother?' Finn asked surprised to see her standing on the other side of his door. 'May I come in, I wish to speak to you alone,' she asked, 'You are alone, aren't you?' peaking her head in the door to see if there was a whore in his bed.

'It is just me here, come in.' Finn turned sideways to allow his mother past before gently closing the door behind him. His room was large and warm. Tankards of ale sat on his desk, two marble stairs led to his bed which was made up of fine linens, a bear skin rug sat centre of the room in front of a large open fireplace. Finn walked towards his desk and took a seat. 'This is about Freya?' he asked.

'Yes…and no,' Mary replied hesitantly. 'I came to apologise to you about my outburst the other day, I would like to say I knew not of what came over me, but that would not be the truth,' she explained. 'I was trying to keep you safe,' she exhaled turning from her son towards the window.

'Safe?' Finn asked.

'Freya's mother Catherine was a dear friend. One of whom I loved dearly. But she was not like other women, or any other person to be precise.' Taking a deep breath, Mary dreaded having to try explain. 'Catherine came from a family of great warriors whose ancestors were cursed for their brutality.'

'Berserkers,' Finn interrupted.

Mary turned to her son, she felt the blood drain from her face, a cold chill ran down her spine and the hair on the back of her neck stood up.

'How?' this was the only word to escape her lips.

'Asger,' Finn said bluntly. 'I know what they are Mother and I care not, if anything being with them provides a shield for me, than that of anyone else.' Finn rubbed two fingers along his temple, as he gazed down at the floor. Finding her voice eventually.

'They will be hunted like animals, people fear what they don't understand, the people who came after them all those years ago will not stop until every last one of them and their supporters die.' Her voice cracked at the thought.

'So you thought that forbidding me to see Freya was a way of keeping me alive?' Finn asked dropping his hand to his lap and looking up at his mother.

'In a way yes,' she admitted.

'Mother, I have as much chance of been killed on the battlefield as I do with associating with the Raghnall's. I understand, you want to protect me and I love you for that but you cannot protect me by holding on to tightly to me. You are afraid having no control over your children's faiths and because of that you are smothering us, can't you see that?' Finn's voice was low and irritable. Mary's eyes welled up, her lip start to quiver. 'No Mother, don't do that.' Finn approached his mother and pulled her in tightly to his chest. 'I will always be your son. But I am not a child anymore Mother. 'Let me be a man.' Leaning in and giving his mother a soft kiss on the top of her head, Finn turned and made for the door.

Walking towards the stables he thought a lot about his conversation with his mother. He could understand her now at least, although her behaviour before still angered him, but he could not think about it now. His little sister needed him, she had asked him for his help. Finn was not one to let his family down when they needed help.

'Finn!' a voice called. Edward ran towards him excited. 'Are you going to teach Cara-Lea how to fight?' Edwards's voice was full of anticipation.

'I am,' Finn answered.

'Can I come watch?' Edward asked.

Finn gestured for Edward to follow him. On their approach to the stables, Edward spoke of a letter Freya had wrote to a man back home and how she spoke of Finn.

'I think she likes you,' Edward said gleefully. Finn grinned, he found his brothers enthusiasm rather endearing.

'Reading a person's mail Edward? Do not let Father catch you,' Finn warned.

Cara-Lea was already at the stables waiting eagerly on her brother's arrival. Taking the horses and galloping from the stables into a vacant meadow that was situated a short distance from the castle, Finn jumped down from Onyx and handed his sister a wooden sword. He thought her how to hold it and how to swing it, after a few practise swings he had his little sister advance on him. Finn defended her strikes easily, he could tell the shock from the impact his blocks was travelling up Cara-Lea's arms as she had to stop and rub her arm after a short while.

'Real swords are worse,' Finn explained. The impact from the strikes can leave you sore for days, when you are first learning.' Giving her arms a rest, Finn had Cara-Lea work on her footwork. 'Your aim is to make your body as small as possible, it can be a harder target to hit and easier for you to defend.' Edward joined in the lesson as he found it to be a great opportunity to learn from Finn.

After a few hours of footwork and striking air, Finn decided to put the twins against each other.

'Show no fear of your opponent, no matter how big or strong they are you will always find a weakness. Use that fear and anger in your body and let it burn within your bellies.' Cara-Lea charged at Edward who was quickly taken aback. Finn watched his sister deliver a horrendous blow towards Edwards head. Edward managed to get his sword up in time to block his sister's attack but the force behind Cara-Lea's strike broke both swords in half. 'Well I guess that is us done for the day,' Finn said astonished at what he had just witnessed.

Later that day the twins watched Finn train the new recruits for their father's army. He was a lot tougher on the soldiers than what he was like on his siblings.

'You're a gutless, pathetic lot, I asked for men to train not a bunch of women,' Finn barked at them. 'You're the saddest bunch I have ever met,' Finn yelled at the young men falling down trying to block his attacks.

'He's got them scared to death,' Cara-Lea watched as the flushed faces of the men in front of her, coward before her brother. Finn was taking on six men at a time and barely breaking a sweat, one after another they all came crashing down face first into the dirt below.

'Heed my every order and you might have a chance at survival,' Finn warned.

Nicholas approached the training grounds. 'Finn,' he called. Finn walked away leaving the men to spar amongst themselves. 'So what news of the new recruits?' Nicholas asked.

'They're unsuited for war, right now they are not even suited to face one another. There is a long way to go in getting them battle ready,' Finn explained.

As the brothers were deep in conversation, the twins thought it best to leave. Cara-Lea went back to the castle while Edward decided to go back to the stables. While brushing one of the horses. Edward could smell something burning, he put down the brush and walked around the back of the stables where he saw some paper being burned, he quickly ran to put out the fire in fear of it spreading. Stomping on the paper he noticed something written one of the pieces of charred paper.

Prepare for the chance of a lifetime, a magnificent new era awaits us. I know it sounds sordid but the rewards will be great when we deliver those Vikings heads. Lure them out, I don't care how you do it just make sure it is done.

Edwards's heart was beating hard in his chest. Someone in his father's realm wanted the Vikings dead. Is this why his brothers were attacked? Why the bandit was smiling when he was put to death? Turning over the paper to see if he could find the seal from the house this letter came but to no avail. The letter had obviously been a lot longer but the fire had stripped it all away. Everything bar the piece he now clutched in his hand. Edward ran from the back of the stables out of fear of being seen with the letter. He had to get this to his father.

Nicholas

A few weeks had passed since Amelia's departure, she had now returned for their wedding. He was thankful that all of the bad blood had died down in his family.

'Not long now,' his mother's voice sang behind him. 'I am so proud of you my son, tomorrow night you become a man.' Lady Olden had spent her weight in gold ensuring the most beautiful flowers and sculptures were to be present on her son's big day. 'Remember to treat her right, I desire a bundle of grandchildren,' she said beaming at her son.

'I will do my best Mother,' he assured her.

Amelia was being kept in the west wing of the castle, where she would not be available to see Nicholas until the next day when they are due to be wed, no doubt she would be getting pampered by her hand maidens, who would be preparing her for the big day.

Nicholas went to go talk to Finn, he had hardly seen the sight of him since Bjorn and the others left. He left for the forest to go find his brother, while all the guests continued to arrive the night before for celebratory drinks.

'I thought I'd find you here,' Nicholas said as he walked up to the cliff where they had killed the Kelpie.

'What gave me away?' Finn asked mockingly.

Nicholas sat on the edge of the cliff next to his brother. 'Tomorrow is the big day,' he muttered.

'You know it's not too late to run,' Finn joked.

'Would you run?' Nicholas asked.

'It depends,' Finn replied.

'On?'

'If it was a bride of my choosing or an arranged marriage,' Finn answered.

'You miss her, don't you brother?' Nicholas glanced at his brother's sombre expression.

'Everyday,' Finn replied.

The sun was setting and a crisp chill filled the air.

'Come lets head back for the festivities, I would rather be warm and drunk then cold and sober,' Nicholas jested.

They arrived home they noticed the house was eerily quiet.

'They cannot possibly be passed out already,' Nicholas said.

Finn laughed, 'Two pint screamers, can't even handle their ale.'

Looking around there was not even a peasant in sight.

'Something's not right,' said Finn, as they approached the Great Hall. Finn put his hand to the door when an arrow shot past his ear missing him by a hairs breadth.

'Run!' Nicholas cried.

The brothers took off running for their lives diving behind pillars and suits of armour to block the archers attack. Finn peaked out from behind one of the armoured figurines to see if he could spot the archer.

'I can't see anyone,' he whispered.

'The walls will shield us from here, they had to be shooting from a distance,' Nicholas nodded.

Both men crept though the halls swiftly as to not alert anyone of their presence. Running upstairs they heard women screaming.

'That could be Cara-Lea,' Finn gasped.

The brothers ran toward the screams.

'Please no!' the voice cried. 'Why are you doing this?' another shrieked.

The door of a room was half open, they could hear men laughing inside the room. 'My father will hear of this! He will have your heads!' Nicholas recognised the voice as Amelia's.

'Your father sent us sweetheart. We came looking for the Viking whore but you will do nicely.'

Nicholas burst through the door tackling one man to the ground. The other turned around swinging his sword down at Nicholas, Finn had blocked the strike by throwing a chamber pot knocking the sword from the bandit's hand.

'You,' the man spat. 'I thought we took care of you back in the forest.'

'Apparently not well enough.' Finn pulled an iron torch sconce from the wall and ran at the bandit brandishing the sconce in hand. Swinging with all his might Finn drove the sconce into the man's jaw, blood spewed from his mouth as he fell backwards to the wall. Nicholas had the other bandit in his grasps, repeatedly driving his head into the solid floor beneath him painting the room in his blood. Finn ran at the bandit again driving the sconce into the top of his skull. He looked around him to see Cara-Lea shaken up and bruised, her dress had been torn to shreds. He ran to her. 'Did they hurt you?' Finn checked.

'Just my limbs and face… I fought like you thought me to' Tears filled her eyes.

'What happened?' Nicholas barked staggering to his feet through the swamp that was the bandits head.

'We were at dinner, Mercenaries and Bandits charged on the Great hall out of nowhere, I don't know how they got beyond the gates. A war broke out in the Great Hall, I tried to escape but they grabbed me and dragged me up here. Amelia was brought in shortly after,' she started crying.

Nicholas gasped looking at Finn, who was dumbfounded by the news.

'What of Mother, father and Edward?' Nicholas asked.

'They were alive when I last seen them,' Cara-Lea answered.

Amelia stood behind Nicholas silent and fearful.

'We need to find them,' Finn demanded.

'I'll go, we have swords now take the girls to the docks and round up as many of the small folk as you can.'

'I am not leaving you to die,' Finn barked.

'Finn listen to me, for our sister you need to find a way out if we both fall, you know what those bastards will do to her.' Nicholas ordered.

Nicholas knew his brother would do the right thing. They picked up the bandits swords and left in search of survivors.

Carefully making their way out of castle Mourne, they heard the horns blow and noticed House Olden banners flying on the road to the docks.

'Looks like we are sticking together after all,' Finn announced.

'If Father is anywhere he is up there,' Nicholas said.

The air was thick and heavy with smoke from the burning houses of the small folk. War cries filled the air along with the sound of women and children's screams. Nicholas ran ahead first cutting down anyone in his path, while Finn kept an eye out for archers, or anyone hiding in the shadows. Nicholas lost Finn in the thick smoke that filled the air, he looked around franticly but could not see his brother.

'Finn!' he cried, it was no use, he noticed soldiers from house Olden not far from him, Nicholas began to run towards them.

'Father!' Nicholas yelled, as he seen Theodore battling the bandits and Henry Preston. Nicholas's cries distracted Theodore momentarily, allowing Henry Preston to knock him off balance. Nicholas watched in horror as the sword swung down to his father's head. He could not bear to lose his father. Henry's swing stopped in mid-air, a sword protruded through his armour.

'Not today, you son of a bitch,' Finn spat retracting his sword from Henrys body.

Amelia's cries echoed through the air, Cara-Lea's hand had found her way across Amelia's face.

'Now is not the time,' she yelled.

'Amelia, you're supposed to be dead,' Mark Preston called, not far from his father's lifeless body. A mercenary grabbed a dagger from his boot and ran at Finn. Plunging his dagger deep into Finns chest. Finn staggered backwards clutching his chest. The screams of Cara-Lea could be heard down at the docks, Theodore ran his blade through the mercenary that stabbed his son. Nicholas ran to block an attack on his father, while a bandit seized the opportunity to take out the infamous Olden boy. He picked up an axe from the corpse of a soldier from House Olden and ran towards Finn, who quickly got to his feet pulling the dagger out of his chest, the bandit hurled the axe at Finn's head and missed. Finn charged at the bandit lunging himself at him, he drove the dagger into the man's neck. Another shriek came from his sister as Nicholas looked over, he noticed Cara-Lea trying to fend off a mercenary. Nicholas ran at the man driving his sword through the back of the man's head. The girls were covered in blood momentarily blinded, they were trying to wipe it away from their eyes. Cara-Lea opened her eyes to find a man running at her wielding a great sword. 'Get away from my daughter, you coward.' a voice called. Nicholas turned around to see his mother repeatedly stabbing the bandit in the back. She stood up and ran towards her daughter, clutching her face in her hands. Another shriek was heard this time from Amelia. Nicholas turned again to see his mother go limp in his sisters' arms.

'NO!' He yelled, fighting his way over to his sister. Finn got there first, he looked down grabbed, the two girls are blitzed his way through the herd of bandits leaving his mother's lifeless body behind, he went running towards the ships and yelling for the small folk to follow him. Nicholas looked down to find his mother had been shot with an arrow through the skull, a surge of rage filled him as he sliced through the men that stood between him and his father. Nicholas decided to stay with Theodore and their men.

'There are too many of them,' Nicholas cried.

'You go I'll stay here and hold them off,' Theodore ordered.

'No I am not going to lose our house to these bastards!' Nicholas yelled.

'Nicholas, this is a pile of bricks your house is your family, have I thought you nothing, go now find Bjorn he will keep you safe trust no one but him, you can take it back again, if you stay we both will fall, let me save your life,' Theodore begged.

'One house, one family,' Nicholas muttered.

'One house, one family,' Theodore replied.

Theodore gave the command to charge at those rushing towards them. Nicholas watched for s split second before running towards the docks. Finn had three ships filling quickly with small folk trying to escape, He was running with a young child towards the boat when a surge of bandits were spotted running towards them. 'We have to go now,' he snapped. One by one the ships start to sail off. Nicholas leapt from the peer onto the ship,

'Father?' Finn asked. Nicholas shook his head.

'WAIT!' a cry came from the peer, Nicholas looked back to see Edward running towards them.

'Edward Run!' Nicholas cried. He watched as his brother ran down the peer leaping towards the ship, he landed hard with a sickening thud. Gazing at his brother's lifeless body he saw it. Edward had been hit with a spear through his chest as he jumped for the ship.

Finn sank to the floor, Cara-Lea dropped to her twin's side cradling him in her arms the tears dropped from her face onto his. Nicholas had stood in shock as he peered at his youngest brother staring back at him through doll like lifeless eyes. A scream came from behind him, Nicholas turned, Finn had Amelia pinned by the throat screaming at her. 'You did this!' He spat. 'You destroyed our home, killed our families and now my brother why should he die and you live!' Amelia gasped for air as Finn lifted her off the floor, off the ship by her throat. Nicholas ran to tear Finn off Amelia's neck but to no avail Finn was too powerful in a blind rage. It took six men to get Finn to release his grip on Amelia.

'Stop this,' Nicholas commanded. 'Amelia was as much a victim in this as we were, her family tried to have her killed along with us. You saw it yourself.' Nicholas tried to reason with his brother who was refusing to listen to anything he had to tell him. 'Right now we need to find somewhere to go to keep our people safe and to grow, and army big enough to regain our home and put those cunt's heads on a spike,' Nicholas bellowed.

'Where do you suggest we go?' Finn asked.

'Rosefort,' Nicholas said simply. 'We have allies there, its impenetrable no army has ever made it past the second wall we will all be safe there.'

Finn stood up with a fire in his eyes. 'You expect me to put Freya at risk?' he asked.

'There is no risk no army can get through, father's last words to me were to find Bjorn to only trust him, and I plan on doing that,' said Nicholas.

'If anything happens to Freya, I will personally remove that bitches head myself.' Finn pointed towards Amelia who was gasping for air on the floor. Finn walked over towards Cara-Lea who remained hysterically crying over her brother's body. He knelt down behind her wrapping his arms around her tightly. 'I'm sorry, I wasn't able to protect him, I swear to you they will pay for this.' Finn kissed his sisters head then bent over his brother's corpse. 'You are with Father now, you will be protected, I am sorry I failed you brother.' He kissed his brothers forehead and shut his eyes, then stood up to remove the spear from his body. 'One house, one family,' Finn muttered over Edwards's body.

The ship remained silent for the night, the sea was angry rocking them back and forth until the early hours of the next morning. Nicholas did not sleep, how could he, this was supposed to be his wedding day, now half of his family have been murdered and for what? He needed answers. He looked around the deck, mothers and their children slept, Cara-Lea was lying across Edwards's body weeping and singing a song so softly Nicholas could not make out the words. Finn was crying silently with his head in his hands, to most people he would have appeared to be sleeping but Nicholas could see his shoulders twitch every now and then. He did not know himself of what he should be feeling, he was numb, angry and upset all at once. He could do nothing but stare at those around him waiting for one feeling to overcome the rest. Amelia's head dropped onto his shoulder as she slept, Nicholas moved her away from him. He knew she was just as much a victim as him but he couldn't shake the hatred he had for her family and did not want to lash out at her in anger. All he could do was keep his head until they made it to Rosefort, so he could give his brother a proper burial.

Gilli

Thankful to be home from Castle Mourne, Gilli woke before first light, he dressed, took his bow and arrows and went hunting. He had grown to know these lands well the past few years, and had a certain fondness for it. The soil was rich and was great for growing crops. The animals loved the grass, and with Rosefort having very little people living in, it meant there was less competition for archers which made it easier to hunt. Hazy rain poured from the sky the wind was blowing harshly, but Gilli knew he would find shelter in amongst the trees.

After setting traps behind each wall, Gilli found himself outside the third wall at Rosefort. The sky was starting to brighten with the light of the sun, the rain had eased off and the howling winds turned into a heavy breeze. Walking only a few metres from the third wall, he noticed smoke from a fire come from the west side of the wall. Reaching for an arrow, Gilli approached with caution listening for any signs of life around him. A figure in a dark cape sat by the fire warming their hands, they appeared to be alone.

'You're late,' the voice called. Gilli froze uncertain if the person was talking to him, or somebody else. 'Well sit down Gilli Iarlsson. I don't bite.' Looking once more Gilli approached the man readily armed.

'How do you know my name?' he asked.

'I know a lot about you, like the fact you were orphaned from a young age, your mother died giving birth to a boy and your father was killed at the battle of Gild Water along with your uncle Arn. Since then you have become part of another family, a cursed family some might call it.'

'If you're here for them…' Gilli started.

'I am here for them, but not in the manner you think, I do not wish to see them killed,' the voice explained.

'If you believe they are cursed, why would you not want them dead?' Gilli asked hesitantly.

'Because as you can see, I am cursed myself.' Gilli watched as the stranger pulled down their hood, a young man stared back at him. Dark doll like eyes met his gaze, short black slightly curled hair blew in the wind as a cold chill ran down Gilli's spine.

'Who are you?' Gilli asked.

'Beigarth Hallisson.' he replied grinning. 'My mother was a volva, alas her gift got passed down to myself. Some call me the seer, others the oracle; those would be the kinder names I have been called,' he explained.

'Why are you here?' Gilli pressed.

'Well since the last village I took up residence in tried to burn me at the stake for witch craft, I thought who best understand my curse as those who are believed cursed themselves?'

Gilli remained unsure of this new visitor to the realm, he eventually agreed to take him to see Freya under the condition that Beigarth's hands were bound and he was stripped of any weapons in his possession. The journey back into Rosefort seemed to take twice as long as usual, tension filled the air, or so Gilli thought as he looked back at Beigarth, who seemed relaxed and content in spite of being tied up like a criminal. Eventually reaching the castle, Gilli led Beigarth to the Great Hall where he knew Freya would be having her morning meal, the floor hall was all marble from the floors and eight pillars to the ceiling with Gold roses painted along the sides of the floors and walls, and sat elegantly at the ends of the pillars. Freya was sitting at the top of the hall with her father, brother, Drew and the two dwarfs.

'Apologies to intrude, I found this man outside the walls of Rosefort around first light, he was alone as far as I could tell and wished to speak to you Freya,' Gilli explained formally, 'My lady.'

Beigarth bowed. 'It is a pleasure to make your acquaintance, I know so much of you yet I am sure you know nothing of me. My name is Beigarth Hallisson, My mother was Rane Hallisson, she was a renowned Volva you may have heard of her?' he asked charismatically.

‘I know your mother’s name she helped train young gifted women like herself, what brings you here Beigarth Hallisson?’ Freya asked curiously.

‘I am fainted to be here,’ said Beigarth. ‘There is a great war approaching sooner than you have anticipated, word of your brother’s survival has spread to all realms, I am afraid your only Allianz has been fractured. Beigarth turned to Bjorn. ‘You have received a letter from Lord Olden not too long ago, about a traitor in his kingdom who was setting up an ambush for you, that is why you did not attend the wedding today?’ he said. ‘I hate to be the bearer of bad news, but your absence there was noted and angered so many that the Preston’s revolted. House Olden stands but a pile of ash and rubble.’

Freya jumped from her seat.

‘How do you know this?’ her voice high and agitated. ‘There has been no word of this from, I demand some truth to these accusations,’ she barked.

‘My lady, my intention is not to upset you, all will be revealed in the next few days the survivors are on their way here,’ Beigarth explained.

‘What did you see?’ Asger interrupted.

‘The sky was filled with fire and thick black smoke as the houses of the small folk and the surroundings burned, I heard voices crying for help and crying of fear, women were raped, hundreds were killed, about three ships full of survivors made it out of the battle. It happened last night, word won’t reach your kingdom for about another day. But that is not the vision I have come to warn you about,’ he explained.

‘What else can you tell us?’ Asger asked.

‘I had a vision not long before Gilli found me outside the walls, I see a great war with great animals, men in furs, red and blue fill the battle field, I see heroes dying. Voices led me here to help that and I could not remove the taste of drying blood from my mouth no matter how much I drank, many of those you love will die, as you reach a point you cannot go on someone you think to be dead, will arise from the grave and win this war for you.’ Asger looked on proudly. ‘It is not you,’ Beigarth explained. Asger looked at the man confused. ‘You have already returned from the dead, the next time you are believed dead you will be, there is no coming back for you now. My lady I beg you heed this warning, there are people you trust who will betray you, who have already done. Be careful about who sits next to you, envy has caused people to kill for less than an empire and you being a woman in such a position of power, men do not take kindly to it, they see you as an abomination but they also see you as weak use that to your advantage.' The room fell silent, Freya walked towards the man in front of her in his dark robes, draped in a black cloak, she took his hands in hers for a moment and gazed into his eyes.

'Gilli release this man's bounds and see that he is fed and housed, I wish to have him placed close to my chambers so I can keep an eye on him.' Beigarth gave Freya a kind smile as Gilli cut his bounds.

Upon leaving the Great Hall, Nari raced behind Gilli.

'I don't trust him, did you see his eyes? They were dead. There is an evil about that man, I am going to keep a close eye on him I don't like him being that close to Freya,' Gilli turned to his friend.

'I know but there is nothing we can do about it, she wants him close to her, just make sure the hounds are with her at all times. You almost missed the meal, where were you anyway?' Gilli asked.

'I was with Hawise,' Nari replied. Gilli rolled his eyes. 'I am going to marry her,' said Nari.

'Did you ask her?' Gilli asked curiously.

'Not yet but I will,' Nari beamed at his friends. Gilli was happy that Nari had found someone but he could not help shake the feeling of dread that came with Beigarth's warning, was it true the Olden's had been attacked? That a great war upon them and even worse that a traitor lived among them? A great war meant great death, scarcely one hundred people filled Rosefort as it was how could they defend themselves if attacked? They would have to do something to gain allies and fast, but who in all the realms could they trust, the Olden's were the only real allies they had if it was true and they had been attacked who else would fight their cause?

Drew

Staying back with Freya and her new guest, Drew found himself growing concerned, why would a total stranger travel all this way to tell tales of destruction if they were not true? His blood ran cold staring at the young doll eyed man who could not have been much older than him the scent of death lingered around them as he stood tall beside Freya. If he was planning on harming her in any way, Drew was ready to attack at so much as a finger twitch from Beigarth, but the strange man did not budge, he barely blinked. He just stood still grinning at Freya as she looked silently upon him.

You want to ask me a question, one you already know the answer too,' Beigarth addressed Freya. 'He lives, but you know that, you have a sense for these things yourself,' he explained.

'You must be hungry, please help yourself to any food that is here, Gilli will return shortly to show you your chambers.' Freya brushed off his last remarks and turned for the door. Drew, Asher and Koi were following quickly behind.

'Who does he mean? Who lives? Drew asked.

'Finn,' she replied. 'I knew he had to be, I didn't get the same feeling of dread I normally do when somebody I care for dies. Just because Finn lives does not mean the rest of the family were so lucky, we don't know who is coming here. After a battle like that, there are sure to be many injured and hungry if it happened last night that gives us at least one day to prepare for them if the winds were on their side. I was soldiers posted at every inch of the land where they can dock, they don't know these lands I want extra horses brought to bring them here, send word to my uncle I need Clara here to help with any injured and I need him here to come up with a plan of defence. There is no doubt in my mind that they will not stop until Finn is dead.'

'Why Finn?' Drew asked.

'Because I care for him and he cares for me. They attacked the Olden's to lure us out, they attacked Finns family, he will not rest until he kills every last one of them.'

'But surely if Nicholas lives he is at risk too?'

'Not as much as Finn, Nicholas is predictable they know what they are getting with him, he is a great fighter but nothing to fear with him other than death, Finn on the other hand is unpredictable, ruthless and skilled with any weapon you hand him. Those Lords fear what they cannot understand, they do not understand Finn or us, that is why to them we all must die.'

'Forgive me,' Koi's voice called up towards them. 'If numbers are our downfall surely we can trap any invaders, are Vikings not known for their traps? Asher and I could start crafting them away from the docks for now that way we can be ready if the enemy is following behind them?' Freya looked at Koi and smiled. 'I knew I liked you for a reason, I will go fetch Father he will be the best person to help out in the making of anything like that.'

'I will rally up the men we have to meet the Olden's when they arrive,' Drew announced. 'I will take some of the hounds too to be safe, the men are not exactly battle ready I would put more faith in the dogs than the men we have.'

After sending a message to Henry Grisson, and setting up a watch at the three docklands of Rosefort, Drew marched out on foot followed by twenty hounds and fifteen wolves towards each of the docklands. On his way to Mountain View, he noticed Asher and Koi scurrying through the long grass with rope and shovels, a small rustle in the grass followed behind them, no doubt it was Rosemary, she had been fattening up nicely since Asher took her but no doubt he would not kill her, he became very fond of that piglet.

Nari was waiting at Mountain View with two men when Drew arrived.

'I brought you some company,' Drew announced. Nari turned to look at the herd of canines that stood with his friend.

'At least you brought something that can fight,' said Nari.

'Aleksia, Anja, Bodil, Disa, Eirik, Kleng, Freki, Olvaldi, Skirnir, Terje Guard. Drew commanded.

'How do you remember all of their names?' Nari asked.

'It's not so hard, when you get to know them,' said Drew.

'Do you believe him?' Nari asked cautiously.

'Freya seems to, and I trust her instincts, besides if he is wrong at least you get to stay out here all day doing nothing.' Drew mocked. Drew turned leaving seven hounds and three wolves with Nari.

Arriving at The Lilly Patch, Drew found Gilli with three men. 'It's about time you got here, I thought I was left to defend this place alone,' Gilli called as he watched Drew approach.

'Would I leave you distressed?' Drew asked.

'Yes,' Gilli exaggerated.

'This is the best I could do ten men on watch now and another ten for the nights watch,' Drew said apologetically.

'It's not your fault, the men are few and far between here, we need more men but we won't find them here,' Gilli reassured.

'Well at least we have these,' Drew turned to the hounds 'Verdani, Tyr, Tollak, Mikkel, Magnus, Lovise, Kleng, Halvor, Forseti, Einar, Carr, Burnaby, Anniken, guard. He ordered. 'I best go take my post,' Drew Turned to go to Helga's Grove.

Finally arriving at his post, he met two men awaiting him, Thorvard Osvaldsson and Edgar Malik. Thorvard was a thin gangly man with long lice infested red hair and known for having a very dry sense of humour. Edgar was average height, built like an ox and very docile, his appearance was the only thing intimidating about him.

'Grayson, Bucky, Gambit, Abbas, Novac, Nighthawk, Alma, Patch, Badr, Pagoda, Sage, Uggi guard,' Drew ordered, as he walked towards a large boulder, climbed onto it and stared out into the horizon.

After a short while, a man approached on horseback, Drew turned to see the horse surrounded by snarling hounds, he whistled, the hounds immediately turned and left the man on horseback.

'Bartholomew to what do we owe the pleasure,' Drew sheathed his sword and approached.

'Good grief why does she insist on keeping these beasts around?' he barked.

'They belong to Freya and if you are wise you do not question her actions,' Drew warned.

Bartholomew was tall with shoulder length blonde hair and a short beard. His armour shone in the light on the sun with his house emblem a hawk soaring with a snake in its claws carved into the chest.

'Why are you here?' Drew asked.

'I have come to see her,' Bartholomew snapped.

'Freya is busy at the moment you should have notified her of your arrival, she may not have time to see you,' Drew explained.

'No time to see me?' he barked.

'But I am sure she has all the time in the world for the Olden beast? I heard all about her escapades in house Olden,' his face grew red like a tomato, his eyes narrowed and his jaw tightened. 'Might I remind you that Freya was never yours to begin with, it is no secret you desire her, but she never promised to be yours, she is a free woman to do as she likes and what she does in her time is no concern of yours,' Drew warned.

Bartholomew shot such a look at Drew, he thought his soul would leave him then and there, the man kicked his heels into his horse's side and took off towards Rosefort.

'You are lucky he's no warlock,' Edgar mocked.

'He could have turned you to stone,' Drew turned.

'I think he almost did. He is going to see Freya?' Edgar asked.

Drew nodded, 'I pity him if he tries to make demands out of her she will have him boiled in oil.'

'Can I have his armour if she does kill him,' Edgar looked eagerly at Drew.

'What would you do with his armour'? Drew asked.

'Sell it and have a good time in the whore house,' Edgar explained. Drew climbed back onto the boulder looking out in the distance, a big change was coming he could feel it in his bones, he had hoped it was for their benefit.

Freya

Standing on the balcony of her chambers, gazing at the people down below her, Freya was briefly distracted and did not hear the door open behind her. She noted a smell of death had appeared in her room and knew Beigarth was standing behind her.

'You feel safe in this castle, behind the parapets of stone, this place is indeed a fortress I have never witnessed such a place before,' his voice called. Freya turned to Beigarth, who had his hood pulled up over his head. 'Why do you hide behind your robes'? she asked.

'I find that my appearance can make most people feel uncomfortable,' he explained.

'I am not most people, you are a guest here, do not feel the need to hide away in the shadows of your hood.' Freya watched as Beigarth brushed his hood from his head. The left side of his body had been badly burned, yet the higher the burns climbed the less damage they seemed fire seemed to have done. 'Why did you come here?' Freya asked.

'I have explained before, I am destined to be here,' he said softly.

'But why here, why us?' Freya found herself more confused the more she thought about it.

'I think the cursed are better sticking together do you not? After all we are less likely to want the others heads for being different.' Strangely his words were making sense. 'Your brother loves you, he does not want you to feel guilt over him protecting you,' Freya looked at Beigarth amused.

'Asger loves to fight, I would have no choice in the matter of his protection, regardless I have made peace with that a long time ago.' her voice amused.

Beigarth's expression hardened in frustration, 'Not Asger, your brother Nate.' Freya felt her heart sink at the thoughts of her belated brother.

'How did you?' Freya began.

'I told you I have a gift…or curse which ever you chose to call it yourself, you were meant to live then and you are meant to live now, you are the one to bring greatness back to your house again not the men.' Freya found herself speechless at Beigarth's words. 'You have a visitor who is eager to see you, I shall take my leave now.' Beigarth turned for the door. Freya stood still trying to make sense of what she had been told.

Lost in thought, she pulled herself together when she heard a knock on her door.

'Lord Bartholomew Hawkland is here to see you my lady.' The servant girl stood nervously at the threshold of the door.

'Thank you Justina, please send him in,' She nodded and quickly hurried to fetch Freya's guest. Almost immediately Bartholomew marched in wearing his shining armour and an angry expression on his face.

'So what is all this I hear about you and House Olden?' he barked.

'That all depends on what you heard my Lord,' Freya spoke disrespectfully.

'I see you have met Finn Olden and his smart mouth on your trip,' he barked.

'Well it was House Olden I visited, I would be very surprised if I met Charles Rupert instead,' Bartholomew slammed the door in the servant girl's face.

'Well that was far from polite,' Freya stated.

'How was he?' Bartholomew asked.

'I am afraid you are not his type if that's what you are asking of me?' Freya explained.

Bartholomew let out a hearty laugh. 'Must we do this every time you visit, I gave you my word, no one else knows about you and Ronald Whitmarsh, although he did avoid me like the plague at the Olden's dinner he left after a day I presume it was to be by your side.' Freya walked towards her bed and leapt backwards onto it. 'You said you needed my help?' Bartholomew asked avoiding her last statement.

‘I do indeed, you see we have very little people living here as it is most are women and children, I need men, soldiers not recruits, I need able bodies and I need them now, I presume you heard about the attacks on my brother?’ She asked. ‘I did, he is fortunate to have survived.’

‘That he is, the attacks did not stop there, word had travelled to me that the Olden’s were attacked the night before the Preston’s were to wed into the family, I know not of survivors, or what state they will be in when they arrive, needless to say if they are on their way here, whoever wants our heads will be following quickly behind them.’

‘But this is Rosefort no one has ever got past the walls,’ Bartholomew was shocked.

‘Anything is possible, and I will not hide away inside waiting for those to starve us out while I have only six good men to my name here, I have sent word to my uncle he should be here soon but I need an army, a great army to put an end to this once and for all, I don’t know how but I know someone involved in these attacks are responsible for the slaughter of my family. I will not rest until their houses are wiped out.’

‘By sword and by shield,’ Bartholomew replied.

‘Live great, die better,’ said Freya as she rose from her bed and approached her friend.

‘I should go prepare my men for war,’ Bartholomew stated, brushing his lips off her hand. ‘I shall return in two days’ time, if those bastards want a fight, we shall give them one like they have never seen.’ Bartholomew swung open the door, smiled at Freya and marched out of her chambers. Everything was starting to come together, if there was to be an attack on her people, she would be ready.

Trying to prepare for new arrivals to the land, Freya grabbed her brother and headed to the animals of the land.

‘I want three large sheep killed, two boars and a cow they need to be ready to be cooked by tomorrow,’ she demanded. ‘Five baskets of vegetables to be picks and five fruit baskets, if the seer is right and the Olden’s are on their way here, they will be injured and starved I doubt they were able to bring anything with them for food.’

‘And if he was wrong?’ Asger asked.

'Then we will have such a feast dear brother that Odin himself would love to come join us.' The vacant properties are to be filled with blankets and other necessities, to start them off. I want the barracks restored to its former glory, we will have men to fill it soon enough, again ensure all supplies for it have been seen too and also tell the blacksmiths to start working on armour and weapons we will need as much as he can craft.' Asger looked upon his sister with pride she had turned from a frail girl to a great leader seemingly overnight.

'And what would you have me do?' he asked intrigued.

'I need you to cut down as many trees as you can I need weapons made and possibly coffins for the dead, get the trees to the carpenter and tell him to start asap, I care not if he is up all night crafting just get it done.'

Freya picked up two large baskets and made her way to the crops, she began filling the baskets full of wheat for the miller. Not knowing how many people were to arrive in her land and with very little people to follow through with the jobs she needed done, she had no problem rolling up her sleeves and helping on the farms, after all she was a farm girl for years, it made no difference to her that she was the ruler of a land now. She had planned to help the cook in the kitchen the next day to prepare the food so everyone could eat, Freya knew what it was like to leave everything you had behind and start again with nothing to your name and she remembered the struggle of it all. Never wanting to be a ruler, all she desired was to have a regular life but since this was what had been destined for her, she vowed to look after her people and to avenge her slaughtered family.

After delivering ten baskets of wheat to the miller, and helping deliver wood to the carpenter, Freya felt too tired to even eat, she skipped her evening meal and went straight to bed. The next morning Freya awoke to a growling stomach, she staggered out of bed remaining quite tired and dressed. Arriving at the morning meal, she could barely keep her eyes open, she picked at her fish, although hungry she felt too tired to lift her fork, she reached over and grabbed a piece of bread, the size of her head and start tearing into that instead. She quickly drank a horn full of wine, desperately wanting to crawl back to her bed she thought of an excuse to vanish for a few hours, but before she could open her mouth she heard the horns blowing fiercely.

‘They’re here,’ Beigarth said softly.

Finn

The boat rocked from side to side, many people had been sick on the hazardous journey across the sea, Finn awoke to the sound of horns blowing he looked down at his sister asleep in his arms. He gently kissed her forehead and moved her against the pillar he had been sleeping at. As he stood he felt the burning sensation back in his chest, looking down his tunic was covered in blood from the fight but mostly from his wound. He noticed his skin had gone pale from the blood loss, his stomach growled angrily he had never gone this long without food. The horns sounded again he turned around to notice the coastline, they had made it. One by one, the people on the ships stood up to see where the noise was coming from, a roar of relief filled the ship they had been the lucky ones, the night they fled from home they lost one of the three ships to the storm.

'It looks like they were expecting us,' his brother's voice called.

'How would they have found out so soon, we are here earlier than we should be, that's down to the weather?' Finn questioned looking towards the emerald isles.

After docking the ships, the small folk followed behind Finn and Nicholas, Finn had his arm around Cara-Lea keeping her close to him, while Nicholas carried Edward's lifeless body with Amelia cowering at his side away from Finn.

'So it is true then about your house?' A voice called. Finn looked up to see a tall broad young man standing at the top of the hill they were climbing, his dark hair blowing in the breeze. Finn did not reply he had never seen this man before, this could be a trap. He watched at the stranger and two other men approached with horses.

'Freya sent these down last night to be safe, she had a feeling you would be here early, you best get on as it is a long walk otherwise.' Finn took the horse by the reins and helped his sister onto it first before mounting the animal.

'Thank you, we had a long journey, I assure you, we are grateful for your kindness,' Nicholas said.

'It is the least we could do, I'm Andrew by the way, but most people around here call me Drew,' the man replied.

'You are Freya's friend,' said Finn.

'I am,' Drew answered.

'What's with the carriages?' he asked.

'For the injured and any dead,' Drew replied turning to Nicholas.

'I will take good care of him I promise,' stretching out his arms. Nicholas hesitated, 'You cannot ride with three people on the horse,' said Drew gesturing towards Amelia.

Drew reached out slowly taking Edwards body from Nicholas and carefully placing it in a lone carriage.

'How far is it?' Finn asked about eight hours for the carriages less for the horses.

Eventually making it to the third wall of Rosefort, Finn felt cow heavy on top of the stallion. The burning sensation in his chest seemed to have spread, his shoulders ached and he felt exhausted. Looking down at Cara-Lea whose head was rocking side to side she had fallen asleep some time ago. Drew called for the gates to be open for the third time, it seemed like an eternity before they were allowed access in. The beauty of Rosefort was evident from the moment he could catch a glimpse in, but he remained too tired to take it in all he wanted to do was crawl into bed in a dark room and sleep. Nari was the first familiar face he noticed throughout the small crowd that gathered in the market place. Gilli had come running out from behind, a carriage full of spears and spikes, he was accompanied by two dwarfs and a piglet. Bjorn and Asger were approaching on foot, they were hard to miss as they towered over the other citizens of the land. He searched the crowd repeatedly but did not see the one person he really wanted to be there.

'Finn!' Bjorn called. 'I am so sorry, we found out after it was… I couldn't believe it…they will pay for this.' Bjorn seemed to be grieving and confused all at once, emotions Finn had known all too well the past few days. Not knowing what to say Finn bowed his head and gave a painful smile of gratitude towards the family friend. Dismounting from the horse, Finn helped his sister down who was still half asleep. Bjorn removed his cape and draped it around Cara-Lea whose dress was shredded from the attacks. 'There is plenty of room here for you all, Gilli and Nari will show you to your new homes, my daughter has arranged a feast, she had the sense of knowing you would all be hungry, it should be ready shortly, listen for the horns, once they are sounded the meal will be ready,' Bjorn announced as he signalled to the two men either side of him to come forward. As the crowd dispersed into two groups, Finn noticed a horse galloping towards them, the rider had a familiar face. Leaping from the horse Freya approached stunned.

'Thank God, you're alive,' she gasped pulling Finn into a warm embrace.

Ah! He winced, she released her hold on him.

'You're hurt,' she examined his blood soaked tunic her face sullen.

'I'd like to say I have had worse days but cannot think of one right now,' Finn explained. His skin that normally radiated warmth and colour was now cold and pale, the blood loss was evident. How he was even standing, had even Finn himself in disbelief. Freya examined the remaining Olden's.

'Your mother?' she asked.

'Killed by archers,' Finn answered dismayed.

'Your father?'

'Died for us so we could escape.' His eyes were full of grief, he fought back the tears as he knew the next question before she asked it.

'Edward?' she muttered, Finn knew by her tone she knew the answer already. Finn hung his head, the guilt of not being able to protect his younger brother haunted him.

'Those bastards killed him!' Cara-Lea snapped. 'We thought he would make it, he jumped for the boat, but by the time he landed he was already…' Cara- lea start breaking down.

'I promise you, here and now. Every last one of them will pay for this,' Freya's expression hardened. 'Come, you must be exhausted.' Freya led the way to the castle.

After everyone had been shown to their room, Finn was left alone with Freya, as she brought him to a room at the top staircase.

‘This can be your room if you like?’ she asked opening the door to a large room filled with a tall marble fireplace with a fur rug and bedding.

‘I thought I would be staying with you?’ Finn asked.

‘I thought you might like your own space, giving what’s happened,’ Freya answered confused.

Finn smiled and entered the room. ‘This will do nicely,’ he announced.

‘I will be back soon to dress your wounds,’ Freya replied as she turned for the staircase. Finn was left feeling relieved, grief-stricken, sore and weary after all that had happened. With his mixed emotions, he didn’t know if he should eat, sleep or brawl. For the first time in his life he felt lost, not knowing what to do, or where to start, falling back onto the bed he closed his eyes and drifted off to sleep.

When he woke it was light outside, his tunic had been removed, wounds had been dressed and he was covered by a fur throw. Pushing himself up to look around he noticed someone had lit the fire in his room, the door creaked open.

‘Good morning,’ Freya’s voice called from the threshold as she signalled two girls in to the room, one was carrying a large pitcher of wine and a gold goblet, while the other was balancing a small feast on a large tray. Finn watched in silence as they placed the food down on the desk and left.

‘You did all this?’ He asked gesturing towards the fireplace and his half naked body.

‘I had some help, but yes,’ she answered. Finn tried to get to his feet. ‘Don’t you dare?’ Freya warned as Finn regarded her amused. ‘You are to be on bed rest for the day.’ she commanded.

‘I am not an invalid, I can manage just fine,’ he answered.

‘You nearly died, I came back to here shortly after leaving you and your lips were blue and you were unresponsive, your wound got infected, lucky for you it was treatable,’ Freya barked.

‘I couldn’t have been that bad if I am awake the next morning,’ Finn joked.

‘You were asleep for three days,’ Freya explained.

Finn was dazed at the thought.

‘Your ribs stopped the blade from piercing your organs, it must have got wedged in there,’ Freya said as she approached him with the food. 'Eat!' she ordered, placing the tray down in front of him.

'If you require me on bed rest for the day, you best join me,' said Finn reaching for a large sausage, he forgot how hungry he was until the food was presented to him.

'I have better things to be doing today than playing wet nurse to you,' Freya replied hastily.

'Wet nurse? Oh I do like the sound of that,' Finn jerked upright.

'I think you're a bit old to be breastfed, don't you?'

'Maybe? There is only one way to know for sure,' Finn shot Freya a sultry smile.

'Eat!' Freya responded, shoving a piece of bread in his mouth. 'I need you to get your strength up. I need Finn the warrior, not Finn the whoremonger right now.' Finn bit down on the bread and tore a chunk off, his eyes never leaving Freya's. 'I have men that have arrived that need training, I have men that live here that need training, I have more soldiers on the way, it has been far too quiet around here something is coming. We have few men even fewer that know how to fight. Edward will be buried today, Nicholas refused for him to be buried without you present you can leave for that obviously but no fighting, no training, and no hunting until you are healed. We almost lost you, I refuse to let that happen again by your own stupidity.' Freya stood and turned to fetch a goblet of wine for Finn, who continued to wolf down his meal. Standing over Finn she handed him the chalice, he noticed she was wearing the necklace he had given her when she left his home a few weeks prior. Gulping down the wine he handed Freya back the empty chalice. She reached out to take it when Finn grabbed her arm and pulled her down to the bed.

'You kept it,' he whispered running his hand over her neck down to the pendant.

'Of course,' she replied, looking stunned. Finn dropped his head and buried it in Freya's neck. He felt her hand run up his back towards the back of his head, gently she ran her fingers through his hair.

'I am so sorry for what has happened to you, if I could change it I would,' she whispered in his ear, leaning in she placed a single kiss on his head.

Many emotions ran through his mind, the grief from the events that took place stayed with him but he was also thankful to have found Freya. He lay in silence curled into her body for a while, he never felt truly at home anywhere but right now in this moment he felt it, this was where he belonged.

Freya eventually moved Finn to go fetch him some clean clothes. She came back with a simple black tunic and trousers. Finn immediately began to change from his blood soaked, shredded trousers into these new clean clothes. Freya blushed and turned away as he stood naked before her.

'Nothing you have not seen before,' Finn reminded her, tugging on the new pair.

'You have no modesty at all, do you?' she asked with her back facing him.

'Why should I be modest?' he laughed. 'There is only us two here… I need your help with the tunic,' said Finn.

Freya turned to him rosy cheeked. He gave her the tunic and sat down on the bedside. She regarded him sternly for a moment before approaching him, placing the tunic over his head and stretching out the arms for him to glide into. After adjusting himself Finn noticed Freya staring down at him.

'What is it?' he asked.

'You wore something similar the night we first met,' she explained.

'The night you hit me,' Finn recalled.

'You deserved it,' Freya playfully snapped. Finn buried his head into Freya's abdomen. 'What is it?' she asked but he did not answer. 'Is it Edward?' her words rang painfully in his ears. Feeling his eyes fill with tears Finn fought them back as best he could.

'I failed him,' his voice cracked.

'You did nothing of the sort,' Freya snapped. 'You are not the reason your brother died understand! Men die in battles all the time, innocent lives are taken in raids all the time. Edward died so quickly he would not have felt any pain there are far more horrific ways to go. This was not you Finn! This was the Preston's and anyone else who fought with them. Your brother would not have even known he died, neither would your mother. She died protecting her children, your father died to save his family, I know you and you would have gladly laid your life down in the same manner but if you had who would have been there for your sister? It is because of you she is alive, it's because of you my brother is alive and all the small folk you saved by bringing them with you… Look at me!' Freya yelled. 'This is not your fault, the people who did this will pay for this I swear it.' Finn reached up and pulled Freya's head down towards his.

'Did anyone ever tell you how desirable you are when you're angry?' he asked pressing his lips against hers.

Looking down at the wooden box in the ground, anger surged through him. 'I will have vengeance,' he spat as his sister stood weeping beside him. Nicholas stood like stone, he had remained emotionless since they left on the ship. Amelia coward behind him trying to avoid Finn's gaze. Ravens flew overhead and perched themselves on the surrounding trees, Finn counted five. He suddenly had the uneasy feeling that he was being watched, looking around he saw Gilli and Nari standing with Bjorn and Asger. Freya stood beside Finn, Drew stood to the side behind him there was a strange man in black robes, his body appeared to be burned he was looking upon Finn with dead eyes his face expressionless. Finn felt his blood run cold, the hairs on the back of his neck stood to attention

'Who is that?' he whispered to Freya.

'That's Beigarth,' she explained. 'He is a seer, he came the night of the attack on your home, Gilli found him outside the walls waiting to be found. He was the one that told us what happened, because of him we were able to prepare for your arrival.' Finn turned back towards the man but he had gone, the ravens began to fly away one by one as the hole was being filled in.

Finn stood in the cold and rain for hours staring at his brother's grave. He was soaked to the bone, as pain crept up his legs and back while his boots sunk further into the mud but he did not mind. He was alone. The rain masked the tears that ran down his face. Freya was right he could not have prevented this, he replayed that night over and over it in his head. Edward died from the hands of an enemy and they would all die at the hands of his brother's.

'Finn Olden!' he turned Freya looked infuriated. 'Are you trying to get yourself killed? Get inside before you do more harm to yourself!' she barked. Marching him through the murky ground towards the castle, he knew Freya was angry with him, he understood he had lost a lot of blood she feared his body would succumb to the cold with the little amount that remained in his body.

Freya marched Finn into the bath house, dismissing the servants she slammed the door behind them. 'Honestly, what did I say about bed rest?' she asked. 'Look at you, you're freezing, the water will warm you up.' Freya ran her hand along his face, it felt like ice. Looking into his eyes, she knew what he was feeling, she knew all too well. She helped him out of his tunic, he could not tell if it was the grief or the cold but Finn felt nothing he was numb, he could not feel her touch against his skin, he did not feel himself, he knew this was a shell she was gazing upon, like Nicholas, Finn had surrendered to the sadness. He stripped down and slowly walked into the large round bath. Freya undressed and joined him, she walked behind him wrapping her arms around his waist, placing her head on his back. 'I know what you're going through, I did the same thing when my family was taken from me. Take as long as you need to grieve but eventually you will have to come back to me,' her soft spoken words got through to him, the warm water slowly thawed out his frozen body. Taking Freya's hand Finn turned to face her. Her deep sapphire eyes caught his gaze, her long curly hair had been pinned up tightly with a few ringlets escaping the confinement of the hair pins. Her voluptuous figure stood naked before him, truly he was blessed to have such a woman love him. He ran his hands from her shoulders down to her ample breasts, gently tweaking her nipples for a moment before his hands found themselves at her tight round buttocks, his lips found their way from her mouth to her breasts as Freya stood flushed as gasping at the sensation. Finn boosted her into his arms, his chest tightened where his wound was dressed he felt the sting of it hit him like the dagger that pierced his body a few nights before, but he paid no attention to it, he had waited long enough, tonight he would have what he desired and he had hungered for Freya since the night he first saw her.

Asger

His uncle Henry had arrived at Rosefort two days prior. Asger always had a certain fondness for Henry, after all the man took him in and thought him how to fight from an early age, he just hated the reunion to be under such bleak circumstances. Cara-Lea had been helping to get the barracks ready with others that came in off the ships, she seemed very inquisitive about the giants that had arrived shortly after herself. Asger thought it was a way of keeping her mind off the horrific events that had occurred. Freya had asked himself and Drew to watch over the Olden girl and help her settle in.

'Uncle!' Asger called happily. 'Hversu ferr?' He noted Cara-Lea looking on intrigued

'Ah! *Asger Allt gott, þakka, En þú*?' his uncle replied.

'*Allt gott, þakka*, you speak the Norse tongue far better now uncle.' Asger beamed.

'How are the men?' he asked looking over Henry's shoulder towards the herd of rugged warriors standing a short distance away.

'Strong, fast and hard to kill,' Henry replied proudly. 'We may be outnumbered but one of my men is worth fifty of theirs, and better yet I have a gift on the way, His name is Shengis and he's a Goggy.' Asger was taken aback.

'Are you certain he will fight with us uncle?'

'I would bet my life on it,' said Henry.

'That is exactly what you are doing with the likes of them.' Asger feared, he knew Freya would have to find out about this, uncertain of how to break it to her, even more uncertain of what her reaction would be, his sister was strange like that receiving news he thinks could upset her might be the news that she embraces.

'Cara-Lea' he called. 'Have you seen my sister today?' he asked.

'I have not seen Freya nor Finn since yesterday,' she explained.

'Why am I not surprised?' he muttered, turning for the castle.

'Asger!' Cara-Lea shouted. 'You were speaking in a Norse tongue a moment ago?' she asked as he turned to her.

'I was,' he answered simply.

'Can you teach me how?' she requested hopefully.

'I am afraid right now is a bad time for me to be giving lessons to anyone other than the soldiers,' he explained as he watched her face sink with disappointment. 'Drew would be the best person to teach you, he is already battle ready which frees him up from training,' he said pointing towards his friend. 'I must go find my sister,' Asger explained kindly as he turned once again for the castle.

Climbing the stairs to the top floor of the castle, Asger marched to his sister's room, he swung the door open to discover she had not been there, the room looked like it had not been lived in, in days. Then he remembered when Finn lost consciousness a few days prior she had stayed in his room monitoring him. He turned towards the stair case, Finn's room was right at the top of them, uncertain if he should open the door or knock he decided to enter the room promptly. To his delight Freya had been tending to Finn's wound.

'There you are,' he sighed with relief. Freya looked up at her brother for a moment before turning back to bandaging up Finn's wounds.

'Do you mind, have you not heard of knocking, I would like to protect my modesty,' Finn jested. Asger was happy to see his friend coming back to himself but ignored his remarks.

'I am afraid our uncle has got mad,' Asger said directing his attention to his sister.

'What has he done now?' she asked rolling her eyes.

'He has recruited, what he thinks is a happy surprise that will arrive here soon,' he explained.

'And what surprise would that be?' she asked finishing up her patchwork on Finn.

'He said he recruited a Goggy.' Asger watched as his sisters stern expression sat staring at him, eventually her face lit up.

'Good we need all the help we can get.'

‘I know I am missing something here, what is a Goggy?’ Finn asked. Pushing himself upright on the bed.

‘A Gogmagog is a giant they are strong but not exactly clever,’ Asger explained.

‘You can relate,’ said Finn, whose face twisted into a sly smile.

‘If you want more wounds for my sister to dress by all means, go on,’ Asger warned.

‘They fight with simple things, Clubs, axes, maces one swing of their weapons can take out a small fleet of men,’ Freya interrupted. ‘Does this one have a name?’ she asked her brother.

‘Shengis,’ Asger replied without hesitation.

‘Are you sure, that is his name?’ Freya asked.

‘Yes I am sure, why?’ Asger asked irritably.

‘He was the prince of the clan of Gogmagogs when we were younger, Mother used to tell me stories about them, with the time that has past he should be king now,’ Freya explained.

‘I had best go practise my curtsey,’ said Finn, rising from the bed fidgeting with his tunic.

‘Here let me,’ Freya approached Finn and helped slip his tunic on over his head.

‘I hate to break up, whatever this is, but there are soldiers to train, and matter of your estate to be dealt with,’ Asger said feeling uncomfortable, being alone in a room with his sister and her companion.

‘I’m coming now, calm down,’ she snapped. ‘You stay out of trouble today, you are not confined to bed rest but nothing strenuous understood?’ Freya reminded Asger of their late Mother, the manner how she spoke to Finn was the same way Catherine spoke to Bjorn.

After Finn agreed to behave himself, Asger and Freya walked side by side down the staircase towards the throne room. A little piglet ran by them in the corridor.

‘Asher!’ Freya called.

The dwarf looked out from the library.

‘I think Rose-Mary is looking for you,’ Freya said kindly. Asher looked up and down the hallway but there was no sign on the piglet.

‘I better go find her’ Asher murmured.

‘Asher, can you be as kind, as to keep an eye on Finn Olden today, I will not have him reopen his wounds again,’ Freya asked sweetly.

‘Anything for you my Lady,’ Asher agreed happily.

‘And Asher!’ Freya called as he scurried away down the hallway. ‘Call me Freya.’ The dwarf gave her a kind smile and she entered the throne room.

‘I best be off to run with the new men, form a pack mentality.’ Asger announced as he turned from the threshold of the throne room. ‘I have asked for Drew to look after the Olden girl today, while I show the men the land.’

‘Just be careful brother, Father has set traps all over the land, to buy us time in case of invasion,’ Freya warned.

‘I know Father’s scent anywhere dear sister as I have come to know these lands, I will not fall into one of our own traps,’ Asger explained, leaving Freya to deal with her duties, it was time for him to fulfil his own.

Cara-Lea

Watching from the side lines as Asger led a group of men off out of the gates, she felt alone, useless. Back home she had a set amount of tasks to complete in a day here they were preparing for war, the men trained hard the women were been shown escape routes out of every part of the kingdom if the inevitable was to occur and the wall was breached. It was evident that the Vikings cared about the safety of their people, they seemed confident in their abilities despite the small army they had. The gates closed behind Asger and his men, as they did she noticed a familiar face smiling at her.

'Edward?' she gasped, this could not be, her brother had been killed, she buried him the day before and yet there he stood a few yards away. She ran towards him, but as she approached he started to walk away.

'Edward,' she called as he walked behind a row of stalls, into a nearby alleyway. She ran as fast as her legs would carry her, catching up to him slowly ignoring the drunkards stumbling around her, this must be another entrance to the tavern she thought. Her brother made his way towards the castle, he was trying to tell her something but what? Rounding the bend of the alleyway's end she tumbled into a passer-by. Her arm throbbed and he knees stung as she pushed herself up off the ground.

'I am so sorry,' she turned to the person on the ground, when he looked up she felt her heart stop.

'It happens,' the man replied as he rose to his feet, his large doll like eyes seemed as if they stared through her. 'He cannot help you, I hope you know that.' His words soft spoken but Cara-Lea felt a chill run down her spine, did he also see Edward? 'They can only come back to warn or adore you, but they cannot tell you what is to come. He seemed happy as he ran by, you can take that as a sign of good things to come, but do not think too much on it, men have driven themselves mad for less,' Beigarth warned.

'What seems to be the problem here?' A familiar voice called, Drew approached Beigarth suspiciously.

'It's my fault, I was not paying much attention to my surroundings and I fell,' Cara-Lea explained, thankful that she had someone else with her now. Drew turned to examine her.

Your garments are ripped from the fall. We need to get you some fresh ones,' He said fondling her torn sleeves. Drew took her by the arm and led her to the castle.

After she had changed she stepped out of her chambers to find Drew waiting patiently for her.

'So, you want to learn how to speak Norse?' he asked. 'Some people find it quite difficult,' he explained.

'Freya's uncle seemed to be doing fine with it,' Cara-Lea replied.

'Yes he is doing pretty well, with the three things he can say,' Drew laughed. 'If you heard him speak in Norse tongue, all he would have asked is, how are you and replied if he is well or not that's about all that man can say,' Drew explained. 'I remember when I was learning I had a handful of sentences to my name, I used to speak all of them together if somebody around here was giving me a hard time, they cannot speak the tongue so to them I was intimidating them while what I was really saying was how are you? I am fine thanks, where is the bathhouse located? And my favourite was barking dogs seldom bite.' Cara-Lea found Drew to be very entertaining, he was the only person to make her laugh since she got here.

'Why is it you are not gone with Asger and the others?' she asked.

'I know these lands like the back of my hand, I grew up here, the men did not and the same can be said of Asger, if we must go to war, we have the knowledge of the land which can prove to be in our favour.' Cara-Lea looked at him curiously, she had never been allowed to sit in on conversations about war or tactics as it was not lady like.

'How does knowledge of the land work in our favour?' she asked Drew.

'Well for example, say the enemy gets off the ships to get to us they must go uphill for a lot of it using up a lot of their energy, so if we knew they were coming and we knew where to disguise ourselves we would have the hills in our favour, it takes a lot less out of a man to run downhill than to run up one.'

'But if you are outnumbered, surely it cannot be that much in your favour?' she asked.

'You may be right there, but our men are worth more than that of normal soldiers, they are stronger, faster and much harder to kill,' Drew explained.

'It sounds like you have just described Finn,' she giggled.

'You're brother has developed quite a reputation for himself, both have, from what I have heard Nicholas is fierce in battle and stubborn he has never giving up despite the odds, while Finn seems to have a certain blood lust, he is loyal to those he loves but also unpredictable a trait many people fear, which is another reason I wanted to speak to you. You need to learn how to fight. A time will come when you will need to defend yourself, when your brothers, or any of us here at Rosefort will not be able to protect you. When that time comes I would prefer for you to be able to know how to fight.'

'Finn was teaching myself and Edward just before…' She felt her heart break a little more thinking back on the days before the attack, they were so happy.

'He is right to have thought you, we will take over. Freya's wish is that all women know how to fend for themselves.'

Cara-Lea found herself highly intrigued by this young man, he was not much younger than her brothers. Nicholas was not long gone seventeen and Finn would be turning sixteen in a few short weeks. He did not come from a well-bred family, her mother's disapproving words ran through her mind in that moment. Drew appeared to be educated and loyal to the Vikings. He had obviously been in battles before judging by the manner of which he spoke. Her old world had crumbled at her feet, her new world was confusing and yet it seemed to amaze her at the abilities of the people in the Kingdom of Rosefort. Asher and Koi came running towards them, their pale faces, looked upon Drew a feeling of Dread came over Cara-Lea at the sight of them.

'The Prestons?' Drew asked.

'Mercenaries,' Asher replied.

'Hundreds of them,' Koi agreed.

They all ran from the castle towards the gates of Rosefort, Freya was on horseback alongside her father and Nicholas. Gilli, and Nari stood alongside the men, Drew pushed his way through the crowd.

'There are hundreds of them,' a quivering voice echoed through the crowd.

'There are less of them now many of them walked into our traps,' Asger explained. Finn ran through the crowd armed.

'You are not going out there,' Freya barked.

'I refuse to stay in here while those bastards remain outside the walls,' Finn spat.

'You are still badly injured forget it! Nicholas is coming with us you stay here, if something happens out there to us I need someone to survive to lead these people. Just do as you're asked for once,' Freya begged. Finn reluctantly stepped back to the crowd.

'So what's the plan?' Asger asked.

'We go out and cut their damned heads off, the Preston's refer to me as a bitch. They are going to find out that this bitch bites.'

Cara-Lea took off on her horse followed by Bjorn, Asger, Nicholas, Drew and her uncle's men. Feeling her stomach churn Cara-Lea knew this is why Edward had come to warn her, she took solace in the fact that she was not left alone that Finn had stayed behind reluctantly, she knew in her heart that Freya had just saved his life. Watching silently for a moment she noticed the two dwarfs run out behind the men with more dogs than she could count. The crowd dispersed, but Finn stood gazing at the gate that was now closing, she knew he wanted to fight.

'Live to fight another day brother,' she said approaching him.

'I should be out there with them,' he muttered.

'You nearly died less than a week ago, you are not able to…' she began.

'I am no use to anyone back here,' Finn barked.

'I have just lost my mother, my father, my brother and my home in the past few days. Do not stand here and ask me for my permission for yours to be the next body I bury,' her voice cracked, tears filled her eyes and her throat burned as she tried to fight back her emotions.

Finn wrapped his arms around her 'I'm an idiot, I am sorry, I will not leave you. You have my word,' he said kissing her forehead. Cara-Lea rested her head on her brother's chest turning her head for the gate, they had just left and it had already felt like an eternity.

Cara-Lea sat in the throne room with her brother who was drinking the horns of wine so fast the servant girls left jugs of it behind for him to save them having to refill every few minutes. The sun was at its highest when Freya led the soldiers out of Rosefort, the sun was not setting. The horns sounded Finn turned to his sister. 'They're home.' she agreed looking at his bemused expression. Finn dropped his horn full of wine and ran from the throne room, Cara-Lea barely able to keep up with him. Nicholas was the first to come riding in, he was drenched in blood luckily judging by his demeanour none of it was his. Asher and Koi came riding in on the two wolves who were also blood soaked from the drippings that came from the dwarfs garments. As more and more people came riding in Cara-Lea could see Finns face sink.

'Where is Freya?' he called to Nicholas.

'It was an ambush, they set up an army of mercenaries outside the gates we got through them with ease, the next set came charging just as we were finishing up on the battlefield again we took them out with ease.'

'What of Freya!' Finn snapped interrupting Nicholas.

'They captured Bjorn, he was injured and managed to isolate himself from the group, Freya seen them taking him and tried to stop it, they caught her too and Drew.' Nicholas hung his head. 'Asger is out now tracking them, they couldn't have gone far.' Cara lea looked upon her eldest brother, for the first time in her life she seen fear in his eyes as he reiterated the events that had taken place. Finn went disturbingly silent, she knew her brother too well, this was the calm before the storm he was going to do something, she could see the wheels in his head turning , she only feared what he might do and who he would do it too. When Finn lost his temper he could easily hurt somebody, he loved just for getting in his way.

Freya

She could not see, found it hard to breathe. They had tied a sack over her head and bound her arms behind her back, her ankles were tied together all she could do was flop around like a fish out of water trying to get loose. She heard the groans from a man in pain, she knew it was her father. He had been shot multiple times with arrows he was a man of thirty eight, not a young warrior like he used to be those wounds could be fatal if not tended too.

'Freya,' a voice called, it took her a moment but she recognised it.

'Andrew?' she asked. 'Can you see anything?' hoping he was lucky and wriggled free.

'No, they've covered my head and bound my limbs,' he explained.

'Shut up!' A voice spat as something sharp had struck her across the back, she heard the same snapping sound and a loud inhale from her friend. She could not see what had struck her but she had guessed a whip of some sort. How was she going to get out of this? Her heart beat so hard she could feel it in her throat, her palms sweating as she tried to free her hands from her bounds but to no avail. Her wrists burned from the rope, her hands where going numb, a tingling sensation ran up her legs she knew they had tied her up tightly, even if she broke free at this rate it would take her far too much time to escape.

'It's me you want, let the men go,' she begged the man that had been bringing them to their deaths.

'I said shut your face you whore,' he spat. 'You better save your breath, you're going to need it, the men have plans big plans for you,' he sniggered.

'Don't you dare touch her,' Drew barked. No response came, her father had not said a word, which was not like him.

Eventually the cart stopped, she heard footsteps approach. They were dragged from the cart, and hauled into a dank cold dungeon. Freya was pushed into a cell and bound. Once she was in chains a guard removed her sack from her head.

She gasped. 'I know you, you were that soldier at house Olden the one who tried to rape that girl,' she exclaimed. He looked at her lustfully.

'You cannot harm me, you haven't got the balls,' she spat. Freya had not feared death not anymore. A sharp pain ran across her face as he struck her again and again. 'You are seriously the biggest coward I have ever seen, it's not enough for you to pick on women but you have to make sure they cannot even fight you back,' her mouth filled with blood her face felt like it was swelling up already, she spat in the guards face.

'You're going to regret that,' he snapped turning for the cell door. Freya watched as he left, she waited anxiously for him to come back but there was no sign of him. The dungeon filled with the echoes of a screaming man.

'Father!' She gasped. 'Let him go!' She demanded. 'It's me you want.' The cries from her father echoed through the cold damp dungeon, it was clear they were torturing him, but with the chains restrictions she could not go to his aid. Freya wished she had her brother's abilities, if only she could change she could save Bjorn. The screaming stopped, after what felt like hours she heard footsteps approaching, the cell door swung open three guards walked in, two dragging behind her father's bloodied body.

'Don't worry, he lives,' one of them said as they strapped him to a table.

'I will kill you for this,' Freya said tears filled her eyes as she looked upon her father's beaten and bloodied body.

'Bjorn the Brave they call him,' the guard from house Olden sniggered. 'Must have a pretty big heart for that title, let's find out shall we?'

'NO!' Freya struggled with her chains trying to break them, one of the guards rushed at her grabbing her by the throat.

'You must stay still, wouldn't want to miss this,' he jeered. She was pinned against the wall, she watched helplessly as one of the men pulled out a dagger from a holder attached to his belt. He held a dagger high in the air, turning to look at Freya giving her a sickening grin before plunging the blade down into Bjorn's chest her father's voice echoed in the dungeon his screams will prove to haunt her. Blood covered his face as he choked for air. She closed her eyes but the men saw and made her open them.

'You must watch,' said the guard gripping her by the throat his hand closed tighter in on her neck the more she tried to look away. She watched as the men passed the dagger around taking turns running the dagger into her father's body and carving out chunks of flesh. Freya feeling light headed and nauseous, vomited all over the floor and the guard holding her up.

'Look what you did to my boots!' The guard snapped as he swung his hand towards her face.

'I'm sorry Father,' she cried hysterically the more they continued. The Olden guard flayed her father's body, picking off pieces of flesh and hurling them towards Freya. One of the men left and brought back an axe, he stood over Bjorn laughing.

'I'm not going to lie, this will hurt,' he said as he drove the weapon into the Bjorn's ribcage splitting it open, the two men took a side each and pulled the Great Norseman apart. The sound of his tearing flesh and shattering bones were muffled by the screams of his Daughter. Finally the Olden guard reached in and carved out his heart. Blood ran from the empty shell that used to be her father's body she dropped to her knees.

'That takes a lot out of a man,' one of the men jeered.

'Come let's eat we will come back for this one, she's not going anywhere.' One by one they took their leave from the cell, leaving Freya bound and staring at the carcass in front of her.

'I'd say we broke her now, did you see her face,' their voices rebounded back to her. Tears filled her eyes once more.

'You are with Mother now,' she whispered.

Footsteps approached after a while screaming filled the dungeons once more, it was not her friends voice, they had more prisoners down here than just them two. She had heard whispering and multiple cries for help. No one would come, Freya knew that. The guard from house Olden entered the cell looking proud of himself.

'I heard you lot were hard to kill,' he sniggered turning towards Bjorn's body. 'He proved to be too easy, I must say I am a bit disappointed, I was hoping for more action than that.' Freya continued to stare at the wall while he was talking. 'Did you hear what I said?' he snapped. Again she gave no reply. 'Oh what's the matter dearie, cat got your tongue? Not so brave with the old man gone? That's okay, I have a little game, see you were right earlier, thanks to you they cut off my cock. But I can find a way to improvised for you, how about the same dagger I used on your father.' He pushed himself against Freya who did not budge, she continued to stare at the wall. 'You smell nice, I can see why Finn likes you, don't worry I can make you scream too.' Freya turned her head to look at the guard, his eyes gleaming with pride, he was calm and relaxed. He would enjoy hurting her. 'Got your attention now lovey? Don't you worry I'll make sure to take this nice and slow.' Freya launched herself at him and sunk her teeth into his neck, his screams were masked by the others that filled the dungeon, He tried to push her off but the more he fought back the deeper she sunk her teeth. Her mouth filled with the blood of the enemy, she jerked her head from side to side until the flesh detached itself from his body. Spitting it out she reached for his keys to free herself. Looking down upon the man on the floor that murdered her father, she watched as he bled out before releasing herself from her shackles.

Not knowing where Andrew was being kept or if he was still alive, Freya refused to leave without searching for him first. She crept down the hallway and peaked in the doors they all came up empty. Taking a corner she looked in one of the cells. A man was sitting on the ground with blood pouring from his wounds, she noticed the emblem of house Olden on his tunic.

'It couldn't be Theodore,' she gasped. He looked up shocked. Freya fiddled with the keys until she found the one to open the cell door. 'I thought you were dead.' she said running to his aid.

'Freya what on earth are you doing here? My children?' he asked worried.

'Three live, Edward did not make it to Rosefort alive,' she said bluntly knowing there was not a lot of time before she was found.

'My Edward,' he hung his head.

'Lord Olden with all due respect the dead can wait to be mourned, we on the other hand need to get out of here and fast.' Opening up his shackles, Theodore sprung to his feet not mentioning the fact that Freya was dripping blood from his jaw. Eventually discovering her friend in a cell tied up a table like her father had been, Freya ran to set him free. 'By the Grace of God you have not been harmed,' she said running her hands along his face. 'We must go now.'

'Careful Freya, they went to get weapons to torture me they could be back any minute.' Footsteps approached the cell Freya hid behind the cell door with Theodore while Drew lay back down on the table, hoping they would not notice his untied restraints. The door swung open missing Freya's face by and inch, the men walked in too self-indulged to notice anything was off. Once they turned their backs to the door Freya swung it closed, the men turned to see Theodore and Freya standing before them. As their backs turned to Drew, he sat up and grabbed the nearest guard's sword from his scabbard and ran him through. The other guard looked on in fear.

'Look at that, he's pissed himself,' Drew pointed at the puddle forming on the ground at the man's feet.

'Kill him,' Freya ordered, peaking out the cell door to see if any more guards were approaching.

Running for their lives out of their prison they now had two swords to fight with. It was an old small castle that they had been kept in no surrounding walls, no defence it looked abandoned, noticing a horse tied up outside, Freya ran to grab it Theodore jumped on with Freya climbing on the back.

'What about him?' Theodore asked looking at Drew.

'You'll be surprised at how fast he can move,' Freya said, kicking the horse to move galloping towards their freedom five archers had spot them and where ready to shoot.

'We are not going to make it,' Theodore urged looking at the firing line.

'Oh yes we will,' Freya shouted looking at Drew. He nodded, as they galloped off towards the archers. A large black Blur ran by them towards the archers.

'Is that a bear?' Theodore gasped.

'Yes and no, I told you he can move fast,' Freya replied, they could hear the screams of the men as Drew ripped them apart. A black horse raced towards them pulling a black chariot.

'Whatever you do, do not draw attention to yourself,' Freya warned as the horse approached faster, a figure in black was whipping the horses upon closer inspection she realised that was no ordinary whip.

'Is that?' Theodore barked.

'Yes it is,' Freya answered trying to avoid starring at the whip made of spinal cords.

'Where in God's name is his head?' Theodore asked as the figure continued on past them.

'He's holding it, Freya explained. 'He's a Dullahan.' Galloping on through the woods she knew they had not left the emerald isles as they had not been brought by ship. The large black bear ran beside them. 'Andrew can you find our way back home.' Freya asked watching the bear run ahead of them.

'Is that a good sign?' Theodore asked. Freya smirked listening out for signs of life.

They travelled for hours before taking a break they were all exhausted, they came across a small farming village where they stayed for the night in the haystacks. At first light they took off quickly as to keep their advantage ahead of those mercenaries.

'We're less than a day's ride before we are home I can pick up out scent from yesterday, the closer we get to Rosefort the stronger it gets,' Drew explained. Galloping towards home Freya started to feel uneasy. They needed the rest last night but it would have giving the enemy ample time to track them. Freya began to hear hoof beats behind them. She knew it was them.

'Andrew take Theodore back to Rosefort, make sure he gets there safe.' she commanded, looking at her friend.

'You're not staying here, you will be killed,' Drew replied.

'Do as I say,' she barked, climbing down off the horse to allow Andrew to mount it. She armed herself with one of the swords. 'Get Theodore back and then come back for me.' The riders were approaching fast she could see them in the distance. 'Go now,' she snapped smacking the horse on the rear for it to take off running. Turning once again to see a herd of riders coming straight for her, they killed her father, they tried to kill her. If she is to die today, it will be on her own terms.

Back from the Dead

Galloping towards Rosefort a sense of guilt hit Drew, how could he just leave his friend like that? She will surely be slaughtered, he could not think like that he had to get Lord Olden back to Rosefort and quickly return for Freya. Drew knew these lands, he knew the quickest ways to get back to Rosefort. They galloped through caves, across rivers and farmland.

'So you're a bear?' Theodore asked.

'In a certain respect, yes,' Drew answered.

'Why did you not change when you were captured, or tied to that table surely you could have broken free?' Theodore was more than confused after everything he had just witnessed.

'It's not that easy, if I turned while they still had Freya they could have got away and I would have lost her, I knew she was still alive in the dungeon, or they would have said otherwise if I turned and they were in the cell with her, she could have been killed. Bjorn was a good man but I had gave my word to him that no matter what I would ensure his daughters safety even if it meant letting him die.'

Approaching the first gate of Rosefort, Drew heard the horns sounding.

'Thank god for those lookouts,' he muttered. 'We should be met at the next gate,' he said reassuringly. Halfway between the first and second gate, Drew saw a group of men gathered in the distance.

'My Boys,' said Theodore. 'I know they are with them.' Approaching the group they noticed the two dwarfs standing in front of the group armed, behind them was Nicholas on horseback with Freya's Uncle Henry and his men. Pushing his way through the crowd, was an injured Finn. Drew yielded the horse and jumped down, Theodore awkwardly dropped down from the animal, his hair was matted and falling in front of his eyes impairing his vision. As Drew was talking the men paid no attention to him, he was filthy, his garments shredded, he had not been held captive for long but it felt like an eternity. The men never let him rest for the first three days, he was kept awake by being punctured with needles and shallowly stabbed with daggers. He had been starved since his capture in order to try and break him but he would not talk.

'Get your father somewhere safe,' Drew's words pulled Theodore back from his thoughts, he looked up to see Nicholas and Finn approach, their jaws had dropped and their eyes bulging as they looked upon him.

'Father!' Nicholas gulped looking upon the weak unkempt man. 'I thought they killed you.' Nicholas was in disbelief. Drew had leaped back on the horse and turned for the first gate.

'Where are you going?' Asher cried.

'Freya is still out there, outnumbered, she stayed behind to buy us time to escape I have to go back,' Finn jumped on Nicholas's horse.

'Where are you going?' Koi asked stunned.

'You heard the man, Freya's still out there,' Finn replied, kicking his heels into the horse he galloped off ahead of Drew. Asher and Koi shared a concerned look, before Koi jumped on a wolf's back.

'Where are you going?' Asher asked.

'The last time I checked we were tied at the head count, I'm going to up my numbers,' Koi laughed, as the wolf took off running.

'Need I ask?' Henry asked Asher as the dwarf climbed upon a hound.

'If anyone is going to have a higher head count it's me!' Asher replied. 'Let's go find Freya,' he said to Christian who ran like lightening, within a few short moments all the men, who had gone to aid the Viking, had disappeared into the horizon.

Drew led the men to where he had last seen Freya, taking every shortcut he knew off to get there, the horses where splattered in mud the trees were dangerous to be charging through if they did not duck on approach they would be whipped off their steeds. The dwarfs found it easy to move around the woodlands, there were less things to throw them from their animals. The closer they got to Freya's last known whereabouts, the more Finn start to have flash backs of the forest near his home. The blood spatter, on the ground and trees, the carved up bodies that were scattered on the ground.

'Looks like the only quick death around here was for their horses,' said Koi, looking at the decapitated remains of the animals.

'This blood trail splits further on, one half going uphill, while the other looks like something large has been dragged down into those hedging's,' said Finn, looking at the brutal scene that lay before him. Christian start barking ferociously towards the hedging's.

'Something's down there.' Asher felt uneasy something was not right, the sound of rattling chains came from a short distance away.

'Do you hear that?' Koi asked, as the rattling got louder.

'What's that over there?' Asher pointed towards the brambles.

'I'm not sure,' Finn replied, looking over he saw something blue flickering. The men armed themselves as they approached. Finn slowly raised his sword ready to strike he saw a figure in black, it seemed to be gnawing on something they start to walk slowly towards the creature they heard a branch snap.

'Christian!' Asher disapproved. Finn Looked up to see the beast had heard the noise it was looking right at them, its eyes burned like the fires of hell, its raven fur stood on end as it bore the long dagger like fangs that dangled from its mouth.

'That's a big wolf,' Finn said, staring the creature down.

'That's no wolf,' Drew replied. 'Don't run!' He beckoned the dwarfs closer to him. 'It will enjoy the chase.' The creature emerged foaming at the mouth it had the body of a wolf.

'Wings! Why does it have wings?' Finn yelled.

'It's a Kludde,' Drew cried. A blue fame flickered around its head, as its massive paws began to tear their way through the earth. With two quick movements it spread its wings and swooped in on Finn, lifting him in the air. His feet left the ground, the creatures claws sank into his shoulders as he struggled helplessly in the air. The calls of his friends had begun to fade underneath him. The creature let out an ungodly screech and released its grip on Finn, who was sent falling from above the trees. Reaching for anything he could to stop his fall, branch after branch broke, this was it he was going to die. A tight burning grasp jolted his body upwards, he was no longer falling but the Kludde had him in its grasp once again. Not knowing if he would rather have falling to his death or be eaten by this beast, he looked up to see an arrow had been wedged in its wing, they were slowly soaring towards the ground as more arrows shot up at the beast. Looking down Finn could see Gilli and Asger armed with their bows and arrows.

'Will you watch where you're shooting those things you nearly got me!' He bellowed. The beast flapped its wings then proceeded to dive toward a large pile of rubble. After landing, it released Finn from its clutches. Finn stood still for a moment, not knowing what to do if he ran surely the beast would catch him but if he stayed he would be its next meal. The beast whimpered as it licked its wounds, this truly was a ferocious looking animal, but it was an animal none the less. Against his better judgement Finn approached slowly. He came face to face with the beast from hell, its warm breath struck his face repeatedly as he slowly reached for the arrow in its wing.

'Easy, I'm trying to help,' he said trying to reassure the beast. Quickly he yanked the arrow from its wing and with a jolt from the beast, Finn was knocked backwards. The creature launched itself at Finn pinning him to the ground, snarling at him.

'Not the face,' he begged as it lunged at him. Finn felt a warm slobber on his face, he looked up in shock as the Kludde stepped off him. 'You're welcome,' he said looking at the beast that trotted over to some boulders to lay down. He looked around there were carcasses everywhere, broken old bones disguising themselves as rocks. 'You live here?' he asked, the Kludde turned its head sideways. 'You don't want to eat me?' he watched as its tail started to wag.

'She went this way!' A voice called in the trees below. Finn rushed over to the side of the cliff and looked down, a group of mercenaries ran through the woodland at great speed.

'Freya!' Finn knew they were hunting her. He looked for a way down but there was no use he was stuck up on a cliff with a Kludde. 'I need to get down there please, they will kill her.' he begged the creature. It pranced towards him and looked down toward the voices, immediately the Kludde began to growl and bark at the men. 'Did they hurt you?' he asked. 'They will hurt someone I care very much about if I don't get down there, please… Help me save her,' he pleaded.

While Asher, Drew and Asger went in search of Freya, Gilli and Koi went looking for Finn.

'Did you see the size of that beast, its paw was the same size as me,' Koi said. 'I must be mad going out here, looking for that thing then again I am closer to the ground and you would look more appetising than me.' Koi mocked turning to Gilli.

'It has already had its meal but it might be looking for a snack,' said Gilli who continually checked the sky for signs of its return.

'Do you think we will find him alive?' Koi asked.

'I have got to know Finn over the past few weeks, he seems more than capable of saving his own arse,' Gilli replied.

'Then why are we out here looking for him?' Koi asked, Gilli looked at the dwarf baffled.

'Do you hear that,' Gilli asked, eventually breaking the silence. They paused, the smell of pine filled their noses, birds were chirping, small animals were hiding, then he heard it again voices, male voices coming from up ahead.

'That has to be those mercenaries,' said Koi.

'Let's go give them a friendly welcome,' Gilli replied.

'There are too many of them,' Koi whispered peering over a bush.

'I count twenty,' Gilli said.

'What's the plan?' Koi asked.

'I'll take the ten on the left, the ten on the right are yours,' Gilli replied.

'Okay…! Which side is right?' Koi enquired.

Gilli turned to the dwarf and laughed. 'Whichever side you want it to be little man,' A sickening screech filled the air, they looked up to see the Kludde descending upon them.

'Is that Olden riding that thing?' Koi cried. The mercenaries turned green, they turned to see Gilli standing across from them in the bushes.

'Get him!' One man yelled, as they charged for the archer. Wielding their swords, they charged screaming as they ran towards the lone warrior. Koi jumped through the bush screaming in retaliation armed with his sword. The mercenaries stopped stunned for a moment and began laughing at the dwarf, who turned to Gilli gobsmacked.

'That was my best war cry,' he said, before turning back to the men shrieking as he ran at them. Gilli's arrows never missed, one by one they all fell to the fatal blow of the arrow. Koi ran at the men cutting them down as he sliced through their legs and driving his sword through their gut. The Kludde never landed, it circled the mercenaries picking them up and dropping them from heights, or tearing them apart in mid-air.

'Freya,' Finn called, looking around anxiously on the back of the beast.

'Finn!' Koi yelled pointing uphill, the Kludde flew off towards a group of bandits.

The Kludde landed near the group of bandits, they turned in fear to see the beast standing behind them. Finn could see Freya stumbling in front of them trying to hold them back. He leapt from the Kludde pulling his sword from its sheath, he felt a sharp pain in his arms, he had forgotten about the injuries he had got from the same animal he had now befriended. The beast turned its head to Finn, it knew he was injured, one of the bandits ran at the beast, who swung around picking him up in its mouth and clamped down, blood ran from its mouth as the bandit screamed in pain, the more he begged for mercy the more merciless the creature was slowly sinking its teeth further into his body before he became lifeless.

'It's the Olden's boy again,' one of the bandits said.

'How many times do we have to kill you boy before you stay dead,' one man snapped.

'At least once more should do it,' Finn replied the men charged at Finn and the beast that stood with him. The swords clanked together at Finn blocked their attacks, the Kludde had charged at a number of men shredding them and throwing down towards Gilli and Koi, who had been making their way towards Finn. Driving his blade through the bandits, he made his way closer to Freya who was fighting off two of the men. With one big boot Finn was sent flying back into a tree trunk, cracking the top of his head from the impact. The bandit approached him, he looked around searching for his sword he had dropped, and he knew he could not get to it in time, the bandit swung his blade down at Finn's head. His arms quivered with the force of the blow as he blocked it with a large rock that had been beside him, kicking the bandit away from him, Finn rose to his feet. An arrow came shooting past his head, finding its way through the bandit's skull.

Finn turned. 'Will people stop shooting arrows at my head,' he cried, looking at Gilli.

Freya felt exhausted, she had been fighting for her life for hours, her arms and legs felt like they had been cast in iron. She raised her sword once again to the men who had hunted her. The first came in quickly leaving his body wide open to attack, Freya blocked his swing, raising her leg she pushed his body away knocking the bandit off balance, swinging her sword upward, with all the strength she had left she drove it through his armour. Staggering to her feet she turned to face the last bandit. Raising her sword she waited on his attack, as he ran for her Freya felt a gust of wind blow by her arm, her attacker had fallen, a simple dagger sat in the dead man's chest. Koi walked by Freya pulling out the knife and wiping it clean.

'I love this knife,' he said, looking up at Freya. She turned to see Finn walking towards her, relieved to see him and knowing she was now safe, she took a deep breath in, everything started to go black as her legs gave in from under her.

Mark Preston

'You let her escape!' he yelled at his men who had lined up in the throne room hanging their heads in shame.

'One woman, an old man and a peasant, were able to get past an army of mercenaries, bandits and soldiers!' He spat. A slow sarcastic applause came from the corner of the room, Mark swung around to see who had the audacity to do such a thing.

'Well done, one hundred and fifty men and only sixty of those returned to you,' Ian Francis, a well-known mercenary approached.

'And now I have heard they have the seer,' he elaborated.

'Impossible! We burned him alive here in the courtyard,' said Mark.

'Really? Well there must be another seer that goes by the name of Beigarth walking around out there, you know those seers are quite common,' Ian interrupted.

'How dare you mock me in front of my men, I should have your head for this!' Mark reached for his sword.

'Go ahead little man, it saves me waiting around for the Vikings to do it you are never going to win this battle. I have fought Vikings in the past, they are animals harder to kill then most men, the women are worse. You have just gone and giving the most powerful one a reason to grant no mercy on your house or these men. Murdering the old man and you seem proud about that, it took three of your men to tie him up and have him killed in front of his daughter, you call them animals. I hope you are ready for what you have just started because they will not stop until every last one of these so called men and their families are dead.'

'What is it you suggest we do?' Eugene asked concerned.

'These men can flee for their lives but you and your brother can run to the ends of the earth they will hunt you down no matter where you run and they will kill you slow, you will suffer a faith far worse than what you inflicted on them and now they have the Olden's fighting with them, they will have more Norsemen coming to their aid. If a woman, an old man and a peasant escaped from their dungeon and a dwarf an archer and an injured Finn Olden along with the woman escaped from the ambush how are your men going to face an army of them?' The room fell silent.

'You speak as if you are not one of these men, I am paying you to fight for my house and you will do as you're ordered,' Mark announced disdainfully.

'I did what you paid for, I helped capture the Vikings and deliver them to your dungeons, you can shove your orders up your arse from now on there is not enough gold in the world that will have me riding to my death for any imbecile who claims their a Lord.' Ian turned for the door.

'How dare you!' Mark bellowed, he watched the mercenary stop in his tracks, he felt his heart race, as the man turned to face him.

'Are you claiming that you are not? You could have become alias with the Vikings, instead you chose to go to war with them, You should have killed Lord Olden, but you chose to keep him alive, not only did you let him live instead of keeping him across in your own home, you move closer to the Vikings with the prisoner and let them all escape. I will take my chances alone rather than under your rule, I should live much longer that way.' Ian turned once more for the door and marched out, quickly followed by a large group of mercenaries and bandits.

'Where do you think you're going?' Eugene asked.

'He's right, you have no clue what you are doing this gold will keep my family fed for a year, with the Viking free and Olden's new pet, I will not stick around to see what else they have joining them,' Alan Roberts announced as he gracefully exited the room.

Mark stood peering at the remainder of the men in the room red faced and furious.

'I want their heads,' he barked.

'Where is he, where is the body of Bjorn Raghnall?' he asked turning toward Eugene.

'His body remains in the dungeons of the Isles, what would you want with his body?' Eugene asked.

'I want his head put on a spike and place with my banner men as we enter battle I was his shredded body sent to Rosefort in even more pieces than that of which it was seen last, I want that Viking bitch to suffer as we did the day our father was taken from us!'

'Have you gone mad brother?' Eugene asked shocked, 'they have our sister, have you forgotten Amelia?'

'She should have been killed the night Father was taken from us, she is of no use to us now, she is one of them and I would rather die than let our bloodline join with those dregs.' Eugene stood still regarding his brother with a look of contempt on his face.

'As you wish,' he replied before taking his leave from the room.

'I want it known far and wide, I will pay double for any information that leads to the extinction of house Raghnall and the capture of the Olden's.' Mark turned to Sir Rolf Doncaster a tall gaunt man who served as his captain of the guard.

'With all due respect my Lord, our informant seems to be doing well by us so far everything we have been told has checked out. I think the gold would be better spent on weapons and acquiring a larger army, we have not got the resources for these people that is evident, if we fight them again with the numbers we have we will perish,' Rolf warned. He watched as mark paced the floor in silence contemplating the situation.

'It would seem we have a situation here indeed, not impossible but a troubling one none the less, you have always proved to have my families best interest at heart and I thank you for that. Send word to the Byrnell's, they wanted the Vikings heads yet have not done a damned thing so far to get them. Lord Byrnell best get his arse out of his throne room and make his way here soon while the Olden's remain in the dark. Soon they will figure it out, if Beigarth has not already told them. As for my sister she is still family regardless when you find her kill her quickly,' said Mark.

'Excellent decision my Lord, what will I do about the men?' He asked nodding in their direction.

'They will eat, sleep and breathe in that barracks, as for numbers every boy that has come of age is to go straight to weapons training, I don't care if it means every male in a family gets taken from their mother's breast, they will fight or they will die. We barged in underestimating the enemy now we know what they are capable of next time they will fall at our feet.' Mark walked around the men examining who he had left.

'It will take time to build a great army that is something I can spare for now,' Mark said.

'If I may my Lord, you cut off the head of house Raghnall, in my experience these types of houses grow back twice as many heads as that that has been severed. The Raghnall girl will want vengeance for her father, I suggest you keep a low profile until your army is ready,' said Rolf.

'That I will, as soon as I do her a courtesy and deliver her father's body back to her,' Mark replied smirking.

Asger

The Howling wind had uprooted trees, blown down fences and made it impossible to train outdoors. The rain beat down hard with shards of ice pelting his skin, the Gods were angry, that he knew. He had heard how his father had suffered at the hands of the Preston men he had vowed to make every last one of them writhe in pain as he would deliver a gruelling death. He had thanked Finn for bringing Freya home even if it was on the back of a Kludde, the beast had been staying in an empty barn with only Finn daring to enter to feed it.

Walking into Freya's room he noticed Clara tending to her, she had seldom left her side since she had been brought back.

'Asger!' she turned to him gleefully. 'I am sorry to say you have just missed her, I gave her a tonic for the pain she will remain in a deep sleep for a while now, although with your family it can be hard to deduce how long, with most people it would be half a day, I know you do not be affected as much.' The jolly plump woman dashed around the room cleaning up the ingredients she used in her concoction.

'How is she?' he asked concerned.

'I have seen her much worse, she will be in pain for a while, he body has been bruised and wounded, her wounds were not deep enough to cause any major concern but it will take her at least a few weeks to recover and she will be left scared both physically and mentally. I believe she was in the room when your father…' Clara dropped her head, gulping back her emotions.

'I am so sorry, Bjorn was a great man.'

'Thank you Clara, you are very kind. I will see him again in Valhalla when it is my time to join him,' His aunt beamed a sweet smile at him.

'You will indeed dear boy. That man who brought Freya back, he cares deeply for her and it would be good for her to keep him close,' Clara spoke softly.

'Finn? He had a reputation when we met for being a person I would not want my sister being anywhere near,' Asger began.

'And now?' Clara asked.

'I can see where he got his reputation from, he has a temper, does not listen to anyone but himself, he is reckless, impulsive and has a mouth that he has no control over. But I have seen him with Freya, he has proven he would die for her, she seems to care for him that is all I concern myself with,' Asger said.

'He sounds like a typical Norseman,' Clara giggled. 'I have seen how he cares for her first hand, I may be an old woman, but that love is very rare to come across in fact the last time I seen someone that devoted that quickly was your father when he met your mother, of course she was having none of him at first but Bjorn eventually wore her down,' she giggled. Cara-Lea entered the room. 'Ah there you are my girl, I will show you how to change these bandages and treat her wounds, it will be much easier for you with Freya sleeping. Asger I must ask you to leave to protect your sisters modesty,' Clara said sweetly.

Upon entering the great hall for his evening meal, Asger noticed the crowd of men divided on both sides of the hall. The Vikings were gathered on his left hand side smashing plates and laughing every time they shattered. To his right sat the Oldens with Drew, the two dwarfs and Gilli and Nari. Amelia was sat at the back of the hall with her head hung low as she ate alone. Asger beckoned Nicholas over towards him.

'Why is Amelia sat by herself?' he asked.

'She has took pleasure in her own company since we got here,' Nicholas replied with little emotion.

'She is to be your wife? Yet you abandon her in her time of need?' Asger asked.

'Her time of need? After what she done?' Nicholas barked.

'She done nothing!' Asger interrupted. 'Her family tried to kill her too. Or have you forgotten that? If we were to all place blame on somebody for their families' actions we would all be on the hangman's noose.' Nicholas glanced over at the frail girl sitting alone, she looked lost. 'The way I see it you have a decision to make. You can either put what happened behind you and start again or free her from her duty to you.' Nicholas did not respond, he looked over at the table where his family and friends sat then glanced back at Amelia. Asger watched as

Nicholas approached Amelia and sat down by her side, smiling to himself he turned to join the other men.

Koi and Gilli were busy mocking Finn by the time Asger had sat down.

'We thought he was dead he was carried away flopping around like fish out of water in the air then the next time we seen him he was flying the thing bareback,' Finn laughed as he chugged a large goblet of ale.

'I'll have you know Luna is a very graceful flyer,' Finn answered.

'I still wouldn't go offering to feed that thing no matter what you called it,' Asher replied.

'Throw her a few pigs and she's fine,' Finn mocked.

'Keep her away from Rosemary!' Asher barked. A roar of laughter filled the room.

Asger noticed Theodore's plate was clean he had not left a crumb. He beckoned over a servant girl and got her to bring him over an extra plate full of food. 'You will sleep well tonight with a full belly and a warm bed,' Asger said warmly.

'You do me a great kindness,' Theodore replied smiling.

'You are one of us now Lord Olden, we take care of our own, drink up,' Asger said handing Theodore a large horn of wine.

'How are you?' Drew asked Finn.

'Despite the fact I reopened my previous wounds and Luna was kind enough to leave her mark on me before she decided not to kill me, I have never felt better,' said Finn.

'I have been told to keep you from training for a few weeks until Clara says otherwise,' said Asger.

'Weeks?' Finn asked shocked.

'Afraid so, you can keep that beast of yours fed and out of trouble while you're passing the time. It can eat anyone it wants as long as it's not one of ours,' Asger warned. 'Drew I need you to take on the women, Freya wants them to be able to defend themselves if it comes to it and any who are willing to fight side by side with the men, we know the Norse women will fight alongside the men but the others will need to learn from the basics,' Asger continued.

'And why don't you take them on?' Drew asked.

'Because if he takes them on, he'll end up fucking them all and they'll eventually all want his head on a spike,' Gilli mocked.

'Not exactly the results Freya would be hoping for,' Nari continued before standing up to leave.

'Where are you going?' Gilli asked?

'My lovely Hawise is waiting for a visit from me. I best not keep her waiting,' Nari replied.

After Nari had left Asger turned to the men. 'So we have a wedding to plan by the look of things.' The men looked at each other dumbfounded.

'Who in their right minds would agree to marry you?' Gilli mocked.

'Not me!' Asger started. 'And I will have you know there are plenty of women who would want to be my bride,' he went on. 'I was referring to Nicholas and Amelia, it would be a good distraction after everything that happened to give them the day they never got and lift spirits around here.'

'I think that you have had enough ale,' Gilli replied.

'I think that is a good idea,' said Theodore.

'Keep the people distracted for a while, I think it is safe to say we will not have to worry about an attack on us for a while,' Asger agreed. 'I best check with Beigarth to be safe, but I agree they have not got the numbers anymore while our numbers are increasing nicely. My only concern is we will need more farmers for when the Goggy's arrive.'

'Good thing you have plenty of them sitting across the room,' Gilli gestured towards the group of Vikings sitting opposite them.

After their meal Asger called Theodore back to him. 'I have a request' he said simply. Theodore looked at him confused. 'While my sister is incapacitated, I need someone who can rule, I will be busy with the men and to be honest I was never brought up to rule, I am a warrior that is all I know, but I need someone I can trust to make the right calls in running this realm until Freya regains her strength,' Theodore smiled.

'It would be a great privilege,' Theodore replied.

'One other thing,' Asger added. 'I know it is not my place but seeing as you both will have some more free time, maybe you can find it in you to reconnect with Finn, I cannot bring my father back but I can take solace in the sense that we mended our rift when I came here to Rosefort, I blamed him on sending me away and the constant punishments I would receive from his hand, while he blamed me on being a "little shit" as he would say always bringing trouble to the door. It was at the later stage after the dust had settled we realised we were both in the wrong and we finally created a bond. I fought alongside my father multiple times after that and learned so much from him as he did with me.'

Theodore smiled. 'I love my children dearly, it is no secret myself and Finn do not always see eye to eye but I agree I should talk to him.'

'I better arrange extra farmers,' said Asger.

'Thank you for everything, you truly are your father's son.' Theodore's words were kind and sincere. Asger found himself feeling a sense of pride after that remark, he was his father's son and he would do everything he could to make him proud.

Cara-Lea

Her arms and legs ached, her hair unkempt and her clothes soiled in blood and dirt, she had never been seen in any state other than perfect back home, looking to be far from well-bred right now she remained content. She had being doing what she set out to do, to be more than a pretty daughter of a well-respected Lord, she had being helping those who needed her, help build up a barracks for the soldiers to come, tending to the wounds of the injured and learning a new language to communicate with a different culture. She had no doubt her mother would not approve of her new endeavours, Cara-Lea had the best education as a young noble girl could get and yet it was far from being educated in her eyes. She was thought to read and write and yet never had the opportunity to use her abilities other than in poetry and song. 'A lady is to be seen and not heard,' her mother's words echoed in her ears regularly, she was raised to be a good wife, to produce children and to keep a household running and for the longest time she believed that was the only option she would ever have, until she met the Vikings.

She had missed the evening meal, her stomach rumbled, but she feared her legs would not be able to carry her down the long staircase, Edward's appearance in the courtyard a few days prior had left her confused and exhausted. Cara-Lea searched for answers for days, leaving her sleep deprived and irritable all she wanted to do was wash up and fall into bed. She began scrubbing her hands and arms vigorously until they turned red raw, finally satisfied they were clean she splashed water on her face and around her neck and chest. She removed her soiled garments and discarded them in the corner of her room before proceeding to fix her hair. Managing to wriggle her way into her nightgown, she felt comforted in the fresh cotton material, pulling back her bed sheets ready fall in and sleep a knock came from her door. 'One moment,' she called as she searched for her robe.

Eventually opening the door she was surprised to see Drew standing on the other side.

'Sorry to disturb you, may I come in?' he asked sweetly.

'Of course,' she replied.

'I noticed you were not at this night's meal,' Drew began.

'I lost track of time, I was helping Clara with Finn and Freya,' Cara-Lea explained.

'I hope you don't mind but I have brought you some food,' Drew replied placing a small basket on the table, Cara-Lea was so taken aback by having him call to her room she never noticed him carry it into the room.

'Thank you, you are very kind,' she said watching as he removed the cloth covering the basket.

'I could not get any hot food I hope this will suffice,' Drew said apologetically. Cara-Lea approached to see a large loaf of bread placed on top of the basket under it sat some fruit and a tankard of wine.

'My father lets me drink wine only on special occasions and no more than a chalice full,' she said.

'Apologies, force of habit with the Norsemen and women,' Drew said. Cara-Lea picked up the wine and poured herself and Drew a goblet each.

'Given recent events, I am sure I deserve to have a little wine,' she said, handing one of the goblets to Drew. Cara-Lea sat and ate and drank until the basket was empty and she was down to her last goblet of wine, her and Drew shared stories and she found herself laughing for the first time since the attack on her house.

'If Freya wants the women to fight I want to train,' she demanded.

'I think you might be taken on a bit much,' Drew replied.

'I can handle it, besides Finn thought me how to swing a sword properly, I just need to learn how to do it when it counts,' she started. 'And you will teach me to fight will you not?' she asked.

Drew smiled, 'As you wish my Lady.'

'Please don't call me that, I have always hated that title, I am no lady, not here anyway, just call me by my name please,' Cara-Lea begged. 'So my brother is to be married after all,' she went on.

'According to Asger anyway,' Drew replied. Cara-Lea's face dropped. 'You do not wish for him to marry?' Drew asked noting her expression.

'It's not that, it's just, it's Amelia,' she began.

'Oh you don't like her?' Drew asked.

'Look what her family did and even then she's spoiled, she's entitled, she's not Freya. I would much rather have Freya as a sister in law than Amelia,' Drew gave a hearty laugh.

'You will never find any one quite like Freya. Amelia isn't all that bad, and after what has happened I am sure her attitude will change, past events would have proved to be a huge wake up call for her. You may not like her now but you never know a time can come where you will be happy to have her around.'

'You sound like you are speaking from experience?' Cara-Lea asked.

'Let's just say Asger was not the most likeable person when I met him, he would stumble home drunk come into my chambers and topple the bed over just because he could, gave me an awful time when I first moved here. But I learned over time it was a defence mechanism with him, he had serious trust issues back then even worse than he does now, he was letting me know he was always around if I fucked up. Eventually he took to me and the torment stopped, he came and apologised to me for it not long after but that went on for about a year before he changed,' Drew explained.

'It sounds awful,' Cara-Lea gasped.

'It wasn't so bad, one day he was so drunk he flipped Bjorn's bed over by mistake, to this day I have never seen Asger run so fast, the only person he ever feared was his father,' Drew chuckled. 'Well anyway it's getting late and I see you're already for bed, I better go myself make preparations for my new female recruits. Goodnight Cara-Lea,' Drew said sweetly, whilst walking towards the door.

'Goodnight Drew, and thank you for tonight,' she beamed a sweet smile back at him and watched as the door closed behind him. This may not be the home she had grown up in but Rosefort had proven to feel more like home with every day that passed. She had no idea why the Vikings had such a terrible name, they had been nothing but kind to her and her family since they had met, the real monsters where those who had ambushed her house taking innocent lives for no reason other than pure greed, she vowed to herself that day on the ship leaving her home she would not die a victim, she would learn to fight to defend herself and others and it seemed that Freya had just given her the opportunity to do just that.

Theodore

After dressing and mentally preparing himself for the day ahead, Theodore made his way down for his morning meal. He had missed the church he had regularly attended all the holy men had been slaughtered the night the Preston's attacked his home and Rosefort had no men of the Christian faith to lead in the word of God. His wife nagging him regularly, a trait he never thought he would miss about her left him feeling broken even more so than the injuries he had sustained. Little Edward, left the biggest hole in his heart, his youngest son slain while trying to escape, he was no threat to anyone yet they took his life all the same. His house crumbled, his people murdered and himself bound and tortured for days, everything he had grown to know destroyed because of one Allianz. Bjorn had saved his life on more than one occasion, he would make sure to repay the favour back by looking after his children now that he had been cut down before his time.

Making his way for the great hall, Theodore noticed two large hounds guarding Freya's room. He had recognised them as Captain and Christian two of the four that had accompanied Freya to his house a few months ago. A loud bang came from inside the room as muffled voices yelled back and forth. Theodore thought it best to go investigate. With the hounds gaze fixed upon him, he slowly opened the door to find Freya staggering around the room throwing anything she could find at whoever was on the other side of the door.

'I told you not to go out there! You could have been killed!' She yelled.

'If I didn't go after you, you would have been killed!' a voice retaliated. It did not take long for Theodore to recognise the voice as Finn's.

'Who cares if I died out there it could have ended all this,' she cried.

'I FUCKING CARE!' Finn bellowed, as Theodore went to enter the room Finn came storming past him, he was so angry Theodore was convinced Finn did not even notice him.

'Apologies, I heard a commotion from the hall, I just wanted to see that you were ok, I didn't mean to intrude,' Theodore explained as he turned to meet Freya's gaze. Her face was bruised and swollen her body from what he could tell had similar wounds.

'It is fine Theodore I am not angry with you,' she answered sweetly as she lowered herself back onto her bed.

'You should be resting, your body has a lot of healing to do,' Theodore warned as he approached. Mandy was watching from the base of the bed, while Toby had been sat under the window.

'I specifically told him not to leave Rosefort and he did it anyway,' Freya said pouting.

'That's Finn for you, believe me I know what he's like. He's reckless and impulsive, once he gets an idea into his head there is no talking him out of it. He has made my blood boil on more than one occasion with his actions. However, if I may he did only go out after I returned with Andrew,' Theodore reasoned.

'Are you defending him?' Freya asked.

'I have seen Finn with you since the day you answered my invite and came to my house. He has never been the way he is with you, with any other believe it or not this is him well behaved, I don't know how you've done it but you have tamed him, at least to a point.'

'You speak of him as if he is a wild animal,' said Freya.

'His mother didn't call him her dark horse for nothing,' Theodore jested. 'I have seen you together both of you would throw yourselves on a blade in order to spare the other, that kind of love doesn't come around every day. I loved my wife but we married out of duty not choice, our love grew over time it was precious to us in our own way but what you have with my son is something completely different not everyone gets so lucky. He will anger you to the point where you will want to kill him, but then he does something that makes you forget about the wrong he did before, he finds another way to get a rise out of you,' said Theodore. Freya seemed to relax talking to Lord Olden.

'I don't want him to die because of me,' she reasoned.

‘Most people would argue the only way to save him would be to break his heart, but those people do not know my son if anything he’d get himself killed with his impulsiveness and his drinking if that were to happen. You have no choice if it comes to it if Finn lays himself down for you that will be his choice alone.’ A sadness overwhelmed Theodore at the thought of losing another son.

‘Not unless I get there first.’ Freya interrupted. ‘Promise me Lord Olden that if it comes to it you will not let him try to save me, get him as far away as possible.’

‘Freya if you fall surely the Preston’s would be obliged to march straight for Rosefort,’ Theodore’s voice was shocked.

‘Exactly, if I fall they will see no threat, they will come here without even thinking about it leaving themselves wide open, I have no doubt their army will be large, but large armies move slowly you would have the best opportunity to kill them all if that were to happen.’

‘You sound just like your father, Freya. I hope it will never come to it but I give you my word I will protect Finn if it does.’

‘Thank you Lord Olden,’ said Freya as she lay back in her bed.

‘I will go and let you rest now,’ Theodore turned and left the room.

Arriving at the great hall, he looked around the great divide in the room was evident his own people on one side and the Vikings on the other, this would need to change if they were to fight together. Finn had isolated himself from everyone, he sat in the top right hand corner of the room partially hidden from view by a large marble statue of a Norseman dressed in bear skins with horns on his helmet and a large bear standing behind him.

Theodore approached his son cautiously. ‘I know that look all too well, I used to wear it a lot when your mother was alive,’ he stated.

‘Father, I think you came to the wrong table, Nicholas is over there,’ Finn spat.

‘I deserve that,’ Theodore replied, placing himself in the seat facing his son. ‘I did not always make myself available to you, I am sorry for that but I am here now,’ Theodore tried to reason with him.

'A bit late now, I am a grown man now. I don't need my father to fix my problems for me… Not that you ever did,' Finn replied taking a large gulp of ale all the while refusing to look at his father.

'You know what your fault is, you may be a man grown but you are still far too young for all of this,' said Theodore. 'Believe it or not I was once where you are now and I know the struggle. It's not easy to be calm amidst all of this. We all have lost a great deal but think of what remains, you still have Nicholas and your sister, you also have these people who have befriended you and a young woman who cares for you and you have me whether you want me or not, I will be around.' Finn looked up at his father with a painful expression on his face, Theodore knew this was a sore subject for him, when Finn got upset he would often lash out.

'Why is it now that you care Father? Why should I try to explain any of what this is to me to you? Every time I came to you in the past you turned me away, but the others you had time for? From the moment I could talk I was ordered to listen, now after everything now you claim you care about me?' Theodore could see his son well up for the first time, Finn fought back the tears by chugging more ale, it seemed the more he tried to repress his emotions the more his jaw seemed to lock.

'I cannot take back the past but I can try to make emends now, but do not think I ever cast you out you are my son. You needed to find your own path in life I could not hand you one, you have found the power to be strong Finn but you are still young wisdom will come to you in time. I am just a man I have made many mistakes you are different from your siblings, completely different, I knew that since the day I laid eyes on you, you had a fierce temper from the day you left your mother's womb. I tried discipline that didn't work, I tried ignoring it that only made things worse, there was no controlling you. You were given your own path in life, one you had to walk alone with no guidance and no one to hold your hand. I have seen you grow from a boy into a man, you learned your craft with weapons and now you can teach that craft you have become a man for all to see and I could not be more proud of you. You ask why I start caring. The answer is I never stopped. Now you want to pull yourself out of that pitiful state you have brought yourself into, in case you didn't notice that was me you stormed by earlier and I can tell you a nagging woman is a happy woman, it means she cares for you. One that smiles and never corrects you is the one you have to watch out for. Eat some bread that should sober you up a bit. You may not be able to train but I need you to scout out the new men and find out what needs to be done with them, we cannot win this if we are a house divided.' Theodore stood up took the pitcher of ale away from the table and placed it over with the Vikings. Finns words cut him like a blade but he dare not show it, not now. He was needed in the throne room amongst the small council which consisted of Gilli, Nari and Asger, they would have to figure out a plan of how to run this house and how to unite the men. This was going to take all day he could tell.

Nicholas

Escorting Amelia towards the barracks he noticed that his wife to be looked rather sullen.

'Are you worried about your training?' he asked.

'It's not that,' Amelia sighed. 'It's just that, I know my brother and with Freya's return and your father's escape, I fear he is going to do something to try and provoke them. He was never shrewd and if he did not get his way he would bellow like a wounded boar. I now know what my family is, I never expected them to become such monstrosities but I do know with Mark now Lord of house Preston things are going to become far worse. I don't know where this hatred for the Vikings came from, it was never there before the day you all went hunting. I fear another house is behind all this but for the life of me I cannot figure out which one.' Nicholas had not given it much thought but listening to Amelia speak it did make sense. The Preston's were indeed a wealthy family but to hire that many mercenaries and bandits and equip them all with weapons and armour both for the attack on his home and the scouts that were sent looking for Freya and Theodore they would have needed help.

'You're right, there is a lot more to this than what we know. We cannot prevent your brother from causing more upset but we can stop him once he reaches these lands, give the matter no more thought and go now Drew is waiting for you,' Nicholas gestured towards the training grounds in the barracks. Cara-Lea had already arrived and was top of the lines, there was a mixture of women from house Olden and from Rosefort nervously standing in their rows. Some seemed more interested in staring at Drew instead of choosing a sword.

Nicholas noticed Finn walking towards the pig farm, he seemed upset. Nicholas watched as the people gathered in the village square made it their business to get out of Finns way as he marched on, he had noticed that Finn had some altercation with their father at the morning meal, intrigued Nicholas decided to follow his brother through the town towards the pig farm.

Nicholas watched at Finn paid the farmer and proceeded with his dagger in hand and cut the boars throats. One by one they fell until he had a wheelbarrow full and busting at the sides.

'I'll get that,' Nicholas called as he watched Finn struggle to lift the cart.

'I don't need your help,' Finn spat.

'You obviously do little brother, you should not be lifting with your injuries, you have been told already,' Nicholas tried to reason with him.

'I'll be fine,' Finn insisted, his arms trembled with the weight of the wheelbarrow, a look of pain etched on his face. 'Arrggghhhh!' Finn yelled toppling the cart. He ran at it kicking it and the lifeless bodies of the boars that had rolled out onto the ground. Nicholas looked on allowing Finn to vent his aggression on the dead pigs. When he eventually stopped beating them, 'I can't do this,' Finn muttered under his breath.

'I told you to let me…' Nicholas began.

'Not the pigs!' Finn snapped. 'This, this fucking life! We are waiting around like these fucking pigs waiting to be slaughtered. We are on the brink of a war we cannot avoid, we have no men, no allies our strongest fighters are dead or injured, I can barely lift a sword, Freya hates me and all we have to show for ourselves is a bloody wall! Our wall back home didn't stop them, why should three?' Finn frantically paced before losing his footing in the mud. 'Great!' He yelled. 'Just fucking great.' Nicholas approached his brother who was lying on his back in the mud

'You're just having a bad day, Freya does not hate you, whatever happened between you two, and you should go talk to her. We have men coming to join our cause, we may be short on fighters now but so are the Preston's you bought us enough time when you went for Freya to rebuild an army. We will take back our home, these things take time Finn and you have Luna now, I doubt anyone is going to try storm in here, knowing she is on your side. We may not be where we need to be, but we are a lot better off than we were and that's saying something. Now get up from the ground and stop your whining, you sound like a woman,' Nicholas reached out his hand.

'I would make a much better woman than you,' Finn joked as he took his brothers hand and staggered to his feet.

'I doubt that longer hair always did suit me better,' Nicholas replied with a kind smile. As the brothers walked back through the village square with Nicholas pushing the wheelbarrow full of pigs, he found it was the right time to fill his brother in on his conversation with Amelia. 'The only problem is I don't know what house would want us and the Norsemen dead,' Nicholas explained.

Finn thought for a minute. 'I wouldn't be half surprised if it was the Byrnell's,' he said.

Nicholas gasped and turned to his brother. 'I know Uncle Richard is a lot of things but are you forgetting Mother was killed we were nearly killed and poor Edward. It makes no sense,' Nicholas reasoned.

'It makes perfect sense to me, think about it where was Richard or our grandfather for the event Mother put on for you? Where were they for your supposed wedding? And do you not find it the slightest bit odd that even after Mother was killed not one person from that household has sent word trying to contact any of us? If I had been away and heard of one of my sibling's deaths I would want to know if it was true or just rumour, I would march out myself and find the family to find out what happened and yet not even a letter from that lot? Even if they are not involved they are dead to me,' Finn's voice was filled with hatred. Nicholas did think it was odd that they had not heard from their uncle or grandfather, Finn had a point even if they were not involved they had a lot of explaining to do, Nicholas tried reasoning with himself that his family would not betray him but then he thought of Amelia she never thought her family would do what they did until they tried to have her killed. His mother always said everything happens for a reason, God has a plan, you would not find out what until it happened now they are in Rosefort. The place the Allianz between households was forged so many years ago, now they are back and only two of the houses stand together it seemed poetic in a way. The thought sent a shiver down his spine if this was the plan to get them all back here, what would the outcome be? Surely only one side would prevail one way or another at least two households were going to be extinct by the end of it all.

Finn

Talking to Nicholas helped calm him. This had been a tough day but he was grateful that his brother was there for him and for the distraction he gave him. Finn never liked his mother's family they were cold and distant towards him because he had all the Olden traits and was considered to be wild and hostile as a child. Every time his uncle came to visit he would bring his siblings a gift from his travels and turn his nose at Finn like he was a mere peasant. It was not until he was older that the house showed interest in him but not as a person, they wanted him as a weapon.

Finn watched as Luna chewed through the carcases of the slaughtered pigs, she tore them apart like she was cutting through butter. Once Luna had finished and Finn ensured she had plenty of water he left for the bath house. Upon arriving he had noticed Nicholas and Drew had the same idea as him, they were both sitting in the large round bath he had not noticed before but the bath had gold carvings all along its edge, the four pillars on entry to the room had the same markings on their ends.

'I thought this place would be vacant,' said Finn as he stripped off his tunic.

'It was, I needed a place to escape after those women…' Drew started. 'I swear half of them cannot even hold a sword why Asger asked me to train them and not Nari I'll never know.' Finn climbed into join them, the three men swapped stories and strategies for a while. Finn was so lost in conversation he never heard the door open behind him. Nicholas began to blush, Finn noticing his brothers sudden discomfort turned around to see a tall, thin, pretty young woman stand behind them.

'Emery, what are you doing here?' Drew asked.

'My father sent for me apparently you need all the able bodies you can get, I got told you were in here and to report to you but I wasn't informed about your friends,' The young woman replied with a seductive grin.

'Training is over until tomorrow,' Drew announced formally.

'Pity, I was hoping to get my hands on some hard steel, I just might have to look elsewhere,' she said crouching down towards a blushing Nicholas.

'He's due to be married,' Drew said before Nicholas could reply. Finn stepped out of the bath and began wrapping a towel around himself when he noticed the young woman approaching him.

'And what about you?' she asked placing a hand on his shoulder.

'Married too?' Finn turned to face Emery, he glanced at her for a moment then smirked.

'Finn is your cousin's companion,' Drew announced.

'Freya? Well she did do well for herself, didn't she? Maybe when you get sick of her you can think of me. My room is just down the hall from hers,' she said in a sultry voice.

'Well you are easy on the eyes,' Finn began to pace around her holding onto his towel. 'But you are far too thin for my liking, I'd split you in half.' said Finn mockingly. Emery's smile turned into a scowl, she quickly looked at Drew then back to Finn before proceeding to storm out of the bath house. Drew and Nicholas filled the bathhouse with the sound of their laughter.

'For a moment little brother I thought you were going to take her up on her offer,' Nicholas said.

'I thought about it, I won't lie. But why would I want a woman like that when I have a psychotic Viking upstairs that likes to use my head as target practise. A normal woman would be boring now no matter how much of a warm welcome her legs offer.'

'That's Emery for you, Nicholas you seem a little shocked?' Drew asked.

'He's not used to women like that,' said Finn.

'Ah yes, Viking women and berserker women are much different from your Christian women. They fight better than most men. They have the freedom to choose who they want to be with, most of the time anyway. They are above men in our culture so they can choose a companion outside marriage and not be judged. The last I heard Emery's last companion was killed on a raid,' Drew explained. Finn feeling the chill now that he was out of the bath excused himself and left to go find himself some clean clothes. Peering out a window on his way to Freya's room, he noticed that Emery was not the only new face that had arrived he counted twenty archers that were standing outside the barracks being examined by Asger.

Eventually making it to Freya's room, Finn took a deep breath before opening the door half expecting an argument when he entered, but to his surprise Freya was sleeping. Of course her hounds had been surrounding her, protecting their master. Christian sat at the foot of the bed, he had noticed Finn, his tail start to wag as he got to his feet to greet him. Finn dropped his towel and went in search of some new garments. A knock came on the door.

'One moment,' he called as he quickly jumped into a pair of trousers, he quickly glanced over to see if the knocking woke Freya but she remained fast asleep. Opening the door Finn found Clara standing on the other side. 'Come in,' he said as he moved aside to let the large woman past.

'I had just come to check on Freya.' she announced, looking at Finns shoulders 'But those wounds look like they need my attention again, sit down,' She ordered. Finn did as he was told and took a seat over by the desk in the corner of the room. Clara placed down some sort of concoction along with some herbs and a small container of maggots. Stripping back the bandages she noticed some pus leaking from Finns wounds. 'That's normal' she reassured him as she began cleaning out his wounds. 'She is lucky to have you, you know?' she continued.

'I think I am the lucky one,' said Finn.

'I have known Freya since she was a little girl, she has always been different, extraordinary even as a tiny tot, she was very inquisitive and intelligent but she has vicious streak in her too don't let the angelic looks fool you dear boy she is not as fragile as many think.' Clara said with a large grin on her face, as if she were remembering some pleasant memory.

'I've noticed this morning at first light she aimed half of the room at my head,' Finn explained rolling his eyes, Clara let out a little giggle at the thought.

'Well you are lucky she wasn't aiming directly at your head or she would not have missed, most likely she was trying to scare you. After her father… I cannot imagine how hard this must be on her. You can only imagine she has lost everyone she holds dear, every last person she loved has died slowly and painfully and some more gruesome than the other, I know that girl like she was my own, she cares for you deeply you can see that by the way she looks at you, she must be terrified to lose you too.' Finn hung his head he hadn't thought of it like that, it would explain why she started pushing him away all of a sudden. 'Our girl is a fighter like you have never seen, even now as she is sleeping, you watch her wounds will heal up twice as quickly as a normal persons, she sleeps to heal, if she is sick or injured her body shuts down to make her sleep, you may notice her body will feel like the doorway to hell when you lay beside her at night. That heat is a good thing it means she is coming back to herself. Asger has the ability to shape shift as some would call it from his mother, Freya never got that ability but she has something greater she is made to last, those bastards may have slaughtered the rest of her family but I can assure you she is different this girl can withstand almost anything.' Clara's words were filled with pride, it was obvious how much she had cared for Freya and Finn thanked her for seeing to his wounds. After Clara left, Finn sat staring at Freya for the longest time, he thought of how he had changed in the short time they met, of how even through her scars swollen face and bruised body that she remained the most radiant beauty he had ever seen. He had never had a woman yell at him before, in fact she was the first person outside of the family that ever corrected him.

After a while Freya began to stir.

'Good evening,' Finn declared passing her a goblet of wine. She looked stunned to see him at her bedside.

'What are you doing here?' she asked.

'You don't think you could have scared me off that easy do you?' he asked shooting her a kind smile. Rolling her eyes Freya reached for the goblet and start taking large sips. 'I had the joy of meeting your cousin today, she seemed to be interested in Nicholas,' Finn joked.

'Emery?' Freya gasped, searching herself for a moment.

'Don't you worry Drew told her off,' Finn reassured her. 'Now since we are both to remain on bed rest and you have nothing more to aim at my head…' he said taking the goblet from her grasp. 'I suggest we make the best of it.' Finn said pressing himself against Freya.

'Finn look at me, my eye is practically swollen shut, my body is bruised. I can't only imagine what the rest of me looks like.' Freya raised her arm to his chest and began to push him away. Finn ignored her moving her hand away, he ran his own around the side of her face.

'You are beautiful regardless, I still find you rather desirable.'

'Not right now,' Freya pleaded, Finn could tell she was feeling a lot of discomfort from her wounds.

'Ok not now,' he replied kindly, both lay down on the bed. Finn thought for a second then proceeded to roll into Freya's chest.

'What are you doing?' she laughed.

'You said no to sex, you said nothing about me burying my head between your breasts,' his answer was muffled as he began to shake his head in between her bosoms, making Freya laugh.

The door to the room swung open, Finn swung his head in the direction of the door to see Emery was sauntering into the room.

'Oh, am I interrupting something?' she asked sarcastically.

'Yes,' Finn snapped.

'No, come in,' Freya replied before turning to Finn, who rolled his eyes and rolled back to the side of the bed.

'I came to check on you cousin, I heard what had happened and wanted to make sure you were okay,' Emery explained kindly.

'I will be fine in a few days, just need to rest up until my strength returns,' Freya said reassuringly.

Emery turned her attention to Finn. 'You don't look very happy to see me?' she asked.

'I'm not,' he replied.

'Finn!' Freya barked.

'That's quite alright cousin, I wouldn't expect anything more from a brute, at least he is an honest one,' said Emery.

'A brute eh? That's not what you were calling me in the bath house when you invited me to abandon Freya's bed and take up in your own,' Finn replied.

Emery's face dropped. 'How dare you! Freya I would never!'

'Like you said, he is honest, now that you see I still live, you can leave now,' Freya's voice was filled with disdain. Finn watched as Emery ran from the room like a scalded cat.

'When were you going to tell me?' Freya asked.

'I didn't think it was important, until she start insulting me that is,' Finn answered.

'I am not surprised, Emery did always find it hard to keep her legs together she has had more companions than I would like to imagine,' Freya said disapprovingly.

'I don't see what the big deal is anyway, sure her face is attractive but she's got a little boy's body, I've got bigger tits than her,' Finn said proceeding to rub his chest with his hands. Freya giggled.

'You are an idiot,' she said.

That may be true, but at least I am an honest idiot,' Finn mocked as he rolled himself back into Freya.

A knock came at the door, before Finn could call out to see who it was, the door opened slowly.

'I am going to have to lock that door,' Finn muttered as he looked to see who entered the room. This time it was Beigarth. Finn rolled off Freya a second time glancing at the burned man in the dark robes.

'Pardon my intrusion my lady but I have an urgent message from your father,' Beigarth explained as he entered the room.

Freya jumped up, 'My father?' she asked frightfully.

'Yes, you see I was down in the library reading through some medicinal notes my mother had left me, when Bjorn appeared to me, he is happy where he is now and he wants you to know he is with your mother and brothers. He does not want you to blame yourself for his death, he said he was happy to go. However, he warned his body will return to you but not due to any kindness. He urges you not to react on emotions. He has a message for you, he said there will be a great battle, there will also be a fire you must enter, your body will burn and you will surely perish from the ashes your spirit will be reborn and a legend will have been created. This is the only way, the dead will win this war,' His lifeless eyes started at Freya as he spoke. Finn felt a chill rush down his spine.

'I won't let her die,' Finn barked.

'Then we will all perish,' Beigarth replied. 'This is your destiny, your death will win this war. Your family name will become extinct the Olden's will live on and they will carry with them your legacy.'

'Thank you Beigarth,' Freya finally spoke, Beigarth nodded and left the room promptly.

'I won't let you die,' Finn snapped.

'All men die Finn, everything that lives will expire at some stage we can't fight our destiny, if God wants me I will have no choice.' Freya tried to reason with him. Finn could feel his jaw lock and his eyes tear up. He fought the tears back.

'I cannot lose you,' his voice cracked.

'You will never lose me, death cannot stop what we have it can only delay it for a while, besides you think I'd let you get everything I have that easy? I'll be back to haunt you regularly you can count on that,' Freya joked. 'Besides we don't know when this battle will be, if it's as great as Beigarth said it will be we have months maybe even years together before it happens, remember both sides are down men, it will take time for any sort of battle to commence,' Freya reasoned as she knelt up on the bed and wrapped her arms around Finn's waist. 'You still find me desirable?' Freya asked in a sultry voice.

'Always, but you told me no remember?' Finn reminded her.

'Maybe I've changed my mind,' Freya replied planting a kiss on his neck. Finn stood up and walked to the door.

'Where are you going?' she asked confused.

'Locking that damned door, they can try interrupt all they want but no one's getting in here.' Finn replied trying to push Beigarth's words from his head, his father's words rang in his ears. 'Everyone knows they are going to die they just don't believe it.' Finn always found that to be true however with his previous lifestyle he had accepted death a long time ago but he cannot accept it happening to the woman he loves, if he can prevent her demise he will even at the cost of his own life.

Freya

She watched as Finn fell sound asleep before she dared move. Beigarth's warning from her father had her mind racing, Freya knew seers had a tendency to speak in riddles and to never take what they said exactly to heart. Her body ached after her sexual indulgences with Finn as she knew it would, but she knew it was the only way she could take his mind off Beigarth's words and give her some time to think. Her stomach growled loudly from hunger, she had not been eating much since she came home, she had found herself too tired and sore to indulge her stomach. You best go find some food she thought as she tried to dress. Freya found her regular dresses and garments too much of a bother to put on, they were all tight and heavy not something she wished to be carting around on her battered body. Looking around the room she noticed Finns tunic lay on the floor near the desk, where he had discarded it shortly after locking the door. Freya hobbled over and put it on along with Finns breeches. His clothes were loose on her but she felt comfortable, they felt much lighter than the heavy dresses she was used to wearing. Leaving Finn snoring lightly in her bed, Freya left in search of food.

The pantry was darker than the rest of her castle, it was cold and dreary with nothing but plain grey walls that greet her. A long table full of unkempt dishes sat to the right of her as she entered the room, most likely from the last meal that would have been served another table sat to her right it was filled with spices and herbs and to her delight a basket full of freshly baked bread sat at the end. She examined the loaves of bread in the basket there was black bread which used to be her father's favourite. Barley bread and Machete bread which was Freya's favourite she adored it as it was made of wheat flour and had a better texture than the others. Picking up a large loaf of Machete bread, Freya noticed some oatcakes had been placed under the bread loaves. At the top of the table an assortment of butters, honey and jams had been laid out, she quickly grabbed the plain butter and strawberry jam and spread generous amounts of both on her bread and oatcakes. With each bite her mouth watered and before long she had devoured the entire loaf of bread and the remains of the oatcakes.

After Freya had her fill her thoughts went to her brother. She admired him trying to bring some joy to the realm with the wedding but Asger was Viking, he had very little knowledge of Christian weddings and traditions. Thinking about leaving him in charge would surely bring tears to Amelia's eyes rather than lift her spirits after all Viking wedding and Christian weddings were two completely different events. Freya would need a lot of help to make this happen the right way, filling an empty basket with some barley bread, butters, jam and some wine Freya left for her room once more. Finn had been snoring quite loudly when she returned so much so that she could hear him while approaching the door. Upon entering the room, Freya noticed Christian had followed her back in, Finn had thrown him out earlier as he had tried to mount him on the bed, tail wagging he pranced over to the bed and lay down beside a sleeping Finn. Freya opened a small case on her desk and took out a set of keys, she then marched over towards a large wooden chest at the foot of her bed and opened it. Inside lay the finest silks of gold, blue, greens and plums she often used to make her own garments, although now a ruler of her own kingdom Freya had never forgot her modest upbringing. She remembered watching her mother as she put together some breath taking garments from just a few materials, after Catherine passed, Clara took over as her mother figure she thought her how to heal and help others she also thought her how to cook and tend to a house hold all the life skills Freya had learned had come from her aunt, who she felt blessed to have in her life. Picking up a large sky blue roll of silk. Freya approached her window and measured up the material to the width of the window. She knew with silk this fine you could see through, that the light of the sun could give a room that beautiful blue tint, blue had been the colour of purity for the Christians however Freya herself had never been fond of the large blue dresses she had seen high born ladies wear on their wedding day, she figured this was she could keep it traditional for Amelia, if she made her dress white it would look blue until she left the room she was to be married in. Then it hit her I have no monk or priest the thought horrified her, how could there be a Christian wedding without a holy man to marry them? That would not do at all. A large snort came from her bed, she looked up to find Finn had rolled himself onto his side and had Christian trapped under his arm. Freya fought back the laughter as she looked upon her confused dogs face, he didn't seem to mind so much after a moment he closed his eyes and went to sleep.

After a short time of cutting layers the blue silk to an appropriate size, a hesitant knock came at the door. Freya quickly ran over to open the door, to her delight Cara-Lea was standing on the other side.

'Come in,' she said gleefully, ushering her friend into the room. 'How are you?' Freya asked kindly.

'Very well, that's kind of you to ask. I just stopped by to see how you are,' Cara lea replied looking sideways at her brother who had been wrapped around one of Freya's hounds. Freya noted Cara-Lea's bemused expression and giggled.

'I am doing much better now thanks to yourself and Clara. That's a long story on the other hand,' Freya pointed at Finn. 'I wonder if he will be that comfortable when he realises its Christian he is sleeping on, I knew I had a lot of hair but…' Freya shot Cara-Lea a playful grin.

'What's all this?' Cara-Lea asked curiously staring at the cut up silks laying on the floor.

'I have been informed that my brother wanted to do your family a kindness and put on the wedding Nicholas never had' Freya began formally. 'However Asger would not know his arse from his elbow when it comes to any Christian traditions, weddings or otherwise. So I have taking it upon myself to organise it considering I cannot do much else in this state anyway. The only problem is it dawned on me I have no priest or monks here they all live outside the walls and I don't dare send my brother or any of the Norsemen they would sooner rob them then bring them back to me,' Freya's mouth pressed into a hard line.

'You are very kind Freya, after everything you have been through no one expects you to go out of your way for us, you have already taken us in, you brought our father back to us, it is us who should be trying to please you,' Cara-Lea's voice cracked a little as she spoke. 'Are they Finns clothes?' she asked grinning from ear to ear.

'They are, you know how bad corsets are, I wouldn't dare to put one on right now I would break another few ribs,' Freya laughed for a second then quickly brought her arm up to her chest.

'Clara said you will feel like this for a while,' Cara-Lea's voice saddened looking at her friend's discomfort.

'Believe it or not I have felt a lot worse than this, you should have seen what state I was in when I came to rule here,' Freya could feel her heart race just thinking about past events.

'I cannot imagine the horrors you faced here, I don't know how you do it, live in the same place you were nearly killed,' Cara-Lea frowned at the thought.

'Roderick was the epitome of evil, if the devil had a face it was his. He raped his servants and the small folk, tore the babes from their bellies and left them to die because it amused him. He had the coal boy sent to the rack where he personally inflicted endless hours of cruelty on him because he took too long filling up a bucket, after every bone in his body was shattered he proceeded to disembowel him while he was still alive, he was only about your age still just a boy not even a man grown. The screaming still haunts me. The simple answer is I took his life to spare my own, but I did it to spare every one of these people that remain here at Rosefort. I knew he wanted to kill me, he would have preferred I sired an heir for him first he wanted me dead to claim my families rightful kingdom, the truth is I found out about his plans before he had me attacked and I made sure he found out I would have rather died than to produce an heir for that monster, turns out the only one that had to die was him,' Freya's words were filled with venom, she could feel her blood boil remembering the beast she was to wed, she could see how upset the thought was making Cara-Lea. 'Don't fret he cannot come back and if Draconian thought me anything, it is no matter how bleak your circumstances appear they can always get better, right now it's just set back we will win this fight you'll see we always do,' Freya reassured her.

'I know, it's just so hard to stay positive with so much suffering,' Cara-Lea pleaded.

'Without suffering there would be no compassion, at the darkest times you will find it takes just one flicker of light, just one little flicker most people will overlook can turn into a light that shines so bright you can see it to the ends of the earth. There is a great deal of darkness in the world, more bad than good it can seem at times but we must not give up hope. For me even in my darkest hour my faith gave me strength I never thought I had, faith in God, in humanity that faith gave me hope, the hope gave me the strength to fight back and with that every other good person I met joined with me and has never left my side and I stand here in front of you because of them.' Freya thought of Drew, Asger, Gilli, Nari, Bartholomew, Bjorn, Clara and Henry those who stood with her through the worst.

'But if the traitor lives amongst us?' Cara-Lea asked.

'Then we will deal with him, I can forgive many things but putting the lives of those I love in peril is not something I will forgive. The Preston's called us beasts, monsters, animals. I will show how much of a beast I can be when I find out who sold us out.' Cara-Lea grinned at Freya's words. 'What? You don't believe me?' Freya asked.

'It's not that, you sound so much like Finn when you say things like that,' Cara-Lea giggled causing Freya to smile.

Cara-Lea helped Freya cut up large layers of blue silk, they used up about half of the roll before Freya pulled out the gold and start cutting up large layers equal to the blue.

'About the priest,' Cara-Lea spoke hesitantly. 'I could go tomorrow if you would like? Outside the walls I mean to find one for the wedding.' Freya stopped what she was doing for a moment.

'It is dangerous outside these walls now, those bandits could still be lurking waiting to strike. But I do need a holy man and God knows I'm in no shape to so much as leave the castle at the moment. If you must go bring Andrew, I trust him with my life and he can protect you if anything goes wrong. No doubt Asher and Koi will want to go too they seem very attached to him.' Freya beamed at Cara-Lea noticing her cheeks flush as she mentioned Andrew. 'You like him?' Freya asked in a giddy voice.

'What no, I… We…we are just friends,' Cara-Lea gushed.

'You have to admit he is quite handsome,' said Freya. Tripping over her tongue for words to say Cara-Lea's face turned crimson as she looked over at her sleeping brother. 'Don't worry, I won't tell him,' Freya reassured.

'Tell who?' Cara-Lea looked shocked.

'Either of them,' Freya said giggling.

A large groan came from the bed Freya peaked up to see if they had woke Finn, Freya's eyes widened and her an awkward smile appeared on her face that Cara-Lea noticed almost immediately. Cara-Lea turned to see what Freya was grinning at, to notice Finn had rolled to the other side of the bed losing his bed furs under Christian and was now sleeping stark naked, she turned away in shock, while Freya fought to contain the laughter that had hit her seeing the shocked and embarrassed look on Cara-Lea's face.

'I'd better be off now,' she muttered keeping her head down and walked almost crab like out of Freya's chambers to avoid seeing any more of her brother than she need to. After she left Freya burst out laughing hurting her ribs and waking Finn.

'What's so funny?' he asked sleepily.

'Your poor sister,' Freya cackled.

'What about her?' Finn asked lifting his head up from the bed, it was then he realised he had not been covered up. He turned quickly to see Christian lying on the bed furs then he looked up at Freya who walked back to the silks, crying with the laughter.

After a few minutes of hearing Freya snigger to herself, Finn decided she was calmed down enough to get up from the bed.

'Are they my clothes?' he asked, standing before her in all his glory.

'They are,' Freya answered red faced from all the laughing she stood up to pour herself a horn of wine. Finn walked over to lock the door of the chambers once more. 'What are you doing?' Freya asked.

'Protecting your modesty,' Finn answered, Freya cocked her head confused. Without another word, Finn charged at Freya who turned and ran off giggling trying to dodge his advances.

The next day Finn convinced Freya to leave the castle with him and get some air. Her face was no longer swollen but still bruised, she held onto Finns arm for support as her legs trembled from time to time from her injuries. They walked towards the barracks where Asger was training the new male recruits. Freya interrupted her brother's lessons to call him to her.

'To what do I owe the pleasure dear sister?' Asger asked, glad to see his sister was healing up well.

'I asked Cara-Lea to go find me a man of God today, which means she has to leave the safety of the walls with Andrew escorting her,' Freya explained.

'And you want me to go ahead and make sure there are no nasty surprises hiding out there for them?' he replied.

'Exactly,' Freya beamed.

Asger turned to his men. 'You, you and you panic…you two come with me.' he said pointing at Gilli and Nari leaving behind a front line of confused men. It was not long before Henry stepped in to finish his nephew's job at training the men.

Freya turned to Finn. 'I want to go to the tradesmen by the first wall,' she told him.

'I'll go get Luna,' Finn replied quickly turning for the barn Luna now called home. Freya could rest easy now she would know where Finn is, be able to gather supplies for the wedding and ensure Cara-Lea and Andrew's safety on their journey today. With Theodore looking after the political parts of her Kingdom for her, she finally felt safe enough to take in a breath, relax and enjoy the moment of having her loved ones around her.

Cara-Lea

Drew knew all the shortcuts in and out of Rosefort, they were outside the third wall faster than she had anticipated. She had not paid much attention to the difference beyond the walls when she first arrived grieving for her family and home. Outside Rosefort was mainly all forest there was one large road leading to the docks that she travelled on not so long ago. She watched as Asher and Koi along with Rosemary ran off into the trees like giddy children.

'They do that a lot,' Drew reassured her. 'But they always find their way back.' he promised. 'Freya wants us to bring back a holy man to perform the marriage ceremony, with any luck I find a monk first,' Drew continued.

'Why a monk?' Cara-Lea asked.

'I don't like priests, a man in a dress telling you what to do, and if you don't agree with them you're going to hell, no thank you. All they while they are more corrupt then the men they look down their noses on. They stay in luxury and pretend they deserve it, big feasts, fine wines, gold chalices and the rest and what do they do to the common man? Tell them how disgraceful they are by doing what they need to, to survive, I have never seen one bring in a hungry family or a beggar off the streets and feed them. I would rather a monk at least they're not hypocrites.' There was a silence for a few moment Cara-Lea had never thought about it like that before, then again she was a high born girl, she was never in a situation like Drew was describing.

'A monk it is, so where are the monasteries?' she asked.

'We follow the two laughing boys and the rustling bushes, they know the way,' said Drew.

They walked for miles, passed babbling brooks, pushed through brambles and mud roads that sucked their feet down into the ground.

'What is your story?' Cara-Lea asked on a whim.

‘What do you mean?’ Drew asked intrigued.

‘I mean I really don’t know that much about you, do I? Since I arrived I have only known you to be Freya’s right hand man and a dear friend of hers but how did that come to be? Where are your family? Have you always served Freya? Where did you learn to fight? And what is going on with you and that Emery girl?’ Cara-Lea’s voice sounded frustrated but it was hard for Drew to tell if it was because of her questions, or because she was trying to keep her shoes attached to her as she got pulled down in the mud.

‘My mother and brothers were killed a long time ago under Draconian’s rule. My father well that’s a good question I never knew him, he left when I was still very young and never returned. Freya found me dying one day I had escaped from the raids, I was starving had not eaten in weeks and was convinced I was going to freeze to death, or be taken by some beast as dinner. After taken me in, Clara worked her magic and Freya seen to it that I was fed and clothed with a roof over my head, Bjorn took a liking to me and sent me to train with her uncle Henry for a time. As for Emery I have obviously known for a long time since I did live under her father’s thumb for quite some time, she is a girl who is used to getting her way and does not like to be told no, I returned to Bjorn after my training and he took me in as another son. When you’re a boy your father, the man who teaches you who you are, mine was never there if it wasn’t for Freya and Bjorn I would have died a lowly peasant boy with no name in the woods, I doubt anyone would have even found me after a time. My loyalty is with Freya and always will be,’ Drew explained.

‘You love her?’ Cara-Lea asked.

‘I do, I always have and I always will but not in the way you’re thinking. It is true Freya’s unique, unlike any other there is no question but she’s like my sister, she’s a good friend. I may seem overprotective at times but she hasn’t exactly had the best of luck with suitors. I’ll admit I was sceptical of your brother, I was even the one who warned her about him, I never dreamt she would return with him. But she reassured me after a while that he was more than his stories and in seeing it first-hand she was right. I have never trusted a soul with Freya, she is the only family that I have but Finn is the only person who has shown that he is worth taking the risk on.' Cara-Lea smiled to herself, she had been so engrossed in her conversation she had not realised she was walking on solid ground once again.

'Finn has a lot of stories that follow him, most of which are true if not all of them, but those that you hear are only one sided. Out of everyone in the family he is the one I run to when I need protecting. The others will fight and die to protect the family but Finn is different it's hard to explain, it's like if anything truly terrible happened to any of us and we needed him he would never stop to sleep or eat he would just keep going until he got us and got us safe. It is like he is not human half the time,' Cara-Lea had a bemused expression etched on her face.

Drew laughed. 'I have to admit he has traits that would resemble that of the Norsemen and Berserkers, the temper for one from what I have heard and the unwillingness to die easily is another.' Finally arriving through the trees and mud Cara-Lea looked down to find she was covered from her feet to her knees in mud.

'Over here!' Asher called waving from a stone wall a few feet ahead. They had reached the monastery at last now it was the difficult part trying to convince a monk to come back with them.

As they walked into the grounds of the monastery a handful of monks saw Drew and froze out of fear, some ran thinking they were there to raid them.

'It's ok we mean you no harm,' Cara-Lea called. 'We are looking to find a man of God to come back to Rosefort with us there are many people there in need of guidance, we have no church, no priests or monks and a lot of devout Christians with no one to turn to,' said Cara-Lea.

A young man looked nervously around him at his brothers all of which looked on in silence. Cara-Lea looked confused as no one came forward to offer help.

'Right so your way failed, my turn,' Drew announced as he approached the flock on monks huddled together. He paced up and down observing them in silence, some men coward at the sight of the giant walking in front of them. 'You'll do,' he said picking up the young monk and turning for the gate.

'Andrew!' Cara-Lea asked stunned.

'He'll be fine, no one volunteered so I made it easy for them,' Drew replied, as he marched out the gate with the young monk slung over his shoulder. Asher grabbed a bible and ran quickly behind Drew, while Koi had been filling his pockets with prayer beads and crosses. When he could fit no more in, Koi ran off giggling and shouted for Drew and Asher to wait for him. Cara-Lea stood speechless staring at the monks who had been left behind.

'I am so sorry about that but we need him, I promise no harm will come to him,' she could feel the blood rush to her face as she took off embarrassed chasing after the young monks kidnappers.

'Are you mad?' Cara-Lea screeched at Drew. 'You just kidnapped a monk,' she panted running up towards him.

'Well I didn't see anyone volunteering to come so I took one, they have plenty left behind,' Drew reassured her.

'That is not the point,' she barked as she looked at the man been carried like a bold child back to Rosefort. He was mumbling something in Latin, a prayer more than likely. 'I am so sorry,' Cara-Lea said to the man who stopped to look up at the breathless girl observing him. 'I promise people are more civilised back at Rosefort,' she continued.

'What do we call this one?' Drew asked as he adjusted the man on his shoulder.

'My name is Gregor,' the monk mumbled frightened.

'It is nice to meet you Gregor,' Cara-Lea said kindly. The words had barely passed her lips when she could hear a roar of laughter coming from the two dwarfs behind her. 'You two are no better,' she snapped. 'Stealing from a monastery of all things.' Both men looked at each other smirking.

'We didn't steal, we borrowed,' said Koi.

'Yeah, how would a monk be any good to us without his bible and beads, you don't want the people thinking you just paid someone to pretend to be a monk you need proof he is one,' said Asher.

'He speaks Latin how many people other than those of God do you know to speak in that tongue,' Cara-Lea said.

'She has a point,' Koi looked at Asher who was clutching onto the bible.

'Oh no, you are not blaming this on me I only took a book, look what you took,' Asher pointed to Koi's pockets.

'Me? At least I didn't kidnap a monk,' Koi said, looking towards Drew. Both men start to laugh yet again and quickly ran ahead disappearing into the forest once more.

'I'm starting to think there is something not quite right with them.' Cara-Lea said as she looked on in the direction they ran.

After hours of walking, they finally made it back to Rosefort.

'I am starving, I hope it's nearly supper time,' she said rubbing her stomach.

As they made their way into the castle Cara-Lea noticed Freya standing outside the great hall with Finn. As they approached Freya had turned to notice their arrival.

'Well what have we got here?' Finn asked looking at Drew who had still been carrying the monk.

'Andrew is that any way to treat a guest?' Freya asked grinning.

Drew lowered Gregor to his feet, the monk stared nervously at Freya and Finn.

'Please do excuse our appearance, we have had a bit of trouble around here as of late, but worry not it has been taken care of, you will be perfectly safe here,' Freya gave Gregor a kind smile which seemed to have put the man somewhat at ease. 'Come you must be famished, we will have you fed then show you to your new chambers. I apologise for the lack of church the last Lord of Rosefort was far from godly he had everything that symbolised hope for the people destroyed, we are working on rebuilding the land to its former glory,' Freya explained as she led the monk into the great hall by the arm.

'Is that any way for a young lady to look?' Finn said in jest, looking at Cara-Lea's shabby appearance.

'I care not how I look right now brother, as long as I get some food in my belly soon. I have not eaten a thing since breakfast.' Cara-Lea replied pushing past her brother into the great hall.

She was famished waiting on the food to be served, she felt cold and slightly light headed and had never been as unkempt in all her years as she had been in her short stay at Rosefort but for once she felt pride within herself. Cara-Lea always wanted to help others, to be more than just a pretty face in a crowd now she was doing it little by little she was doing something useful with her life. She would have her meal, go wash up and fall into her bed tonight with a sense of accomplishment.

Ian Francis

The sea had been rough the past few days, rocking the ship to the point he was certain it would capsize. Finally to his amazement they had arrived, able to dock their ships at Lilly Patch, Ian sent for Annabelle Preston, who had been sleeping in a cabin below deck. She emerged a short time later groggy and nauseas, no doubt from their unpleasant journey.

'Well I got you here, now where's my pay?' Ian asked impatiently.

'We are not there yet, the deal was you take me to Rosefort then you get paid,' she answered stubbornly.

'It's not far from here, you'll be there before nightfall,' said Ian.

'Good, then you'll be paid before the day is out,' Annabelle replied marching off the ship.

Ian looked on in shock for a moment before running after the high born Preston girl.

'Look Lady, I don't know what you expect me to do, if you are right and your sister lives with them and has not been butchered like a pig for what your family done to the Olden's and the Vikings then maybe you have a chance in there. Maybe they will even take you in and protect you like you hoped, but if they see me I am as good as dead. I helped capture them remember, I am the reason their families have been killed, they will boil me in oil or feed me to the wolves while my heart still beats in my chest.' Annabelle looked at the mercenary amused.

'Is that what you are worried about? I will explain to my sister that you helped me escape the clutches of my brothers and yes, you aided in the capture of many people but you were not the one to torture Bjorn those men are dead, you know my brother's plans, you know how many men he has and what houses joined with them. They will not kill you while you can be of help.'

‘So I help them and then they kill me that’s much more comforting,’ Ian said sardonically.

As Ian as his men made their way towards Rosefort nervously, they watched as Annabelle Preston marched on like a warrior into battle.

‘Look at her prancing ahead with her head held high like she was the queen of fucking Sheba,’ Alan Roberts announced to the men.

‘Why shouldn’t she hold her head high, after all she is the only one here not guaranteed to have it cut off?’ Ian replied.

‘It’s a bit quiet around here, too quiet for my liking,’ said Alan.

‘You think that after what happened, they would be more on guard?’ Asked Iwan Fitzmaurice, a young mercenary who had fought with both men for the past four years.

‘I think they are, it’s too eerie out here I have a feeling we are being watched,’ Ian answered cautiously glancing around without making it look too obvious.

‘An ambush? What do we do if you’re right?’ asked Alan.

‘That depends on whose trap it is we have just walked into,’ Ian replied.

Rounding the mountain side which led into one of the many forests in the land, the group had to condense to two men abreast as the roads where narrow. The trees shook in the wind, the shrubbery rustled and the ground slowly sucked their feet into the mud, it was hard to hear if they were being followed. Iwan had slowed down to help Annabelle through the grounds as the rest of the men trudged on. Hearing a whistle Ian turned in the direction of the noise, with that he and his men were raised off the ground with great speed. When he realised what had happened it was too late, they had been caught in a net and every one of the men who had been armed had dropped their swords when they set the trap off.

It wasn’t long before two halflings jumped out of the bushes shouting. They had been armed with spares, Ian watched as they picked up the weapons that had been dropped and examined them.

‘For goodness sake,’ Annabelle pouted. ‘You there,’ she called. ‘Let us down this instant,’ she demanded. Both men turned to look up at her.

'Oh, we'll let you down alright,' one said.

'Just as soon as the Kludde gets here,' the other smirked.

'The Kludde? I take it you know the Olden's then?' said Ian. A look of surprise came across their faces. 'What do you know of the Oldens?' one asked.

'I know this right here is Annabelle Preston, her sister was to wed Nicholas Olden. We have travelled here to give her safe passage to her sister.'

'If you're Amelia's sister, prove it, what's her middle name?' One of the men asked.

'Elizabeth,' Annabelle answered proudly.

Ian could hear the two dwarfs muttering.

'Is that true?' one of them asked.

'I don't know I never asked her,' the other replied.

'She seems pretty sure,' a voice called from a short distance away.

'Koi! Asher!' both men seemed excited as they looked on at a man emerging from the gathering of trees and shrubbery.

'What have you been told about staying close to the group?' The man asked the two dwarfs.

'Sorry, but we found these in our trap and they say they know the Olden's.' Ian watched as the man turned to look at the net.

'Nari?' Annabelle asked. 'It is you,' she said after a moment her voice excited.

'Annabelle?' Nari asked surprised. 'What are you doing here?'

'Escaping my brothers,' she replied.

Nari had cut them down and offered to walk them to Rosefort. Koi and Asher refused to hand over the weapons and ran off towards the others who had been waiting for them up ahead. Annabelle knew only two as Ian listened to her talk she had known the man who found them and she knew one of the archers that had been waiting to see where their men had disappeared too. Gilli, the archer, seemed to be more suspicious and on guard of them then Nari had been. He had walked behind the group with his weapons at the ready along with two other men Ian heard them being referred to as Thorvard and Edgar. Nari walked alongside Annabelle leading her by the arm while Koi and Asher had run ahead excited that their trap actually worked.

When they reached Rosefort, the sun had been starting to set Ian tried to take the image in as he feared it would be the last sunset he would ever see. They passed through one isolated gate after another, at each one he was convinced they would be shot down. Eventually being marched into the castle, Ian felt his heart beat in his chest so hard he thought it would break through to the surface. The waited in silence in the throne room as the two dwarfs ran off to fetch Freya. The throne room was exquisite it had red and gold painted walls with a large gold Chandelier that hung gracefully from the ceiling. Two thrones set side by side at the top on the room both gold with red material crafted into them. A large red drape fell from the ceiling behind the thrones and fell gracefully behind them onto the steps on the floor beneath. A large red carpet filled the middle of the room from the doorway to the steps that led to the thrones. Gold carvings were etched into the white marble ceiling and the Raghnall banner hung proudly on both sides of the room.

The doors opened as Freya was announced, the two dwarfs ran in excitedly ahead of her with a pig quickly following at their heels, they stepped to the side when they reached the bottom step which led to the thrones. Freya walked in eloquently, she had been badly bruised from what Ian could see. A surge of guilt rushed over him, he had been paid to capture Freya and her father, he had killed people in the past that much was true but torture was never something he was comfortable with. Ian would often take lives and not think twice about the person but when he was paid to kill he would make sure it was quick. Two men walked on either side of Freya, one was a beast of a man, built like a bear and just as tall with shoulder length black hair and a tightly trimmed beard he was wearing a loose white tunic and black britches with matching boots. Ian had remembered him, he was captured alongside Freya and Bjorn by another group of mercenaries, it had been a much easier task than they had thought it would be, however, Ian had expected the man wanted to be captured, he had fought many men in his life to know a man of that stature was not so easily defeated. The man to Freya's left Ian knew without giving him a second glance, he would never forget Finn Olden's face. He had witnessed him in the past, in bar brawls and heard the stories of him in battle. He was known as a man who could not be killed yet today his injuries were evident, he walked with a slight limp his body battered and bruised like Freya's and yet he walked with a sense of purpose. Finn held himself well, and although he must have been in a lot of pain he did not show it his stern expression on approach to the steps of the throne had many of the men intimidated. Ian was not surprised looking at the other mercenaries after all many had tried to kill that man and everyone who had tried had been killed. Ian watched as the men separated and stood either side of the steps, guarding the Viking girl. Finn had been shorter than the other man but if anything he looked more aggressive. Freya took her seat on the larger of the two thrones and stared at the group in front of her without saying a word.

'My lady, we came across this group on duty they claim to be here to see the lady Amelia,' said Asher.

'What is it you want with Amelia?' Freya asked coldly.

Ian watched as Annabelle pushed her way through the men to the top of the group.

'Freya, do you remember me?' she asked.

'Annabelle?' Freya answered concerned.

'I have come here to escape the clutches of my brothers, I knew not of their plan to attack house Olden and have been a prisoner in my own home for weeks. If I had stayed any longer they would have killed me, I came here seeking refuge for myself and these men who have delivered me here safely.' Freya paused and looked at the group that stood behind Annabelle.

'Why is it you think your brothers will try to kill you?' Freya asked glancing back at Annabelle.

'Because… I am with child.' Annabelle hung her head and for once she was not the confident girl Ian had agreed to bring to Rosefort.

'You think they will kill you because you will have a child out of wedlock?' Freya asked formally. 'They tried to have my sister killed for a lot less, that and it's not just the child that will guarantee my death, but it is who the Father is.' Freya glanced at Finn and back to Annabelle.

'And who is the Father?' Freya asked.

'Your brother, Asger.'

There was a silence in the throne room, one that she had never had before in her rule. Suddenly, all eyes were on Freya who had been obviously caught off guard. Ian watched as the

Viking girls face dropped at the news that her brother had sired an heir with the enemy.

'That's it we're fucked,' Alan whispered.

'I quite liked having a head,' Ian answered.

Freya stood from her throne and walked towards the crowd of mercenaries.

'I know these men,' her voice sent chills down Ian's spine. 'They were involved in the battle that had my father and I abducted.' her voice filled with venom. 'Why should I grant them refuge when I should have their heads?' she asked as she paced around them slowly.

'It is true these men were paid to fight for my brothers but they left his side when they discovered what kind of men they are, they have assured me that they want no part in my brother's plans and they wish to fight for you instead,' Annabelle pleaded.

'Why should I believe them?' Freya asked.

'If they were working for my brother, I would have been taken back and buried alive for even trying to leave, they offered me safe passage and have got me here in one piece as promised. They will be living under your watchful eye and I am sure if any of them prove to be anything but honourable to their word that you will see to it that they are punished accordingly.'

Ian watched as Freya walked away to seek council from her men, the more they turned to look at them the more he was sure he would never see the sun rise again. The archer marched over and readied his weapon while the large beast of a man approached. 'You lot, come with me. Any funny business and Gilli here will shoot the eyes out of every last one of you.' As they turned to follow the beast of a man Ian noticed a pack of hounds and wolves snarling at the doorway of the throne room, he was thankful that it was just them and not the Kludde. They must have agreed to spare the men if not he was sure they would have been dead by now but the question remained where were they being led to? And what was to happen to Annabelle who had been left behind in the throne room?

Nari

Watching the group of men being led out of the throne room, he waited patiently for Gilli to march up behind them. Gilli had his bow and arrow at the ready, pointing it towards the crowd of intimidated men that had been following Drew. Nari never understood how it was that Drew and Freya seemed to communicate with one another without ever saying a word.

'Where are you taking these men?' Nari asked Gilli.

'No idea, I'm just following Drew's lead here,' Gilli confessed.

'How is it he seems to be able to read Freya's mind? They never say anything in these situations yet know exactly what the other one is thinking?' Nari asked confused.

'You'll drive yourself mad trying to figure that out. No one knows not even Asger. Best to leave these things to them if they wanted us to know, I am sure they would have told us by now,' Gilli explained.

He had a point Freya was not one for keeping secrets from her men but even still Nari noticed that out of everyone, Drew seemed to be the only person she trusted completely.

'Do you think they ever?' he asked Gilli hesitantly.

'What Freya and Drew? No… I mean I don't think so they never let on if there was ever anything going on,' Gilli answered perplexed.

'Yeah, I suppose you're right, I guess nothing would be going on especially with Finn around,' Nari replied.

He followed Gilli to the tower, where all accused were kept for their crimes until sentencing. He had not stepped foot in here in two years. Rosefort was a rich land but since Freya took over the realm there were very few people left to it, after Roderick Draconian's reign of terror had slowly picked the people of the land off one by one and after the takeover all that rebelled or that had any loyalty to Draconian were put to death. There had been no need for the tower since then. Gilli and Nari watched in silence as Drew ordered the men to stand upright against the wall, for a moment Nari thought Gilli was going to have to execute them there and then but it seemed a bit drawn out for an order handed down by Freya. Having thought that these men were responsible in one way or another for the untimely death of Bjorn the Brave. Had she sent these men to be mentally tortured before putting them to death? It was true she seemed a bit unhinged since her father was murdered, at this point it would be of no surprise if she had turned sadistic towards anyone she considered her enemy.

The silence in the room was deafening. Some of the men look around frantically, it was obvious they were fearful while others stood like stone staring down the men that had lined them up. The tension in the room even had Nari on edge and he knew he would not be harmed, Drew stood centre of the room staring down the men. The tower door swung open, Nari jumped and quickly looked over at who entered the room to his surprise Beigarth had been the one sent here. Nari's blood ran cold he had not taken to the seer since his arrival at Rosefort. He watched as the walking corpse of a man approached the line up on mercenaries. He paced up and down the line occasionally, stopping at the odd man and examining him before moving on to the next. The room felt like ice, a cold chill ran down Nari's spine as he looked on, his fingertips grew numb with the cold. Glancing around at Gilli and Drew, he had seemed to be the only one effected by the chill.

'You there, why have you come here?' Beigarth's voice sent shivers down Nari's spine as he addressed one of the men.

'I came to bring the Lady Annabelle to her sister,' the man answered nervously.

'Surely you were paid for your efforts?' Beigarth asked amused.

'I was,' the man nodded.

'Then why stay?' Beigarth asked, slowly approaching the man.

'We have nowhere else to go,' the man explained.

'But you have a family Ian, a wife and a son, surely you have a home to go to?'

The man froze when he heard his name he did not respond just stared helplessly back into the dead doll like eyes that had been looking upon him. Beigarth turned for the door, Nari noticed a sickening smirk on his face as he walked away.

'I know why you are here, even if you do not. These men come here for sanctuary and it will be granted to you at a price. You must fight for Rosefort but you knew that already didn't you Ian.' Beigarth's voice made even Nari feel sick. 'These men will set you up in your new quarters. However I should warn you, rape is not condoned here for those of you who participate in the act and value your manhood, I suggest you take your knives and cut it off now, for it will be far more merciful than Freya if you are caught committing the crime. You know who you are,' Beigarth said facing the men once more, he quickly scanned the room once more before lifting his hood to shield his face and taking his leave.

The men were shown to the half built barracks, where they were shown their tents and left under Henrys supervision. Nari knew Henry too well, the man may be old but he was a force to be reckoned with. He would have the skilled berserker's on sight watching over the new recruits, they would be put through gruelling training starting before first light. They would be marched around in the cold and rain for hours, holding tree trunks above their heads some may even dislocate their shoulders from the weight they have to carry. They would run forty miles a day and if they could not run the whole way, they would be dragged by the other men. They would live on gruel for the next six weeks with four hours sleep a night in their bodies. Henry would break the men, everyone broke eventually Nari took three weeks for Henry to break, Asger took twelve weeks the longest anyone has ever gone until they hit breaking point. Some men were so broken they were only good enough to carry the banners and cook for the soldiers, the rest emerged vicious killers that would be trained up in hand to hand combat, swordsmanship, and archery everyone had a specialty but everyone knew how to use every weapon available to them. Henry separated his men into learned killers and born killers, it was no secret the born killers were his favourites Asger being the top one, Gilli and Nari where put into the learned killers they had developed the skills but they were more under developed than those who the bloodlust came naturally to. Looking across the barracks at the women training with the practise swords, Nari had noticed Emery who was by far the most skilled fighter out of them all, young Cara-Lea who seemed to be picking things up quickly, Amelia was also out training with the women to Nari's surprise she had been practising with Hawise. Hawise was a slender girl of average height with wavy dirty blonde hair and a long face. Her eyes were small, chocolate brown in colour and her lips thin. Nari had been in love with her since they came to Rosefort, she was skilled with a blade however Emery far surpassed her with her years of training on top of Hawise's year with the blade. A large shadow passed overhead distracting him from his thoughts, he looked up to see Luna flying above them, no doubt with Finn Olden on her back. Nari had not approved of the beast coming to live at Rosefort, Kluddes are dangerous, they are known to eat people and yet there it is, flying around without a care in the world from most of the townsfolk. He knew Freya would not listen to reason about the beast, after all she had brought wolves, wild boars and bears to Rosefort without one attack being had but this was different, no Berserker could transform into a Kludde, the other animals could not fly nor have a flame around its neck. Luna was here for one reason, to feed. Nari could not tell what made him more uncomfortable the seer or the Kludde, both made him feel uneasy and he would not trust either and now a Gogmagog was only days away from reaching them, this land was going to be a sanctuary for monsters, how could they possibly take charge of a kingdom with so many creatures taking up residence here?

Beigarth

Content with himself, Beigarth marched through the halls in search of Freya. He had tried the Throne room, to no avail she had already left, Asger and Annabelle were the only two left to the room and sticking around for that conversation was not something that had interested him. He tried her chambers, but when he arrived he found only Loki the puppy spread out in front of the fireplace, curled up with a piglet he knew only too well as Rosemary. It was true the dwarf seemed to take a liking to that little pig but for the life of him Beigarth could not figure out why. He searched every room in the castle, all but one the pantry. As he briskly walked to the far end of the castle, never minding the many wolf cubs and hounds running the halls, Beigarth had noticed every person he had passed had moved from his path quickly as if he was some beast sent to kill them.

A roar of laughter filled the cold stone corridor, the door to the pantry was half closed, but as he went to enter the room he had noticed a white substance on the floor. 'Flour?' He thought, as he slowly pushed the door open. Beigarth immediately noticed Theodore and Freya sitting down on the floor, there was something in between them that he could not make out from where he stood.

'Ah Beigarth! Can you do me the kindness of shutting the door please?' Freya asked light heartedly. Beigarth done as he was asked.

'There we are,' Theodore announced holding a small barrel. Beigarth looked at Freya to find her holding a young bear cub.

'He had got himself stuck in here trying to get to the jam inside,' she explained.

Koi and Asher ran out from behind a stack of shelves covered from head to toe in flour.

'The other one is free m'lady.' Asher said breathlessly.

‘Thank you boys!’ Freya replied amused, she then turned her attention to Beigarth, who knew she was waiting on his report on the mercenaries.

‘Those men will be of good use, to you my lady. They are intimidated of Drew and Finn so it would not hurt to keep them close by for the first while at least, however some men are less than noble there are a certain few who enjoy the raids and rape that comes with their line of work. I have warned them that none of that is condoned here,’ Beigarth said quite formally. Freya gave him a kind smile as she rose to her feet holding the bear cub.

‘Well done,’ she said, as she gazed around the room anxiously. ‘I have been meaning to talk to both of you for a while now, we all know open war is upon us and despite the fact that we are doing our best to keep things light around here until we get the numbers the people are no fools. Death is certain for many even if we miraculously get the advantage in numbers we will lose a lot of our own. With myself and Asger having the biggest targets on our backs we have a higher chance of being killed in battle. If I die out there, I want Rosefort to be under four rulers, should I die and Asger live I want him to be the commander of the army, he never wanted to rule but he can fight better than anyone I know. I want Finn as the face of the realm he has a name alone that will command respect and I trust him to make the right decisions by the people. Andrew is to take over the security of Rosefort, he knows these lands better than anyone and he can spot a weak point in our defence with little more than a glance, do not let his kindness fool you he is incredibly intelligent and a fierce warrior and Theodore I want you to be Finns hand. We both know he can fight but he has not got a head for politics or money, Nicholas was raised to be a Lord Finn was not you will need to take control of coin and pretty much anything else Finn will take no interest in.’ Beigarth nodded approvingly, Theodore smiled down at Freya searching for the words to say back to her.

‘And what should become of us?’ Koi asked.

‘If you die, surely we will have no place here?’ Asher asked mournfully. Freya turned to them giggling.

‘My friends, you will always have a place here, this is your home now, no one would dare put you out or risk having me come back to haunt them,’ she said reassuringly.

The door to the panty burst open. Gilli stood in the threshold, his normally bright complexion was now sullen and his skin had turned a grey like colour.

‘Gilli! What?’ Freya began.

‘There is no time, you must come with me,’ he ordered Freya, who quickly put down the bear cub and done as she was asked.

Asher, Koi and Theodore followed Freya down the hallway just as confused as she was. Beigarth knew what had happened, he had seen it happen and he had warned Freya. Today was the day that would set this war in motion. Before he knew it, they were marching through the town square a large crowd had been gathered around, they parted as Freya marched through them.

‘Bartholomew?’ Freya gasped as she seen her friends concerned expression.

He had been standing near a large chest that had been placed in the centre of the crowd.

‘I just arrived ahead of this being delivered, but I beg you please do not look inside that chest,’ the pain in his expression turned Freya’s stomach, she brushed past her friend and gazed upon the blue and brown chest that sat just beneath her feet. Blood ran down the sides of Beigarth could feel Freya’s heart stop as she realised what was in there. He could feel the shivers that crept down her spine and the hairs on her neck stand to attention. He wanted to shield her from this, but he knew he could not, all he could do is watch on and feel her pain that he wished he could take away. She opened the clasps on the chest, inhaling deeply before lifting the lid open. The smell of decay filled the air immediately causing some of the townsfolk to vomit, others cried out in horror, Bartholomew stood frozen looking upon his friend, waiting for a reaction. Beigarth watched as she stared blankly down at the chest, her father’s face was the only thing they had left intact. His body had been dismembered, maggots had been crawling along his body parts, Bjorn’s eyelids had been cut off so his blank stare was the first thing you could see when looking at the trunk. His famous red hair and beard lost in the swamp of blood and excrement that had purposely been thrown in to dishonour the noble Viking. Drew and Clara had pushed their way through the crowd, the normally joyful woman let out a cry, when she seen what lay in the trunk, her eyes filled with tears as she clutched her chest.

'Asger?' Freya asked turning slightly towards Drew.

'He has seen, he changed and took off out the gate somewhere,' Drew answered.

Freya turned towards the trunk again and slammed in shut. 'I want my father's remains cleaned, have a boat prepared for his send-off,' She demanded, right away the carpenters ran off to get started. Her voice was cold and her eyes blank and dark, the light behind them had gone out.

'Beigarth I want every person who fights for us in the throne room within the hour, Drew find my brother and bring him back to me in his human form.' With that the crowd dispersed, Gilli and Bartholomew carried the large chest behind Clara, Drew had called for the gates to be opened and left quickly. Beigarth had passed the order down to the soldiers to round up all who would fight for them as he quickly stalked after Freya.

Beigarth followed at a distance as to not alert Freya to his presence. She had marched back up through the castle coming out the other side, passed the strawberry fields and into a small woodland. She stood staring blankly for a moment, Beigarth took the opportunity to move closer to her. He had hidden behind a large tree and looked on patiently.

'I'm so sorry this happened to you, I'm sorry I could not stop it, I cannot break out there, not with a traitor still amongst us. But I swear to you I will avenge your death. It seems like just yesterday you told me how proud you were of how I have grown. You once asked me to forgive you for your mistakes but I couldn't. I never got to tell you I couldn't forgive you because there was nothing to forgive, you done everything for us, you gave up your title and home and humbled yourself as a farmer and trader. You protected us from everyone who had tried to harm us. You were not there when Mother had been killed but that was not your fault. You saved me from Roderick, you saved Asger's life by sending him away. When most men would rule after what happened, you stepped aside and gave me Rosefort. I thank you for all you've done Father, now you can be with the family, with Mother. Are you looking down upon me? Are they proud of who I am? I know I am just your little girl but I swear it by all that is and ever will be Mark Preston will die at my hands. It's so hard to say goodbye when it comes to this…but we will meet again someday. I no longer have you here for your guidance, I wish I could speak to you just one last time. I would have loved to see your reaction knowing Asger is to be a Father. I miss you every day so for now I say goodbye until we meet again. I love you Father and no matter what happens with me in life you will forever be in my heart.' Beigarth watched as tears fell from Freya's eyes and streamed down her face, he heard the cracking of her voice, the pain in her words filled him with sorrow to the point where he felt himself feeling choked up. To his surprise, for once he was not feeling Freya's sorrow but his own. It had seemed in the short time he had lived with her, he had grown to care about the girl. Beigarth carefully retreated from the woodland back towards the castle to give Freya some time alone before she had to be in the throne room. As he walked back he thought to himself, Freya is destined to perish in battle, one were Mark Preston survives. His mother always thought him not to meddle with what he has seen she said, 'Once there is death, there will always be death, no matter how much you might like to change it.' But what if knowing what he knows there was a way to change things. A way of making it that Freya can live and Mark Preston will die.

Nicholas

He watched as the throne room filled, with Berserkers, Vikings, and Christians. Everyone from Noble birth to the common peasant gathered. The room was covered in a sea of faces, which made it hard for him to pick out his own men from the rest. Amelia stood at his side clutching his arm, Nicholas could tell she was fearful, she did the very same thing on the journey to Rosefort after the Attacks on his home. The noise of the chatter in the throne room suddenly came to an abrupt halt. Silence fell, at first Nicholas thought it was Freya that had entered but on closer examination he turned to see Drew and Asger march towards the top of the room quickly followed by Beigarth and Finn. Finn marched through the room as if he was entering a great battle, examining the faces as he approached the top of the room, finally meeting Nicolas's gaze Finn moved towards his brother.

'Where is she?' Finn snapped.

'We're not sure, she took off shortly after, called for us all to be here within the hour,' Nicholas explained.

'Your girl is strong, she would not break even under the circumstances,' said Theodore.

'However one thing troubles me, what happened to the men that delivered the chest?' Amelia asked.

'You don't need to worry about them,' Finn replied coldly.

Nicholas knew what that meant. 'How did you know?' he asked.

'Asger,' Finn replied sharply before turning for the stairs where Drew and Asger waited.

The silence in the room was deafening, as the wait for Freya seemed to be endless. Eventually she was announced and quickly marched through the sea of faces towards her throne, but she never sat down, she stood staring blankly at all that had come. It was a shock for Nicholas to see her so expressionless, she looked almost cold as if she was made from stone.

'You all know why I brought you here today,' she began. 'Not so long ago my father was murdered, slaughtered like an animal by order of Mark Preston.'

Nicholas felt Amelia's grip tighten on his arm, he placed his hand on hers trying to be of some comfort.

'Today his remains were sent to me, to try and anger me enough that I march not only myself but everyone here today to our deaths. But that is not something I am going to allow to happen. My name is Freya Raghnall, daughter of Bjorn Raghnall, the rightful king to North Shore and I will have my vengeance. As some of you know there is a traitor that lives amongst us, this person is responsible for the ambush on my brother Asger and the Oldens, as well as the destruction of Castle Mourne and my father's death. Believe me, when I say we are getting so close to finding out who you are. My uncle tells me that not all men are working together, the Vikings don't like the Christians, the nobles look down on the peasants and the Berserkers don't like anyone. This will change, or those of you who are too stubborn to work together will be put to death. There is one sure fact, the Preston's hate every last one of us. Do you think they care that we are different religions or ranks in society? We are doing them a favour, fighting amongst ourselves. My brother is pagan and I a Christian, our mother was a berserker of not so noble background while my father heir to the throne. In our family alone we were divided with beliefs, if one family can put such differences aside and fight together surely you can, or it will all be your lives. Why should we make it easy for the enemy? Are you going to lay down and let them win?' A roar came from the crowd. 'Are you going to fight together and stand united?' Amelia jumped as another roar came from the crowd. It was the first time Nicholas had seen everyone agree. 'Good, because you are not alone in this war, we have allies Bartholomew here, has agreed to fight by our side as we speak two hundred of his finest men march to join us.' Another roar from the crowd followed Freya's words. This was great news indeed, Nicholas knew their numbers had depleted greatly in the past weeks.

The doors to the throne room swung open, everyone turned to see who had dared interrupt Freya at this time. Nicholas was horrified to see a large brute trying to squeeze through the doorway, he must have stood thirteen feet tall, his body rippled with strength. His face was hideously ugly, he was a terrifying creature indeed. Amelia's felt like they would pierce through Nicholas's skin, as her grasp tightened significantly. Nicholas had heard tales of these beasts they were said to be sons of demons with the strength of more than twenty men.

'Ah Shengis, I was starting to wonder when you would arrive,' Henry's voice echoed through the room, full of excitement. Freya calmly walked down towards the Brute. Nicholas watched as she curtsied to him.

'You're grace, I am Freya Raghnall, I thank you for taking the time to come here to Rosefort. Your journey must have been very tiresome. Come we have much to discuss.' Freya led the beast out of the throne room leaving everyone dumbfounded.

Asger dismissed everyone in the throne room and made his way to the barracks, no doubt training around here was going to be done far more often with much stricter rules to abide by.

'What do you think?' Finn asked Nicholas.

'I think I finally understand how Asher and Koi feel around us,' he answered.

'Oh yeah? Well if you feel like us, how do you think we feel?' Koi interrupted. 'She's probably going to have to feed that thing an entire farm as it is,' Koi continued.

'Rosemary!' Asher gasped running from the throne room. Koi rolled his eyes before following his friend.

'So… Freya seems to be taking things very well?' said Nicholas.

'I'm not so sure, she's good at wearing masks. How well would you take it if it was you that happened too?' Finn asked.

'You're right. Well at least some good came off today, we have more men riding for Rosefort as we speak and if Freya can charm the Gogmagog, we start with a huge advantage,' Nicholas could feel the relief in his voice at his words.

Cara-Lea appeared through the now dispersing crowd. 'Amelia can you come with me, I need to get you measured for your dress,' she asked kindly.

'What dress?' Amelia asked curiously.

'Your wedding dress, Freya has been organising the event for days we just got the material in, since our training is over for the day, we have time don't you think?' Cara-Lea gave Amelia and Nicholas a kind smile, she took Amelia's hand and led her away.

'How is she taking this?' Finn asked.

'Not so well, I think she fears Freya will want her head because of the actions of her brother,' Nicholas explained.

'She needn't worry. If every person was to be blamed on a family members actions I am sure we would all be dead by now,' Finn said reassuringly.

'That's true, you would have had us all at the end of the hangman's noose, with your past actions, I'm surprised you never made it there yourself,' Nicholas mocked.

'Came close a few times actually,' Finn joked. 'But every time they wanted me dead, they just looked at my face and said he's too devilishly handsome to kill.'

'You and your vanity brother, I will never know how Freya puts up with you,' Nicholas laughed.

'It's the face, I am sure of it,' Finn gave his brother a sly grin.

Both Finn and Nicholas made their way to the barracks where the men were in weapons training. Asger had always trained the berserkers as he could shape shift like them but today he had a mixed group. Nicholas looked on astonished at how the men were actually standing together training as one rather than in split groups. He listened as Asger explained the enemy to them, after spotting Finn and Nicholas he pulled them up to speak to the men.

'From what we have seen of you, and of the Prestons we can say it matters not, that some of you fight in armour, chainmail or even that others fight with no armour at all. You are all a target to them,' Nicholas began.

'They are cowards, dirty fighters so throw your rule book out the window, your weapons training is merely a guideline. Nicholas and I were unarmed when they first ambushed our home. Nicholas killed a man using only his hands and the floor below him. I had a chamber pot and a wall sconce while the man attacking had a sword. You need to look at everything as a weapon or your dead,' Finn continued looking at the line-up of men.

'The Preston's are cowards but that does not mean the same for their men and we know they have powerful allies, although we cannot confirm who that is just yet we cannot treat them as just the one threat. They will try provoke you and if they succeed, they have you trapped and you die. If you fight honourably you die, as much as I hate to say this our only advantage is your carnal instincts. They will expect us to fight a certain way, or at least those in armour who are known to them. You need to change your fighting style to win this thing, they know only traditional Anglo Saxon fighting styles they know little to nothing of the Norsemen or the Berserkers,' Nicholas explained.

'You need to fight like animals to win this, especially if numbers are against us, we can only guess what their numbers are and who they have fighting for them so always think of your numbers being less than theirs, it will give you that advantage to think ahead. For a man is only fighting a losing battle, when he has not prepared for the enemy. If the numbers are in their favour we make them come to us,' said Finn.

After talking to the men and leaving Asger to their training, the brothers took off for the castle once more.

'I was thinking, we cannot contribute many men since most were slaughtered in that ambush,' Nicholas began.

'Go on,' Finn replied.

'Well before Freya, were you not sleeping with one of the Whitmarsh girls?' Nicholas said raising an eyebrow at his brother.

'Have you lost your mind?' Finn snapped. 'You want me to go back to Elizabeth Whitmarsh? Have you met Freya?' Finn asked disgusted.

'I'm not saying take her to bed! I could see you being hung drawn and quartered for that.' Nicholas mocked.

'Hung, drawn and quartered would be a welcomed send-off compared to what she would do to me,' Finn warned.

'I am sure Freya knows all about your past indiscretions, it is not exactly your best kept secret little brother. Surely if it meant talking to Elizabeth, she could persuade her father to fight with us?' Nicholas reasoned.

'Freya may know about my past but that does not mean I need to bring it up and sit it under her nose. Did you not hear how she got out of those chains when she was captured? What she did to that man's throat?' Finn dropped his hand towards his groin.

'You are not afraid of a woman now, are you?' Nicholas asked mockingly.

'Any woman who can rip a man's throat out with just her teeth deserves to be feared. Can you imagine what she could do to the rest of you, if she is capable of that?' Finn's voice cracked. Nicholas laughed, continuing to walk ahead of his brother.

'We will find another way,' he said. 'I am sure somebody else here has ties with the Whitmarsh's. If we find out who, we can have them plead our case while you get to keep your cock attached,' Nicholas said smiling.

'That's all I ask, you may mock me but when it is your balls in a vice, I doubt you will be so eager,' said Finn.

Drew

Trudging through the rows of fields at the back of the castle, as much as he tried to distract himself with the beauty of his surroundings, Drew could not forget what he had seen today. Bjorn Raghnall was the father he never had. Bjorn was the one who raised him, thought him how to fight and what it meant to be a man.

He always said, 'These men that go around with a sense of entitlement, swinging their pricks around are not men. A real man is humble, that is not to say he cannot take pride in his achievements but there is a fine line between being proud of yourself and being full of arrogance. Arrogance is what will have you killed.' Bjorn's words ran through Drew's mind so clear, it was almost like he was standing in front of him speaking to him. He also remembered Bjorn's warning, that Drew may be blessed with his height build and strength and of course his ability to change form but he must only use that power when he needs to defend himself or those he loves. Most people saw Bjorn the brave and thought of a caged animal who had escaped, it was true he was a vicious man an absolute force if you went up against him but that was not the same man who took him in. The man that raised him was kind and full of life.

'What are you doing out here?' a voice called. Drew turned to see Gilli approach.

'Patrolling,' Drew answered simply.

'It has been a queer day, don't you think?' Gilli asked.

'Aye, that's one way to look at it. How is Asger?' Drew asked.

'Taking his aggression out on the men in the barracks. The poor bastards will be lucky if they can walk by sun rise,' Gilli mocked.

‘Shengis is proving to be quite the motivator already, I have never seen so many men on the verge of shitting themselves at once,’ Drew joked.

‘Whatever Freya’s plan is, it seems to be paying off so far? Honestly, I think she only brought him here so she can scare the traitor out of hiding. That and let’s face it no matter how many men the Preston’s have to fight for them one look at a herd of Gogmagogs and they’ll take off leaving a trail of scutter behind them for miles,’ Gilli laughed at the thought, for the first time today Drew felt himself smile. Gilli always had a way of making light of even the worst situations.

As they lost themselves in conversation walking back towards the castle Gilli noticed Finn and Nicholas.

‘What have you two been up to?’ he asked.

‘Checking out the barracks and generally pissing about’ Nicholas answered.

‘Would either of you know who, if anyone, is friendly with the Whitmarsh’s besides my brother that is?’ Nicholas went on.

‘I told you to drop it!’ Finn snapped.

‘Are we missing something here?’ Drew asked.

‘Genius here thinks we can convince the Whitmarsh’s to fight with us,’ Finn explained.

‘And what’s the problem?’ Gilli asked.

‘Finn bedding Elizabeth Whitmarsh quite regularly before Freya that is,’ Nicholas replied, searching Drew and Gilli for a reaction.

‘Does Freya know?’ Drew asked.

‘It doesn’t matter if she knows, or not if she finds out Finn’s been canoodling the Whitmarsh girl she will string him up by the bollocks,’ Gilli interrupted.

‘There is nothing going on, nor will there be with me and Elizabeth. That all ended when I met Freya,’ Finn demanded.

‘And he said that would happen anyway,’ Nicholas said in jest.

‘I think I heard Freya mention Bartholomew being acquainted with that house. Maybe he could convince them to fight alongside us, that way we get our numbers up, but the women of the house can stay back where they belong and away from Rosefort,’ Drew explained.

‘And Finn gets to keep his manhood, see all works out in the end,’ Gilli laughed.

‘We should go talk to Bartholomew, any idea’s where he may be?’ Nicholas asked.

‘No idea, he usually doesn’t stay here at all but with his men on the way I am assuming he will be setting up camp somewhere in Rosefort, best ask Freya,’ said Gilli.

‘Although, that’s easier said than done today of all days, the only one she has let near her so far is Shengis. Finn you would probably have the best chance approaching her right now, after all you do share a room now,’ Drew explained.

‘Technically he has his own room.’ Nicholas began.

‘I just choose not to sleep in it,’ Finn interrupted.

‘Until Freya locks you out of her chambers,’ Nicholas joked.

Tonight Dinner was sombre and quiet, unlike most other nights. The men who were trained ate inside, while those who were in training were stuck outside in the cold damp air with nothing but gruel to look forward to. Drew sat at the end of the table leaning onto his hand, staring down at his plate of pork pie which had been barely touched. He had not had much of an appetite, nor did he have a thirst for ale, his goblet remained full. He felt a gentle touch tap him on the shoulder, as he turned around, he noticed Cara-Lea placing herself in the seat next to him.

‘How are you feeling?’ she asked kindly.

‘Never better,’ Drew answered.

‘I doubt that, you have not touched your food, or your ale,’ Cara-Lea said concerned.

Drew picked up his goblet and drank the contents. ‘There you see, I was just a bit preoccupied,’ said Drew trying to shake off his mournful feelings.

‘You don’t have to lie to me, I know Bjorn meant the world to you.’ said Cara-Lea placing her hand on his.

‘I think we need more drinks,’ Drew said, calling for his goblet to be refilled.

‘I did not see Freya at dinner, I hope she is okay,’ Cara-Lea said concerned.

‘She is probably just having her meal in her private quarters tonight, after all that has happened I can’t blame her for wanting to be alone for a while,’ Drew said reassuringly.

As the night went on, the hall start to empty slowly but surely Drew had not touched his food but was making his way quickly through the ale. The night grew hazy with the large amounts of ale consumed. Awaking the next morning just as the sun had risen in the sky, Drew felt like he had been through the wars. His head felt like he had been punched repeatedly by Shengis and his stomach in knots. He sat up groggy in the bed, it took him a moment to realise he was naked, but that was not unusual of him after a night of too much ale he was seldom able to dress in his bed clothes. Feeling movement in the bed he glanced over to see a thick mass of dark hair in the bed next to him, had he brought Cara-Lea back to his chambers with him? Had she succumbed to the ale like himself and not realised what she was doing? How would he explain this to her? After all she was still very young and innocent. Drew cautiously reached for the bed covers and slowly drew them back from her face. He had looked on in surprise to find it was not Cara-Lea in his bed. The woman that lay beside him he had known for quite some time. How did this happen? How did he end up bringing her back to his chambers?

'Good morning handsome,' the young woman said with a lethargic voice.

'Morning Emery,' Drew replied, looking around for any indication of how he ended up in this mess.

Finn

Awaking to the light of the morning's sun, Finn wished he could stay in this moment. Freya was still sleeping in his arms. She looked so peaceful he dared not wake her, yesterday's events were sure to have taken their toll on her. They ate their meal in her private quarters, all the while she barely said a word. He dogs must have felt her pain as they were not their usual playful selves. They lay on the floor quietly, only moving when Freya did, they did not let her out of their sight, not that they ever did. She had gone to sleep in silence, as Finn lay behind her wrapping his arm around her waist trying to provide her with some sort of comfort. She never said a word, acknowledging his presence only by lacing her fingers between his and drifting off to sleep. Finn noticed when he woke that she was still clutching his hand. Slowly glancing over her shoulder, Finn noticed a hint of a smile on her face. He lay back down careful not to wake her, this was the happiest she was going to be for a while, he would not take these few moments away from her.

Finn had arranged for their breakfast to be brought up to Freya's private quarters this morning. He had also arranged the monk to come up to console Freya. She had spoken of how her faith had helped her through the dark times in her life, Finn had hoped that Gregor may be able to help her through the ordeal of losing her father in ways he himself could not.

Finn could hear the clanking of chalices and plates from the next room. No doubt the girls had been setting up their morning meal for them, with no concept of how noisy they actually were. Toby start growling at the noise, before Finn could tell him to stop, Captain Start barking loudly, waking Freya and almost deafening Finn as he was close to his head.

'What's going on?' Freya asked through a tired voice.

'I was trying to arrange a peaceful meal for you today, in your quarters but apparently nobody around here knows how to do things quietly,' said Finn, scowling at Captain who dropped his head.

'Thank you, but I really do not feel like eating right now,' Freya said turning back to her side.

'I understand this is hard for you, but you need to eat something even if it is only something small,' said Finn trying to reason with her. 'If you are feeling unwell after then come back to bed, I will take care of things today,' Finn placed a gentle kiss on Freya's shoulder, before sliding from the bed.

Finn dressed quickly, looking over at Freya's seemingly lifeless body in the bed, he knew he would have to force her up. He went and found a dress and carried it back to the bed.

'Come on now, you must eat,' he urged.

Freya stared blankly up at him refusing to move.

'I didn't want to do this but you left me no choice,' he said as he bent down and picked Freya up, carrying her through to the next room where their food had been awaiting them. Freya punched and yelled until Finn dropped her down in a chair.

'I said I am not hungry,' she barked.

'Tough, the food is here for you, now eat,' Finn snapped.

'I am not even dressed,' Freya yelled as she tried wrapping herself in her bed covers.

'Whose fault is that then?' asked Finn.

Freya rolled her eyes and scowled at him from across the table. 'Why are you even here? I don't want you here,' she snapped.

'Well we can't always get what we want,' said Finn brushing off her comments.

The table had been set with Freya's favourite breads along with jams and butters laid out for her to use. Finn had arranged her favourite deserts to be made and presented for her. There were bowls of fresh fruit dripping with honey, sweet custards and an assortment of strawberry, cherry, apple and plum tarts.

'You did this?' Freya asked in a more calm tone.

'I arranged it, yes,' Finn answered bluntly.

He could see Freya begin to weep, although she was trying her best to conceal it. Finn stood up, and walked around to her, kneeling at her feet he looked up at her. Freya tried to avoid his gaze as the tears streamed down her face. Wiping her tears away with his thumb, Finn forced her to meet his gaze.

'I'm sorry this happened, I'm sorry I wasn't there for it. I promised you I would never let you hurt again and I could not keep that promise. But I swear to you, when I get my hands on Mark Preston he is going to feel pain such as he has never even imagined,' Finn said calmly.

'I'm sorry for what I said. I don't know what to do, that was my father and I could not help him, I could not save him,' Freya said with the tears building up in her eyes at the thought.

'Listen to me, this was not your fault. Do not for a second think it was, this was his doing and only his. I swear to you I will make him pay.' Finn ran his hand from Freya's face to the back of her neck, he gently pulled her towards him and kissed her passionately.

The door opened as Drew cleared his voice. Finn turned towards him.

'Does nobody believe in knocking, around here?' he asked frustrated.

'I came to see how you are, I was worried,' Drew said to Freya, ignoring Finn's remarks. He closed the door behind him as he walked towards the table.

'Oh, do join us,' Finn said sarcastically as he seated himself at the table once more.

'Don't mind if I do,' Drew replied picking up a cherry tart.

'Please help yourself,' Freya signalled to Drew, there was plenty of food laid out at the table that they could spare to have one more person join them.

'So how are you?' Drew asked concerned.

'I'll be fine,' Freya said simply.

'Eat,' Finn said as he handed her a strawberry tart.

'So, was I right about the Whitmarsh house?' Drew asked turning to Finn.

'What about them?' Freya asked curious.

'Finn and Nicholas thought they would be good allies, a means of getting our numbers up for battle,' Drew explained.

'And?' Freya asked.

'We thought you might know of someone who is on good terms with them,' Finn said quickly.

'I suggested Bartholomew might, did you not once say he was associated with them?' Drew asked Freya.

'I did, but surely the Whitmarsh's would help out the Olden's if asked after all they were at your brother's feast were they not?' Freya asked Finn.

'Well…er…yes they were but you see, if I was to ask I fear it would not work out so well,' Finn explained.

'And why's that?' Freya asked.

'It involves one of the Whitmarsh girls, Elizabeth I believe,' Drew said grinning at Finn whose eyes had widened in his head and skin drained of all colour.

'Because Finn used to fuck her you mean,' said Freya.

'Exactly!' Drew agreed.

Finn looked on in horror. 'Not recently I haven't!' he demanded. Freya giggled at the sight of a gobsmacked Finn.

'You can calm down now, I am not going to have you sent off to be castrated and it was before our time after all,' Freya reasoned. 'I will speak to Bartholomew, I am sure if he can do anything to help, he will,' said Freya.

Finn was thankful Freya did not take offence to the news of his past with Elizabeth Whitmarsh, he took a large gulp of wine and stuffed a large piece of bread in his mouth.

'So Drew,' Finn began after swallowing the contents in his mouth. 'When were you going to tell Freya about you and Emery,' Finn asked with a mischievous grin on his face. Drew looked at Finn stunned.

'I obviously know about Andrew's past with Emery, Finn, it's not exactly a well-kept secret,' Freya explained sipping on her goblet of wine and picking at her bowl of honey covered fruit.

'That may be sweetheart, but I was referring to last night' said Finn sitting upright in his chair.

'How did you?' Drew began.

'You and Emery again? Andrew seriously, was it not messy enough the last time,' Freya asked.

'I don't know how it happened, I had drank too much ale on an empty stomach and blacked out. One minute I was in the Great hall will Cara-Lea the next I woke up next to Emery,' Drew explained.

'How did you know this?' Freya asked Finn.

'When I was going down to arrange this lovely meal last night, I seen him stumbling back to his room with Emery practically in his lap, you can thank your lucky stars that it was Emery and not my sister you brought back to your chambers,' Finn warned.

'Enough, Cara-Lea is nearly a woman grown, I am sure when she chooses a mate your approval will not mean so much to her, besides if that was the case she could do far worse than Andrew here. She could end up with someone exactly like you, or the way you used to be I should say,' Freya warned.

Finn looked at her not at all pleased. 'Well, this has been an eventful morning,' Finn said as he rose to his feet. 'I'm going to go see what other surprises are in store for me today, I may be lucky, Luna may try to devour me,' He said scowling at Freya, who was smirking up at him.

Finn marched from the castle, his little outburst reminded him he had to go and feed Luna before she decided to go find her own meal. As he arrived at her secluded barn with a wheelbarrow full of pigs and chickens, he heard her growls coming from within. Finn called out so she knew there was no threat. Opening the barn door Finn noticed her tail wagging frantically when she saw him.

'Here you go girl,' Finn said closing the barn door behind him and emptying out the carcases in front of her. Immediately she started ripping them apart, within a few short minutes there was no trace of any of the bodies that had been brought in to feed her. Finn rubbed her head. 'Good girl,' he repeated rubbing her behind her ears. Luna started to lean into Finn's leg. 'Easy' he warned, the beast acknowledging his voice sat upright 'That flame can burn me you know' he said pointing out the blue flame around Luna's neck. He walked to the side of her to inspect her injured wing. 'Healing up nicely, I must say,' Finn said rubbing her back. He could not explain it, it was true Luna saw him as her next meal when they first met, but they bonded very quickly after she decided not to eat him. Finn had a certain fondness for Luna and he had to admit, being the only person to ever tame a Kludde made him feel a great sense of achievement even if he could not explain how it was he tamed her. The same way Freya has seemingly tamed him. He knew his reputation would start to be torn down, but that did not matter to Finn he knew he did not have to prove himself anymore, for all those thinking he had gone soft, he knew they would be in for a big surprise if they were tempted to cross him. Having Luna around would keep people weary of him, that he knew. After all the two men that delivered the chest with Bjorn's remains came to an abrupt halt when Luna approached them, Asger killed one man in his animal form while Luna finished off the other who tried to escape. Finn knew there were more than likely scouts around spying on them, but no one dared to approach.

Finn was pulled from his thoughts as he heard a voice outside the barn frantically screaming his name. Finn ran outside to see Asher on the back of a hound that was running towards the barn, he looked panicked.

'Asher, what is it?' Finn asked concerned.

'Your sister, she's in trouble,' Asher yelled.

Finn took off running after the hound and the dwarf that had turned to run back across the farmland, eventually coming to the outskirts of the town square where nothing but derelict old houses stood, this part of town had been empty Rosefort was taken over by the Raghnall's. Hearing a scream come from one of the houses, Finn burst through the door without a second thought. Three of the mercenaries that had come to Rosefort were standing in the room one had Koi by the throat, it was obvious he was trying to help Cara-Lea, he looked badly beaten and his skin had been opened up just above his eye, Asher quickly ran over a bit the leg of the man holding his friend. The hound Asher had been riding on, had attacked the man nearest the door.

'There is nothing to see here,' the third called to Finn.

'Where's my sister?' Finn demanded.

'I don't know who,' the man began.

'Cara-Lea!' Finn called.

A loud crash came from the floor above.

'I didn't know she was your sister, I swear I never touched her' the man begged.

'Nor will you,' Finn barked.

Finn was unarmed, he noticed the man's hand reach for a dagger at the side of him. Finn launched himself at the mercenary dragging him to the ground. Asher's distraction had worked with the other man and Koi was now back on his feet. Asher had taken the mercenaries belt and now had it wrapped around his neck slowly lowering him to the floor, as Koi kicked at his legs. The hound continued to maul the third mercenary whose body no longer fought back, it was limp on the ground as the hound continued the assault. Finn had the mercenaries wrist in his grasp he continued to bang it off the ground trying to make him release the weapon. Ian Francis ran in through the doorway plunging his dagger into the mercenary's neck.

'Are you alright?' he asked Finn.

'My sister,' Finn gasped staggering to his feet.

'She's up there,' Koi shouted relentlessly kicking the mercenary that had beat him, while Asher maintained his grip on the belt around his neck. Ian bolted upstairs and Finn followed, he heard a sickening thud hit the ground. Cara-Lea came running down the stairs towards him.

'Finn!' she cried, throwing herself into her brother's arms.

'It's ok I'm here now,' he said reassuringly.

Finn walked his sister downstairs and not a moment too soon. They barely cleared the stairway when a body came tumbling down them. Finn approached the body, he recognised the man he was amongst the sea of new faces Annabelle brought with her to Rosefort, another mercenary.

'You tried to rape my sister,' Finn said coldly to the trampled man, whose only reply was to spit in his face. Finn dragged the mercenary to his feet. 'I could pop your eye out right here,' Finn threatened pressing the dagger under the mercenary's eye.

'I say bleed him like a pig, like his friend there,' Koi spat looking over at the man Ian Francis stabbed, that was still clinging to life as he bled out.

'Kill him Finn!' Cara-Lea demanded.

Ian's footsteps came down the staircase slowly.

'And what do you think?' Finn asked Ian.

'A quick death would be too good for the bastard,' Ian replied coldly.

'Very well, then,' Finn replied. 'You know you brought this on yourself, right,' said Finn, as he stared blankly into the mercenary's eyes.

Tightening his grip on the dagger Finn drove the blade through the mercenary's eye, the screams echoed loudly enough to serve as a warning to anyone within earshot not to make the same mistake. Ian handed over his dagger to Finn who took it and plunged it into the other eye. Koi and Asher searched the mercenary looking for another weapon, when they found it another dagger hiding in the back of his tucked in tunic. Finn took the blade and cut him from his groin to his stomach before pulling the blade away.

'I never liked him anyway,' Ian joked, walking towards the door.

'He'll be dead soon,' Koi spat struggling to follow.

Asher took Koi's arm and placed it over his head to help support his friend.

Finn turned to Cara-Lea, 'I'm sorry you had to see that.' he said.

'I'm not,' she replied 'the things he said they would do to me…with the blade,' she explained.

Finn felt his blood boil at the thought. 'I would never let that happen to you,' he promised. 'Here,' Finn said handing her the dagger.

'What's this for?' she asked.

'The next time someone tried to harm you, you drive that into their neck, or eye, or anywhere you can to get them away from you, understand?' said Finn.

'Where am I supposed to keep this?' Cara-Lea asked.

'No place, I want to know about,' Finn joked leading her out of the old house.

Finn took his sister and Koi to see Clara, he told her what had happened, and she assured him she would let Henry know at once. Back at the castle it was oddly quiet, there was no sign of Theodore, or Nicholas nor Drew or Freya, or even Gilli or Nari. Finn went to his chambers to clean up, he did not want to concern Freya with his appearance, he was scuffed up and his clothes bloody. Just as he was about to undress he heard a voice behind him.

'What happened?' Freya's voice asked coldly.

Finn turned to face her, he was trying to avoid upsetting her. 'Nothing that I couldn't take care of,' he answered bluntly.

'Don't!' she warned. 'Don't try to brush this off, four men are dead, murdered brutally now what happened,' Freya snapped.

'It wasn't that brutal,' said Finn.

'I seen the bodies Finn!' said Freya.

‘Okay, you want to know what happened, those mercenaries tried to rape my sister. Asher and Koi seen them advance on her and pull her into the derelict part of town, Asher came to get me while Koi went to try stop them. When I got there I couldn’t find Cara-Lea and Koi was beaten badly,’ Finn explained.

‘Then how did you get out alive and they were butchered?’ Freya asked.

‘One of the hounds attacked the one nearest the door, Asher and Koi teamed up on another, while I was left to struggle with the third. Then that mercenary Ian came in, he must have heard the commotion, he helped me then ran up to save Cara-Lea before I could. When she was safe and that one was left…I knew what he would have done to her, or you or any other woman if he got the chance, men like that don’t just rape a woman Freya, they torture them before they kill them,’ Finn explained.

‘So you took it upon yourself to butcher him first,’ she said coldly.

‘I’m not sorry, I would do it again. If you want to arrest me or have me put to death go ahead but you knew what I was when you met me,’ Finn said.

He felt defeated, there was no way Freya would look at him the same. She would only see another monster like the kind that slaughtered her father. Sitting on his bed, Finn placed his head between his hands. Freya said nothing, for what felt like forever. She stood still staring at him, Finn felt her eyes burn a hole right through him. Freya approached Finn, hearing her footsteps walk towards him, he looked up not sure what to expect he knew it would not be good. Finn met her gaze as she stood above him, to his surprise, her eyes were no longer cold and the hurt that he had seen in them earlier that day had also disappeared. He knew that look, it was the same one she had given him the night he took her to the hot spring back home. It was the same look she gave the night he took her in the bath house. He stared at her in awe as she climbed onto his lap, he was not going to be punished but rewarded for his actions. Then he remembered what he had said Freya knew what he was, she had from the day they met, maybe even before. He no longer had to fear his temper around her, she accepted Finn the way he was, Freya knew he could commit savage acts to protect those he loved, she must have realised he would do the same for her. As she undressed his body,

Finn found himself lost in the moment. He had had many sexual conquests in his past but never had anyone lured him in like Freya, she had a passion about her that made it exciting leaving Finn always craving more. As her body pressed up against his, Finn lost himself in the euphoria of the moment, then a troubling thought hit him. If Freya could accept him knowing how violent he could be, what kind of woman did that make her?

Cara-Lea

Cara-Lea waited for Koi to finish being patched up by Clara.

'How are you feeling?' Asher asked kindly handing her a cup of wine.

I have had worse done,' she replied. 'Thank you, for finding Finn for me,' she said sweetly.

Asher blushed 'Of course, we couldn't let those fiends bring any harm to you.'

'I hope Koi is not too hurt,' her voice concerned.

'Koi, never. He's had far worse done to him than a bit of choking, in fact I think he enjoys that,' Asher joked.

'There now, good as new,' Clara's voice said gleefully from the next room.

A few moments later Koi emerged, his cuts were cleaned and he was bandaged above the eye. 'I'm so sorry this happened to you,' Cara-Lea felt her heart sink looking at the little man.

'I'm not, this will go over great with the ladies,' Koi joked. Cara-Lea bent down and kissed them both on the forehead.

'Shall we go eat?' Asher asked excitedly.

'That sounds like the best offer I have had all day,' said Koi.

'You two go on ahead, I'd better change first, I would not like to be seen in torn garments,' said Cara-Lea.

Back in her chambers, she stripped off her torn garments and examined her body, her neck was covered in rope burns from where the brute tried to choke her out. Her left breast had been bitten so hard she had the indentations of his rotten teeth embedded into her skin, she felt her face swollen from where she had been punched and slapped repeatedly. Her stomach felt sore from where she was punched, her legs were already starting to bruise. She noticed her thighs were discoloured, in parts from where she had been knelt on, kicked and pried at. Though her body was battered and bruised, she felt mentally and physically exhausted, Cara-Lea was thankful that she never stopped fighting. Thankful that Koi and Asher had followed her and forever grateful to them for finding Finn when they did.

Dressing in loose clothing, remembering how Freya did it after her attack. She fixed her hair and washed the blood off her face and hands. Proceeding to wipe the dagger her brother gave her clean, she placed it in the pocket of her garments and turned for the door. Walking down the long narrow corridor from her chambers, Cara-Lea did her best to hold her head high and not succumb to the pain of her injuries.

'Cara-Lea' a familiar voice called. Looking around she was greeted by Amelia.

'Oh my Lord,' Amelia gasped seeing the extent of Cara-Lea's injuries.

'It looks worse than it is,' Cara-Lea reassured her.

Amelia looked at her for a moment drinking in the sight of the battered girl that stood before her.

'You need wine, lots of wine,' Amelia said encouragingly. Cara-Lea laughed for a moment that was cut short when the pain in her abdomen made her wince.

'Wine sounds like something I need right now,' Cara-Lea agreed. Amelia took her by the arm and they strolled down towards the great hall together.

Dinner was a bit livelier tonight, the room was still divided by the different groups but not as much as usual some of the Vikings sat with the berserkers, some Christians sat in amongst the Vikings while others stayed in their closely knit groups.

'Well that's a start,' Theodore said looking over towards the groups.

He had tried to speak to Cara-Lea quietly for a moment but the room filled so quickly he never got the chance to properly check in with his daughter. Knowing his intentions, Cara-Lea reassured her father that she was ok, with no more than a few bumps and bruises and praised Finn, Asher, Koi and Ian for coming to her aid. After hearing the rumours about Drew and Emery, Cara-Lea did her best to avoid both of them. She sat at the opposite end of the table next to Amelia and Annabelle and for once enjoyed their company. The girls told tales of what they have been doing since they last saw each other. Amelia poked fun at Annabelle for her circumstances and all three laughed it off. Cara-Lea paid no attention to how much wine she had actually been drinking. Before she knew it she was drunk, excusing herself from the table Cara-Lea tried to act sober while she tried to escape from her father's sights. Stumbling up the corridor, she could feel eyes watching her. Remembering the dagger she slipped her hand in her pocket readying herself for another attack. 'Aim for the neck.' she told herself, knowing full well she would not be able to fight off another assault. Gripping the dagger tightly she could feel her heart race as she heard footsteps catch up with her own.

'Cara-Lea,' the person called. She knew that voice and she did not want to see him right now.

'Cara-Lea,' he called again. She walked on pretending not to hear him. She felt a large hand grip her arm, turning to face him she felt anger surge through her. Drew's shocked expression looking on the young girl who had looked like she had been through a battle said it all.

'Emery is back in the Great hall waiting for you,' she snapped.

'What, where is that coming from?' Drew asked.

'From my lips obviously! But it's hers you're more interested apparently,' she said trying not to slur her words.

'Are you drunk?' Drew asked taken aback.

'So what if I am, what's it to you?' she asked stumbling slightly on her own feet.

'You sound like your brother when you're drunk,' Drew said bluntly.

'So?' she spat.

'You need to go sleep it off,' Drew warned.

'Maybe you need to go sleep it off!' said Cara-Lea.

'You're acting like a child,' said Drew.

'Exactly! Is that not what I am a child!' She snapped.

'What are you talking about?' Drew asked.

'Well I'm sorry that I am still waiting for my breasts to fully come in, not all of us are as blessed as Emery you know.' stumbling back again.

Drew caught her. 'Is that what this is all about?' Drew laughed.

'I don't know maybe you should tell me,' Cara-Lea replied sardonically. 'Where are you going,' she barked as Drew led her up the staircase slowly.

‘I’m making sure you don’t kill yourself trying to make it up the stairs,’ he replied.

‘I can walk myself,’ she said, pushing Drew off her.

‘You have nothing to cushion the blow if you fall,’ Drew mocked.

‘Oh so now I’m too thin, well the insults keep on coming now, don’t they? Come on tell me what’s the next one? That I have big feet? That I’m too short? Go on big man do your worst,’ she yelled.

‘You sound exactly like Finn when you have had too much wine,’ Drew mocked.

‘Well at least one of us does,’ she argued.

‘That would only make sense if I was related to you,’ said Drew.

‘Well maybe you are, how would I know,’ said Cara-Lea stumbling back into Drew.

‘Right, that’s it you’re too far gone,’ he said picking her up and climbing the staircase with her.

‘Look at you, with your broad shoulders and large arms, you disgust me.’ she said gripping his bicep. Drew just laughed it off. ‘Why aren’t you talking to me?’ she asked. ‘How dare you ignore me when I’m fighting with you,’ she snapped. Drew grinned but remained silent. ‘I hate you,’ she whimpered.

‘You wouldn’t be the first,’ Drew replied throwing her over his shoulder.

As soon as they reached her chambers, Cara-Lea felt nauseous. Drew placed her down on her bed and passed her a chamber pot. After a few moments of vomiting Cara-Lea felt the room spin uncontrollably, even with her eyes closed she felt ill from the motion. Laying on her side clutching the chamber pot she closed her eyes and fell asleep.

Waking up the next morning Cara-Lea felt her body ache all over, she felt cow heavy from utter exhaustion, her mouth was dryer than the wine she had delighted in the night before and her stomach remained nauseous. Struggling to lift her head from her pillow she glanced around the room, the chamber pot she clutched the night before had been nowhere in sight. Flashbacks from her argument with Drew came back to haunt her. ‘Oh no’ she exclaimed at the thought. Lifting a pillow she placed it over the back of her head as she buried her face in the bed.

‘Good morning!’ a voice called cheerfully. Cara-Lea poker her head out from beneath the pillow to see who was in her room. Amelia had placed herself on the side of the bed, she had a large smile on her face and was holding a chalice of wine.

‘Drink this, it helps,’ she said sweetly handing Cara-Lea the goblet. Cara-Lea awkwardly rolled out from under the pillows and bed covers, eventually managing to sit up.

‘My head,’ Cara-Lea mumbled as she took a sip of wine.

‘I remember the night I first drank more than I could tolerate. The outcome was not far off yours,’ Amelia joked. ‘I was not as lucky as you. I didn’t have a kind man to look after me, instead I woke up next to a pool of my own vomit. You can imagine how horrified I was to find out I had drank myself into such a state,’ said Amelia.

‘What do you mean? What man?’ Cara-Lea asked confused.

‘Andrew,’ Amelia said kindly. ‘He stayed here all night to make sure you didn’t choke in your sleep, he helped clean you up and emptied out your chamber pot and everything. You’re lucky to have a man like that who cares for you, I doubt your brother would even do that for me,’ she joked.

‘Drew stayed here?’ Cara-Lea asked.

‘Yes all night, he only left for the new line up of training the berserkers have. As well as working as a team Henry is taking the individual skilled groups to work on their abilities, he was gone by first light, but he had knocked in to my chambers to ask if I would keep an eye on you,’ Amelia explained.

‘I don’t understand. I was so mean to him and my behaviour, oh! I am mortified just thinking about it,’ Cara-Lea said.

‘I remember not too long ago, I came to you crying over my behaviour as a spoilt brat, you corrected me then, I deserved it. No man who does not care for you would do the things he did last night. Any man who would do that for you is a hard one to lose. Trust me, if Nicholas has not abandoned me yet, there is hope for everyone,’ Amelia joked. ‘Would you be willing to come with me to meet Freya today she wants my opinion on the wedding decorations,’ Amelia asked.

‘Any situation where I can avoid men today is a welcomed one,’ Cara-Lea joked.

‘Well I best let you get dressed, I will come back shortly for you and we can go together,’ Amelia said sweetly as she turned for the door.

Asger

Standing in the desolate woodland outside the walls of Rosefort, Asger watched as the untrained Berserkers tried to attack the warriors. Looking on at Drew, who blocked a group attack with ease, wolves, boars and bears were been sent soaring through the sky, as one after another ran at the colossal black bear caught their attacks in mid-air. Looking around with every opponent on the ground, Drew slowly made his way back to Asger, slowly changing back to his human form until he stood tall peering over at the battered berserkers.

'You know why he could do that? It's called discipline!' Asger snapped. 'Something none of you have. You want to fight? To go into open war? Yet you cannot even defeat one man, you make me sick.' The berserkers looked on, hanging their heads hearing Asger's words. Ordering them back to the barracks he stood like stone in the middle of the forest, until the last man had run off with his tail tucked in between his legs.

'You're angry?' Drew asked calmly.

'Of course I am angry, did you not see that, it was an appalling effort. They would have us all killed! Not one of them used any form of stealth. The Preston's would hear them coming a mile away and open fire before we could reach them,' said Asger.

'Well they have only been training for a short time, they were not all that bad,' Drew replied.

'I have seen women fight better than that,' Asger snapped.

'Well that's not a fair comparison, the women who fight with us are even fiercer than the men, you know that,' Drew explained.

Asger said nothing in reply, he stared grimly into the far off distance. 'Just admit it, Annabelle Preston arriving here claiming to be carrying your child has really pissed you off,' Drew mocked.

'How did that even happen?' Asger muttered.

'Well generally it happens when a man and woman…' Drew began.

'Not that, I know how that happened, I mean how did this all happen? How did we end up here, like this?' Asger asked.

'No idea,' Drew laughed. 'But since we are here, we might as well make the most of it. After all we wouldn't be in the situation if it was not destined,' said Drew.

'You sound just like Freya when you speak like that,' said Asger.

Walking back to Rosefort the two men joked about past events. They spoke of how they met, of growing up together and training together, they were not brothers by blood but by circumstance.

'So are you going to marry her?' Drew asked.

'Marry who?' Asger asked shocked.

'Annabelle Preston,' Drew stated.

'No, I will never marry,' Asger said bluntly. 'I will provide for her and for my child, I will take care of them but I will not marry any woman just to leave her a widow a short time later.' Asger explained.

'You don't know that,' said Drew.

'I know our kind has been dropping like flies. We are a cursed clan Drew, not so much in our capabilities but because people tend to fear what they cannot understand and our kind will always be seen as a threat.' Asger's lips pressed together and his brow furrowed at his own words, he knew there would always be people like Mark Preston, desiring to have their heads.

'We are not animals they think we are,' Drew reasoned.

'We are far worse, animals don't stay up plotting how to kill another, they do not use strategies and armies like we do, and nor they kill for survival. They kill for food or to defend themselves or their packs, we are far worse than animals we are monsters,' said Asger with a heavy heart.

'We are not mindless animals brother, we fight to survive, they attack us, they slaughtered our people, raid our towns, rape our women. Yes we plan attacks, and we kill just as many of them as they do us but we do it to protect our own, we may be the beasts that many fear, but they Asger, they are the true monsters not us,' said Drew.

Back at the barracks, Asger kept a distance on arrival as Henry was busy screaming at the men, 'nothing new there' he thought. Examining the crowd, he had notice the mercenaries had been beaten, their faces bloody, their clothes had been torn and muddy. Some had been left half naked and shivering, every mercenary except one.

'Why was he spared?' Asger asked Thorvard.

'He helped Finn Olden yesterday,' Thorvard answered in a low voice, trying not to attract Henry's attention. 'Gruesome sight all the same, they won't be forgetting that for a while,' he went on.

'Henry brought them to the bodies?' Asger asked.

'No, he brought the bodies to them,' Thorvard answered, gesturing towards the back of the barracks. Asger walked around to see what had happened. A cold chill ran down his spine as he grew closer to the bodies. He could see what Thorvard meant, this was a sight even the most hardened warriors would be uncomfortable by. One man whose body looked as though it was mauled had been left hanging over the wall of the military base. 'That was most definitely the hound,' Asger thought. Gazing at the body he could not tell who the man even was, his face had been chewed so badly he barely had half a face left on his skull, his neck had been ripped open and his left hand severed by the jaws of what attacked him. Another man whose face was recognisable had been nailed to a large pallet of wood, this one was far less gruesome, as he had only been stabbed in the throat and bled out. Walking further down the wall, Asger noticed a third man hanging more loosely than the other mercenary. His eyes were so badly blood shot he had no white left in them, it was obvious he had been strangled. Finally the last man was tied onto a rack, but Henry had not used a typical flat rack for his presentation no he had one that was shaped like a wheel. The mercenary was left bound and secured onto it by the arms and legs. His head turned towards the passers-by. His eyes had been carved out of his skull, his belly had been sliced open all the way to the groin while his entrails hung from the corpse, lacing themselves around the wheel.

'I did warn them,' Beigarth said approaching Asger.

'You have a fine ability of sneaking up on people,' Asger said turning to Beigarth.

‘Well it’s not like I could knock to announce myself,’ said Beigarth pointing out the fact that they were indeed outside.

‘You are a seer? Tell me do you see us winning this war?’ Asger asked hesitantly.

‘I can see a great many things Asger Raghnall, some things are never set to be as they appear, I can only see what is destined and what has been decided. Some men that will fight for you are destined to die regardless of the attempts they make to prevent that happening. While others will die based on their decisions, some wars are meant to be won but this I am afraid, is only an outcome the leaders choose. I have seen both sides win, and both sides fall. It is true some men have a destiny they cannot break, but others like yourself are the deciding factors in their faith. I believe that if you are wise and don’t let the enemy get into your head you will win this war, but only you can make that happen,’ said Beigarth as he smiled and walked away, leaving Asger staring at the mercenaries.

Theodore

His eyes felt heavy and uncomfortable from reading through multiple books to do with Rosefort's finances, he thought once he had found them all through the mess that had left from Bjorn it would be a simple enough task to carry out, but he was wrong. Bjorn had saved Rosefort so much money on farming as he and the other Norsemen took over the task of that and with half of Rosefort's population dead due to the Raghnall's take over they had less mouths to feed, and people to house. Bjorn was never much of an organised person nor a book keeper, and his penmanship looked like chicken scratches. Rosefort looked like its finances were on the up and up since house Raghnall's reign, however, if there was to be a war, hundreds if not thousands of men, a Kludde and now Gogmagogs to feed, they would need to increase taxes to make ends meet. That would just be food alone, they will need weapons, armour, horses and the rest. The Olden's wealth had been left at castle Mourne when they were invaded. The safe holding the kingdoms wealth was impenetrable, if only he could take back his home he could make a vast contribution to this war. Alas he would need men, a lot of well-trained hardened warriors to take back his family home and to get them, he would need gold.

Strolling out of his quarters Theodore decided to take a walk outside the castle to clear his head and give his eyes a break. He could not help thinking that if Edward was still alive he would have not only organised those books for him but he would have read them all and found a way to benefit their cause. Edward had a gift, he was always a great thinker and he could find a silver lining in anything no matter the circumstance and see things that men with twice the experience could not. Nicholas was intelligent and fierce but mainly in the matter of war. Nicholas was a born leader but he had the mind of a soldier, he would need advisors at this court to help him with political and financial matters. As for Finn his gift was not dying, he was intelligent but he was led by the heart and not the mind, his mother would say he had a great mind locked away in that head of his but he was too stubborn to use it. Theodore has seen Finn take on up to eight men at once and walk away with little more than a few scratches and a bruised ego. If Theodore was to ask Nicholas to look over the books, he would reach the same conclusion as his father, but if Finn was asked to look over the books he would most likely burn them out of frustration.

Lost in thought Theodore had found himself outside of the chapel that sat opposite the castle on the opposite side of the gate. He heard loud voices and a lot of banging, curious he decided to go inside and see what was going on. Immediately he was greeted by Gregor the monk and Freya, behind them Asher and Koi had been helping to clean the church, it was evident that it had been vacant for quite some time, a thick layer of dust covered the chairs and the floor, cobwebs hung from the ceiling and all the furniture. The once marble carvings of angels on the walls had started to turn black.

'Theodore!' Freya called happily when she noticed him standing in the doorway. Upon hearing his name he approached slowly glancing around him as he strolled towards her. 'I know it's a disgrace, before you say anything,' said Freya noting the look of disgust on Theodore's face.

'What happened here?' he asked.

'Roderick was never one for men of the faith, in fact he had them all impaled and placed on the surroundings of the church. This place has sat dead for years, I wanted to open it again when I took over but no priest would come here after what had happened. Now, with Gregor here we can finally have a church for our people again. Obviously, it needs some work but I am sure we will have it up and running by the wedding,' Freya said optimistically.

'The wedding is in a week is it not?' Theodore asked.

'It is,' Freya smiled.

'Forgive me my dear, but how on earth do you expect to have everything ready by then?' Theodore asked.

'I took over Rosefort when nobody expected me to, I took the life of the monster Draconian when all others had failed to do so and I have Finn settled down, he is no longer bed hoping or being found in the company of whores. I do believe if I can achieve that above everything I can do this,' Freya said with such confidence Theodore could not help but to laugh.

Asher and Koi were running around with broomsticks trying to remove all the cobwebs in their reach. Some of the servants had brought in large pales of water and sheets of cloth, Theodore watched as they placed down the items and walked out of the church.

'Are they not here to clean?' Theodore asked.

'No, they have too much to do, with getting in the foods needed and flowers made up for the wedding. We are going to clean in here ourselves,' said Freya.

'But there are only four of you,' said Theodore looking around baffled.

'No, there are six of us now and Finn and Nicholas have offered to help,' said Freya. '

My sons cleaning? This I will have to see to believe,' said Theodore.

'Believe it old man,' Finn's voice called from behind him.

'Is it so hard to believe that we can be of use?' Nicholas asked mockingly.

'Well not me, you, yes,' Finn replied.

'Do I seriously have to separate you two already?' Freya asked smiling.

'It wouldn't help, they both have big mouths, you would still have to listen to them,' Theodore said in jest.

'What needs to be done?' Nicholas asked ignoring Theodore's comments.

'Everything!' Asher's voice called out.

'You can start with scrubbing the floors.' Koi yelled from the opposite end of the church.

'Fine by me,' said Finn, picking up a pale of water and walking up towards the Alter.

'Careful now, you might burn being up there,' Nicholas called.

Finn walked on not turning back to his brother, instead he raised his free arm and flipped his middle finger upwards.

'Finn Olden is that any way to behave in a church,' Theodore yelled. Freya started giggling.

'I am sure the good monk here has seen far worse by now, besides until we have this place cleaned I doubt we can refer to it as a church, the sight alone would bring shame upon anyone wanting to refer to it as one,' Freya said sweetly.

'What's the matter brother, afraid of a little manual labour, should I go fetch you a blouse?' Finn called to Nicholas.

Gregor himself even cracked a smile hearing that remark. Nicholas scowled at Finn, marching over a grabbing a pale of water he was about to start walking to towards the Alter, to join his brother.

'Actually Nicholas, if you don't mind you are quite tall, can you maybe help wash the walls? The carvings have just about vanished under all that dust,' Freya asked kindly. Gregor began to wash down the seats of in the venue, while Freya polished the chalices and the ornaments that had been locked away in a dusty box at the top of the Alter. Theodore watched for a moment as Finn scrubbed the floors on his hands and knees, Nicholas washed down the walls, and Asher and Koi ran rampant with the brooms on the floors of the church, sweeping all the dust outside the doors. He could not believe that Freya had this big of an impact on Finn in particular, who was content with scrubbing the floors like a common servant. Theodore could never get Finn to even wash the blood off his hands half the time after a brawl and here he was being helpful. That was all Theodore needed to see, picking up the last pale of water Theodore walked towards the doors of the church, he would start there, then move for the walls and meet Nicholas up the top at the Alter by the end.

After endless scrubbing, the group finally had the church stripped of dirt, it needed another go over to make it immaculate but it was a lot better than it had been earlier. Theodore felt his arms burn from the hours of constant scrubbing, for the first time he realised how tiring the servant's jobs were, they just cleaned one small church but the servants clean an entire castle as well as attend to everyone in it.

'Thank the Lord that's done,' Nicholas said rubbing his arms.

'It wasn't so bad, keeps the arms fit,' Finn said posing, in a way that showed off his muscles.

'The mercenaries are coming here to take over, Henry has them all ready to scrub this place spotless, and they have been awake for over a day now. I think this is my uncle's last punishment for them before finally letting them rest tonight,' said Freya.

'I'll go gather the people and have them wait at the docks,' Nicholas said, excusing himself.

'I better go feed Luna or she will go hunt down her own meal.' said Finn. 'I'll meet you at the docks,' he said turning to Freya who simply nodded. Bjorn's send-off was today Freya wanted to wait until the sun was setting to do it.

Walking towards the docks with Freya, Theodore thought she could use the distraction from what was about to take place.

'I went over the books today, well everything I could find at least. It seems that Rosefort is doing rather well financially thanks to the changes your father put in place.' Theodore hesitated for a moment, he was trying to distract her from her father's funeral but brought him up without thinking. 'I…eh…that is to say… With so many men marching to our aid in this war, it will cost a lot to feed them, never mind provide weapons and armour and of course training,' Theodore said recovering from his blunder.

'I was thinking about that,' said Freya. 'The Norsemen have agreed to farm the lands at no cost to our kingdom, since we have provided them and their families homes and with land of their own, however Rosefort in known for producing the best cattle, fruits and vegetables because of the rich soil that grows here in the Emerald Isles. Anyone who wishes to buy from here that is not living in the realm will have to pay the cost plus tax on the items they wish to buy,' Freya said proudly.

'Well that will certainly help as to trade here is quite popular. I was also thinking with so many ships coming in and out of your docks due to the trade, we could charge an extra sum, in order for their ships to be able to sit out there. Not an extreme amount of course, we would not want to turn the traders off coming here, just a little extra. The coin gathered can go into the men's training or production of weapons or armour,' Theodore said.

'I will admit I have never thought of that, but yes, anything to work in our favour. Anything within reason that is,' said Freya.

Theodore found himself lost in conversation with Freya about matters of the realm, he was surprised to find out how knowledgeable and tactical this young woman was.

Before he knew it he was standing at the docks. A Viking long boat sat gracefully on top of the water. It was beautifully carved, the banner of house Raghnall hung proudly from the mast. Before long it looked like everybody who lived in Rosefort had gathered. Everyone from peasants to nobles lined up to look upon the magnificent vessel that would take Bjorn the Brave on his last voyage.

'I never understood that tradition much, I mean it's such a magnificent ship what a shame to burn it,' Annabelle Preston's voice said in the background.

'You know the tradition of the two coins to pay the ferryman?' Amelia asked her sister.

'Yes?' Annabelle answered, Theodore could tell from her voice she was confused.

'Well this way, Bjorn has his own ship, he does not have to pay passage to anyone to get to the other side, this way he sails straight through,' Amelia said proudly.

Theodore found himself pleasantly surprised by her answer, it seems living amongst the diverse cultures had a profound effect on Amelia. The sun was getting ready to set, Theodore watched as his friends body was carried onto the ship. Clara had wrapped Bjorn in a sheet, it was rumoured that she had done her best to put his body as much together as she could but with dead tissue that would have been quite a difficult task. Asger draped the banner of their house over his father's remains, while Freya placed his things around his body. A servant girl had asked to accompany her old master to the next life, she had just come from her ritual. Standing just before the ship, she smiled and closed her eyes as her throat was slit from ear to ear and her body was laid down beside Bjorn's. Theodore knew this was the way of the Norse people, but he could see a few Christians who looked horrified at what he had just seen. He watched silently as the ship was cast off, heading into the sunset. Gilli fired a single flaming arrow at the ship, for a moment Theodore thought he had missed. Suddenly, a large flame grew from the deck of the ship and spread ferociously, climbing from the deck up the mast and to the house banner. The crowd start to disperse, but Theodore remained, he wanted to wait there a few moments longer, just enough time for him to be alone and say goodbye to his beloved friend.

A New Beginning

A week had passed since Bjorn's send off, leaving a great excitement in Rosefort. Cara-Lea, Amelia and Annabelle took the Norse folk under their wing and showed them how to dance and explained the Christian wedding traditions. Theodore arranged housing and food for the two hundred men that had come to Rosefort's aid. Finn opted to train with the berserkers, now that he was regaining his strength, he was one of the few men with his background that was able to go toe to toe with them, so much so that even Henry was impressed. Not all those from Berserker decent could shape shift, some like Freya had the animal instincts and the power behind them to do serious damage despite the fact they remained in human form. Nicholas led the Christian men in their training, those who were battle ready fought alongside the Vikings and berserkers, those who were not had to go through gruelling training leaving them battered and bruised on a daily basis. Asger had thrown himself into a leaders role, he had been training with the men as well as teaching those who needed to be brushed up on their skills. Gilli had been teaching the bow men some new tricks of his, he said that if they could take out a berserker with an arrow a normal man would be as easy as cutting through butter. Cara-Lea seemed to take to the arrows a lot faster than the other women she trained with, her swordsmanship improved drastically over the short time she had been training with Drew and Nari. Freya and Clara had been busy finishing Amelia's dress for the day of the wedding, Clara was left to tend to the dress alone on more than one occasion while Freya saw to Shengis who had agreed to aid her in her fight against the Prestons.

The wedding day was finally here. The castle was buzzing with excitement, looking out the window of her chambers Freya could see dozens of marquees set up just outside the castle grounds. The church was glistening in the sunlight, they had scrubbed inside until it shone, while the grounds of the church had been cleaned and the overgrown garden which once lay at the entrance had been tended to. Finn walked into the room, pulling Freya from her thoughts. Finn had been dressed in an elegant fawn coloured tunic with light beige embroidery a dark brown belt draped around his waist with matching breeches tucked in to dark brown boots. His clothes were expensive, Freya could tell by looking at the material alone. She admired how Finn could scrub up, he had a remarkable way of dressing simply yet he was always immediately appealing to the eye. His usually fair complexion had been darkened by the long hours of training in the sun. Freya had been dressed in gold. The sleeves of her dress were fitted to the elbows then loosely overlapped her forearms and hung over her hands. The bodice was tightly fitted to her curvaceous figure, while the skirt swung loosely from the hips. The middle of the skirt had gold embroidery and beading covering the paler gold fabric which lay underneath. The sides of her skirt had dark gold and yellow needlework framing her hips and highlighting the two toned fabric of her dress. She had a large braid starting at the top of her hair-line running down the centre of her head meeting her curls which loosely fell down her back.

'I value my breath, I wish it was not so easy for you to take it away,' Finn said gazing upon her. Finn approached unwrapping a small item in his hand.

'What is that,' Freya asked.

'This? This is nothing sweetheart. Something I saw that I thought you could wear today.' Finn said signalling for her to turn around. Freya felt Finn drape something around her neck, looking down she could see a simple gold necklace with a large yellow diamond sitting in the centre.

'It's beautiful,' she said staring down at the gift.

'Not as beautiful as the person wearing it,' Finn said kissing her lightly on the shoulder.

Arriving at the packed church.

'It looks like we got here just in time,' Finn joked as they walked to the front row.

Gregor stood nervously staring at the people of the land, everyone was wearing their best clothes even Asger had cleaned up immensely, Finn had noticed as he looked around the room.

Nicholas was standing at the top of the Alter with Gregor. He had been dressed in a fine white silk shirt with a black vest, black breeches and shoes to match he kept it simple like his brother, although his white tunic looked blue from the light shining through the blue silk which gracefully draped from the windows. A harpist played from the back of the church, as soon as they heard the music everyone got to their feet. Amelia entered the church with Asher and Koi standing on either side, they had agreed to give her away today. Her dress was made of the finest silks that puffed out from the hips. The corset was white with Gold needle work, other than that the dress was kept quite simple. Amelia had a long silk cape draped over her shoulders that matched her dress, Finn had notice she was wearing the necklace his mother had given her before the attacks on his home. Asher and Koi elegantly gave Amelia away leaving Freya and Finn impressed, it had been the first time they had taken anything serious since they had met them.

After the ceremony a large banquet had been set up in the largest marquee, a large pig on a spit greeted them as they walked into the tent, Koi had to reassure Asher that it was not Rosemary they had cooked. An endless supply of gifts were presented to Nicholas and Amelia by the guests before they sat down to enjoy their meal. Jesters, musicians, bards and much more all entertained during the festivities.

'I must say Freya you really have out done yourself today, setting this up on such short notice.' Annabelle said approvingly.

'Freya has a way of making the impossible, possible.' Finn beamed proudly.

'She always has had that gift, I have to give it to you this is not half bad…for a Christian party,' said Asger, Freya smiled at her brother and shook her head.

'I'll take that as a compliment coming from you,' she replied.

'Do you think you will ever marry yourself?' Annabelle asked.

Finn stopped midway through drinking his wine, his eyes shifted towards Freya.

'I don't know, I have not given it much thought to be honest, maybe someday,' Freya answered.

After the meal the group moved into a different marquee, where the dancing took place. Impressed that the Norsemen especially Asger was not swinging their partners around the tent like he had at House Olden, now he was much more gentleman like, rusty but they only had a week to learn these new dances. As they constantly changed partners, Freya found herself partnered with Drew.

'What's wrong?' Drew asked as soon as he was by her side.

'Nothing, why would anything be wrong?' Freya asked.

'I have known you long enough to know when you're hiding something,' said Drew.

'I have a bad feeling I cannot shake, like the one I got with Roderick and the raids.' Freya explained.

'How long have you been feeling like this?' Drew asked concerned.

'Not long, since dinner ended. I think with everything that has happened and knowing the traitor is still out there,' Freya explained.

'You're instincts have yet to be wrong Freya, you are wise not to brush it off. I will take Asger and a few of the men on guard and look around the grounds just to be safe,' said Drew. Freya nodded in acceptance.

'Just please be careful, it could be nothing but.'

'I know, it's best to be safe. Which is why I'll take Asger before he drinks any more ale or wine,' Drew said mockingly.

Changing partners again Freya was back with Finn, looking over his shoulder as they danced she noticed Drew approach her brother.

'So about what Annabelle said earlier,' Finn said.

'About today, I did do a good job if I do say so myself,' said Freya.

'You did an amazing job, but you know that's not what I was talking about,' Finn said.

'The marriage thing?' Freya asked.

Finn raised an eyebrow and smirked.

'What? Don't you think that I am husband material?' Finn asked mockingly.

'I never knew marriage was something that interested you,' said Freya.

‘It wasn’t, at least until I met you, then I figured I could make an honest woman of you,’ Finn said sardonically.

‘Are you asking me to marry you Finn Olden?’ Freya asked beaming.

‘Well not right now…but maybe someday. I already have you Freya, I am in no rush to force you into something you do not want. However, it would be nice to make you mine permanently,’ said Finn.

‘Maybe, we will see. I should warn you, I will not be the typical wife,’ said Freya.

‘That’s good, because I will be far from a typical husband,’ said Finn spinning Freya around, it was then she noticed Asger and Drew leave the tent, her heart sunk as she watched them disappear from her sight.

Drew and Asger walked from the marquee up towards the barracks. The night was quite aside from the noise coming from the wedding, which could be heard up to the village square.

‘Do you smell that?’ Drew asked as they approached the barracks.

‘Blood,’ Asger said bluntly as his mouth pressed into a hard line and his brow furrowed.

Entering the gates of the barracks they noticed pools of blood which had looked black in the dark of the night, the scent of death grew stronger. Two bodies had been sprawled out on the ground.

‘These men were on guard duty tonight,’ said Drew gazing down upon their lifeless bodies.

‘There are two ways around this barracks I’ll go this way, you go the other way. If the bastards still here he will have no way out,’ said Asger picking up the dead men’s swords and handing one to Drew.

After splitting up Drew walked by one dead mercenary after another, until he came to Henry’s display of bodies. He heard gurgling from behind the wheel, the dead rapist was tied to, approaching with caution he came to the feet of the man before realising who it was. This warrior had his throat slashed, but not deep enough to cause immediate death, kneeling down beside him he asked.

‘Thorvard what happened?’

‘Forgive me, I did not know,’ he whispered.

‘Who did this to you?’ Drew asked anxiously.

'Hawise, and Nari, please Andrew, forgive me,' his words growing weaker.

'There is nothing to forgive old friend,' Drew said as he watched Thorvard fight for his last breath.

'Drew!' Asger called, Drew stood up his blood boiling.

'Henry's dead, throat slashed, no doubt from an ambush,' Asger said furiously.

'Nari,' Drew said with venom in his voice.

'Nari? How do you know?' Asger asked stunned. Drew turned and pointed towards Thorvard's body. 'Why would he do this to us?' Asger asked angrily.

'I don't know, but I will kill him,' Drew growled jumping past Asger, he had changed into his bear form and ran for the gates. Asger knew more men had been stationed out by the docks if Nari was the traitor he would know where the men were stationed, without them to protect Rosefort they would surely be at the mercy of the Prestons.

Running frantically towards the docks, Asger noticed a trail of dead bodies, most of which had their throats cut. There was no telling where Drew had run off too, he was worse than a demon when he lost his temper. Asger thought quickly that Nari would need a quick escape from the land, surely he would know the bodies would be discovered quickly. The nearest dock would be the smartest option for someone to plan an escape, hearing a commotion Asger turned.

'Put it down Gilli,' Nari called.

Asger looked over to see Gilli had his sights set on Nari, bow and arrow at the ready.

'You betrayed us,' Gilli snapped.

'I don't want to kill you, put the bow down.' Nari demanded. Asger knew his friend would never let Nari leave. He started to approach, when he noticed a figure move through the tree's behind Gilli. In one swift movement Hawise grabbed Gilli and ran her dagger across his neck.

'NO!' Asger screamed.

Nari and Hawise turned in fright to see Asger standing yards away from them. Asger could not control himself, the betrayal, the death of his best friend, his father, the rage shot through his veins as he felt himself turn. Within seconds he had taken off running after the traitors. Growing closer he had them in his sights, the large black bear that had left him in the barracks had jumped out of the nowhere tackling Hawise to the ground. He could hear the blood curdling screams from her as she was being ripped apart.

Nari turned for a second. 'Hawise!' he screams, filled with agony, but he did not stay to mourn her, he noticed a large brown bear running towards him with his teeth bared. Narrowly escaping Asger by climbing into boat and rowing off into the sea Nari stared blankly back at Asger, who let out a roar filled with frustration as he watched Nari escape.

Arriving back at Rosefort, Asger carried Gilli's body to his chambers in the castle and laid him out on his bed. Drew watched from the doorway covered in blood. He had sent one of the servants to fetch Freya. Drew felt his eyes fill with tears, he had grown up with Gilli, and both had been raised by Bjorn along with Nari. Sinking to the floor, Drew dropped his head to his hands.

'I'll kill him, I swear when I get my hands on that cunt I'll rip his fucking head off,' Drew spat.

Hearing footsteps coming up the corridor Drew turned to see Freya rushing towards the room.

'Gilli!' she cried staring at her friends lifeless body laid out on his bed. 'Who did this?' Freya demanded.

'Nari.' Drew answered running his hands through his hair towards the back of his neck.

'How could he do this to us? After all we've done for him?' she asked.

'I don't know and I don't care,' Asger said, his voice had grown cold. 'He is a traitor, and when our paths cross again, we will show him exactly what happens to his kind,' said Asger turning to his sister.

'A group of our men are dead, most of the mercenaries. We don't have an army. Now thanks to Nari and Hawise we are farther from it then before. Face it, he's won, it's over. The only solace I'll take in this is I took that bitch's life,' said Drew.

'This is not the end, this is only the beginning,' Freya answered, knowing in her heart that this war had not even started yet.

She would have to bury her friend and her father in the space of a week. There were more clans out there like them, even some that were considered fearless, she would grow her army to be like one the world has never seen. The Raghnall's were considered animals by the highborn families who attacked them yet they have never seen their true capabilities. The Preston's would be the first to realise how dangerous the wrath of house Raghnall was. Mark Preston has won this battle with the help of the traitor Nari, but the war was far from over. In fact the war has only just begun.